A Hand-Book of Volapük

A HAND-BOOK OF VOLAPÜK

and an ELEMENTARY MANUAL of its
GRAMMAR and VOCABULARY,
prepared from the Gathered Papers of
GEMMELL HUNTER IBIDEM JUSTICE;
together with an Account of Events Relating to the
Annual General Meeting of 1891 of
the Edinburgh Society for the Propagation
of a Universal Language.

Edited for the First Time by
DR. CHARLES CORDINER
*Emeritus Professor of Phrenology
at Fraserburgh University.*

MENAD BAL PÜK BAL

WITHDRAWN

EDINBURGH
PUBLISHED BY POLYGON
WEST NEWINGTON HOUSE
MMVI

First published in Great Britain in 2006 by
Polygon, an imprint of Birlinn Ltd
West Newington House, 10 Newington Road
Edinburgh EH9 1QS
www.birlinn.co.uk

ISBN 10: 1 904598 67 6
ISBN 13: 978 1 904598 67 1

British Library Cataloguing-in-Publication Data
A catalogue record for this book is available
on request from the British Library

The publishers acknowledge subsidy from the
Scottish Arts Council towards the publication of this volume

Typeset by
Antony Gray, Oakfield Road, London
Printed and bound by
Creative Print and Design, Ebbw Vale, Wales

Contents

Preface

"The Roslin Mystery"
BY PROFESSOR CHARLES CORDINER

Since the successful conclusion of the affair of The Dilatory Calvinist, my promising young pupil, Mr. Sherlock Holmes, has been wont to correspond with me in many cases, some of which must forever remain protected from the public gaze, for they involve the very highest personages of the Realm. However, I understand that he is detained in Switzerland on important business, so I am unable to offer a full explanation for The Roslin Mystery, which I now lay before you as the Preface to a far less interesting work.

The facts, which will be familiar to readers of the police-reports in *The Scotsman*, are as follows: on the morning of Wednesday, the fifteenth of April, 189–, the Reverend Barnetson of Roslin in Mid-Lothian made a gruesome discovery in the policies of his Free Church Manse. You must know that his garden is a righteous one, being divided equally between: a variety of shrubs and restrained plants framing a considerable area of grass; and a utilitarian vegetable plot, which is tended faithfully by his wife. At each corner of the square of grass stands a solid pole to support a drying-line, each pole made of cast-iron, painted emerald-green against the weather, and shaped at the top in the form of a pineapple. It must be observed that the famous Chapel of Rosslyn is visible from the front door of the Manse: some hold this proximity to have a bearing upon the mystery. It goes without saying that I do not.

At around seven o'clock on this bright, but blustery, April morning, the general servant, Isabelle McLaggan, went out to the garden to hang out some clothes which she had just put through the mangle in the scullery. Distracted by a blackbird which was worrying worms in the shrubs, she did not lift her eyes until the very last moment. The sight, which she then beheld, robbed her of speech, and consciousness: hanging upon one of two diagonally-opposed drying-line poles was a blood-stained cloak, a helmet, gloves and a curved sword; hanging on its opposite partner, a man's coat, stained with gore. Blood had coursed down the poles and discoloured the surrounding grass.

The maid, not unnaturally, fell to the ground in a swoon, as is not uncommon in females whose skull has an melonoid shape. About fifteen minutes later, Mrs. Barnetson, wondering where the girl had got to, and requiring her assistance for the stirring of the porridge, erupted into the garden, and came upon the grisly scene. Having the contours of her skull quite differently from the maid, she did not faint, but screamed loudly and long; at such a volume, indeed, that the local police-constable, Mr. Ross, who was passing down the road on his bicycle, in pursuit of a master-criminal from Roslin Glen, immediately rushed round the side of the house to investigate the disturbance.

Having rendered assistance to the maid, and to the outraged feelings of Mr. Barnetson, who had emerged from his study of the Book of Ezekiel, the constable examined the gory stage on which this melodrama had unfolded. Apart from the blood-stained clothes, the constable observed, written on the back wall, in large letters incarnadine, the incomprehensible words "*NIVENKOS! OVIKOBS!*" There were also sundry shattered pieces of wood, and two broken wooden wheels. And, in the centre of the grass, a tin box, such as a man might use to keep safe his important documents. This strong-box had evidently been hurled to the ground with some force, for it stood with one corner embedded some three inches in the damp turf. Its lock had burst open, and the lid was twisted. A number of papers lay scattered about on the grass, some muddied, others bloodied, many more snared upon the thorns and branches of the surrounding bushes and trees.

Being himself an enthusiastic follower of my protégé Mr. Holmes, Constable Ross very correctly did not disturb the scene with his boots, and watched that no one else should destroy any evidence which might be contained in the slightest broken blade of grass. Standing on a spot which he judged would provide him with the widest panorama of the scene, he looked carefully about him. He noted down the words scrawled on the wall. He observed the prints of two pairs of boots, crossing to the back wall. Inspecting the wall more closely, he discovered, from various scrapes and marks, that two men, bleeding profusely, had climbed the wall and jumped over into the field behind it; there were two sets of foot-prints and two trails of blood leading across the field to the railway-station, which lies barely one hundred yards distant.

And then, as he turned his attention once more to the drying-green, his eyes lighted upon a third figure, an ancient man, half-concealed in the upper part of a rosemary-bush at the side of the garden. The old man was alive; but neither then, nor since, did he utter a single sensible word, or react to any external stimulus.

*   *   *

On account of my reputation in the district as the sometime mentor of Mr. Holmes, a fact to which I may have alluded already, Ross immediately despatched a boy to Mavisbank House, where I had been commissioned to conduct a scientific survey of the relative skull-shapes of the Residents; he requested my urgent attendance at the scene. I was at my breakfast when the summons arrived, but, such was the gravity of Mr. Ross's message, that I stopped only to drink two last cups of tea, before Henry Smail, whom I retain here as my coachman, drove me in my carriage to Roslin. I have named my carriage The Nemesis; under my guidance, Mr. Smail has painted it in black with silver wheels, with silvered curtains to the windows, and a large pair of golden wings at the rear of the roof, by which we may fly faster to our destination. Mr. Smail has also done me the goodness of painting the likeness of flames bursting from above the wheels, to indicate our aspirations to swiftness. The whole effect is emphasised by a mechanism for low suspension, built for me by Mr. Cosworth of Penicuik, which gives the appearance of soaring above the surface of the roads. We travelled, therefore, at a smart pace, and came within barely twenty minutes to the Manse; by then, the entire population of Roslin had been alerted and was gathered around the gate. As is frequently the case with the more impressionable classes, a non-sensical rumour was already circulating that the mysterious forces centred on the chapel had, once more, exacted human sacrifice. Ross had the whole thing under his control, however, and a passage was made for me so that I could examine the scene in more detail.

I found the back garden exactly as described above. I confess that, in my long and distinguished career as Professor of Phrenology at the

Marischal College of the University of Fraserburgh, I have never seen, or heard tell of, a more macabre spectacle! Indeed, in my eighty-one years of life, I have never set eyes on, or had reported to me, a more grisly sight! It was abhorrent in the extreme. However, I gathered my powers of logic and, taking care not to disturb the ground, I made a careful examination of each of the drying-poles in turn. I could tell at once that the clothes belonged to men, one being around fifty years of age, with thinning red hair, the other being dark in appearance, aged perhaps twenty-five. From a close examination of the trousers, I determined that the younger one was probably a medical man from the Colonies, and a dedicated smoker of cheap cigarettes; while the older man, owner of the cloak and helmet, had the gait of an artist, the skull of an artisan, and the digestion of a neglected bachelor.

Realising that the strewn papers could hold valuable information, I ordered Ross to gather together as many of them as could be found. He himself garnered those which were within the policies, meanwhile recruiting an eager band of by-standers to search the neighbouring church-yard, surrounding woodland and lanes for any which might have escaped. Having done this, Ross made it his business to pursue the trail to the railway-station where, it was confirmed, two men of dishevelled appearance had indeed boarded the early train for Edinburgh; but no one had thought to apprehend them, despite their curious appearance: Mr. Lorimer, the Station-Master, had not wished to challenge two such desperate-looking men.

For my own part, I turned my attention to the many pieces of garishly-painted wood which were scattered about, and deduced that together they had once formed a small carriage, or perhaps a large hand-barrow. Some Oriental characters were painted upon the surfaces, and I determined that I should consult on the meaning of these, at the very next opportunity, with the gentleman who supplies me with opiates.

It is well that I have trained my mind over many decades to detect small items which are commonly over-looked by others, and most particularly the Police. For it was only thus that I observed, hanging from a dismal frame for the disciplining of beans, a bag which was found to contain a considerable amount of oats. Mrs. Barnetson denied hysterically that she had ever seen this bag before, and swooned. But my growing suspicions were confirmed not many minutes later, when I hit my foot upon a metallic object embedded in the lawn, which discomfited me for a moment. On closer examination of my badly-scraped leather over-shoes, however, my annoyance turned to pleasure when I found the impediment to be a brass horse-shoe; and, not far off, I quickly discovered three of its companions, two of brass, one of common iron.

I made my way to the bush in which the shrivelled old man was still perched, and tried to engage him in conversation: to no avail. The Ancient stared steadfastly before him, dribbling slightly, his leathery hands clutching the handle of a stick. The size and shape of his skull interested me greatly, for his craniognomy spoke to me of a mighty mind and a courageous character. Reaching up, I probed his temples carefully, and examined the solid ridge at the back of the skull. I considered him to be Mediterranean in origin, owing to the extreme tanning of his skin. His poor dress, too, marked him out as a foreigner, being of a cut unknown to me; and my responsibility as a man in the public eye requires me to take note of the modern fashions, to be *à la mode*. Knowing a little French, Italian and Spanish from juvenile Tours of the Continent, I plied him with some phrases – largely, I confess, revolving around the quality of hotels in these parts and the potability of the waters – but obtained no reaction of any sort.

This was very frustrating! Here was one who may have seen the entire tragedy unfold before him, like a man in the front row of Her Majesty's Theatre; and yet he neither spoke, nor gave any sign that he was aware of my presence. It is my experience that, in such cases of shock, a lively dose of strychnine and brandy does the trick; but I had, alas, omitted to bring any along with me. I asked Mr. Barnetson to extricate the old gentleman from the bush, and place him on the bench which stood in the middle of the vegetable patch. As he did so, we were both quite startled to find that the bush was alive with dozens of mice, which fled squeaking in all directions at the disturbance; there was great consternation among the female on-lookers, but all the mice escaped into the surrounding countryside, pursued by a loud extemporised sermon from Mr. Barnetson, on the matter of Plagues and Vengeance; never to be seen again. When the old man was free, I tapped him firmly upon his chest in an attempt to force his attention; as I did so, I noticed a piece of paper protruding from a pocket of his top-coat. Gently, I prised it out, eliciting absolutely no reaction from the old man, save that he dribbled copiously upon my kid-glove.

On the piece of paper were written the following words or letters: "*Ebo payagobs e pacödobs, ibo dels ebeigoloms kü äyagobs. Eketobs, ab esötobs libön. Elitobs adelaliti nabik su vegi nefinik kel dugos äl odelo; e sikod efalobs.*"

I have not been able to make much sense of these words, which seem in some way related to the curious exhortations painted on the wall. I present them to you simply as more details in this great mystery. Perhaps a Professor of Languages will find enough, in the pages which will follow my Prefatory Remarks, to decipher the code in which they are written. My colleague, Dr. Chartres, has been in telepathic contact with the world-renowned archaeologist, Herr Professor Sigismond Bugarschitz of Vienna, on this very matter, but so far without illumination. If any academic Reader decrypts these words, then perhaps we can publish together a paper in one of the Journals of the Institutes. Until then, much that is baffling will necessarily remain so.

After an hour of the most careful observation of the drying-green, I concluded that a horse and its cart were central to this whole mystery. I had discovered wheels, oats, horse-shoes. I had discovered three men apparently hurled some distance through the air, and suffering appalling injury as a result. My mind, prowling hither and thither like the wolf, had also noted the proximity of the Roslin Gun-Powder Works, those many Satanic Mills which lie along the banks of the River Esk, grinding innocent materials into the smokeless powder of War and Mutual Destruction. I recalled also that the horses used by the Gun-Powder Works were always shod in brass, to prevent sparks. Is it not probable, I propose, that a cart had left Roslin Glen to deliver the periculous wares to one of the near-lying coal-mines, to Bilston perhaps, and that, as they passed down the road outside, a spark from that single iron horse-shoe, over-looked by some careless stable-lad, had ignited the materials. The cart, its occupants, and the unfortunate horse, would thus have been blown high into the air, over the roof of the Manse, and into the back garden. Two of the men, no doubt dazed and bleeding, had fled the scene; their older companion plunged into the rosemary-bush, which was as soft as the many cushions in my *equipage sportif*; and so survived unscathed. As for the horse, alas, all that remained were its four shoes and its nose-bag: doubtless, its mortal remains are even now being scavenged by hoodie crows and snarling dogs.

(I am obliged to pour ridicule over the tentative explanation of my ill-trained colleague, Dr. Lyon, who later reminded us that the Greek hooligan, Phaeton, had driven the chariot of the Sun, failed to control the horses, and had been struck from his carriage by a thunderbolt from Zeus, falling into the River Eridanus, afterwards to be mourned by his sisters, who were transformed into trees and their tears to amber. Lyon expects us to believe that something similar occurred in the air above Roslin, with the River Esk standing in for the Eridanus! The man is clearly an imbecile.)

The Reverend Barnetson argued stubbornly against my scientific deduction: he stated that not one of the residents of the Manse – being himself and his wife, their sombre sons, William and Horatius, and their friend and lodger, Miss Napier, a school-teacher – had heard any explosion, noise or ill-mannered disturbance, such as would have been the inevitable accompaniment to such an accident as I have outlined. But, as I have said and taught on many occasions: if we work solely from the facts, the one deduction at which we arrive, however improbable, must of course be the correct one. Upon my close and insistent questioning of young Master Horatius in a secluded spot, he admitted tearfully that his family are heavy sleepers. And so I rest my case.

*   *   *

Since the bright morning had by this time turned to a cold, overcast day, with the threat of drizzle, I decided to return home for more tea. I satisfied myself that the correct Police authorities had been alerted, and were even then on their way from Edinburgh by the fastest possible transport. I then summoned Smail to return me to Mavis-bank. The young man willingly came from the crowd of by-standers and loafers to find me. He seemed hardened enough to the sight of gore and horror: he is, after all, a native of Jedburgh, and I suppose they do things differently in those border-lands. However, he cried out with surprise, and turned to me: "Surely, sir, those belong to Mr. Justice and Mr. Bosman! Do you not remember?"

I confess I had little memory of the more recent events and visitors to Mavisbank, being wrapped up entirely in my measurements and craniological deductions. I am prey to periods of distraction, arising from my dedication to Science. It is a habit I have passed on to my very capable young student and Alumnus of Fraserburgh's Marischal College, Mr. Sherlock Holmes. It was therefore impossible for me to recall the two individuals of whom Smail evidently had strong memories. Without flinching, he stepped up close to the two garments in turn, as they creaked and dripped slowly in the gathering breeze. "Yes," he confirmed, examining the trousers of the darker and younger of the two missing men. "This is poor Dr. Bosman! And that is his friend, Mr. Justice. I wonder . . . " I observed my young friend's eyes wandering over the rest of the garden, until they lighted upon the Methuselah seated among the new potatoes. "God save us all!" he cried impropitiously, and to the icy disapprobation of Mr. Barnetson. He pointed in excitement, "And that is Sir Thomas himself, as lively as he ever was!"

After this moment of melodrama, I persuaded Constable Ross that the old man be allowed to return with myself and Smail to the comfort of Mavisbank House. I surmised that, if I were permitted to trepan his skull, I might relieve pressure on the brain therein, and perhaps get some sense from him. I have found this treatment to be a remarkable cure for many ailments and vices, most successfully with the wayward youths of Inverallochy. And what a paper I could write on such a subject! My already illustrious career would be crowned in glory! I itched to approach him with my craniometer. Therefore, we wrapped him in a horse-blanket which Mrs. Barnetson was good enough to provide, and coursed homewards in our low-slung Nemesis.

*   *   *

Over the next few days, the police detectives considered the matter as best they could. They discussed the case amongst themselves; they trampled over the Reverend Barnetson's garden until it resembled – so I am told – a field of battle; they came to talk to the ancient man known as Sir Thomas. They did not consider my opinions of any value; and I offered them none in return. At last, they retreated to their temple on George the Fourth Bridge in Edinburgh, and considered the whole case "a mere local curiosity", quite outwith their narrow sphere of interest. If Constable Ross is to be believed, the detectives were far more excited by the newspaper reports of an audacious robbery of the mails from the Dover to Calais ferry by a gang of ruffians led by a young gentleman of seventy-two years of age.

After the departure of the detectives, Constable Ross was able to furnish me with all the papers which had been gathered up from the scene of the mystery; the Edinburgh Police having determined that they had little or no bearing upon the horrible events of the night of the fourteenth of April. Some of the papers were in shocking condition, being – as I have suggested – covered in blood and gore, or ripped to tatters by the hawthorn and the gorse, nibbled by squirrels, shredded by hedgehogs, or pecked by birds.

But, with the desultory assistance of my contemporary Dr. Felix R. Lyon and the young Irish cleric Dr. William Chartres, I was able to piece together a document of passing interest, written by the afore-mentioned Mr. Justice, which is now presented for public examin-ation as *A Hand-Book of Volapük*. Mr. Justice evidently had advanced plans for the publication of this work, having prepared title-page, a List of Contents and an extensive Appendix. It is my duty to publish Mr. Justice's work by proxy, although I have no great hopes of its success.

* * *

Several chapters are missing from the original schema for the work. It is clear that some of the more uncouth residents of the Esk Valley had used the paper as an unexpected windfall with which to replenish their supplies for out-houses or "cludgies"; that the local grocer, Mr. Glover, has found it convenient to wrap his carrots and cauliflowers in such papers as fluttered into his yard; that birds and other untamed beasts of the wood had found the material most suitable for lining their nests; and that peasants had found the paper useful for lighting their pipes and poisoning the airs with their tobacco fumes. By a strange and opportune chance, the papers which are missing relate principally to the proposed final three chapters of Justice's *magnum opus* – to wit: The Frequentative and Aorist Forms; The Prepositions and Derived Prepositions; Idiomatic Expressions, and *Miscellania*. My colleague Dr. Lyon has taken it upon himself, therefore, to assemble all the relevant and incomplete papers into a single final chapter: I cannot condone this liberty, but I do not feel responsible for it. A "Transaction", or discussion-paper, mentioned by the evasive Mr. Justice *à propos* "Writing for the Blind", has also gone astray: perhaps all the missing pages will turn up as linings in kitchen drawers!

In considering the papers of Mr. Justice which follow, let it not be forgotten that I am a Scientist, trained in the study of the Human Skull, and a master of my subject. I never considered myself to be a Literary Executor or Editor, and have neither the patience to undertake such a task, nor any pertinent training in the Art – or otherwise – of Language.

If there are mistakes in any of the papers which now follow, or if the work seems obscure, it is none of my doing. I have ceded full responsibility for examining the linguistic details in the papers to Dr. Chartres, being a self-proclaimed student of two European tongues. For his part, Dr. Lyon has been asked to furnish logical explanations for some of the gaps in the text; to this end, he has consulted with Dr. Iain Hutchison, the Chief Resident of Mallendo College in Mussel-burgh, whose several insights into the beneficial effects of ozone cannot have failed to escape the attention and admiration of every Rational Man in Scotland.

And now, I have my own interests to pursue. I have not yet had the opportunity to trepan the skull of the old gentleman, Sir Thomas; and I understand that a lady from Edinburgh is to come soon, for to return him to his lands in Cromarty. The only words he has uttered, repeatedly, and to my distraction, are:

> Baltumlulsefol mugs ebinoms,
> Glekalodik in sil esenoms.
> Efidoms lieni,
> Emekoms vamik bedi,
> Obik vab e mugs efaloms.

Mr. Smail suggested that the doggerel resembled a "Limerickal"; I have no idea what he means by this, although Dr. Chartres, a native of Ireland, may find hidden signification. But if the opportunity for phrenological examination should slip, I will not be discomfited: my studies on a grander scale will be more revelatory. It is my belief that all the troubles of this present month can be traced back to villains of a certain craniological type. If we were to examine the skulls: of the natives who caused the recent Disaster at Manipur; of the agitators and fomenters of the General Strike in Belgium; of the organisers of the International Conference of Mine-Workers in Paris: then it is my premise that there would be but a single shape and size of skull common in all cases. I shall scrutinise all the newspaper reports for clues. My work is of the utmost importance to the survival of Western Civilisation: I would therefore ask to be left alone in future.

Mavisbank,
May, 189–

Chapter 1: Sounds and Letters

Notes from a Lesson given to the Workers of the
Harbour of Refuge, Peterhead. February 1891.

Binob üt, kel ko man nedeilik vöno etävob . . .

bin(ön)	to be
-ob	suffix denoting the first person singular – "I": thus, "I am"
üt	that very person
kel	who
ko	with
man	a man
ne-	prefix to denote the negative, "not", "un-"
deil(ön)	to die
-ik	adjectival suffix: thus "undying", "immortal"
vöno	once
e-	prefix to denote the Perfect, or Past, Tense
täv(ön)	to travel, to journey
-ob	first person singular – "I": thus, "I did travel"

I am he, who once with an immortal man did journey. From the comely town of Cromarty, hard by the shores of the Cromarty and the Moray Firths, we travelled at a patrician pace, in comfortable companionship, in deepest dialogue. To Nairn we journeyed, and then whither business called me: to Forres, to Elgin indeed. From Fochabers, we shunned the road of temptation that leads to Keith, and hastened to the coast, to Cullen and Portsoy; to the twin towns rich in fricatives, Banff and Macduff; each and every one set as a jewel in the necklace of the cities of the North. On this journey, we did not reach the Crown Jewel of all, the sapphire in the brooch, the Broch, the famous town of Fraserburgh; but rather turned our way southwards, to timeless Turriff. And came at last, as all men must do, to Peterhead.

*   *   *

You must know that I follow a trade which takes me to some of the farthest outposts of Civilisation, modest places where a man with skills such as mine are called for only on an occasional footing. For I am a repairer and tuner of church-organs. In a big city, such as Glasgow or Edinburgh, men of my profession vie for business as a matter of life or death; under-cutting each other in an attempt to secure the next job, driving each other and themselves into poverty and despair. But for those of us prepared to journey out of Edinburgh, there are rich pickings in the smaller places. I have established a list of towns which have need of my services, perhaps once a year, strung along the Fife coast, up beyond Arbroath and Montrose, beyond Aberdeen, where a huge land of opportunity opens up; also to the South, into the more obscure Borders towns. I have rivals, sure enough, in Dundee, in Aberdeen and in Inverness; but I have built up my business by the quality and quantity of my work and I am a hard man to oust from my contracts. Why, you might ask, do I not make myself resident in some more convenient spot, such as Aberdeen? Certainly, it might be more comfortable, and I could be called on more rapidly in a time of trouble and unexpected catastrophe. But I find that Edinburgh pleases me better. There is an excellent network of railways which will take me to the smallest village in the shortest possible time, should there be an urgent situation; and I can be summoned at the shortest notice by a letter with a penny stamp.

After thirty-three years at this trade, as apprentice and master, I have established a list of over two hundred customers; if I visit each one just once in two years, then I can lead a comfortable and quiet life, venturing out on these lengthy tours of the hidden country, perhaps three times a year; returning to Edinburgh to pursue my own interests. There is a great sufficiency of work in tending to broken reeds, rotten bellows, abused manuals, and the other depredations to which the organs in small churches are subjected. I admit that my work at this trade, and my frequent journeys into the wilderness, have cost me personal happiness, and encouraged me to actions which I now regret; but that is not the matter of this Hand-Book.

*   *   *

In late January of 1891, I set off for the North from the Caledonian Station in Edinburgh. As usual, I bought a third-class ticket to Inverness; and then travelled by cart and foot to Cromarty, where my first job awaited me. From there, I would make my way southwards, as I have indicated in my preamble to these notes, in the style of the poet Virgil, taking in a number of towns to the north of Aberdeen, the coast-line from Montrose to Dundee, and two small places in the Kingdom of Fife.

My journey was uneventful, up until the time I was about to leave Cromarty. The wind-chest had split in four places, no doubt due to the perpetual dampness which comes in on the church from the cold seas. I repaired it as best I could, given the small amount of money which I had been offered for the job. Having done that, there were three pedals in the pedal-board to be replaced; and finally a dead mouse to be retrieved from the third rank of pipes. This last task took me four hours, since it is no easy task to extract small items from such a perpendicular place. I was still in the church as dusk fell, playing a medley of the tunes "O Tannenbaum" and "The White Cockade", by which performance I am used to ensuring that my work is complete. Having established that all was in order, I dusted down the wooden surfaces of the organ one last time, and left the church.

Outside, it was cold. The Firth sent in a biting wind, and the bare branches of the trees shook and rattled against each other. Almost all natural light had faded from the sky. The clock in the town struck five, hopeless, dejected, gloomy, dispirited, sombre, and the chimes carried away in the gale. Any man subject to superstition and illogical fears might have found himself tipped over easily into terror by the short journey across the graveyard which surrounds the church. I, however, revelled in the solitude, and in the contemplation of mortality and the transience of the human life; and wondered whether to take a whisky or a beer with my supper, which I foresaw would soon be steaming on a board before me. When a shape suddenly burst out from behind a grave-stone and stood before me, a lesser man might have taken fright. But I realised quickly that this was no bogey, merely a dog. As it did not bark, I continued my way down the path towards it. The dog turned round and trotted in front of me. As we reached the gate which led out into the road, it stopped again, turned to me. And bared its teeth. I took one step forward. It growled. I took one step down a path leading to the right. The black dog stopped growling. As I made to dodge past it out into the road, it bounded back in front of me and encouraged me, with its fierce snarling and open jaws, to precede it down the other path. After a few yards, we turned past a stunted tree which grew there, and came across a small shed or building. Its door stood ajar, and a dim light shone out through the narrow opening. Wondering whether some gardener or sexton might be hard at it, I pushed back the door to peer in.

I was surprised to find that, in the damp and mouldy building, something the size of a small van or large privy, an old man was feebly tapping his way up and down, a heavy stick held before him. I coughed gently, so as not to startle him. He whirled round, lost his footing and slumped with considerable noise against the stone sarcophagus, which took up most of the space.

"The Pox and the Devil!" he snarled. "What's your purpose, slithering about like the Viper?" I stepped forward to help him to his feet, as he seemed irretrievably entangled in his coats and his stick. He pushed me off, and, with considerable cursing, staggered to his feet. "Eh? Eh?" he repeated, poking at my chest with a talon.

I am not used to such an ill-welcome; but excused him for his advanced years. I explained as best I could who I was, what I was doing in the church, and that I had seen the light.

"On espionage, then? Well, there's no forgiveness for you. Step in, step in – there's a wind howling that will bring my testicles up with a clang if you do not close the door!"

I did as I was bid, and closed the heavy wooden door behind me. Inside, it was surprisingly snug for a shed. Four or five candles were burning, and the scent of melting wax I found most comforting. It was silent, too – all sound of the wind outside was stilled, as if the external world had ceased to exist. I examined my new acquaintance, and he likewise examined me. He was very old, and his face was weather-beaten – indeed, his hands and the bottom of his legs, exposed where his trousers fitted badly, were also gnarled and of the deepest mahogany colour. His clothes were most surprising: they were of considerable antiquity, and I cannot remember having seen anything of their sort in all my days, even in some of the more isolated villages of the North-East. If he was, as I conjectured, an octogenarian or nona-genarian, then I supposed that his coat, his waistcoat, his trousers and boots were of the fashion when he was quite a young man. On his head was deposited a large wig, also of a bygone age, which had, perhaps because of his fall, slipped sideways upon his massive skull to expose a most depressing want of hair. Such white threads as still clung to his head were long and feathery.

"Behold, then, an Ancient." The old man leered at me. "Are you so impudent with all those you encounter? Or only with those gentlemen who display the stigmata of longevitious years?"

I averted my eyes as best I could, and studied my surroundings. I now realised that I stood inside an ample tomb, or mausoleum. A large stone coffin was placed upon some hidden supports; I peered underneath it, thinking to see the dog which had herded me hither. But the dog had vanished utterly. The lid of the coffin was covered in piles of yellowing paper or parchment, covered with scribbled words, some of which had floated to the floor in the draught. There was a tin bucket in a corner on the floor, from which an unmentionable sour stench arose. And the walls were covered in red and gold and black paint, depicting scenes vaguely reminiscent of war and derring-do. The illumination was not sufficient to let me see all the details. But the pictures extended from the floor to the roof, from end to end, and, as I admired them, they seemed to make the place larger, loftier, more spacious. I found that I could stand up tall and stretch my arms out, even stride up and down, but did not find a single obstacle. The old man sat on the coffin and watched me.

"So, Mr. Justice," he said, after a few minutes. "And how can you beneficate me?"

I was so startled to find that he knew my name, that I stood and gaped at him, presenting the appearance of an imbecile of the orthodox tradition.

Evidently exasperated at my continued silence, the old man struck me several times forcefully upon the lower legs with his stick, which – I confess – caused considerable pain. My cry echoed around the tomb as if it were a palace or the great hall of a mighty fortress.

"Let me facilitate the affair, then, since you are dysphoric and dysphonic," he muttered crossly, fixing me with one of his coal-black eyes. "You are evidently a traveller. You manifest a sophistication in your habiliment and in your posture. From Perth or Edinburgh, then?"

I nodded, marvelling to myself that he could describe me as a sophisticate – evidently, he had been deprived of good company for many years.

The old man looked at me with a keener interest, scratched his chin and muttered something to himself – "One *jetée* of the dice," were the words I caught. "Sir," he continued, "I have an erethitic proposal to make to you. I have neither amicable connection nor familial presence any longer in this town of Cromarty. And I have a flagrescent inclination to ride once again to the Cities of the Plain, and, in particular, Edinburgh. If you agree to my companionship on your perambulations, I will naturally recompense you handsomely."

I was cautious enough at this proposal: I had always found that travelling-companions lengthened any journey I made, for I soon tired of their conversation. But his offer of money, despite the long-windedness and obscurity of his language, made me consider otherwise. After all, I reasoned, if we did not suit each other, one or other of us could turn off the road. I therefore asked, could I know his name perhaps, since he knew mine?

"I am, evidently, Sir Thomas," was the short reply, which sufficed.

And it suffices also to say that, after some close, but civilised, bargaining, we struck an agreement, which would advance my own ambitions in equal measure to his. It will be noteworthy only, that, in negotiation of the accord, Sir Thomas expressed an enthusiasm for Universal Languages.

"I have a great interest in the wealth of language," he informed me. "In my youth, I fought many valiant campaigns in France, Italy and Austria, and the expressions that are utilised in these lands for our agreement are far more more idoneous than 'contract', which mercantilistic term you have employed. In Austria, for example, courtly people make a distinction between '*Verständigung*' and '*Verständnis*', of which the posterior, I believe, expresses our agreement more pikestafficiously. And in France, the word '*agrément*' in its plural form is far more pleasant to the otocystic organ. So," he declared, clasping my hand, looking at me in a manner I considered rather too sly for a man making a contract, "let us swear an oath, as gentlemen, to uphold our *Verständnis* and our *agréments*!"

And so we shook hands on our contract. From the feel of his hand, he was indeed an Ancient, and I secretly doubted that he would survive the troubles of the long journey. He must have caught a hint of my concern, for he advised me that he had money to hire a cart or carriage for any parts of the road which tired him or me. "But I am a fortitudinous Scottish warrior!" he shouted defiantly, as if to warn me off any concern for his antiquity, striking the flagstones with his stick. "Not one of your latter-day weaklings, not your effeminate, anaemic, flaccid, infirm, lily-livered, decrepit milksops, depraved curs, dunghill-cocks, teat-sucking poltroons, lachrymose debilitati, these numskulled zanies, the witless muffs that military men have now become!"

Recoiling under this onslaught, I stepped out again into the dusk, and proceeded to my lodging for the night. I was surprised to find that it was only ten minutes after five when I reached the inn, and could not account for the slow passage of time. Even more curious was the fact that the wind had died down completely in those few minutes, and that a moon, almost full, now blazed out from a cloudless sky upon the silent town of Cromarty. But I was grateful that I had not missed my supper; and that the black dog was nowhere to be seen.

*   *   *

On the following morning, having been paid for my work by the grateful Minister of the church, I found my new companion by the gates to the graveyard, carrying a small wooden box with a strap crossed firmly over his chest, and we set off as best we could towards the south. After only two hundred yards on the road, however, it was evident that Sir Thomas had over-gauged his old-fashioned strength. We would walk at a very slow pace for twenty yards, and then he would feel obliged to stop, leaning on his stick, distracted – apparently – by the depth of his own conversational powers; but in reality, gasping for breath and trying to rally the failing vigour of his legs. At length, fearing that we would not reach the next wind-scoured farmyard, let alone Inverness, in the day's journeying, I appealed to his sense of nobility, by proposing that we travel in style, by hiring a cart to take us to a ferry which would bring us close to Fort George, on the southern shore of the treacherous Moray Firth.

"Ah!" exclaimed Sir Thomas, shaking his stick in my face and sneering the while. "Then you have lost the utility of your limbs, you impotent maggot? When I was of your age, and older yet, I could march for forty, fifty miles in a day, with all my arms and armour, my breast-plate, my sword and shield, fight a duel with three, sometimes four, skilled swordsmen, and still throw off my journal abiliaments and deliver amatory justice to a well-proportioned woman in the evening! Away with you, you par-boiled degenerate! Take my nobles, find a willing conductor – but do not superlucrate him!" As I stood looking blankly at him, he aimed a swing of his stick at me: "Do not pay him too much, you loggerheadistic minion! Be off!" Regretting already that I had agreed to make him my travelling-companion, I took the silver coin which he pulled from his ragged coat, and set off back to Cromarty; where I engaged a boy with a cart to take us to the ferry at Rosemarkie, where we hailed the ferry and boarded.

It was a grim day and the racing tide on the Firth threatened many times to overwhelm us. But, with Sir Thomas insulting the poor ferry-man all the way, and chastising his fellow-passengers, two clerical gentlemen who shrank visibly under his verbal assaults on their "Presbyterian asininities, mongrel Calvinist dogmas and sanctimonious hypocrisy", we made it safely to the far side; whereupon the two Kirk representatives scuttled off into the gloom of the afternoon, the ferry-man rowed to a safe distance from the shore, and shouted profanities and spat in our direction; but kept his fee; whereupon we engaged another ruddy-faced youth to drive us to the convalescent town of Nairn. Unfortunately, the youth's horse was greatly afflicted by wind in the gut, and expelled loud farts in our direction every ten yards or so, such that we were obliged to cover our noses and mouths with scarves to avoid the stench. Sir Thomas was greatly insulted by this, and expended a great deal of energy in shouting at the horse for the length of the journey. The horse, however, was not in the least discomfited at being the subject of abuse; being, on the contrary, greatly encouraged in its efforts by the raucous reception. Our driver was interested in all the words which poured from Sir Thomas' mouth, and mightily pleased with the entertainment. Thus, we rolled into Nairn, where the horse resided and was evidently – to judge from the shouts of welcome in the narrow streets – well-known as "Cracking Charlie".

It was the bad fortune of Mr. Humble and Mr. Kneale, our two ecclesiastical companions on the voyage over the Firth, to find themselves in the same elegant inn as ourselves that night. As soon as he saw them, Sir Thomas was up and at them again, growling like a dog with a touch of the heat, proclaiming himself to be *Christianus Presbyteromastix* – eater of Presbyterians! – belabouring the ears of all within, with a vocabulary that few had heard and fewer still remembered. At last, a braver man than most, with the anatomy, aspect and bearing of a blacksmith or forester, called across the room for him to keep his peace. At this, to the surprise and relief of everyone else, the old gentleman guffawed, raised his glass to the dare-devil, and toasted "The King, the Bitch, and the Bombastic Braggarts of Scotland"; to which everyone acquiesced, with some muttered questions as to "which King?", "which Bitch?". Sir Thomas then turned his attention to a slightly over-ripe bar-maid, addressing her innermost secret curves with some witty and bawdy quatrains, in which similes drawn from the sphere of grain-farming were prominent; and when he expressed to the *belle-dame* a desire for "visuriency" and "tacturiency", both Mr. Humble and Mr. Kneale fled precipitately from the room; all of which brought the entire company to a peak of untrammelled enthusiasm. The evening ended in the uproarious singing of bawdy songs, considerable liberties being taken by Sir Thomas upon the person of the bar-maid, and in a devoutly expressed agreement amongst the men of Nairn that the Cromartarians were not such simple loons after all.

As we retired for the night, I asked myself for the twentieth time that day, whether I had been wise in attaching myself to this troublesome old man. But when I considered what he had told me of his schemes for a "Universal Language" in the church-yard at Cromarty, and his solemn promises of assistance in my struggle, I knew I had found in him the card with which to trump the play of Dr. Bosman, once and for all.

*   *   *

We therefore travelled, in the style to which Sir Thomas rapidly became accustomed, to the towns aforementioned, in each of which I would spend a day repairing the effects of time and the cold North-East climate upon poor, run-down, abused church-organs, and a night listening to the ever-more-daring boasts and lewd propositions with which Sir Thomas would ambush and solicit the people of each town.

In the town of Elgin, the nature of Sir Thomas' wooden box was revealed. It had become apparent, in our several days of travelling, that Sir Thomas valued the box highly. Imagine my surprise, then, to be awakened in the early hours of our second day in Elgin, by

Sir Thomas proudly displaying the contents to me, illuminated by a sputtering candle: "Behold the children of Adam and Eve!" he announced, a little enigmatically. I rubbed my eyes, for I had been disturbed from a deep sleep, and peered into his box. There, I saw a nest of straw, and two pairs of beady eyes looking back. It was evident that there were two small brown mice in there; and beside them, a small trembling mass of fur which, on closer inspection, turned out to be a clutch of baby mice. "Twelve of them," said Sir Thomas, with tears in his eyes. "They will be named after the children of Adam." Adam and Eve, it later emerged, were the rodent parents.

We travelled on from Elgin, and Sir Thomas held the box, in which the mouse family now lived, with the greatest caution, throwing a rage if our cart or train was too shaken. At New Deer, the entire family of twelve was displayed to the customers of the inn, and their gender determined. There were eleven females in the brood and one male; the latter was named, after careful examination by Sir Thomas, "Gargantua". At which remark, all the customers and Sir Thomas were helpless with mirth.

When my business at Old Deer was complete, rather than spend the night in the rather poor inn which was kept there, we made our way by a rather dilapidated train the few miles to Peterhead, where I had to keep another appointment; it being a Wednesday night, and I had promised to address yet again the assembled brothers of the Self-Betterment League, whose ranks were composed of men assisting in the building of the Harbour of Refuge against the North Sea.

For it is not my main purpose in life to repair the ravages of time and smooth the tones of rustic organs; but rather to promote the Universal Language of the Future, the World-Language, *Vol-a-pük*. To which end, besides my position as General Secretary of the Edinburgh Society for the Propagation of a Universal Language, I give lectures and lessons to those who ask, up and down the east coast of Scotland and its hinterland.

This was my fourth visit to the Self-Betterment League of Peterhead in the past year, and a small number of the members had made considerable advances with the grammar and the inflection of nouns and verbs. However, the vast majority had still not grasped the simplest basic pronunciation of vowels and consonants. This was largely due to the fact that the men here had come to Peterhead from all points of the compass, from the farthest Western Hebrides to the rocky tips of the Broch, from the icy shores of Shetland to the deepest dales of Yorkshire, from Wales even and beyond. With this huge variety of men came a huge variation in the pronunciation of, for example, the letter "r", or the simple words "book" and "church". I had determined, therefore, that I would not leave Peterhead until I had brow-beaten these coarse men into correct pronunciation of the simple essential sounds of Volapük.

*   *   *

The town of Peterhead is a pit of despair, for it has little to recommend it on a winter's night, or indeed on a summer's day, its main boast being the splendid new Prison. I was advised, by one of my students who had taken great pride in the construction of that fortress, that its main block, containing 208 cells, was built of concrete, and measured 150 feet long, by 40 feet wide and 40 high. There was, for the more recalcitrant prisoner, a separate "Cell Block", in which eight convicts might be held in seclusion. I understand that most of, the prisoners, who began to arrive there only three years ago, are from Glasgow, and few more than thirty years of age: this is indeed a sad reflection on the social conditions in that forsaken city, and a cause for concern amongst those who would improve the lot of the Common Man. Since many garrotters are amongst the convicts, for the ease and peace of mind of the fishing community which surrounds the Prison, no man is permitted to escape, the outer wall being 18 feet high and topped by a triangular coping, which does not lend itself to easy purchase. The very gate, which I have seen, is of stout oak, measuring 12 feet by 12 feet. By day, prisoners may be seen, under strictest guard, working far out upon the breakwater; but it is my opinion that it will be many years yet before the harbour is completed.

Notwithstanding the bleak aspect of the town, this night in Peterhead was a great success. Between the hours of seven o'clock and nine, we were hard at it in a draughty room in Constitution Street. I attribute our success partly to the intelligence and wisdom of the men who were willing to learn; partly to my skill in setting out the lesson in easy stages, and paying close attention to each man's native accent and way of pronunciation; and partly also to the fear and desperation which arose in my students as Sir Thomas stepped among them, encouraging, shouting, harassing, beating where necessary a rhythm on the floor with his stick and sometimes – I regret – on the arms and legs of my pupils. But the method of instruction is not for debate, only the final result. For this Hand-Book, therefore, I reproduce:

Lesson One: How Volapük is to be Pronounced.

The alphabet of Volapük contains twenty-seven letters: **a ä b c d e f g h i j k l m n o ö p r s t u ü v x** y and **z**. You will see that the letters **q** and **w** have been omitted and three new ones (**ä, ö, ü**) introduced from another source, which is the German alphabet.

As native speakers of English, you should forget how you normally pronounce this alphabet: do not say "(h)ay", "be", "see", "dee", "ee", "eff" and so on, but follow the rules set out below.

In learning to pronounce Volapük, the first difficulty is to avoid sounding the vowels **a e i o u** like their English names **A E I O U**.

Always think of them and speak of them by their Volapük names.

The Volapük syllables:	**pa**	**pe**	**pi**	**po**	**pu**
are **not** to be read as:	pay	pea	pie	po(t)	pew
but like the English syllables:	**pa(h)**	**pay**	**pea**	**po(le)**	**poo**

Read them over carefully several times, then drop the **p** sound and repeat **a e i o u**: "ah, ay, ee, oh, oo".

The adding of another consonant at the end does not change the vowel sound; therefore, **pet** is pronounced "pate" (not "pet"); **pit** is pronounced "peat" (not "pit"); **pot** rhymes with "goat", not with "got"; **put** rhymes with "boot", not with "but".

Clearly, much will depend on how you pronounce such words as "father", "food", and so on. If Mr. Davis from Lanarkshire addresses his male parent as "faither", rather (or raither) than "father", then he cannot be asked to compare the pronunciation of the vowel "a" to that word; he must perforce use "dad". Similarly with the word "food", which can be closer to "fid", depending on which part of the Kingdom you come from.

So: practise these vowels a few times – "ah, ay, ee, oh, oo" – and then move on.

The new vowel **ä** is to be pronounced quite simply as the short "e" in "get", or "wet". Do not be confused: the Volapük **e** is the long one, as in "they", the Volapük **ä** is the short one.

The vowel **ö** is pronounced as the vowel in "word" or "sir". Have a care not to rhyme "word" with "turd", or "sir" with "cur", however much your Republican feelings may drive you. The vowel is half-way between "e" – as in "bed" – and "o" as in "boat": say the word "boat-bed" very quickly a number of times until you find the happy medium. The lips being drawn back as if to say **e** ("bed"), try to say **o** ("oh").

And the vowel **ü** is pronounced as in the Scottish "who" or "rude" or "food". The lips being protruded as if to say **u** ("oo"), try to say **i** ("ee").

I asked Mr. Johnston to attempt to pronounce the new vowels, since he was girning and complaining and threatening to leave. "Mr. Johnston," I proposed, "would you step up here and repeat after me . . . " Of course, the man was quite hopeless at any subtle distinction between the vowels, excelling only at **ü**. He felt out-manoeuvred at the subtle intonation of **ö**, and all his attempts at "sir" and "bird" came out as "surr" and "burrd". His premise was that the language was unpronounceable by "any decent man", in which judgement he found a passionate supporter in Mr. Witherspoon, a man of very few merits. Alas, he found no other person in the room to support him, for they knew him to be uncouth. Mr. Johnston – like our own Mr. Gunn in Edinburgh – was a firm believer that English would do for Everyman, "be they white, black, or just plain foreign". Mr. Theodor Witherspoon, for his part, was outraged that the alphabet had no place for a "W", or – apparently – the short "I", the short "O", or the sound "TH", which four absences placed his name at a sore disadvantage. It was in vain that I argued with him, and others who murmured support, that these sounds were omitted in order to allow for those nations who were incapable of pronouncing such sounds; "We look to a Universal Fraternity," I re-iterated. I had intended to explain to my class that the letter "R" was greatly frowned upon in Volapük, since it would cause difficulty to our friends in China and Nippon; but I considered that we had gone far enough down this road and thought not to endanger such advances as we had made that evening.

As it happened, ten minutes of energetic coaching from Sir Thomas, whose consummate mastery of the new vowel-sounds startled me, was enough to render both Johnston and Witherspoon as eager and adept as any at the new rules of pronunciation. Under a withering onslaught of epithets, the two "lobcocks" were discouraged from their "blightery", and encouraged to become "linguafascinated"; none of these words attached to the comprehension of anyone in that cold room, but their significance was clear enough.

Of the consonants, the only ones likely to cause difficulty are **c**, **g**, **j** and **z**.

- **C** is to be pronounced as either "ch" or "j" – I admit there is some confusion in this, one that even a lengthy debate at the Great Assembly of 1889 did not adequately resolve. With the able assistance of Mr. McLean from Uist and Mr. Leask from Ayr, I attempted to show how the letter could be pronounced, simply by asking them to say the word "church" and then the word "judge". In McLean's mouth, the syllable sounded the same for both words; whereas Mr. Leask had no difficulty in making a distinction. However, both versions seem quite permissible for all practical purposes.
- **G** is only ever to be pronounced as in "got", and never as in "George".
- **J** is deceptive. It is never pronounced as in "judge" (even allowing for the Hebridean variation on this). It is always pronounced "sh", as in "**sh**oe".
- Finally, **z** is to be pronounced as "ts", as in "lo**ts**", "boa**ts**", and not as in "zoetrope" or "haze".

Let us consider the following English words spelt, as nearly as possible, in Volapük letters:

A magistrate: **cöc**. A farmyard fowl: **gus**. An adjective describing an ill-considered idea: **herbrend**. The edible parts of the pig: **ham**, **bekän**, **brens**. A number of different animals: **jip**, **goz**, **bors**. The endless call of a summer-time bird: **küku, küku, küku.**

It will be best at this stage to spell your own names as if they were words of Volapük. For example, my name is **Gämäl Höntar Öbidäm Cöstös**. Some innocent hilarity may be gained from writing names of ordinary people, or ordinary objects, upon a blackboard. Consider the labourers George Hartson and John Shanks, both ordinary men, with never the slightest claim to sophistication between them; and consider now their exotic names: **Corc Harzön** and **Con Janx**. Even **Tiodor Vödärspun** and **Cems Constön** were given a veneer of interest as a result of this evening's work.

Two further rules are to be observed:

Firstly, that the accent is always on the last syllable of a word, unless it ends with the hyphenated suffixes **-li** and **-la**. For example: **getom**; **getom-li?**; **if getom-la** (I get; do I get?; if I were to get).

Secondly, that two vowels coming together are sounded in separate syllables; as **laut** (*la-ut*, lah-oot), **geil** (*ge-il*, gay-eel), **sied** (*si-ed*, see-aid).

And follow the good advice of Mr. Sprague (to whom I will introduce you shortly): "When you meet with a new Volapük word, do not 'jump' at its pronunciation by guessing what the letters might spell in English, but consider each sound. If it is necessary to analyse it, do so in the following manner: begin at the last vowel; sound it alone; prefix a consonant; affix another consonant, if any, until the last syllable is sounded. Then build up another syllable in the same way; sound the two together, accenting the last. Then the next syllable, sounding all three, accenting the last. And so on."

Thus, to read the word **jivolapükatidel**: (a female teacher of Volapük)

e	(h)ay	**a**	Ah
de	Day	**la**	Lah
del	dale	**lapükatidel**	lah-pükáh-
i	Ee		teadále
ti	Tea	**o**	oh owe
tidel	tea-dále	**vo**	Vo
a	Ah	**volapükatidel**	voláh-pükáh-
ka	Kah		teadále
katidel	kah-tea-dále	**i**	Ee
ü	-ü-{see above}	**ji**	She
pü	Pü	**jivolapükatidel**	she-voláh-
pükatidel	pükáh-teadále		pükáh-teadále

The End of the First Lesson.

The evening of instruction for the workers at Peterhead ended at around nine o'clock, in high good humour; and we retired to a nearby public-house at the command, and generous expense, of Sir Thomas, to spend the rest of the evening in practical exercises of the Volapük Pronunciation. After two pints of Mr. Whyte's 80/- Ale, Sir Thomas chalked a rhyme on the board behind the bar, normally reserved to record the credit extended to regular patrons. The verse, which he announced was entitled "Jill and Joe O'er Hill and Dell", is reproduced here only for a didactic purpose and should not be understood in any immoral manner. It runs as follows:

> Jill a grit o mitten,
> An Jill, Joe am fain tizz;
> Hill lear on jizz,
> An fills cuss raisin.
>
> Jill part her in Dinah it,
> An greet pox hill big in;
> Dell filter ask we king,
> An dell haul in Diella it.

And it proved of gradual and huge entertainment to those who had attended my classes, as slowly and painfully they read it aloud; but the other customers were ill-humoured and dismissive, frowning at the nonsense-rhyme and telling us to "keep the noise down!" There were, amongst the customers, some guards from the prison; it was evident that there was a bitter enmity between the workers on the harbour wall and the warders from the convict prison, both considering themselves to be of the higher class of worker; and the arrogant requests of the Warders for some peace and quiet, aroused only a fiery defiance in their rivals.

At length, the landlord himself decided that there was something amiss with the verse, and rubbed it from the board. This led inevitably to precipitate behaviour on the part of some of my students, ably led by Sir Thomas, who stood on a table at the back of the room, shouting encouragement: "Up and at them! *Avanti*! my valiant heroes! *Los! Los!* Peel these vapouring infencibles limb from limb, my unflinching autochthons, my bellicose swashbucklers, my mettlesome myrmidons! Prove yourselves as dreadless hondersponders, as indomitable janissaries, as armigerous mercenaries! Discomfit these wasps, genitalectomise them, my palestrical skirmishers! Besquatter the walls with their sangrial liquids!" Simultaneously, he laid about himself with his stick, dust flying from his wig, cracking any head and whacking any hand which came within reach.

The landlord sighed and shook his head, picked up a bucket of cold water from behind the bar and, without moving from his stance, expertly cast the contents across fifteen feet of air, to douse the brawling parties in the centre of the floor; and returned to his business of polishing glasses. Obviously, he had had a good deal of practice in this discipline; however, Sir Thomas was there again, urging on the dripping warriors.

In due course, a pair of constables burst in through the door, and the disturbance was soon quelled. At the first sign of the men in blue, I noted that Sir Thomas hopped nimbly from the table-top, huddled himself up in a corner, and looked the very picture of aged frailty and distraught decency; the constables treated him with respect, and refused to believe the landlord or the outraged prison-warders that the feeble patriarch had had anything to do with the outrage; and provided him with an escort to the lodging-house where we had taken a room. For my part, I ran from the public-house to seek shelter with one of my students; and spent a most uncomfortable night sharing a cold bed with him.

Transactions I: An Historical Introduction

*Being a copy of an Open Letter to the Brothers and
Sisters of the Inverness Trades Linguistical Society,
Written on 3rd February, 1891, at Portsoy.*

Menad bal – pük bal!!

Glidis, o flens löfik e sufälik! Greetings, dear and patient Friends! In
your letter of September last, you asked me to write to you with an
outline of the history of The Edinburgh Society for the Propagation
of a Universal Language.

I have decided to prepare a Hand-Book of the pre-eminent Universal
Language, Volapük. You can rest assured that this book will be a central
work of reference to all students of Volapük, put together by an Author
immersed in the subtleties and scope of that Holy Grail of Modern
Times, the Search for a Universal Language. When the book is finally
published, the Reader will find, as he or she progresses, that an
understanding of the fundamental rules and vocabulary of Volapük
will be easily and swiftly acquired: this is attributable simply to the
clear-headedness of the Author and his ability to make obvious the
most difficult ideas. Since I am that Author, it is plain that I understand his strengths and I can make that claim without fear of contradiction.

This present letter, then, will serve two purposes: firstly, to reply
adequately to your request of last quarter; and secondly, to be an
Introduction to my book, which I expect to be published to the very
greatest scientific and popular acclaim.

But before I discuss with you the imperative for a Universal
Language, and guide you on a safe road past the bogs and screes
prepared for you by the partisans of lesser languages, let me pause
briefly to warn you against Dr. Henry Bosman, of Edinburgh. This
man is none other than a snake, a viper, a serpent, a reptile, an asp, an
adder in the bracken, whom you should by no means trust, though he
come to you waving the banner of The Edinburgh Society for the
Propagation of a Universal Language, voicing words of blandishment,

and offering untold riches. It was but last month that he and I crossed swords once more at the regular meeting of our Society. He, proposing a motion that "the Society notes with disfavour the General Secretary's promotion of Volapük, and recommends the expulsion of the General Secretary from our ranks"; I, counter-proposing "that the members of the Society distance themselves unanimously from the Chairman's provocations and remove the Chairman from office for his attempts to promote Esperanto by under-hand means". After the vote was taken by the members not yet steeled in the scientific methods of Linguistics, and no definite decision taken, I followed Bosman and his tiny coterie down the narrow streets of Tollcross and, with the aid of my comrades Mr. McKelvie and Mr. McKelvie, was able to strike a blow for Fraternal Universality, by the application of kicks to the thighs and blows to the back of the head, all under cover of darkness and with secure concealment of our identity behind mufflers. Bosman showed his lack of comradeship when he treacherously called upon the assistance of a police-constable walking nearby, and demanded retribution from the Agent of the State. We were fortunate to retire in good time, and are determined to carry forward the struggle for One Language and One Humanity, against the machinations of those who oppose us!

Blods e sörs! Brothers and sisters! Is it not our greatest hope and dream that Men should live with Men as brothers, and Nation with Nation as friends? At the end of the nineteenth century, Humanity has surely scaled heights enough to see with a clear eye that the future lies, not in war and mutual destruction, but in co-operation and friendship; not in the brandishing of weapons of annihilation, but in stretching out the hand of peace. Even within Nations, we must recognise that there is nothing of Humanity in the exploitation of many by a few; for a Nation which cannot conduct its domestic affairs in an amicable and fraternal manner also cannot hope to deal with other Nations as friends; similarly, a People which cannot deal with other Peoples as friends, cannot hope to have Justice at home.

Look around you at your own neighbours and fellows: with some of them you have grown up, perhaps, boy and man. But others have come from the countryside or from more distant parts of the land, even from other countries, from France, Italy, Prussia, Russia perhaps. Now ask yourself what it is that binds these people into your community?

Is it their mode of dress? No, for each man and woman dresses richly or poorly according to taste and wealth, in different styles according to their provenance and inclination.

Is it their facial appearance? No: for some are ugly; others, perhaps the female organist in some Tay-side church, possess an astounding beauty; and the vast majority are plain of feature.

Is it then the colour of their skin? No, for some are pale, others swarthy, some may even be black or brown or yellow.

Is it their trade? No, for we can see men who work with their hands, and others with their minds, and some with no trade at all, mere wealthy bowel-worms crawling in the body of society.

Is it their intelligence? No, no and a third time no! – for some only are of high intelligence, with whom a man might discuss serious philosophy; and many others are of mean intelligence, not questioning the world and the heavens; and some others, such as a certain gentleman of the medical profession, are so stubborn, so vicious and self-preserving, that they rarely use the intelligence given to them.

No, we recognise this – that it is *language* which unites your neighbours with each other and with yourself: all members of a community will, one way or another, speak the native-tongue of the country in which they reside. Admittedly, some are teuchters, with a rough and barely-comprehensible manner of speech, as is the case here in Portsoy; others display Sassenach or European accents; still others stumble over words longer than a single syllable, albeit in their native tongue. But the words and the grammar, however feebly grasped, are our common link. You make friends with the newcomers when you speak with them, using a tongue that both parties comprehend. If there is no common language, there is no common wealth.

For that reason, the Author advocates this solution to the troubles of the world: *"Menad bal – pük bal"*, which means: One Humanity – One Language. Let this be your first lesson in Volapük, my eager friends of Inverness – *"bal"* – the number, one; *"menad"* – Humanity, or Mankind; *"pük"* – speech, language.

The declared intention of my work is to introduce Readers to the basic ideas, grammar and vocabulary of this inspiring world-language. By the time you have completed all twenty of the lessons in the Hand-Book, you will have joined the growing battalions of those struggling for fraternal relations between the Nations of the World.

Let us outline the general purpose of this Hand-Book and History: it is principally to provide a thorough grounding in the language known as "Volapük". *"Vol"* – world; *"pük"* – language: *Vol-a-pük* therefore means "world-language". The Author will guide you, surely and with due regard to the strengths and weaknesses of your varied intelligence, to the acquisition of the basic fundaments and cornerstones of grammar. He will, with a skill honed in many years of teaching, introduce you to Tenses, and Cases, and Genders, and the inflection of the Verbs. And finally, he will share with you a Vocabulary, a Promptuary of the most useful words of the new language.

The Author has based his lessons on those provided by the illustrious Mr. Charles E. Sprague of New York, in his "Hand-Book of Volapük" which appeared three years ago, to the greatest acclaim. I have written to Mr. Sprague, requesting his permission to use some extracts of his grand work; but although my envelope was addressed and the letter couched in the best Volapük, I have not, as yet, had an answer. No matter: the treasury of Volapük is open to all, and I am certain Mr. Sprague will not object to my use of his text.

Having recognised my American comrade's contribution, I will now give a brief summary of the origins of Volapük, taken directly and without apology from Mr. Sprague's Introduction:

"This 'world-language' was invented and first published in 1879 by Johann Martin Schleyer, a German, and a priest of the Roman Catholic Church, who had become a very accomplished linguist. The system is entirely his production, and has not been modified in any essential point.

His aim was, first, to produce a language capable of expressing thought with the greatest clearness and accuracy; second, to make its acquisition as easy as possible to the greatest number of human beings. He resolved to seek these ends by observing the processes of the many languages with which he was acquainted; following them as models wherever they are clear, accurate and simple, but avoiding their faults, obscurities and difficulties.

[. . .] For some time after [the appearance of Herr] Schleyer's grammar, his adherents were few, and his project was ignored by the scientific and literary world. It spread first to Austria where it awakened considerable interest, and where the first society for its propagation was formed at Vienna in 1882. Until 1884 its adherents outside of the German-speaking countries were very few and scattered. In that year it invaded Holland and Belgium, and a great many societies sprang up in those countries. In 1885, Dr. Auguste Kerckhoffs, Professor in the School of Higher Commercial Studies, at Paris, introduced it to the French nation by several articles, lectures and treatises. This created a great sensation in France and a strong National Association '*pour la propagation du Volapük*' was formed, which numbers such men as Francisque Sareey, Emile Gauthier, and Dr. Allaire.

Prof. Kerckhoffs aroused enthusiasm, not only in France, but in other countries where his works were circulated. Spain was the next, followed by Italy and Portugal. During 1885 and 1886 the countries of the North – Sweden, Denmark and Russia – also received the new language. Thus, the extension of Volapük has been geographical, and the English-speaking peoples are the last of the great European races to be affected by it. In each country, as a rule, its popularisation has immediately followed the publication of a grammar peculiarly suited to its people.

Prof. Kerckhoffs, some months ago, estimated the number of persons who have studied Volapük at 210,000. This may be somewhat too high, but the number is certainly very large. In Vienna alone, the classes during the winter of 1886–8 were attended by 2,500 students; 138 societies for its cultivation have been organised in different places.

Eleven periodicals are now published, devoted primarily to Volapük, at Constance, Breslau, Madrid, Paris, Vienna, Munich, Puerto-Rico, Stockholm, Aabybro (Denmark), and Antwerp, the youngest being four months old, and the oldest, six years. Most of these contain articles in the language of the country, as well as in Volapük; but three of them, one being a humorous paper, are exclusively in Volapük.

The bibliography of the subject (as given at length in *Le Volapük*, No. 10) comprises 96 books in 13 languages. This does not include articles in periodicals, nor Schleyer's single-sheet compendiums in various languages, nor works merely announced as forth-coming.

Two General Assemblies, or Congresses, of the advocates of Volapük, have been held: the first at Friedrichshafen, in August, 1884;

the second at Munich, in August, 1887. The third is to take place at Paris, probably in August, 1889.

The Congress of 1887 established a three-fold organisation: a General Association of the supporters of Volapük (*Volapükaklub Valemik*); an Academy of Volapük (*Kadem Volapüka*); a Central Organ (*Volapükabled Zenodik*). Schleyer's own *Weltspracheblatt*, published at Constance, was designated as the organ, and its name has been changed accordingly. Each of these organisations has its officers, Schleyer remaining at the head of the whole movement. The Director of the Academy is Prof. Kerckhoffs; his colleagues number, at present, 17, from various nations: Germany, Austro-Hungary, Spain, Italy, Portugal, Holland, England, the United States, Russia, Syria. The Academy is expected to edit the standard dictionary and grammar, to authorise new words, to adopt any necessary changes, and to give their sanction to approved works of instruction."

Let there be no doubt in your minds: my Hand-Book of Volapük, which will shortly be made available to all men and women in Inverness, Dingwall, Ullapool, and beyond, will turn upsides-down your view of the world; it will provide answers to questions which you had never thought to ask; it will divert you down new avenues of speculation and purpose. In the end, we expect that it will thoroughly inspire you to join in the fraternal struggle for Democracy in this Nation and for Peace in this World. One Humanity requires One Language:

Menad bal – pük bal!!
Your Brother in Correspondence,
Spodan olsik blodiko,

GEMMELL HUNTER IBIDEM JUSTICE
February 1891

Chapter 2: The Numbers

Notes on lessons given on the Road from
Aberdeen to Arbroath. February 1891.

Of our journey from Peterhead to Aberdeen, there is nothing of note to relate. It passed without any further incident requiring the attention of constable or magistrate, although a trail of mature broken hearts and injured spirits lay in our wake. Sir Thomas and I passed some fruitful hours in exploring some of the basic points of the pronunciation of Volapük. But my abiding memory of these days was that Sir Thomas never once stopped talking; it was as if he had been locked away for centuries, without a living soul to speak to. It was greatly wearing.

At Inverurie, we transferred from cart to railway-train, which brought us to the railway-station, foetid with the smell of fish, at Aberdeen. As we came into that city, Sir Thomas was moved to reminisce about an "old co-linguisticator", by the name of George Dalgarno, who had studied in the University there, and who had – so Sir Thomas said – "outshone, like a meteor in the asteristic firmament, all others of his class". With a distant look in his eye, Sir Thomas asked me if I knew what had become of Dalgarno: I had to confess that I knew nothing of the man, beyond his famous "Ars Signorum" and "Didascalocophus", and some collaboration with Mr. Wilkins; at the mention of the name Wilkins, Sir Thomas became enraged to undue degree, and we changed trains at the Station in poor spirits.

Between Inverurie and Arbroath, I had seven organs which required my attention. Our route therefore took us to the quietest of places – by railway first to Stonehaven: which mode of travel seemed to give Sir Thomas considerable anxiety, for he could see neither rhyme nor reason for our forwards movement at all, let alone at such terrifying speed. Even allowing for his residence in Cromarty, I began to wonder how much he had kept away from human society. We travelled on to Inverbervie; then by cart or horse to Johnshaven, Laurencekirk, Fettercairn, Friockheim and Lunan. Sir Thomas provided a silver or gold coin for each stage of our journey, so we travelled in some comfort. Noticing that he dispensed his wealth as if he were

Royalty itself on tour, I asked him how he came to have so deep a bag of coins with him. "Longistatic debts, Mr. Justice, antiquagenitive arrears," he replied with a smug smile on his horrible brown face. "In recent months, I have visited the spawn of Mr. Cuthbert of Draikies and the insolvent bastards of Mr. Leslie of Findrassie, where I have sought compensation, retribution, indemnification, and nullification. The debts of the fathers have been recouped from the sons, even to the twelfth and thirteenth generations! Turn and turn and turn again, and out comes all the sediment, like a remuage in Verona!"

I thought to keep silent on this, considering that, with the temper and moods which I knew of Sir Thomas, I might hear more than I wished of his methods of calling in old debts, and their likely incompatibility with the laws of the land. However, as we had some way to go between Johnshaven and Laurencekirk, he had started on a theme of his own, which required no interruption from me. "Did you know, sir, that I can trace my intemerate ancestry to Adam through the paternal line, and to Eve through the maternal line? One hundred and fifty-two pregenitors, and I can prove them all!" Perhaps I displayed my disbelief too openly, for he struck out at me with his walking-stick, and proceeded, over the next two miles, to recite to me, in reverse order, the names of his father and his father's father and his father's father's father, and so on; and sure enough (I lost count after reaching ten), we came to Adam. But that was not all, for he set to with his mother, and her mother, and that mother's mother, until, after two miles more, we arrived at Eve. What struck me was that, if his father was descended from Adam, and his mother from Eve – was there some close-breeding at work here? But I found no opportunity to pursue this thought: no sooner had he finished with his mother's family-tree, than Sir Thomas demanded to know of my family – who was my father and his father before him. Alas for my pride, I could go back only two generations on my father's side (for my great-grandmother appears to have mislaid her husband), and only three on my mother's side. My travelling-companion was overcome with amusement at this, spouting tears of mockery and poking me with his annoying stick. "That is why I have a cornucopia of crowns and guineas, you slubberdegullion, and you wear the empty horns of *hoi polloi*!"

Thinking to distract him from this disrespectful pursuit, I proposed
that we while away the miles in counting to one hundred and fifty-two
in Volapük. Almost immediately, Sir Thomas was swept away by his
enthusiasm for this novel Universal Language; for all his faults, he was
a true student, a seeker after knowledge. "Let us commence, and
proceed with no interruption!" he agreed, and settled in his saddle to
learn. And so we commenced and proceeded with

Lesson Two: The Numbers.

1	is	**bal**	6	is	**mäl**
2	is	**tel**	7	is	**vel**
3	is	**kil**	8	is	**jöl**
4	is	**fol**	9	is	**zül**
5	is	**lul**			

Thus, if a man is – fortunately – "man" in Volapük, then one man is
"bal man", two men is "tel mans", then on to "kil mans", "fol mans"
and so on. There is no easy way of remembering these numbers, so I
would ask you to repeat them in groups of three until you have them
firmly in your head: **bal tel kil; fol lul mäl; vel jöl zül.** Remember to
use the correct pronunciation!

If it helps to remember them, notice that the vowel in each
successive word is **a e i o u** and then **ä, e, ö, ü.**

We rode slowly down the windswept roads of Angus that afternoon,
taking it in turns to shout out numbers. We thought of: **bal** balloon;
tel tales; **kil** keels; **fol** foals; **lul** loons; **mäl** females; **vel** failings; **jöl**
shillings; **zül** starlings. We saw: **bal** farmer; **tel** tails; **kil** queans; and so
on.

Sir Thomas composed a small ditty which helped us on our
journey, one in which a lady of easy virtue set out of an evening with
nine dresses, only to find that she was divested of these one by one by
her lover, until but the thinnest of these remained. Greatly pleased
with himself, he insisted on roaring this out as we approached the
tiny hamlet of Garvock, and – to my deep shame – on completing
the song with a line where the lady wore no dress at all, and the
consequences thereunto. I will not repeat it, for the number zero is
not part of our lesson: the Volapük word "**nos**" suffices. A more
innocent round may be used by my students – I would suggest the

song of "green bottles", or of the farmer, the dog and his meadow?

Counting repeatedly, we at last spied Laurencekirk on the moor ahead of us, where, on the following day, I had my work to do. A grim place, this town, swept by blasts from east and west. Apart from the long main street, which stretched for an incredible distance, there were three churches and one railway-station, providing the country-folk of that district with a means of escape to the wider world. I laboured at my task in the most promising of the three churches. Many years ago, perhaps, there had been great money spent on this place, for the organ was a massive one with no fewer than forty ranks of flue-pipes, and the speech which could be persuaded from these pipes – in bygone days – must have brought all sinners to their knees. Alas – no more; for half of the pipes were encrusted with rust, and spoke no more, and the ivory faces of the stops had yellowed and cracked; there was a great swell-shade which was split top to bottom as if by the anger of a Vengeful God. For ten years past, my only task at this organ was to conceal its irreparable demise: in the secrecy of a dark night, I had removed the original pedal-board and the manuals, and put in their place a simple harmonium, whose sound wheezed out faintly from the simple metal reeds, while the organist pedalled away furiously to maintain a flow of air. But the Minister would have it no other way – only, he, I, and the organist, Mr. Farquhar, had any idea that the magnificent structure of the original organ spoke no more, and that the sound came from a cheap harmonium buried in its frame, like a parasite. Perhaps the congregation simply imagine that their hearing has worsened, year by year.

I learned later that, as I perpetuated the deceit this day, Sir Thomas had forced the acquaintance of a rather impressionable spinster living in the town, Miss Jamieson, and had plied her so much with his flattery, and promised her – doubtless – treasures from every sphere of existence, that she willingly sat down and embroidered in white thread on the mittens he wore to warm his hands, one on the reverse of each finger: **bal tel kil fol lul mäl vel jöl zül**. All that Sir Thomas had then to do was remember that **bal** was one, and **zül** was nine; and he had to hand, as it were, a cardinal mnemoneutic (or *aide-memoire*) of the very best order. I recommend this ingenious solution to anyone wishing to master the numbers in Volapük. The man was intent, that night in his cups, on telling me the full impertinent details of his dealings with Miss Jamieson and her many skills; but I hummed to myself a Socialist anthem and would hear none of it.

*   *   *

As we progressed then from Laurencekirk to Fettercairn, we advanced to the higher numbers, which are made in the simplest manner possible – just make the integers plural, by adding an **-s**, as follows:

10	is	**bals**	60	is	**mäls**
20	is	**tels**	70	is	**vels**
30	is	**kils**	80	is	**jöls**
40	is	**fols**	90	is	**züls**
50	is	**luls**			

To arrive at numbers composed of tens and units, simply join the two parts with an "**e**": so, **balsebal** is 11; **balsetel**, 12; **telsebal**, 21; **lulsevel**, 57; **zülsezül**, 99.

Again, repeating the numbers over and over will drive them into the memory; and so we found as we came down upon Fettercairn for the night. What a place is Fettercairn! Filled, it seemed at first glance, with towers and castles and triumphal arches. Sir Thomas was greatly taken by the comfortableness of the buildings, and declared that he would, upon his return journey, settle there, for it seemed "an eximious location", whose "dimensions of continuate quantity" he greatly praised. We admired, as the sun went down, the arch in memory of the Queen and her Consort; and the Town-House; and the church upon its low-rising hill. In the church, I had some small repairs to make to the wind-chest and a blocked reed-pipe; otherwise, my work here was limited to a general removal of dust and cobwebs, a polishing with soda of the stops and the keys on the manuals; and some adjustments to the pitch of the pipes. For here, no doubt in memory of the Queen and her Consort, standards had not been allowed to slide.

The following day, as we passed down the road, Sir Thomas shifted his ambition from a baronial seat at Fettercairn, to a sandstone mansion in Edzell. But the splendours of that latter town did not divert us from examining the larger numbers as we jolted along in a cart towards Friockheim, as follows:

Tum	is	a hundred

Mil	is	a thousand
Balion	is	a million

When using these higher numbers, simply precede by one of the units: **baltum**, 100; **teltum**, 200; **kilmil**, 3,000; **folmil foltum**, 4,400; **lulmil lultum lulselul**, 5,555; **balmil jöltum zülsebal**, 1891; **jölsevelmil mältum lulsetel**, 87,652.

Unfortunately for me, Sir Thomas decided that he would reinforce his aristocratic superiority by repeating yet again his paternal and maternal lines, in full, this time with the Volapük numbers attached, until he reached Adam, his forebear at number **baltum lulsekil**. I should make it quite clear that Sir Thomas meant, by "Adam", not the patriarch of the mouse-family, which squeaked and rustled by turns in his wooden box, and was fed with crumbs from the table and with cheese; but the purported father of all Men. Those of you among my Readers who have so many ancestors may amuse themselves by emulating my companion's feat; do not, please, do so in my presence.

The End of Lesson Tel.

From Friockheim, where, to my surprise and pleasure, no scandal erupted from our overnight residence, we made our way in great comfort to Lunan. Sir Thomas had found a man who was taking his master's carriage back to Montrose; the man was a discharged soldier, and Sir Thomas had tracked him down at the Masonic Lodge and had plied him with stories enough of war, battles, plunder and camaraderie, in the end to persuade him that we should ride inside, as the rich and the noble of the land. It was a bleak and blustery day; the wind howled across the land, a grim vista of fields and fields and fields; stinging rain and sleet clattered at the windows of our carriage. There was a great air of peace and tranquillity upon Sir Thomas when he had fallen back upon the cushions within and wrapped his legs in a blanket; a flask of brandy kept him warm enough.

He desired some intellectual stimulation – "Instruct me more in numerology!" he commanded. To oblige, I told him all that I knew of the Leibnitzian Scheme, which was represented in Edinburgh by Professor McInnes. This is not the place to go into great detail; I have provided matter on this elsewhere in my Hand-Book. But it whiled away the hours as we splashed and lurched through the miserable roads from Friockheim. Indeed, Sir Thomas was on one occasion so pleased with my story, that he broke into loud and helpless laughter, inflamed by brandy, so riotous that it scared the overhanging crows, and obliged the driver to stop the coach, fearing for the life of his revered Colonel. It was only after the application of considerably more brandy, and a cool blast of the winter sleet upon his brow, that our ancient friend recovered sufficiently for the journey to be continued.

Towards the end of the journey, our driver decided to pause in the shelter of some trees, while his horse rested, and a particularly wild blast of wind raked the land. Sir Thomas invited him inside the carriage, and we shared a flask of rather poor brandy (the coach-man's). As we kept ourselves warm, Sir Thomas decided to regale us with a numerical riddle, an "octastich", or verse of eight lines; each of which he drew carefully upon the steamed glass of the carriage-windows, a quite bewildering series of numbers, which I need not reproduce here. Needless to say, neither I nor our poor driver had any insight into the riddle; which was a cause of exaggerated mirth for Sir Thomas, whose pitiless mockery of us forced even his greatest admirer, our coach-man, to brave the elements once more. Then we resumed our journey, Sir Thomas' numbers fading under the cloud of our breath.

And so we reached Inverkeilor, and took residence with the Minister of the place, Mr. MacPherson. I feared for our accommodation and more so for my contract with Mr. MacPherson, for Sir Thomas was in fiery mood after his journey: the "Chance Inn" on the main street, which was the only alternative place to sleep, gave every appearance of a gambler who had failed his last chance. As good fortune would have it, however, there were no ladies present to pour oil on his flames, MacPherson maintaining an entirely bachelor establishment, upon a small hill over-looking the wild German Ocean and the wide sweep of the coast. Our after-dinner hours were spent in a debate on Sir Thomas' own vision of a Universal Language, a language, he claimed, which had a mere two hundred and fifty root words, on which the rest of the vocabulary was so arranged that its exact meaning could easily be deciphered.

Mr. MacPherson was politely sceptical about this claim, but quite outraged – as indeed was I – by the assertion that this language would afford "such concise words for numbering, that the number for setting down, whereof would require in vulgar arithmetic more figures in a row than there might be grains of sand containable from the centre of the earth to the highest heavens, is in it expressed by two letters"; and further that, "what rational logarithms do by writing, this language does by heart; and by the adding of letters, shall multiply numbers, which is a most exquisite secret in this language: every number, how great soever, may be expressed by a single word." Sir Thomas leered at us triumphantly.

"A single word of two letters, Sir Thomas?!" exclaimed our host, in righteous outrage. "Why, that is absolutely impossible! Consider this – we have twenty-six letters. With two random letters, I can make only the square of twenty-six – which is, if you will allow me—" he paused for thought. "Which is barely six hundred and seventy-six!"

Sir Thomas not unnaturally waved this objection to one side, as being of little consequence. "One single word," he re-iterated. "The letters thereof matter naught. One word alone for any number you choose to calculate." MacPherson being something of a mathematician, a game then commenced, in which he would calculate huge numbers and fire them at Sir Thomas; who sat calmly in his chair and fired back single words, with as many as sixteen or seventeen syllables, which he claimed were the representations of MacPherson's series. To the Minister's great amusement, Sir Thomas' skills at mental mathematics were a fair match for his own, and the game developed into a regular arithmetic contest.

Thus, the evening passed. I excused myself early, claiming that I needed my rest for the work on the following day; and left the pair of them in mutual delight, as they began to debate the numbers of pronounceable words. Monsieur Mersenne, declared Sir Thomas, in his "*Harmonie Universelle*", had calculated that there were thirty-eight million million possible words, and that the number of pronounceable combinations of letters could be adequately expressed only in a number containing no fewer than seventy-three digits. The magnitude of these numbers, I fear, merely stoked the fires of Mr. MacPherson's enthusiasm, and his voice was raised throughout the night in wild debate. I do not know what time they retired, but neither was up and about when I crossed over to the church on the morning.

I laboured that day upon the pitiful organ. Here, there were no grand stops to pull, only simple wooden sliders, by which the put-upon organist would open or close the passage of air to the reed-pipes. One would have thought that the organist must have been a dervish with arms and legs of Malay rubber, for he had the task of pedalling furiously to maintain a pressure of air, sliding the slats in and out to open and close the serried ranks of pipes, and, as if that were not enough, playing the tune. But I knew the organist well enough, and he was a decrepit gentleman of eight and eighty years of age, who could barely walk a dozen yards. Late that afternoon, when my own work was finished, Mr. MacPherson was so generous as to take us to the hamlet of Lunan, to show us the ruined castle and the tiny buildings of the village, and then to its equally tiny station so that we could catch a train into Arbroath. Seated in the tiny waiting-room, out of the continuing wind, but assailed by draughts, Sir Thomas announced that, in gratitude for a most intellectual entertainment, he had provided the Minister with a pair of expensive jewels. I was doubtful as to the wisdom of this, knowing that men of the cloth are frequently perturbed by manifestations of worldly wealth.

"You ill-bred scatophage!" cried Sir Thomas. "I talk of emerods, not emeralds! Have you no wits in that Cromwellian cranium?" He struck me forcibly with his stick and sulked. I rubbed my leg and silently reviewed murderous options. Then the train arrived from Stonehaven and we boarded noisily.

Tidüp kilid (Lesson Three): Days, Months and Ordinals.

Sunday	**balüdel**	January	**balul**
Monday	**telüdel**	February	**telul**
Tuesday	**kilüdel**	March	**kilul**
Wednesday	**folüdel**	April	**folul**
Thursday	**lulüdel**	May	**lulul**
Friday	**mälüdel**	June	**mälul**
Saturday	**velüdel**	July	**velul**
		August	**jölul**
		September	**zülul**
		October	**balsul**
		November	**balsebalul**
		December	**balsetelul**

To pass the brief minutes until we arrived at the well-lit, bustling city of Arbroath, I muttered the days of the week to the rhythm of the rattling wheels: **balüdel; telüdel; kilüdel; folüdel; lulüdel; mälüdel; velüdel.** This was enough, after a mile, to shake Sir Thomas from his mood and ask to learn them. I needed only tell him that the word for "January" was **balul**, and he recited to me, word-perfect, the remainder: **telul; kilul; folul; lulul; mälul; velul; jölul; zülul; balsul; balsebalul; balsetelul.**

Thus we had the **dels** and the **muls**. All that remained, as we pulled into the station, was to indicate the Ordinal Numbers,

First	**balid**
Second	**telid**
Third	**kilid**
Fourth	**folid**
Nine hundred and ninety-ninth	
	zültumzülsezülid

and so on; and we had come to the *Fin tidüpa kilid*.

* * *

We stayed one night at Arbroath, where I had a small repair to make to an organ; we passed that night in the Grand Marine Hotel, a mean little place with no view of the sea to speak of. Sir Thomas was outraged and disbelieving when he discovered that it was a Temperance Hotel, and that no intoxicating drink was to be had in the place. But it was the only hotel open at that time of year, so he obliged us to step across the road to a public-bar named "The Brimming Sea of Haddock", a place whose lack of customers and general air of gloominess dampened the spirits of even Sir Thomas. He tried hard to lift his humour, with two or three whiskies and a song of the round, whose words consisted simply of the numbers eleven to ninety-nine, recited backwards, to a lilting Schottische, ever faster as he neared the end. It was, I have to admit, quite rousing in its way – *zülsezül, zülsejöl, zülsevel, zülsemäl, zülselul, zülsefol, zülsekil, zülsetel, zülsebal,* züls!, *jölsezül, jölsejöl,* and so on; at the end of each decad, he would shout out the name, bang the table and toss another glass of whisky down his throat. But the round played greatly on the nerves of the only other person in the room, a thin, tall, leery-eyed individual with a huge lantern jaw and red nose. Who rose unsteadily from his seat, and called for silence.

Sir Thomas, interrupted at *kilsefol*, looked round slowly at the man.

He stared at him for a full minute, saying nothing. The man, wilting visibly under this gaze, fell back into his seat, muttering "It's only right, it's only right . . . ", and gazing sadly into his empty glass.

"Do you presume, you bravashing surquedist, to give me my orders? You demand that I should forthwith fall into quiescence?" He glared at the poor man, but made no movement with limb or stick. His wig was slightly askew, but otherwise he was a perfect picture of tyrannical dignity. No answer from the man being forth-coming, beyond a side-long glance from an inch above the rim of the empty glass, Sir Thomas continued, his eyes always fixed upon the offending party: "Your temulency does you no honour, sir! It dulls the senses, it ignites the baser passions into flames of foolishness, it dampens the aspirations, and causes common soldiers to forget their station!" He looked hard at the man. "To forget their station," he repeated very slowly and very distinctly.

The man, to his credit, stood up slowly, and, swaying slightly from the waist upwards while his feet felt for a firmer purchase, his eyes cast down, stated clearly, that he "Meant no insult to a gentleman". "I apologise unequivocally for my interruption, which, I fear, was prompted no less by the imbalance of my judgement caused by too much beer and too few potatoes, as by my desire to finish an analysis of the outbreaks of Rhoncholepsy in the Parish of Kirkbuddo, succeeding upon the Wars of Napoleon." He looked up. "Once again, sir, I offer my humblest apologies." With that, the man melodramatically offered the semblance of a bow, no doubt in intended obeisance, which toppled him forwards across the table. There was a sharp rending of cloth, and an anguished cry of "Oh! Oh! – my jaiket!"

Sir Thomas, to his great credit, stepped forward hurriedly and raised the man to his feet again, patting him gently on his torn sleeve. "A bottle of your best brandy for my dissentaneous friend," he commanded the man behind the bar, who, impassive throughout, complied silently.

I noted then, and I would note it again now, that I found Sir Thomas' over-generosity with long words and secret vocabulary very trying indeed. Here was a man, who claimed to be the champion of a Universal Language, using words that no one apart from himself could understand. On more than one occasion, I took him to task for his language, which built a barrier between himself and all others. But

I had nothing for my pains, besides long discourses, couched in Greek, French, Latin and – for all that I knew – invented words, in which he argued that any language could be "Universal", as long as it was understood by all; and all that prevented the great unwashed from understanding his words was their lack of learning – "a matter, sir, to which you have turned your attention, I believe".

After a few minutes, therefore, we were seated more comfortably, a group of *kil*. We introduced ourselves, and found that our new friend was none other than James Shaw, compiler of *The Scottic and Aberbrothic Encyclopaedic Cornucopia*. Mr. Shaw was kind enough to offer us of his store of cold potatoes, to which he was very partial, and of which he maintained a steady supply about his person. We declined politely, although Sir Thomas accepted some for his mice; which did not prevent Mr. Shaw himself from consuming four or five large tubers in the following interesting hour, with considerable relish. As he did so, Sir Thomas declared himself most anxious to hear about this encyclopaedic work, which Mr. Shaw had been compiling for thirty years, since – as he informed us – he had graduated *cum laude in minoribus partibus* from the ancient University of Aberdeen. Following the example of the great John McTaggart, the compiler of the Gallovidian Encyclopaedia, his ambitious work now ran to nigh on fifteen thousand entries, ranging from the well-kent to the quite forgettable. Mr. Shaw, by the application of free brandy now our most loyal friend, reached into the satchel which he carried with him and read to us some articles he had most recently written: on the sixteen species of shell to be found on the beach at low-tide; on the Declaration of Arbroath of 1320; lines from a spontaneous oral address by the very great Mr. McGonagall to the "Smokie"; several hundred words apostrophising the recent visit of Dr. Johnson; more obscurely, the number and names of the army of maids employed at Hospitalfield, and the number and names of the army of Hospitalfield gardeners held in her arms by one Jane Keillor; the luminescent wonder of the Bell Rock Lighthouse and the fabled speed of its pigeons. And so on. And so on.

For his part, Sir Thomas was now charm in corporeal form. He listened attentively, he raised his eyebrows in admiration, he laughed where laughter was due and widened his eyes if amazement was called for, he filled his guest's glass again and again. And finally suggested that the eager encyclopaedist might wish to write an article on the spread of Volapük in Arbroath and the surrounding parishes. Understandably, our man was as keen as a dog on the scent of a rabbit: he whipped out a pen, a traveller's ink-pot and some spare paper, and scribbled down the names and pronunciation of the numbers from *bal* to *zül*, and the decads through *bals*, *tels*, *kils*, *fols*, *luls*, *mäls*, *vels*, *jöls* to *züls*. He noted our names carefully, and that of the Reverend MacPherson. Then he signed his article so assiduously that he made only two mistakes before arriving at: "*Cems Jo*". Under my guidance, Sir Thomas superscribed the article with its number *balselulmil bal*, and we drank a toast to the assured success of Mr. Shaw's undertaking. At which point, the man abandoned himself once more to tears, lamenting that not one publisher in the whole of Scotland was willing to contemplate his work; that he had lost a fortune in sending parcels with his manuscript, taking trains to Edinburgh to leave his card at the great publishing houses there; and had at last been driven to drink.

"Mr. Shaw," stated Sir Thomas solemnly, placing an arm around the man's heaving shoulders. "Mr. Shaw – it is a common truth that these Scottish publishers are unquiddical posteriophiliacs and ovilickerists to a man. You need not be dispirited by their unreclaimable ignorance." Mr. Shaw looking puzzled, our friend elaborated, in a needlessly-loud voice: "Buggars and sheep-shaggers, my good sir!" The eyebrows of the landlord were raised by one quarter of an inch, perhaps in keen interest; but he said nothing. For his part, Mr. Shaw nodded in painful understanding and blew his nose, then looked hopefully at his comforter.

"It is for you," continued the old man, "to complete your work at – shall we say? – fifty thousand articles. Do not tender it to them now – it is like the Pearls before the Swine. Wait until the grape is sweet and the vintage is ripe, and then you will have them clamouring at your very gatehouse for the privilege of selling your Aberbrothic wine! You will be vindicated!"

Mr. Shaw's gratitude for this encouragement knew no bounds: he made swift notes on the concealed character of Scottish publishers, which he vowed would be elaborated in a new and revelatory article on "Journalistic Perversions". Then, pulling ever-more sheaves of papers from his satchel, he passed around the first pages and the

"Introductory Remarks" of his work, promising that we would in due course receive an honourable mention therein. The title of his work was as follows:

The Scottic and Aberbrothic Encyclopaedic
Cornucopia, on a PLAN Entirely NEW,
Consolidating, for the FIRST TIME,
Various Detached Parts of Knowledge:
Historical, Geographical, Legal, Local,
Universal, Ecclesiastical, Civil, Military,
Commercial &c. TOGETHER with a
Description of All the Towns of Angus and
the Significant Parts of Forfar-Shire;
a General HISTORY and Account of the
Different Towns, Villages and Estates;
and an Account of the Lives of the Most
INTERESTING Persons
of the North-East of Scotland

all of which, in a rather uncertain manuscript, barely fitted on to the cover of his work. We admired it greatly, however, and our chance meeting ended in pledges of undying friendship. As the town-clock in Arbroath struck ten, he dodged out into the night, clutching his precious satchel, the empty bottle, some torn cloth and a hatful of dreams. No sooner had the door swung closed behind him than Sir Thomas lapsed again into a most unseemly rage of laughter and mirth, which he took with him back through the sober portals of the Grand Marine Hotel, and which lasted him throughout the night and into the following day, which was *folüdel* (Wednesday), *del balsevelid* (the seventeenth day) *de telul* (of February).

Transactions II: The Edinburgh Society

Written on 9th February, 1891, in Turriff.

It only remains to add to the brief history of the adoption of Volapük, that the Third General Assembly of its advocates, which I had the privilege to attend in 1889, was the most triumphant yet. This is not the place to describe my adventures in detail, of how I travelled to and from France; but only to give you some idea of my conflicting emotions in travelling across the French countryside, understanding barely one word in ten of those addressed to me by the natives; and then of arriving in the huge and beautiful capital, at the hotel designated to accommodate the Assembly, where I understood everyone perfectly, be they from the farthest reaches of Russia, from Arabia, from Algeria, Spanish America, Vienna, Italy or Spain; the very waiters and porters, cooks and messenger-boys who attended to our needs, spoke exclusively Volapük. For five days, we were a World Unified, friends separated by national borders, but with one Ambition and one Language.

The work of the Congress was arranged such that there were General Meetings each morning, during which certain propositions and items of order were discussed and voted upon; in the afternoon, small groups would consider the many urgent tasks ahead for the Association, and hammer out tactics and strategies – in these meetings, I was fortunate enough to find myself with a number of like-minded comrades – in the newly-established *Volapükaklub Dugöfik* – who considered the work that must be done to translate into Volapük the books of Shakespeare, Virgil, Goethe, Dumas, Marx, Zola, Kautsky, not to mention all the books of the Bible. Another group, led by Dr. Vallienne, comprised painters and authors, poets and sculptors, who considered the application of Volapük to original creations (some of you may already be familiar with Dr. Vallienne's rich and popular work of murder and mystery in America: *Mölod e Kofud in Melop*). At length, after our evening-meal, a number of entertainments were arranged, always in the common language, comprising songs, both amusing and uplifting, small dramas, comic turns, and – on the last night – a "gentlemen-only" entertainment, which was of a most instructive nature in its depiction of the Passive and Active Voice of Volapük verbs, and of the subtle distinction between the Imperative, Optative and Jussive moods.

I came away from Paris barely eighteen months ago, greatly enthused by the sights I had seen, the people I had met and the work which lay before us; but aware also that, within our strong community, some traitors lurked, ready at any moment to spike our guns, to build barricades against our onward march, to divert us from our goals with sophistry and withdrawing-room arguments. We had been advised at the Congress that a number of deluded persons had turned away from our Movement and thrown in their lot with the group formed by Dr. Zamenhof, for his bastardised language known as "Esperanto". Already, it seems, the *Weltsprachverein* of Nuremberg had deserted, as a man, to this poor rival, lured by promises of easy victories and simple solutions. Little did I realise then that I travelled in the close company of one, named Bosman, who nurtured in his dark breast a similar treachery!

On our return to Edinburgh, in September 1889, I set about the formation of the Edinburgh Society for the Propagation of a Universal Language. My Readers will note the lack of the word "Volapük" in the name of this association: this was not of my doing, but rather that of my erstwhile comrade, Dr. Henry Bosman, of whom I will give a fuller account elsewhere. Bosman argued, with his silver tongue, that to have the name "Volapük" in the title would immediately place a barrier between ourselves and those whom we wished to attract to the Society – those people who had an interest in a Universal Language, but who were perhaps dabbling in other, less fit, languages, such as Greek and Latin, or Solresol and Nal Bino, Celtic or Hebrew. Since we knew of these people already, it seemed – at the time – a reasonable compromise; and so I agreed to it.

And so the first meeting of the Society in Edinburgh took place on the twenty-second day of September, 1889. Over two dozen individuals attended the Inaugural Meeting, and a number of office-holders were elected – myself as General Secretary, Bosman as Chairman, Mr. William Gunn as Treasurer, Mrs. Keenan (a woman who enjoys her food) as Refreshments Secretary. Those who became Members of the Society at that time were – it should be emphasised –

drawn from all strata of society: there were professors, a minister of the church, medical doctors, librarians, teachers, clerks, ladies' nurses, shop-assistants, a farmer, several carpenters, one rat-catcher, two educationalists, and one man well-respected in the Mid-Lothian perfumery trade.

The Society soon devised a Programme of educational lectures and talks, delivered and chaired by each individual member. It was in the course of this Educational Programme, to the accompaniment of shortbread, Dundee cake and tea prepared (and largely eaten) by Mrs. Keenan and her occasional assistants (Mrs. Turpie, Miss Hutchinson and Mme. Muriset), that the true nature of Dr. Bosman was exposed. The man had turned renegade and was in furtive communication with a cell of discredited Esperantists in London; at their instigation, he was agitating under a cloak of secrecy to convert the members of our Society to the simplistic and inflexible aims of "*Doktoro Esperanto*". At our first Annual General Meeting, which was held in April of 1890, the battle-lines were drawn, and a bitter struggle was waged between myself and Bosman: Bosman vied for a change to the name of our Society (to "The Edinburgh Society for Esperanto") which would reflect his narrow interests; I myself adopted a principled position, arguing that a change in name (to "The Edinburgh Society for the Introduction of Volapük") would follow qualitatively from the quantitative changes in our understanding of the nature of Universal Languages.

However, apathy and antipathy among the remaining members resulted in no alteration to the name, nor to some changes to our Constitution which I considered vital: so much for Bourgeois Democracy, easy prey to lethargy and hostility!

Katel Kilid, the Third Chapter:
The Derivation of Words

*A Lesson given to The Didactic Society of Newburgh
Linoleum Workers. Telul 1891.*

Having completed my professional work (or *organergonotika* as Sir Thomas affected to describe it) in Arbroath, we travelled, dipping yet again into the bottomless purse of my companion, by second-class carriage to Dundee and thence across the dangerous bridge over the River Tay. We were accompanied on this trip by none other than Mr. Shaw, who had – as he confessed – missed our company after the fertile meeting in The Brimming Sea of Haddock. Filled with enthusiasm for Volapük, Mr. Shaw now insisted that his name should henceforward be written "Mr. Jo", so I will henceforward oblige.

Mr. Jo was scarcely a fit companion for a professional person such as myself, smelling, as he did, of stale beer and spirits, and with a disconcerting hourly habit of eating cold boiled potatoes from a vade mecum-larder of old newspaper, kept in an inner pocket of his greasy coat. The man took a keen interest in, and maintained a wonderfully detailed memory of, all facts and figures, and could (and did) recite the full railway time-tables for trains to and from Arbroath, summer and winter, week-days and Sundays. His astonishing ability to mop up and store large amounts of information did not, alas, extend to a familiarity with social courtesies.

Sir Thomas was willing enough to have another companion, regardless of – perhaps even because of – his disturbing personal habits. As the train rattled along the northern shore of the mighty river, I undertook to teach our new devotee the principles of the Volapük numbers and their immediate application to the days of the week and the months of the year. Before we had come past Broughty Ferry, we had Mr. Jo and Sir Thomas harmoniously chattering out the names of the month: "*balul telul – kilul folul – lulul mälul – velul jölul – zülul basul – balsebalul balsetelul*". There was a remarkable co-incidence of the rhythms between these names sung out loud and the rattling of the wheels over the rails and points, and the whole effect was rather pleasing, at least to ourselves; the old lady who shared our compartment had a rather different view, I believe, since she muttered grandly to herself and shot us evil glances. But she was not so old that she was immune to an onslaught of charm from Sir Thomas, who, noticing her annoyance, adroitly smacked a surprised Mr. Jo over the head and ordered him to be silent, before ensnaring the lady in a web of honeyed words, silken flattery and ill-disguised suggestions of a scandalous nature. I pretended to sleep, resting my head against the cold pane of rattling glass. The old lady was gallantly handed down to the platform at Dundee, where she slyly issued an open invitation to Sir Thomas alone to visit her in her home whenever he was back "in town". As for ourselves, we had to change trains and wait an hour for one travelling south over the ill-famed bridge.

As we cooled our heels on a windy platform, I made the mistake of asking Mr. Jo if he had any local names for months of the year, hoping to score a point or two by contrasting a proliferation of local dialect names against a standard, universally-understood and simple set of names. Mr. Jo knew of no local ones, but promised to research the matter on his return home; in the interim, he surprised me rather by coming up with the French Republican names for the months, which he had learned from an old man of St. Vigeans, whom he had interviewed for his knowledge of by-gone "Aberbrothic" Radicals (of which, it seems, there were many). His fascinating exposition, sadly, was rudely interrupted by the fulminations of Sir Thomas, calling down the wrath of God and the Gods upon the heads of the Gallic Voluptuaries and all their Republican Corruptions, for to punish the State of Disgrace into which the perfidious French had fallen. Which episode brought us over the fearful bridge.

*   *   *

From Wormit, my trade obliged me to travel to the small town of Newburgh. My two companions were willing to accompany me, and so we engaged a carter, who had a case of champagne to deliver to a debauched gentleman in those parts. Sir Thomas expressed a very lively interest in the bottles, and soon he and the carter – a serious man of middle years – were deep in an earnest discussion on the measurements of champagne bottles. Mr. Jo, anxious to increase the number of articles in his Encyclopaedia at the fastest possible rate, avidly scribbled down the information thus yielded concerning Splits, Magnums, Jeroboams, Methuselahs, Salmanazars, Balthazars and Nebuchadnezzars. I openly scorned this, for it was manifest that a unit of measurement restricted to champagne bottles would be of little use to the ordinary man, or in comparing one bottle against another. I suggested the Volapükian term *liät*, meaning the metric litre, as the single unit of measurement, against which all liquid measures could be rated.

"A lee-et!" exclaimed Sir Thomas derisively. "What would a red-blooded man want with a 'lee-et' of champagne, heh? A lee-et leetle!" He shook with laughter and poked our carter in the ribs, as encouragement.

"No, sir," I answered calmly. "You mock me to no good end, Sir Thomas. A litre or two of champagne does just as well as a Magnum. What is a Balthazar – the equivalent of sixteen champagne bottles, approximately sixteen Litres, maybe? So, instead of a 'Balthazar', we simply say '*balsemäl liäts*'. By a happy co-incidence," I pointed out, "it is almost the same word: Balthazar – Balsemäl! Why need we have all those out-dated, unmemorable descriptions, when a simple standard unit would do? We should adopt a *liät* for a litre and *met* for a metre."

Sir Thomas and our carter, both, were outraged at my suggestion, which I had delivered solely in the spirit of scientific enlightenment. A bitter argument ensued, during which a whole variety of absurd names for units of measure were bandied about – by Mr. Jo, Sir Thomas, and the carter, who, as demanded by his trade, had a vast knowledge of the weights and measures of dry and liquid goods. From the simple ranges of: drops, ounces, pounds, stones, hundredweights and tons; gills, pints, quarts and gallons; inches, feet, yards, poles, chains, furlongs and miles; we were soon at loggerheads over the dubious merits of lippies, pecks, firlots, bolls, chalders, bushels and quarters; divided by the rivalry between gills and mutchkins *versus* gills and pints; bemused by how many mutchkins would be in a chopin; and then Mr. Jo chipped in with the Jesus, the Royal and the Super-Royal, the Folio, Octavo and Quarto, for sizes of paper. But when the carter, Mr. Gauld, boasted openly that there were forty poles to a rood, four roods to an acre, and that a pole was equivalent to thirty and one-quarter square yards, I could contain my feelings no longer.

"What kind of nonsense is this?" I demanded of my enlivened companions. We were rolling sedately along the high road, with a panorama of the Tay beneath us, having just passed the church at Flisk. "Have you stopped to listen to yourselves? What nonsense you babble! – how can any ordinary man understand these words? An Englishman will measure his pint differently from a Scotsman, a German will measure his paper differently from a Frenchman; and who knows how the Turks and Indians might weigh out their grain? How can we even comprehend each other, let alone engage in peaceful commerce, if the simplest words for measurement are so different? And, having mastered the words, how could the common man then master the arithmetic?"

It is as clear as crystal that a standard approach to measurement can only advance Civilisation; and that anything else would leave us in the grips of parochialism, nationalism and fearful ignorance of the practices of our fellow-man. From the loins of fear springs antipathy, fully-armed; from the blazing eye of antipathy, the urge to war and oppression.

My friends, alas, disagreed: Mr. Jo, with expressions of regret, for the loss of encyclopaedic articles which such standard-isation would bring in its wake; Mr. Gauld, anxiously, for the anticipated anarchy, and collapse of trade and commerce in Fife, Perth-Shire and Angus; and Sir Thomas, as was to be expected, for the loss to the "richness and omniformity of the Linguistical Amalthea". Many were the times that I regretted having contracted with him for this journey. But our agreement was binding upon us both, and we were tied together for its duration. On this occasion, however, his disagreement with me led to a swipe from his stick, closely succeeded by a struggle, during which the two of us tumbled off the back of the cart into the road; thereby frightening the horse, whose precipitate flight from the scene of trouble placed the cargo of champagne in immediate danger. Mr. Gauld brought the animal under control after about fifty yards (or – should I say? – ten poles, or two and one quarter chains, one quarter, maybe, of a furlong!). Mr. Jo leaped from the cart at the first sign of the nag's disturbance; from this safe distance, we could hear Gauld shouting imprecations, naming us all as imbeciles, and giving us notice that he considered our hire to be finished. Our luggage was ignominiously ejected from the cart, and Mr. Gauld went off at a smarter pace than heretofore towards Newburgh, whose smoking chimneys we could just observe in the distance. In the stony field next to us, a gathering of crows cackled and hopped impertinently, eyeing Sir Thomas' wig with great hope of profit.

It was around noon, and Sir Thomas wanted his meat. When Sir Thomas wants meat, he affects a sore head, and loses the use of his lower limbs. The matter of Weights and Measures was driven from his mind, and he wailed piteously that he should be taken to Newburgh, to see what an inn could offer him. Between us, Mr. Jo and I managed to carry Sir Thomas, his box of mice, our luggage and all our other movable paraphernalia the three or four miles, across the hill, down to the river, past the water-mill, past the ivy-clad ruins of the abbey at Lindores; to our destination. We arrived there at about two o'clock in the afternoon, to find that the keeper of The Mugdrum Siren judged it to be "well past dinner-time", and that we might whistle. Sir Thomas, however, latched himself on to the innkeeper's wife, a thin, sour-looking woman, whose brown hair was turning to steel, victim no doubt of years of thankless marriage; and with honeyed words and unlikely charm, softened her as a man can soften putty, until, within minutes and in open defiance of her scandalised husband, she retired to the kitchen to produce a handsome lunch for the three of us.

*   *   *

It being late afternoon before we were replete, I left Mr. Jo and Sir Thomas to stroll outside the inn, along the banks of the River Tay; while I called upon Mr. Brewster, the Minister of the Parish, to examine the work which I was contracted to perform for him on the morrow. He was glad to see me, for I do not think he has much company in these parts, and detained me to discuss the world of books, of music and of ideas. I mentioned to him that I had a meeting arranged for that very evening with "The Didactic Society of Newburgh Linoleum Workers", to advance their knowledge of Volapük. I noticed that he blanched and shuddered slightly at the mere mention of the name of this body of men; but he said that he would be pleased to come and learn about a new language, being himself – as he confessed modestly – tolerably familiar with the grammar of Greek, Latin and Hebrew.

Accordingly, at eight o'clock; and accompanied by Mr. Jo who was anxious to gather information on the making of linoleum, for the product was, he stated, greatly appreciated in the vestibules and kitchens of Aberbrothic; I repaired to the meeting-room of the Tay Institute on the Main Street, and found myself once more in the company of half-a-dozen desperate men. No sooner had I entered, than Mr. Brewster slipped in behind me and, smiling politely at his wayward parishioners, slid into a chair at the back of the room. Sir Thomas had found alternative employment for the evening, which I expected would involve the inn-keeper's wife; but I did not enquire after any detailed plans; and was pleased to be free of him for a few hours.

Tidüp folid (Lesson Four): Radicals, Derivations and Compounds.

My discussion with the Didacts of Newburgh was the fifth in a series which had begun a year previously. The men had shown themselves to be quite adept at the sounding of consonants and vowels, and we began the evening – to Mr. Jo's great joy – with a rendering of a selection of the numbers from one to one thousand and one, which passed off without too much incident.

It was time to explain to my eager students the process by which words and vocabulary were to be derived in Volapük.

Radicals.

I explained to them that the simplest ideas are represented by words, or "radicals" of one syllable. (I noticed the flush of anticipation and of hidden excitement which passed over the face of Mr. Brewster, as the word "radical" was used.) For more complex ideas, radicals of two syllables may be used. On rare occasions, a radical may possess more than two syllables, but this was highly unusual. More likely, a Volapük word of more than two syllables will be a compound word, to which we shall pass later. Thus the word **vol** is the simple concept "world" and **pük** is the simple concept "speech": **Volapük** is not a radical word (except in its implied threat to World Order!), but is a compound of two radicals.

The radicals have been taken principally from the following languages: English, Latin, German and French. More material has been taken from the English than from any other language, and this ought to make the language more easily mastered by the natives of Newburgh, Newhaven, New Deer or New York. The simplest words: **man**, **dog**, **kat**, **bed**, are much the same in English as in Volapük. But, I warned, the English words are often modified in adapting them to Volapük.

The Derivation of Words.
With the laudable principle behind it, that words should be capable of pronunciation by Brothers and Sisters from every part of the globe, Volapük may alter the original words it uses. This is done in four ways:

1. The spelling is changed, so that the pronunciation is preserved or nearly so:

Jip, **sheep**	Löf, **love**
Kipön, **to keep**	Giv, **give**
Kömön, **to come**	Sin, **sin**
Gudik, **good**	Juk, **shoe**
Bot, **boat**	Cif, **chief**

2. Consonants are dropped or changed, when there would be any difficulty of pronunciation. The consonant **s** will be avoided where possible, and certainly if it occurs at the end of a noun, since the suffix **-s** is used to denote the plural:

Vol, world	**Pükön**, to speak
Tat, state	**Ted**, trade
Täv, travel	**Tif**, (thief) stealing
Lol, rose	**Jol**, shore
Fit, fish	**Klöf**, cloth
Mug, mouse	**Nud**, nose

3. The letter **r** is specially avoided, **l** being frequently substituted:

Glen, grain	**Glet**, great
Bil, beer	**Telegaf**, telegraph
Blod, brother	**Flen**, friend
Katel, chapter	**Lam**, arm
Led, red	**Fol**, four
Bluf, test, proof	**Fögetön**, to forget

4. As radicals should seldom begin or end in a vowel, the consonants **n** or **l** are added, or the letters are transposed, or, in some
cases, a completely new source-word is chosen:

Pel, pay	**Lep**, ape
Love-, over-	**Nidian**, Indian
Nelijik, English	**Nulik**, new
Del, day	**Fin**, end

My students were pleased with this explanation, and I introduced
them to many new words in this way. I was gratified to note that some
of them even wrote down vocabulary – painfully, slowly, with much
licking of pencils – in small notebooks. Mr. Brewster made no notes at
all, but maintained an interested look. However, one man – and there
always is one in any class – demanded to know why the word for a
"rose" was rendered as **lol** in Volapük. James McGinty, for it was he,
could see no sense in it. Mr. Brewster egged him along: "A rose," he
quoted, chuckling, "by any other name, would smell . . . " I thanked
Mr. Brewster for his kind intervention and told McGinty in no
uncertain terms that that was how it was. Some nations Oriental
could not utter the letter **r**, and we had to hold back the letter **s**, for
reasons previously mentioned. Mr. McGinty was about to argue, but
his fellow-students told him to sit down and hold his peace; and the
incident passed.

We then moved on to:

Compound Words.

From the radicals, other words may be formed by compounding, that
is: by prefixing and by suffixing. A compound noun is formed by
inserting the vowel **a** between the determining word and the principal
word.

Volapük,	**the Universal Language**
Potamon,	**postage**
Pükatidel,	**language-teacher**
Flentapük,	**the French language**
Yagadog,	**a hunting-dog, hound**
Nulayel,	**New Year**

Put simply: the first part of the compound word may be considered as the determinant, and usually the meaning of the compound may be expressed by placing the determinant after the principal word (the determined) in the adjectival form. However, the meaning of the compound word is more specialised than just a relationship between noun and adjective. **Pük vola** may mean a language of the world, or any language of the world, while **Volapük** specifically means the language which will, ultimately, be understood through the whole world. Similarly, **dog yagik** means a dog which can hunt, any dog at all which has at least three legs, one eye and a muzzle, while **yagadog** means a dog bred for hunting.

In a few compound words, the syllables **as**, **i** and **o** are used as connectives, instead of **a**, but there is no settled rule:

Vödasbuk, dictionary
Pölivegam, wandering astray (**pölüdön** to lose, **veg** the way)

Sometimes three nouns may be compounded together, but care must be taken not to produce words which are too long, for then they would be hard for another person to decipher. In situations where this is likely to arise, I cautioned, make more use of adjectives. A lengthy compound word is likely to be very precise:

Volapükatidel, a teacher of the Universal Language

At this point in the evening, Mr. Brewster rather unhelpfully suggested that the noun to describe a maker of machine parts for a linoleum-press would probably be, in Volapük, a very long compound word indeed. I think he meant it as an expression of his interest in my lesson, rather than with malicious intent. And, although Mr. Brewster's presence was barely tolerated in this room, by men who were naturally suspicious of the cloth, his suggestion was eagerly picked up by my students, ever anxious for a distraction. We spent an interesting few minutes trying to establish the word for "linoleum", and finally agreed that it should simply be *linom*; and I made a mental note to advise the Academy in Paris of this word, for it might be a new coinage which would have to be ratified. From there, we passed on to "machine", which I knew to be the word *cin* (the word *jin*, of course, meaning "sheen" or "shine"). But we then strayed into quite unknown territory for "part" and "press". At length, however, we came up with the word **linomapedacinadilabumel**, having rejected the ungrammatical **pedalinomadilacinel**. In the spirit of scholarly research and in order to keep my students engaged, I asked Mr. Jo to make a note of this word also, that I could send it to Paris at the earliest opportunity. The length of the word made a good impression on my class, and their zeal made a mighty one upon Mr. Brewster.

The evening was well-advanced by now, but my class were eager to hear more. Before I proceeded, I handed out a sheet of the most common words in Volapük and asked them to learn them before my next visit. Sadly, this simple request was met with sour looks and grumbling. Ignoring this, I also invited them to consider the creation of other compounds, following the model of our recent success.

And then came the rather more difficult aspect of this lesson – the acquisition of vocabulary which does NOT derive from English. I explained to them that it was simply not possible to take all words from English and adopt them for the Universal Language. The English word "end", for example, could not be employed, since it began with a vowel; and since Volapük words already existed for the letters "end" prefixed by the available consonants (bend, fend, lend, mend, and so on), then we had to turn to another language – in this case, French: **fin**. Similarly, the word for "hunt" was proscribed, the combined consonants "nt" being frowned upon because of their proximity, we had to turn to the German to acquire the word **yagön**.

Thus, we had a cosmopolitan source for quite common vocabulary:

Bled, leaf	**Dil**, part	**Dol**, grief
Dom, house	**Dügön**, to lead	**Gel**, a church-organ
Huit, oyster	**Jek**, terror	**Ka**, than
Kanit, song	**Lapin**, robbery	**Lel**, iron
Miel, honey	**Nif**, snow	**Pianik**, gradually
Saun, health	**Spat**, walk	**Tor**, bull
Veg, road	**Vut**, or **zun**, anger	**Zil**, aim or goal

Not surprisingly, when I advised that a list of such words was a very long one, the individual lights of enthusiasm vanished like the flame of a candle in a sudden draught. It was noticeable that, after one or two words from the above list had been jotted down, pencils and notebooks were put away, slowly and deliberately. Even Mr. Jo caught the new mood, and ceased his writing.

"There will be some homework to do, then?" asked Mr. Brewster, brightly. "Mnemonics, repeating one's lessons until they are second nature, and so forth?" He rubbed his hands in anticipation at hard mental effort.

I agreed, but decided that this was probably the best time to close the meeting. I stressed to my class that they must work hard at their new knowledge, and they filed out silently into the night. Mr. Brewster thanked me for a most interesting couple of hours and, wrapped warmly in his muffler, coat and hat, strode off as one who has, after a gap of many years, been in society for an evening's entertainment, and found society not to be lacking.

Fin tidüpa folid.

As I packed away my materials, and Mr. Jo packed away his, and engaged with a cold potato, we were joined by Sir Thomas. He was, as is frequently the case after an evening spent at his own pleasure, in high good humour, and wished to learn as much of the vocabulary of Volapük as he could. I presented him with short lists of words, which he immediately learned and was able to repeat to me. The man was, to my chagrin, the perfect pupil. "As I have stated in my own books," he advised me, "the greatest matter of all is that, of all the languages in the world, a Universal Language is the easiest to learn. Why! – a boy of ten years old should contrive to learn it in a month! And for a gentleman of my years—" He waved airily as if a thousand words of new vocabulary was of no consequence to him.

Being still rosy and flushed from his pastime of that long evening, he wanted to know the Volapük word for a "strumpet". I could at first give him no clear answer, but, after great encouragement from my questioner, I came up with **lädül nestimik**, a dishonourable young lady. This was not very satisfactory to Sir Thomas. He wanted to know the word, then, for a "trull". I gave him the same reply. What about a "fornicatress"? The same. A "Cyprian", a "wanton", a "hussy", a "slut", a "cocotte", a *"fille-de-joi"*, a "woman of easy virtue"? He demanded the words for a "Delilah" and a "Jezebel". At each question, I could only refer him coolly to the previous answer given.

"This is highly unaccommodating, Mr. Justice!" he exclaimed, laughing uproariously. "If a learned man needs to describe a fallen woman in every delineation of her character and with the full weight of voluptuary excoriation, surely a learned man should have a selection of more than two lack-lustre, equivaluated, anaemical words? What kind of language is this? It is not universal enough, you miserly wretch!"

Playfully, no doubt, he smote me with his stick on my testicles and thrust his red face up at me. I detached myself with dignity, trying to explain that the whole beauty of a Universal Language, as he himself would no doubt agree, was its ability to convey ideas with the simplest, most commonly understood words. "Oh, simple!" he agreed. "Oh, yes. But what could be more readily understood than – shall we say . . . drunkard, boozer, tippler, reveller, toss-pot – terms of affectionate approbation easily understood by even the greatest soaker, toper, Bacchanalist and lush, and each having its own slight shade of meaning?"

I demurred, anxious to get away to my bed. But Sir Thomas was not to be dissuaded. He turned to Mr. Jo and asked him to explain the difference between the words "naughty, sinful, vicious, evil and malicious"; at which task our companion acquitted himself reasonably well; and then he challenged me to come up with five words in Volapük which would adequately translate these words. "Do them justice, Justice!" he howled with inebriate laughter, rolling about the bench until he fell on the floor, insensible.

With heavy hearts, we carried him down to The Mugdrum Siren, up to his bed, to lie beside his beloved mice; and we retired.

*   *   *

The following morning, I repaired to Mr. Brewster's church and was soon knee-deep in the mechanics of his organ. Here, at last, after the ill-concealed poverty and ruin of so many organs of the North-East of Scotland, was an instrument worthy of my attentions! No cheap harmonium, no nine-rank squeeze-box, with broken keys, loosened stops, and rusted pipes as the last resting-place of generations of mice. Here was an organ of the first order, with fifty ranks of gleaming flue-pipes, ranging from the thirty-two-feet pipe down to the six-inch pipe; a magnificent swell-shade, activated by the swell-pedal which could glide open or closed at a moment's notice. The bellows which pumped air to the wind-chest was not worked by the organist, but rather by a small boy kept specifically for that purpose, and whose

Sabbath suit was no doubt ruined by the sweat which must have poured off his brow, as he sought to slake the thirst of the mighty pipes. The speech of the Principals was felt in the bowels, and that of the Flutes and Strings as clear as a bell. I set to with enthusiasm, to oil and to dust, to tune the pitch, and to screw down tight.

It appeared that Mr. Brewster's parishioners gave him very little to do, for he found that he had an hour or so to spare, and wished to spend it in my company, enquiring after the nature of the citizens of Volapük. Malevolently, perhaps, and with my mind bent to my present chore, I did not disabuse him of his belief that the Universal Language was spoken already by a Nation somewhere over the sea. As I polished and screwed, I painted a picture of a land filled with happy people, speaking a language soon to be known to all men; a people who had existed prior to the Tower of Babel, and whose speech was dimly understood, in their sleep, by men and women of all other nations. "And the whole Earth was of one language, and of one speech," murmured the Minister to himself. "Now, Mr. Justice," he then asked earnestly, "what do you think of this? I have it on very good authority that, last autumn term, a mermaid was washed up on the shore at St. Andrews, where she was found by a number of Divinity students. Now, would that mermaid have been one of your Volapükians, do you think?"

I hazarded that it might be possible, and asked Mr. Brewster to describe the mermaid in more detail. But, either he had no more details, or he blushed even to think of them, for he shook his head. Already, his mind was racing down other roads.

"I slept little last night, Mr. Justice, so enlivened was I by your excellent class. Now, it seems to me that I could perhaps make a small contribution to your great project, by preparing some texts to assist in translations."

I paused to drink a cup of tea which Mr. Brewster's maid had brought over, and thanked him for his kind thought. What did he have in mind? I enquired.

Alas, it seemed that Mr. Brewster had not properly grasped the essential nature of Volapük. What he had in mind was not the preparation of exercises which would help the Scots to learn Volapük, but rather the translation of texts from English which would allow the Volapükians to learn our customs. "They should be Moral, Mr.

Justice: Moral Texts, lessons in Christianity; a description of the many and splendid benefits of being part of the British Empire; a guide to Constitutions of the Temperance League, the Little Mothers' Institute, the Commemorative League of Lystra. Let us encourage them to share our morality, as we share their language!" He had a collection of neatly-printed texts at home, from the famous "Temperance Library" issued by Messrs. Dobie & McIntosh of Edinburgh, which would certainly provide adequate material for translation. Was I interested? Would I commission him?

The man was not to be distracted, so I urged him on; and with such encouragement, he skipped off to his study to begin the Great Labour.

Transactions III: Solresol

Written on 24ᵗʰ February, 1891, at Inverbervie.

I mentioned in a previous Transactional item, that The Edinburgh Society for the Propagation of a Universal Language devised a Programme of educational lectures and talks. At Bosman's suggestion, all members who had paid their dues were permitted to deliver a one-hour talk and discussion on the merits of their preferred Universal Language. "Democracy," advised Bosman sententiously, "must be seen to be our guiding principle." Which sentiment was heartily applauded by all, although I had my doubts about the wisdom of so much – too much – democracy. There is, as you will be aware, the Democracy of the Bourgeois, and the Democracy of the People: what distinguishes them is the tendency of the former to wallow in the bogs of procedure, and of the latter to march steadfastly along the metalled road towards a known goal, looking neither left nor right, and certainly not backwards.

Thus it was that, at the regular monthly meetings which followed, in the back-room of Mr. Aitken's billiard-hall in Hill Street, we benefited from the following talks:

- By M. Edmond Muriset, an impenetrable discussion of *The Merits of Solresol*, illustrated frequently by blasts on the bugle played by his compatriot, M. Coens;
- By Mr. Louis Desdemoni, an excited diatribe on *The Advantages of Italian and French*;
- By Mr. John Flynn, a wearisome insight into *How I Learned Nal Bino*;
- By Prof. Hamish McInnes, an obfuscating explanation of *Leibnitzian Number Systems and Their Application to Non-Verbal Communications*;
- By the Revd. Mostyn Goodfellow, a naive *Prospectus of Greek and Hebrew, the Universal Languages of the Ancients*;
- By young Mr. Issachar Clark, a rather inaudible and garbled *Account of Esperanto, "Our Hope for the Future"* (I later discovered

that Mr. Clark simply read aloud, without full comprehension, from notes prepared clandestinely by Dr. Bosman);

* By Miss Lillian Hepburn, a short and angry scolding on *Latin: The Common and Common-Sense Solution – Why Should Anyone Want Anything Else?*;
* By Mr. William Gunn, an abrupt *Plain English*;
* And by myself, a clear and detailed dialectic of *The Acquisition of Simple and Effective Skills in Volapük.*

But, in the interests of True Democracy, and to show that I have retained an open mind throughout this struggle which – I trust – will shortly have an advantageous outcome – I will, in the following Trans-actional Items, briefly summarise what I understand of some of the more obscure Universal Languages. You will understand, *blods e sörs*, that I can refer only to my notes from the lectures which have been mentioned; if my notes are in any way faulty, it is the result of poor communication by the lecturers themselves – *quod erat demonstrandum*!

                              *   *   *

A very early attempt at a language is still represented in our Society by the two Frenchmen, M. Walther Coens and M. Edmond Muriset. Coens owns a small perfumery business, located in Gilmerton, and is known, amongst the wits of our Society, as "Toilet Walther". M. Muriset owns and runs, with his wife, an establishment for the Board and Education of Young Ladies, in Newington, and contrives as a side-line to offer the services of his wife in Translation and Private Tuition.

For reasons which I can only suppose are to do with their nationality – which is, of course, in contravention of the Third Paragraph of the Constitution of our Society – they champion the work of Jean-François Sudre. The primitive language developed by Sudre is known as Solresol, and in its time, it grew very popular; but has been left far behind by the brilliant work of such men as Schleyer. In essence, Sudre's language was based upon the seven sounds of the musical scale, sounds that we learn as very small children in school – "doh", "reh", "mee", "fah", "soh" (or "sol"), "lah" and "tee".

All words in his language would simply be combinations of these seven basic sounds – thus: "lah reh fah" might suggest a factory for making scent, as we are continually reminded by M. Coens. The initial sound in any word would denote its philosophical category – thus, "doh" would denote that a word was in the domain of the physical and moral aspects of man, "reh" would denote the domain of family and dress, "lah" for industry and commerce, and so on. By simple mathematics, one can arrive at some twenty thousand possible words, using only five syllables, and almost one million using seven syllables.

Muriset's paper to the Society extolled the "beauteous flexibility" of the modes of expression in Solresol – explaining that a language using only seven syllables could be spoken; could be sung; could be played on any musical instrument; painted in the seven colours of the rainbow; even, interposed Coens excitedly, could it be expressed in a series or combination of smells. (Mr. Gunn, uncouth as ever, enquired whether a message could even be farted? At which sally, the Reverend Goodfellow marched out of the room in disgust.) Blind people could be persuaded to understand by a simple touch to one of their fingers for each sound; blind amputees by the application of different scent-bottles to their noses. Muriset warmed to his theme, waxing uncontrollably enthusiastic about Solresol. By some stroke of fortune, the bells of a nearby church began to play as Muriset read his paper; his colleague, Coens, stood up and called a halt: "Hush!" He listened, hand behind one ear; then blushed; and asked M. Muriset to continue. It later emerged that he believed the bells to have made a lascivious remark about Miss Hepburn, the spinster whom M. Coens secretly admires.

Another member of the Society, who attended only three of our meetings, was inspired to jump up at the end of Muriset's contribution and propose that telegraphs and telephones might be persuaded to play tunes to announce the names of both the caller and the receiver. We suppose this gentleman to be deep in further telegraphical experimentation, for he has never returned since that evening.

In the interests of completeness, which I am persuaded should be an attribute of this Hand-Book, I will conclude this sketch of Solresol with a note on its grammatical categories. These are distinguished by an accent over the first, second, third etc. syllables. Thus, if there is no stress, then the word is a verb; if the stress is on the first syllable, then the word is a noun (or thing); if on the third, then a noun (or person), on the fourth, then an adjective, and on the fifth, then an adverb. (Quite how M. Coens would contrive to stress one of his scents, I cannot determine, but I await our next open discussion with some anticipation, for to challenge him with this very question which has only just occurred to me.)

As for antonyms, these can simply be illustrated by the following anecdote: Madame Muriset was put quite in a swoon by the appearance, at a window of their grand house in Crawfurd Road, of a man in cunning disguise. It was late on a wild All Souls' Night, and the visitor's black coverings and concealment of face suggested to her, and to a gaggle of brainless young ladies acquiring the rudiments of language fit for a French *salon*, the sudden and imminent termination of the life of her beloved Edmond. However, the visitor was there only to advise her quivering husband that Solresol was no longer a relevant matter for discussion at the meetings of our Society. But to conceal his identity, the caller introduced himself simply as "Doctor Solmi", knowing that in Solresol, the opposites of words are made by reversing the order of syllables – the word for "good" is "*misol*"; but, such is the fragile nature of his Solresol, that M. Muriset seemed not to understand the name nor any of the message! How frail is the distinction between such moral extremes, that it is dependent on a simple transposition of letters and syllables! In any event, Mme. Muriset was convinced – in great part, no doubt, by a clue deliberately let fall on the front step by their unknown visitor – that the nocturnal *provocateur* was their compatriot, Walther Coens.

*   *   *

Since that night, the only two speakers of Solresol in Great Britain have ceased to speak to each other.

Katel Folid, the Fourth Chapter: The Cases

A Visit to the Workers Improvement Association in Dysart.

Kilul, Balmil Jöltum Zülsebal.

Tidüp lulid (Lesson Five): The Declension of Nouns.

Mr. Reekie, Mr. Bleloch and Miss Coqually attended to me carefully as I explained, in Dysart, for the tenth time, the Declension of Nouns. I explained, for the tenth time, in Dysart, that a noun in Volapük had to be declined in order that you might determine whether it was the subject of a sentence, or the object; and, if the object, whether it be a direct or indirect object. In Dysart, for the tenth time, I met obstacles as I shall hereinafter explain.

For example, the sentence "the man gives the dog the bone" contains a subject (the man), an indirect object ([to] the dog), and a direct object (the bone). In Volapük, we have these three nouns which cannot readily be distinguished without being *declined*. This was a major obstacle for Mr. Bleloch, who could not understand why anyone "with their head screwed down tight" could not immediately see from the sentence which noun was which. "The dog," he argued, "will not give the bone to the man. Nor will," he advanced, "the bone give the dog to the man, nor the man to the dog. So," he reasoned, to the unvoiced approval of Miss Coqually, "the man has to give the bone to the dog. What, in the Name of the Wee Man, could be the trouble?"

For his insistence on simplicity, I decided to make life more complicated for him. "Mr. Bleloch," I suggested, "how about the sentence: 'The man leads the boy to the woman'? What can you do with that?" Mr. Bleloch, after considerable mockery and hilarity, considered it obvious even to a blind beggar what he could do with that; but conceded that his earlier argument held no more water. So he was courteous enough to listen further to my arguments.

Some vocabulary is required here: **man**, the man; **dog**, the dog; **bom**, the bone; **givom**, gives. "The man gives the dog the bone", without declining – or marking – the noun, would be: **man givom dog bom**. Or it could be: **man givom bom dog**. Or indeed: **bom dog man givom**. All word-orders are possible, Mr. Bleloch. So, Mr. Bleloch, we must distinguish. We decline, as follows:

- The subject will have no modification made to the noun: **man**.
- The direct object, or Accusative, "the bone", needs the suffix **-i**: **bomi**.
- The indirect object, or Dative, "(to) the dog", needs the suffix **-e**: **doge**.

Thus: **man givom bomi doge**, leaves no room for doubt. The dog is the recipient, the bone is the gift, and the man the donor. In our other example, **man dukom puli vome**: the man leads the boy to the woman.

To advance further in our studies, we consider the Genitive Case, the "of". If the man were to give the dog's bone to the cat – only for the sake of argument, Mr. Bleloch! – then we need to make it clear that the bone belonged to the dog and not the cat (at least initially, for after the event, clearly, the reverse would hold true, although the dog might care to contest the point). For this, we use the suffix **-a**. Thus: **man givom bomi doga kate**.

The case-endings, put simply, are the first three vowels, **-a**, **-e**, **-i**, corresponding to the Genitive, the Dative and the Accusative. Neither Miss Coqually nor Mr. Bleloch had a great deal of time for this, but Mr. Reekie persevered, albeit with no visible result.

We advanced falteringly to plural endings. Everyone was contented with these, for it was simply a case of adding a suffix of **-s** to the singular noun. Thus: **dogs, kats, boms**. Miss Coqually found this agreeable. I then came back at her with: **mans**. At which, she reared up and remonstrated: "*Mans*, Mr. Justice!" she demanded. "What kind of blether is that?" I explained that the blether was simply to make the language easier to learn. If all plurals were simply the singulars with an **-s** attached, then what possible difficulty could there be? Compare this, for example, with "men", "women", "children", "geese", "mice", "feet" and so on. Mr. Reekie, at least, nodded brightly in sympathy.

Let us summarise our case-endings and then proceed to a little exercise with some new vocabulary.

	Singular	Plural
Nominative (*or* subject)	-	-s
Genitive	-a	-as
Dative (*or* indirect object)	-e	-es
Accusative (*or* direct object)	-i	-is

Exercise 1.

Decline these nouns through all eight cases:

Fat, father	**Man**, man	**Dom**, house	**Blod**, brother
Dog, dog	**Mug**, mouse	**Gan**, goose	**Kim**, who
Pul, boy			

Remember to accent the last syllable, and to pronounce the vowels correctly!

There was considerable prevarication from my students at this, so I started them off with:

Fat	**Fata**	**Fate**	**Fati**
Fats	**Fatas**	**Fates**	**Fatis**

We barely completed, in unison, the declension of **blod** before Mr. Bleloch complained of a sore head, and Mr. Reekie was leafing furiously in previous pages of his notepad, a sure sign of his confusion. I considered it my duty to pay no attention to their inward struggles, and passed on to

Exercise 2.

Wherein I urged the class to express the following in Volapük:

- The boy's mouse.
- The house of the dog.
- For the men.
- The geese.
- To a father.

(Let the Reader note that the answers to the exercises in this Manual are provided at the end of the Book. But let him not be idle, and view the answers before exercising the mind!)

How we struggled, that evening, in the windy town of Dysart, by the grim north shore of the Firth of Forth! Mr. Bleloch had decided, for the tenth time, that the declension of nouns was an *effete* foreign custom, unworthy of his consideration. Miss Coqually gazed out of the window, overwhelmed, for the tenth time, by the thought that "men" should be **mans**: "Men" was a concept that embraced a number of pleasant and secret thoughts, while **mans** really did not raise a similar echo in her young and fertile mind. Mr. Reekie tried very hard, as always, but did not quite master the significant difference between dative and accusative. I encouraged Miss Coqually a little, for she was not a bad person, by introducing her to the case known by academicians as the Vocative: when you address someone, or something, then the interjection **O** should be used before the noun, and an exclamation-mark should be used as a suffix. **O vom!**, I cried provocatively in her direction. She burst into tears, claiming that I was a bully and a gullering brute. Mr. Bleloch (subject) lent (verb) her (dative, indirect object) his (genitive) handkerchief (accusative, direct object) and cast (verb) threatening (adjective) looks (accusative, plural) at me (dative). "Have (verb) a care (accusative), Mr. Justice!" (vocative), he muttered. I sighed adverbally and passed on to

Exercise 3.

For which, a mere nine words of additional vocabulary were required:

> **Logom**, sees **Blinom**, brings **Labom**, has
> *(Why these words end in* **-om** *will be covered in a later lesson.)*
> **Fut**, foot **Jip**, sheep **Pul**, boy
> **Steab**, Pound (Sterling) **Pin**, fat

Now read in Volapük and translate into English:

- **Man labom dogi.**
- **Dog logom gani.**
- **Dog blinom gani mane.**
- **Man pin labom gani.** *Etcetera.*

For the more diligent student, additional phrases for translation can be seen in my Appendix, "Key to the Exercises". I would urge you to immerse yourselves in these exercises; these should be undertaken daily.

But it was a lost cause, a task of Sisyphus. No sooner had my students conquered one word, than they fell down at the next. **Man** did not give them too many difficulties, until it was declined – and then it seemed to become a logical and intellectual impossibility. Mr.

Bleloch complained, Miss Coqually whined and Mr. Reekie found difficulty in expressing his difficulties: "Thon thing, I dinna ken fit ye cry it, thon thing, ye ken?" he would repeat over and over again, furrowing his brow. For each phrase offered up, it was I who had to complete the translation. The evening unravelled slowly and steadily.

I had been coming to Dysart on every trip I made north, and some more besides. A dozen visits I had made there, and my bright expectation of a class, which began with a roll of twenty students, had declined to bleak disappointment surrounding a class of three. At least, I could hope, at least, three still remained. But they were neither the brightest of my twenty, nor very willing to learn. Was this to be my Revolution of Language, the bright harbinger of a new dawn? I thought not.

When, for the third time of asking, Mr. Reekie failed completely to translate *Fat givom dogi pule* correctly, I lost my temper.

"'The fat man pulls the dog to the woman? Mr. Reekie, you're a fool! What is so difficult about this?" I demanded to know, slamming my fist down on the table. "Just how complicated do you think it is? Four cases is all I ask you to learn, with only three extra letters to choose from? What is it that you cannot understand? I have taught you this ten times already, and every time I teach you, you choose to forget it!"

Mr. Reekie had the good grace to look shame-faced at this, but Miss Coqually bridled up. "Aye indeed, Mr. Justice," she agreed. "You have taught this to us ten times already. But do you think we have no other worries in our lives, no other troubles? Do we perhaps not have a crippled father to look after, and a grandmother who cannot sit in her chair without falling out, and a crowd of brothers and sisters to keep in line? Do you think I have time to go out of an evening and seek out my fellow-students and talk Volapük to them? We need to practise, do we not? It is what you have always told us!" And at that she burst into tears. Mr. Bleloch glared at me and called me down for "a pernickety misery and a heavy-handed doup", which I did not take to be a compliment.

In the midst of all this uproar, Sir Thomas arrived from his supper. He had been dining out with a maritime man we had encountered on the train from Kingskettle. He had evidently dined very well, and of the five courses served up, perhaps four had been composed entirely of fermented liquids; for he stumbled on entering our class-room and fell over with a clatter. Miss Coqually, a tender-hearted soul, had started up at the accident, seen an old man lying on the boards, and had rushed forward to help him up. Resting his huge head in her ample bosoms, Sir Thomas had feigned weakness for a good five minutes, and then had made a very solid feint of requiring her continued ministrations. Every inch the ailing grandfather, he patted and stroked his nurse tenderly on the leg, several times, as a man might squeeze a chicken he intended for his supper, and thanked her profusely. Then, with the assistance of Messrs. Bleloch and Reekie, a chair was found, into which he was placed, and from which he affected a great interest in the continuing argument.

I conceded readily that it might be found impossible to practise Volapük every day and every week. But encouraged them to make use of every spare minute to repeat the lessons. "Remember – just four cases: Nominative, Genitive, Dative and Accusative. *Dog, Doga, Doge, Dogi.* The Dog; Of the Dog; To the Dog; For the Dog. **a, e, i.** It's a simple rule."

Simple enough, one would think, were it not for the peculiar duties, diversions and distractions which an ordinary life in Dysart seems to attract, like iron filings to a magnet. From Sunday to Saturday, there was, it emerged, no time: no time on *balüdel* because there was bathing to be done in hot tubs, and a church to visit, and dinners to cook; there was no time on *telüdel*, because there was a wage to earn and then there was supper to cook, and clothes to be washed; there was no time on *kilüdel*, because there was a wage to earn, and then there was supper to cook, and the kitchen had to be scrubbed down, and the scullery floor washed, and the sheets to iron; there was no time on *folüdel*, because there was a wage to earn, and then there was supper to cook, and grandmother to attend to, and bread to bake; there was no time on *lulüdel*, because there was a wage to earn, and then there was supper to cook, and brasses to clean, and the chickens to feed; there was no time on *mälüdel*, because there was a wage to earn, and then the fish to gut, and there was supper to cook, and more clothes to wash, and the steps and the yard to sluice down; and there was no time on *velüdel*, because there was a wage to earn, and then there were provisions to buy, and food to prepare for *balüdel*, and the children to teach their letters, and maybe a dance to go to at the Mission-Hall. During all of this – which of course came from Miss

Coqually – Mr. Bleloch nodded sympathetically, although it was certain that he had never before in his life raised a finger to cook a meal or wash some clothes.

Mr. Reekie's tale was no improvement. Every day of the week, except *balüdel*, he had to work at the iron-monger's shop, and every evening he had to tend to his ailing mother, and every night he would join in the work of the Salvation Army, for he was a charitable soul. Little opportunity, then, to engage in stimulating Volapükian dialogue with a passing stranger or a fellow-student. And the first day, of course, was a Day of Rest, and he rested religiously: this was no time to be found recklessly practising the four Cases and the Personal Pronouns, let alone acquiring by heart the curious vocabulary of tongues.

Sir Thomas listened to all of this with a beatific smile upon his shrivelled face. I had supposed that his smile concealed drunken oblivion, but I was shown to be wrong. As Mr. Reekie finished his Lament, Sir Thomas sprang from his seat and applauded vigorously. "Now," he exclaimed, turning to me in triumph. "Now you can see why they cannot acquire knowledge, Mr. Justice. How do you judge that, eh? These poor abecedarians, they cannot learn for want of comfort!"

I ventured to suggest that they would not rise above their discomfort until they had prepared the way for Equality and Socialism, by promoting the Universal Language; but Sir Thomas shouted me down: "Nonsense, Mr. Justice! Nonsense, moonshine and quatsch, drivel, dreck and sophistry! Macaroni and merde, Mr. Justice, mere trumpery and stultiloquation! Blattery and blightery! I propose that you dismiss these worthy catechumens, and hereinafter attend to me."

My students proved highly appreciative of this idea and began to array themselves in coats and scarves, to brave the winter storm which was now raging outside. Sir Thomas, meanwhile, took me to one side and began to whisper to me in his most honeyed tones.

"Now, young sir, we have an *agrément*, you and I, and it is time for me to fulfil my part of that bargain. You have brought me further south than I have been in many a long day, and I am grateful. Captain Mitchell has shown me the very portals of the great City of Edinburgh; that Vesuvius of the North, the Seat of Arthur, beckons to me now. And, with your assistance, I have been introduced to the company of such women as I beheld only in phantasy, and I have consumed suppers fit for the King. And now I see I must render you assistance,

for your instruction breaks upon slothful otiliths and petrified hearts."
I recollected that our Contract did, in deed, have two signatories and
thought that perhaps it was time for mutual benefit. I acquiesced.

"I have in mind, then, a thaumatical sport, Mr. Justice." As my
pupils left into the night, Sir Thomas produced, from some vast
hidden pouch in his own coat, the following items of clothing: a long
bolt of silken cloth, which turned out to be a cloak, black as the
night; a helmet, fashioned of iron, with a silver face-plate; and huge
gauntlets, made of soft red leather. "Apparel yourself in these," he
urged, man-handling me into the gloves as he spoke. I did not ask
any questions, but slipped the cloak over my shoulders, and the
helmet over my head – it covered my eyes and nose, like the mask of
some ancient warrior. Sir Thomas turned me towards a mirror; I
saw, standing before me, the very portrait of an Avenging Spirit. I felt
an uncontrollable urge to stamp and posture; I did so. I strutted
again, for it felt as if a fire had blazed up in my very soul, and that hot
blood flowed through my limbs. I struck a pose such as a Leader of
Men might strike, and I stamped my foot a third time.

Sir Thomas chuckled. "Now you have some power, Mr. Justice!"
He paused. "And what is your name?"

I knew what was my name. My name was written in the stars at
night when the heavens were as deep as death, and was written in the
waves of the sea which broke upon the cliff and swallowed up all
who stood idly there. My name was: Cödel Yagöl. He who, hunting,
judges. The Hunting Judge. The Avenging Angel, the Teaching Tyrant,
I was indeed He Who Must Prevail!

Sir Thomas patted me on the back, provided me with a heavy
scimitar – for, he advised me, "a judge cannot mete justice without his
sword" – and urged me to be off. I strode from the room into the
night, where the snow lashed my helmet, and my cloak whipped and
cracked behind me. The streets of Dysart were deserted on such a
night; the sea crashed invisibly under the black night.

My eyes, I found, were under an assault. But not of colours; for all
colour had been leeched from the night, and everything was black or
white, or a single shade of grey in between. A light in a window which
might gleam yellow: white. A red sign swinging above an inn: black.
The green glow of the sea: grey. And every thing which lay before me
had a small label attached, as one might see in a child's picture book:

the sea was clearly labelled "Sea"; the sky, "Sky"; each and every star, "Star"; the streets and wynds, "Road"; and so on. For a minute or so, I spun around on the spot, like a top, my attention drawn now here, now there by the distracting lack of colour and the super-abundance of labels. I looked back into the meeting-hall, newly constructed and kindly rented to us for the evening by the Masons of Dysart, gazed past the object labelled "Door" and sought out Sir Thomas. A "Man" standing there waved encouragement to me.

Then, to my right, perhaps a hundred yards off, I saw movement, labelled "Student": it was Mr. Reekie, making his way home, head bowed against the wicked wind and the stabbing sleet. Half-running, half-striding as with Seven-League boots, I made after him, came up behind him silently, overtook him as he reached the little square under the Tolbooth.

"Reekie!" I called out, holding up my gloved hand to stop his progress. The man was utterly petrified, having had no fore-warning of my coming. He fell back against the wall, bathed in a reddish glow, arms held up to protect himself. "Who are ye?" he stuttered. "I have nae money, I am a simple man, ye ken!"

"I do not want your money, simple man!" I shouted, if only to raise my voice against the storm; but also because it felt good to be shouting. "I demand your attention!"

Mr. Reekie was nothing, if not attentive.

"Reekie," I ordered. "As you value your life, and your sanity, and the life of your old dear mother, give me the house—"

"Onything, onything! Ma hoosie, ma money, onything!" he wailed.

"Give me," I continued, "the house, *dom*, in all its eight cases."

Mr. Reekie was, perhaps surprisingly, word-perfect: "*Dom, doma, dome, domi, doms, domas, domes, domis*," he cried. "*Dom, doma, dome, domi, doms, domas, domes, domis*," he repeated in anguish. "*Dom, doma, dome—*"

"Good, Mr. Reekie, excellent!" I applauded. "And now decline for me the words for man, mother, brother, dog, mouse, and goose."

Mr. Reekie was keen and needed no prompting, other than my sinister presence.

"*Man, mana, mane, mani, mans, manas, manes, manis, mot, mota, mote, moti, mots, motas, motes, motis, blod, bloda, blode, blodi, blods, blodas, blodes, blodis, dog, doga, doge, dogi, dogs, dogas, doges, dogis, mug, muga, muge, mugi,*

mugs, mugas, muges, mugis, gan, gana, gane, gani, gans, ganas, ganes, ganis."
There was no way to stop Mr. Reekie. He had it all there in his head. It
just needed Cödel Yagöl to help him realise that. (The Reader of these
lessons may take Mr. Reekie's answers to be entirely correct, and may
mark their own answers accordingly.)

"And what about 'Who', Mr. Reekie?" I demanded of him.

The answer was swift: "*Kim, kima, kime, kimi, kims, kimas, kimes,
kimis.* Who, whose, to whom, whom, and all the plurals thereof, yer
honour!" Never had I seen a man so terrified, and yet so lucid in this
thinking.

"Let me walk you to your house, Mr. Reekie." I offered him my left
arm, and my cloak swirled in the wind. He took my arm meekly.
"And, as we go, perhaps you will translate for me just a pair of brief
phrases. Let me see . . . how about 'the man's father'?"

"*Fat mana,*" came the reply, almost instantaneously.

"For the boys?"

"*Pulis.*"

"To a mouse?"

"*Muge.*"

"Of the dog?"

"*Doga.*"

"And finally . . . of the geese?"

"*Ganas!*"

I could see that Mr. Reekie's strength was almost exhausted by these
exercises, all of which, I had to concede, he had done with not one
error. We came to a building labelled "House", and he let himself in
the "Door". From indoors, a quavering voice called out – "Donald?
Are you being seduced by a woman again?"

I left him to recover his wits, and make an explanation to his mother;
and I hastened down the streets to the house of Mr. Bleloch. I would
have known where he lived, even had I not been there before, because I
had the power of Cödel Yagöl! As I strode through the darkened streets,
I saw people talking to each other, and from their mouths issued
banners of white, bordered in black, and each banner held the words
that they spoke. Every object was clearly distinguished from every
neighbouring object, by virtue of a clear solid line. On the ancient
Tolbooth, which I understood to be the town-house of that
community, the entire wall was decorated with the legend of Echo and

Narcissus, and the faces thereof were of the eminent persons of Dysart; with such attention to detail that every square inch of stone had been covered in tincture; and all done in grey, black and white. This was a Dysart that I had never seen before, so clear was it, so simple.

Finally, I tracked down Bleloch to his cottage over-looking the extensive salt-pans; he sat whitely upon the seat of his lavatory in the shed in the yard at the back. Draughty at the best of times, his out-house was the vortex into which all the storms of the world now poured, as I threw open the door and stood before him; judging, being not judged; hunting, being not hunted; asking questions, being unquestionable.

As had been the case with Mr. Reekie, Mr. Bleloch was a reformed character when tested by my stern voice. Before five minutes had passed, I – and my Readers, should they turn to the chapter headed "Key to the Exercises" – had the answers to all the questions in Exercise Three. Barring a minor error, in translating *dogis* as a genitive singular – for which I smote his bare pale trembling knees with the flat of my scimitar, and soon encouraged him to a correct translation – I could never have asked for a quicker and more obliging student.

"Good, Mr. Bleloch, very good," I said, patronisingly. "Perhaps you can crown your achievement with the correct answers to . . . "

Exercise 4.
If I state that "The man has a dog and gives it to the boy", then would you please answer, in Volapük, the following questions:

- **Kim labom dogi?**
- **Kim givom dogi pule?**
- **Kimi man givom pule?**
- **Kime man givom dogi?**

Mr. Bleloch was no sluggard here. Quick as a flash, he was able to provide the correct answers.

And, since Mr. Bleloch had understood that the order of words was almost irrelevant, the case-endings being correct, I tapped him smartly upon his neck with my scimitar, as a sign of high approval. Bleloch fell into a faint upon the iron-hard floor of his cludgie. I left him, rapped upon the bright grey kitchen-window of his house, calling out that a man needed assistance. I proceeded on my way, filled with the spirit of

Education and inspired by a paternalistic pride in my students. Truly, Cödel Yagöl was a Being of Great Power and Influence, and I had cause to be thankful for my Contract with Sir Thomas!

As ten o'clock struck, I hunted down Miss Coqually. I came across her quite by accident, concealed in the windy ruins of St. Serf's Tower, a massive keep standing firm against the gale; and evidently a trysting-place for the *inamorata* of Dysart, for she was with a Lothario. I had expected her to be at home by now, making marmalade, passing blankets through a mangle, or scrubbing the staircase; but I was not surprised by my encounter, for it is my duty to Judge unflinchingly, and not to turn aside at the frailty of Humanity. She stood bathed in black light, words of tenderness visibly passing between her and her companion as letters pass through a grille.

I saw that her hand was labelled possessively with the name of her young man. He was, it appeared, Mr. Hector Moffat, late of Dunfermline, and a rising star in the local branch of the Fife-Shire Bank and Savings Company. I supplied the eager Mr. Moffat with some vocabulary for his beloved, and demanded that Miss Coqually finish

Exercise 5.

in which she was to express the following sentences in Volapük. In each sentence, I cautioned her, there was at least one word which ought to be put in the Accusative Case. Mr. Moffat was no fool, and managed to supply his belle with the right vocabulary at the right time; I foresaw that he would soon be a man of some significance in the town of Dysart.

- The fat man has seven geese.
- The four dogs have twelve feet.
- Who has three hands? *[A riddle, of course!]*
- The boy's father *[father of boy, I cautioned]* gives a hundred pounds to the man. *Etcetera.*

Fin tidüpa lulid.

In order to discourage laxity amongst my Readership, I have provided the full exercise, along with Miss Coqually's answers, at the end of this Book, after some instructive interludes. You may be assured that the young lady's answers were entirely flawless: women, even flighty ones in the firm embrace of a romantic attachment, having – it seems to me – a far greater capacity for exactitude than men. After his efforts, Mr. Moffat felt abandoned by his strength, and Miss Coqually, for the second time on that momentous evening, was obliged to provide an ample cushion for the head of a swooning man. I left them to their mutual comforting in the pouring black rain and strode back to our lodging at the top of the hill, where Sir Thomas waited, with an enigmatic smile upon his face, to reclaim the cloak, the helmet, the scimitar and the gloves.

"A profitable evening, Mr. Justice?" was all he asked, as he tucked away the instruments of Judgement, and the world reverted to its usual colouring and vague borders. I believe that it was my upright posture, my burning sense of achievement, my piercing eye, which provided a unspoken reply.

*   *   *

I should note that Mr. Jo was no longer with us, having decided, as we prepared to leave behind us the village of Kingskettle, that the shores and braes of Aberbrothic called out to him with a siren song. With lengthy lamentation, he had bidden us farewell earlier in the day. As a parting gift, Sir Thomas had passed him a piece of parchment, dating, he said, from four hundred years ago, on which an Ancient Volapükian had penned a love-poem to his beloved. Mr. Jo clutched it to his breast, tears of gratitude in his eyes, and then stowed it safely in his satchel, along with the many new articles he had composed for his *magnum opus* during his formative travels in Fife; and the skin of a three-day-cold potato; he swore energetically that this gift would soon be a poem uttered by swains the length and breadth of Angus and The Mearns. As we made our way from Kingskettle towards Dysart, in the train, Sir Thomas recited the full verse to me. As he finished, a young Minister, sharing our carriage in the innocent hope of good company, buried his head in *The Perth-Shire Presbyter*, affecting a hearing disorder:

> *"Vai, sör!" ji kraid, to ji wos not daunhartäd,*
> *"Yuv slöpd tru mai get önd left mi öndön!"*
> *"Fir not, mai swit ledi, at vot ai hav startäd:*
> *Bitvin yur tu cix let mi sötöl mi daun,*
> *Tu plau yur fain filz önd so öntöl don!"*

In the opposing corner to our Minister, however, a man with a large beard and weather-beaten face laughed heartily, and introduced himself as Captain Mitchell, of the Burns Line, Retired. Sir Thomas and he were soon engaged in loud comparisons of "interesting" verse, which obliged them both to recite samples of the same, much to the Minister's chagrin and my own embarrassment.

In a rather fruitless attempt to bring the conversation back to a more respectable tone, I recalled to Sir Thomas' attention a discussion which we had had on the long road between Newburgh – from which town we had departed by horse, leaving many new friends behind – and Kingskettle. I alluded to the Robert Burns Memorial Supper, which The Edinburgh Society for the Propagation of a Universal Language had held one year previously, celebrating the democratic spirit of the Ayr-Shire poet with renderings of his most famous songs in Volapük and lesser languages. It had not been a success.

The Members had fallen into argument at the very first song: "My Love is Like a Red, Red Rose". The correct translation of this would have been: "*Jilöfel oba binof Lol Ledikün*" (female-lover mine is a rose most red). But some mean-spirited people present, chief among them Dr. Henry Bosman, laughed outright and said it sounded no more like the great Burns than the cawing of a crow sounded like the trill of a blackbird. The man had no feeling for the true art of translation!

As the Burns Supper proceeded, and the bottles of whisky which circulated took their toll, we had arguments over "Ae Fond Kiss" ("*Eit kid löfik* . . . "), of which the first line was translated agreeably, by myself, but whose further lines ended in a bloody nose for Mr. Flynn; the metamorphosis to the letter "l" of the many fricatives in "Green Grow the Rashes-o", led to considerable hilarity amongst the more superficial minds ("*Lids glünik glofoms*"), and some discussion of the nature of the Vocative Case amongst the more earnest intellects; but the evening ended in uproar as we came to the finale, "Auld Lang Syne", since no one could offer an agreeable interpretation of the first three words in the original, let alone a translation. Old acquaintances and old enmities were renewed, hand-shakes turned to punches and slaps, and cups of bitterness were hurled through the air.

The Captain, thinking of his supper at that time, had inquired after the translation of the famous address "Tae A Haggis" (of which Sir Thomas had heard nothing, but, on being illuminated, was greatly desirous of hearing more, proclaiming the haggis to be "a roisterous boorish dish, doubtless with aphrodisiastical qualities"). I had no translation to hand, not having been asked this on any previous occasion; after some reflection, I proposed "*Lenpük stomake jipa*"; which, even I had to admit, was rather mundane. Sir Thomas had proposed "*O feinik hagit*"! I had demurred then; but as our train slowed down, Sir Thomas recruited the opinion of both the Captain and the Minister, and, in their ignorance of the finer points of Volapük, they sided with him.

Upon our arrival at Dysart Station, Sir Thomas strolled off, arm in arm with the Captain, to his residence in the grounds of Dysart House, leaving me to my own amusements. Which I pursued until night-fall, when I engaged my remaining three students in battle, as heretofore noted, for the tenth time.

Transactions IV: Petty-Bourgeois Phantasmagoria

Written at Newburgh, on 11th March, 1891.

I make notes here of a rag-merchant's bag of "other languages", each proposed by some as the Universal Language to which we should aspire. My notes are necessarily short.

Nal Bino:
Of the infamous language of Monsieur Verheggen, promoted by John Flynn, I understand little and expect to learn nothing. It inhabits the stagnant, brackish back-waters, far from the fast-flowing currents of living language, with no hope of a future, along with Streiff's "Bopal", Mr. Andrews' "Universology", Bauer's "Spelin", M. Dormoy's "Balta", and the ludicrous "Chabe Abane" from M. Maldant. John Flynn's explanation of Nal Bino was interesting only for the spectacle it presented of a man lost in the swamps of his own mind.

If I may take time for an aside here, let me list out an additional number of risible petty-bourgeois phantasmagoria, models for language which reflect nothing but the narrow interests of nation-state mandarins. This list will give you some idea of how easy it might be to be diverted from a strong movement, rooted in the Will of the People:

- "Pantos-Dimou-Glossa", drafted by De Rudelle in 1858.
- "Lingua Lumina", invented by Dyer in 1875.
- "Monoglottica", invented by Ferrari in 1877.
- "Weltsprache", by Volk and Fuchs in 1883.
- "Blaia Zimondal", invented by Meriggi in 1884.
- "Langue Internationale Neo-Latine", drawn up by Courtonne in 1885.
- "Langue Naturelle", by Maldant; "Pasilingua", by Steiner; "Weltsprache", by Eichhorn, all in 1887.
- "Lingua Franca Nuova", by Bernhard; "Kosmos", by Lauda; "Lingua", by Henderson, all in 1888.
- "Anglo-Franca", by Hoinix; "Myrana", by Stempfl, in 1889.

- "Nov Latin", by Rosa; "Mundolingue", by Lott; and "A Catholic Language", by Liptay, all in the past year.

Esperanto:

Little enough need be said of Esperanto. It is but a poor imitation of Volapük, mal-nourished, and too simple by half. It will trickle into the sands of disuse and vanish into oblivion.

However, in the spirit of scientific study and the Democratic Voice, I will provide you with some knowledge of the following rules for Mr. Zamenhof's thin broth:

- Nouns end in *-o*
- Adjectives end in *-a*
- Adverbs end in *-e*
- and Infinitive verbs end in *-i*

The definite article "the" is yielded by one inflexible word *la*. Thus, "the man" is *la viro.*

Plurals are rendered by adding a suffix of *-j*, which is pronounced as the "y" in "yellow". "The green tree" is *la verda arbo*, while "the green trees" is rendered *la verdaj arbo.*

The opposite of a word – the "un-", for example in "un-friendly", is contained in the prefix *mal-*. Thus, "friendly" is *amika*, and "unfriendly" is *malamika.*

For pronouns, we have *mi* (I), *vi* (you), *li* (he), *ŝi* (she), *ĝi* (it), *ni* (we), and *ili* (they).

The present tense of a verb is formed by removing the *-i* suffix from the infinitive, and replacing with *-as*; thus, *li venkas*, he wins. For the other tenses, the future is formed by the suffix *-os*, the past by *-is*. Thus, *la patrino parolis*, the mother has spoken.

There are some other grammatical and syntactical rules, but the whole thing is crude, simplistic, and devoid of any potential for creativity. And in order not to divert us from the task in hand, I certainly do not propose to bring these to your attention. It is manifest that the language of an Esperantist – "one who hopes" – is beyond hope. Dr. Bosman and a handful of deluded persons support Esperanto in Edinburgh; but the man has no moral fibre, no experience, and will be thwarted in his ambitions.

English, Italian, French, Greek, Hebrew and Latin:
As for the other languages proposed and expounded, I will deal with them briefly and easily. The modern languages – English, French and Italian – have their own champions, each one of whom simply represents the interest of a Colonial Power or the dominion of one Nation over another; and for that very reason we cannot permit them.

Why not, say some, return to the ancient languages – Ancient Greek, Latin, Hebrew? After all, it might be argued, these were the languages which permitted the rise of great religions and great literature, and which were understood by scholars the length and breadth of Europe for centuries. Indeed, Greek and Latin were the languages which arose from the Babel of the Dark Ages and began the re-construction of "civilisation" in Europe.

I will tell you why not:

Greek is the language of ancient democrats and slave-masters; and now it is too much associated with obscure learning;

Latin is the language of military conquest and the subjugation of nations; neither it nor Greek has kept pace with the world. What is the Latin for – a "railway", a "steam engine", "The United States of America"?

Of Hebrew exactly the same might be said; with the added difficulty, that the script for writing Hebrew would not come easily to the vast majority of Europeans. It is said – by some, and in particular, the Reverend Goodfellow – that Hebrew is the language of Adam, that it is the language which could halt the scattering of the peoples and their languages upon the face of the Earth, bring an end to the confounding of the people of Babel, who had realised that almost nothing was impossible to them. A JUST GOD, I think, that confounds the aspirations of the peoples of the world! But Hebrew is too ancient a language – and you cannot bring the Ancients back from the dead.

None of these archaic languages, therefore, will serve the purpose of the coming twentieth century. The rules of their grammar are complex and not easily learned. The vocabularies are exhausted, clumsily altered by usage, like a building of centuries' standing that has been altered for different purposes of trade every ten or twenty years; I would cite my neighbour's house as an example of the depredations wrought upon a simple building by even one generation of painters, plasterers, bricklayers and joiners; and these languages, as my neighbour's house, are quite unfit for continued usage.

*　　*　　*

I trust that my notes on the "Transactions" of the Edinburgh Society will illuminate for you many of the problems associated with, and reasons for, the introduction of a single language for all of Mankind. Special note has just been made of various alternatives to Volapük which have been proposed, and my Book offers a serious and penetrating discussion of their fundamental weaknesses; so that the Reader, with a cool and rational mind, may observe for himself the idiocy, the imbecility, and the utter lunacy of these flawed alternatives. Through the Reader's experience, we expect that the factionalists within the Society will be exposed, and the way will be clear for Volapük, as the single Universal Language, to be promoted in Scotland.

Katel Lulid, the Fifth Chapter: The Persons

Afternoon Tea with the Members of
The Edinburgh Society for the Propagation of a
Universal Language. March, 1891.

Kilul, Balmil Jöltum Zülsebal.

Four words on the Leviathan that is the Forth Railway Bridge: it is too high, and too dangerous – *tu geilik, tu pöligik*. It cannot endure many winters, as the ill-fated bridge over the Tay did not endure. I have not travelled on it since it first opened one year ago, and will continue to avoid it, so long as the time-tables of the Railway Companies permit. There is no sound reason why it should stay upright. For this reason, when the new day broke, and the wind was but a fresh breeze playing upon the grey waters of the Forth, I proposed to Sir Thomas that we cross to Edinburgh by ferry-boat, rather than by train. To my surprise and satisfaction, he did not seem averse to the idea.

I discovered shortly afterwards the explanation for his agreement; that his Cornucopian purse had been almost emptied, and that he had little enough money remaining for comfortable travelling such as we had enjoyed thus far. Trains, horses, carts and carriages had been our mode of transport from Cromarty down to Dysart, the very length of the Eastern Coast of Scotland, all thanks to the gold and silver coins which cascaded from his horn of plenty. But, to raise the fare to cross the Firth of Forth, we had to rely on my own modest savings. It was only by listening closely to his odious abuse (which I usually ignored) throughout the course of the day, that I discovered that he and Captain Mitchell had been in the company of card-players, a breed for which the coast of Fife is justly infamous. These scoundrels had raised the stakes at each succeeding hand, and finally detached Sir Thomas from his riches. He was now destitute; Captain Mitchell had also been subjected to a decline in his fortune, but not, apparently, so dramatic. When I confronted Sir Thomas with this discovery, he was, at first, violently aggressive, then violently sub-missive, and finally he laughed it off: "I will send a cartapaciatory request to Cromarty and we will have supplementary riches before the week is out!" he claimed.

Thus, we made our way, upon a conveyance owned by his intimate (and impoverished) friend, Captain Mitchell, to Burntisland; where, wrapped up in a large number of blankets and coats, and with his hat tied firmly over his wig, Sir Thomas embarked with me upon the boat which took us to Granton. Captain Mitchell accompanied us on the short stage to Burntisland, and on the road there was a good deal of lewd laughing and calling out at women as we passed. But, once we had left dry land and come out into the open seas, Sir Thomas' demeanour changed; his face turned ashen-white, and he was obliged to lean overboard. After which episode, he sat in a corner, cursing the enthusiasm of men for sailing upon the sea, and in particular that Captain Mitchell who had filled his stomach with drink, and the "bastard conspiration of gnarring cut-throats and assassins" who had bested him at the card-table.

I determined to divert my friend's attention from his woes, by teaching him the Personal Pronouns. He listened, but – perhaps because of the choppy seas and the regular thrashing of the salt spray – seemed unusually slow to take in the new knowledge.

Tidüp mälid (Lesson Six): The Personal Pronouns.

A pronoun is the word which stands in place of a noun – he (in place of "the man"), she (in place of "the woman"), we (in place of "we people"), you and so on.

The pronoun of the FIRST person is: **ob**, I; and in the plural, **obs**, we.

The pronoun of the SECOND person is **ol**, you or thou (singular); and in the plural, **ols**, you (or, in the uncouth mouth, youse).

In the THIRD person, there are no fewer than four pronouns, with distinctions of gender and of animation:

- **om** for masculine, he; or for an animate "it" which has previously been mentioned;
- **of** for feminine, she;
- **os**, neuter, "something", inanimate or abstract, it;
- **on**, collective, one (as "one says"), people, "they".

But, in the plural, only **oms** and **ofs**, they.

To remember all the personal pronouns, I urged my companion to use the mnemonic word OBOLOMOFOSON. Sir Thomas fixed his eye upon the heaving roofs of Edinburgh above the waves, and muttered OBOLOMOFOSON to himself, over and over again. OBOLOMOFOSON – it seemed to distract him. I would recommend the mnemonic to all who suffer from sickness of ship, train, carriage or alcohol, to mothers in the pains of labour, and to army-men about to suffer an amputation of the lower limbs. Repeat: OBOLOMOFOSON over and over to yourself, and you will find yourself calm; and incidentally, you will also have committed to memory all the Personal Pronouns of Volapük.

Sir Thomas had recovered sufficiently, by the end of the voyage, to demand to know the difference between the "it" embodied in **om**, and the "it" implied by **os**. It is a question frequently asked by my students and it is very difficult to explain. But I explained that, in the sentence: "The Beast emerged from the Pit and my eyes beheld *it*"; "the Beast" could be either feminine or masculine, and is definitely animate: so we would use **om** to translate the "it" which relates to the Beast. Whereas, "the train crashed down from the railway-bridge and with horror I watched *it* sink into the waters" contains an "it" which is neuter, inanimate; and I would express this in Volapük as **os**.

Fin tidüpa mälid.

*   *   *

The huge and busy harbour at Granton soon took us in and we clambered ashore. Sir Thomas, determined to out-do any other passengers, stopped and flung himself down to kiss the cobbled ground, much as if he had sailed with Raleigh or Cook in circum-navigation of the globe; rather than a crossing from Burntisland. Then he sprang up and looked keenly about him, rubbing his hands in anticipation. "Conduce me to the parades and piazzas of Edinburgh!" he commanded. I suggested to him that we would be obliged to walk; he refused. "You cannot ask an old gentleman like myself to walk all that way," he whined, in a loud enough tone to attract the attention of a number of fish-wives, who immediately took his side and – with words I hesitate to commit to print – castigated me as a worthless son and heartless scoundrel, to treat my frail old father like that.

Realising that I was embroiled in an argument in which I would not even be heard, I led Sir Thomas by the arm, away from the sympathetic mob, to the railway-station, and purchased two third-class tickets for Waverley. We soon arrived there and, turning a deaf ear to the laments which were raised against me, for all to hear, I obliged Sir Thomas to walk up Market Street, down George the Fourth Bridge until we gained the Meadows, which we crossed, at the pace of a snail or slug, to come to my residence in Carlung Place.

By this time, it was late afternoon, our journey on foot from Waverley having taken well over two hours, with frequent occasion to rest and complain. I lit a fire in the grate, placed Sir Thomas in my second-best arm-chair, and made a pot of tea. I expected him to complain that the drink was not strong enough, and I was not disappointed. I advised him that tea was all that was to be had, my neighbour and moral guardian, Mrs. Forbes, disapproving of the use of drink within her dominion. With that, Sir Thomas reached into some secret pocket; I heard the clinking of coins; he pulled out a crown and obliged me to walk round the corner for a small bottle of brandy. "But be sure to conceal it!" he warned me, grinning from ear to ear, choking with mockery: "The Harpy perchance will snatch it!" I carried out his wishes, not without some misgivings; on my safe return, I took the opportunity of his new good humour to enquire where he had found another store of money.

He was startled that I should even ask: "You do not expect me to husband my wealth so poorly that I would reduce my drinking-purse for the sake of travel?" He fortified his cup of tea with another generous dash of spirit. "You are not a man who has travelled much, then? No, no – I have kept a respectable sum for such emergencies as this," he confirmed comfortably, and patted his coat. "One purse for the travel; one purse for the drink; and another – " he patted another obscure corner of his moth-eaten coat, which chinked heavily in response, " – for the ladies!" He giggled again, unpleasantly, and held out his cup for more tea.

I fore-saw a rather tedious evening ahead, and realised just then that I had no idea how I was to deal with Sir Thomas, now that I had brought him all this way. Our contract required me to bring him safely from the wild lanes of Cromarty to the more genteel streets of Edinburgh; this I had done. For his part, he was to assist me in ensuring that The Edinburgh Society for the Propagation of a Universal Language adopted Volapük, and no other, as its preferred language. I had had a glimpse, on that wild night in Dysart, of how he could help me. But here in the familiar surroundings of Marchmont, our contract seemed to lack reality, immediacy.

But my thoughts were interrupted by a knock on my door. I opened. It was young Lizzie, the daughter of my landlady. A girl of perhaps nineteen or twenty, she was employed as pupil-teacher in one of the local elementary schools. She was a pretty, tall girl; but spoiled, in my view, by her adherence to the faction led by Dr. Henry Bosman, champion of the simplistic scheme of Esperanto. Sir Thomas, however, seemed to shed several decades from his age as he saw her, and invited her in. To her credit, Lizzie looked at him with unconcealed disgust and addressed her remarks to me.

"Did you know, Mr. Justice, that Professor McInnes has died?"

Of course, I did not, and I was quite shocked. The Professor, even although he might suffer from delusions as to the correct way of promoting a Universal Language, was polite and intelligent enough. Lizzie advised me that he had died on the previous Sunday, peacefully in his sleep. She had had the news from Mrs. Turpie, the Professor's house-keeper. The funeral was to be to-morrow, Lizzie told me, being Wednesday, the eighteenth of March.

I thanked the girl for her news, and she retreated back down the stairs to her mother's house. Sir Thomas rubbed his hands. "Nothing makes my heart pound heavier than the funeral rites of a great man," he advised me. I did not believe him, having seen, on our east coast travels, just what made his heart beat strongly – stirring up trouble, drinking to excess, and rutting rudely after the fair sex. However, I kept my opinion private; and made the domestic arrangements necessary for the evening and night; while Sir Thomas inundated me with little-known facts about the obsequies, exequies and epicidiums of the peoples of Austria, Italy and Spain.

*   *   *

The following day was very windy, but dry, and we made our way to the New North Church at the junction of Forrest Road and Bristo Place. On our way down to the street, we narrowly avoided an encounter with Lizzie Forbes and Dr. Bosman, who had emerged below us into the stair from Mrs. Forbes' domain. Sir Thomas called out to Lizzie in his impetuous manner, and she turned round to say "Good day, sir", with a cool politeness; but Dr. Bosman, beyond puffing some of his infernal cigarette-smoke in our direction, said nothing at all and hastened on his way.

Knowing that we would miss the funeral service if I obliged Sir Thomas to walk, we boarded a tram, and arrived at the church ahead of our neighbours. There was a good crowd there – faces I knew from the Society, almost all of whom had turned out to pay their respects – as well as others, whom I took to be colleagues of the Professor from the Edinburgh University. Mrs. Turpie was at the centre of a huddle of elderly ladies, offering their condolences, and speculating, no doubt, on the contents of the Professor's Last Will and Testament.

The funeral service did not go well. The Minister, a Dr. Wallace, emerged at eleven o'clock, when the service was due to start, and advised us that his organist had failed to put in an appearance. Was there anyone here who could play the organ? To my deep embarrassment, Sir Thomas proclaimed publicly that we had in our midst the finest organist ever to visit Cromarty, and propelled me forward. There was no way of avoiding it, Dr. Wallace being overwhelmed with gratitude and seizing me by the arm; we went inside and I was seated at the organ and invited to play. What Sir Thomas did not know, and what now became alarmingly obvious, was that I knew only the two tunes, neither of which seemed particularly apposite to the occasion. However, I determined that, if the Professor should be celebrated, he might as well be celebrated with enthusiasm, and set to. I began with "O Tannenbaum" and the Minister eagerly ushered in the mourners. To the tune of "The White Cockade", the coffin and last container of Professor McInnes was carried in by six imposing gentlemen, and was positioned at the front of the church.

Allowing for the lack of a skilled church organist, all proceeded with decorum for several minutes. We prayed, we listened to Dr. Wallace's thoughts on Life, Death, the Might-Have-Beens and the Hereafter, we sang a Psalm without the accompaniment of the organ; we prayed again, and then we sang again, Dr. Wallace asking me to oblige. Not knowing quite what to do, I rattled off "O Tannenbaum" again; but to our very great consternation, John Flynn, our great Irish exponent of Nal Bino, burst into song, for he recognised the tune as the one adopted for the Socialist anthem, "The Red Flag". There was considerable outrage at this, once the congregation realised what the words signified. The Minister asked me to desist, John Flynn was escorted from the body of the church by three of the pall-bearers, shouting as he went that, "though cowards flinch and traitors sneer", the time was ripe for the over-throw of Capitalism and the Liberation of the Oppressed. "The Professor would have had it so!" was his parting shot, as he was flung into the street, and the heavy door slammed shut behind him. Sir Thomas, who had found himself a comfortable nest of simpering elderly women, eloquently voiced the general outrage of the assembly, then settled back once more to enjoy the funeral-rites.

It was now that Dr. Wallace made the fundamental mistake of asking the Professor's friends if they had any brief words to say in memory of the man. I felt it was my duty, as General Secretary of the Edinburgh Society, of which the Professor had been a tireless and much-loved member, to make a considered and well-balanced statement; one, indeed, which I had prepared on the previous evening. I stepped up therefore to face the congregation; it was fortunate indeed that I had had the foresight of being at the organ, for I found that I had several seconds' advantage over a keen irruption of people with similar intentions – foremost among them being, not unnaturally, Dr. Bosman. But I could also see M. Walther, Mr. Desdemoni, Mr. Gunn and several others, all jostling for position as they entered the lists in the centre aisle. Seeing that I was temporarily master of the situation, they halted their advance, fidgeting tremendously.

I offered up my eulogy to the Professor, remarking on his great intellectual abilities and noting that, despite his preference for the numbering systems of the philosopher Leibnitz, he was, to my sure and certain knowledge, barely a week or two away from recognising the supremacy of Volapük over all other languages. What a tragedy it was, then, that he should have been struck down, so close to the Annual General Meeting at which, we must be certain, he was about to endorse publicly the unquestionable claims of Volapük.

Woe for the dignity of the occasion, for these vipers in the nest, Bosman, Muriset and Gunn voiced their impotent outrage at my views, and tried to shout me down, their voices raised in unseemly wrath. Dr. Bosman, in particular, was so aroused that he ran down the aisle, thrust me to one side, and defiantly voiced his opinion that, quite contrariwise to the claims of "this charlatan" (by which epithet he referred to myself), the Professor was in fact on the verge of coming over to the camp of Esperanto, in recognition of the simplicity of that language. I countered this absurd claim by stating the very obvious: that the Professor was no lover of simple solutions and had no time for the "Lowest Common Denominator", as he often referred to the populists' pandering to the common masses.

Then a small band of Leibnitzians suddenly emerged from the shadows at the rear of the church, academics to a man; I had heard that the Professor had had fellow-thinkers, but had never encountered any of them. Yet here they now were, five or six of them, blinking in the unaccustomed light, shouting out anathema and castigating us all for sullying their fond memory of a great Mathematician and Thinker. "Prime numbers are indivisible!" seemed to be their battle-cry. Of course, at this, Sir Thomas was not to be restrained. The man seemed to find in the rumour of war and the promise of war, the very elixir of life. He sprang up from the midst of his admiring ladies, rattled up and down the pews, encouraging now this side, now that faction, in the fight of words and fists which had broken out in earnest. In vain did a despairing Dr. Wallace appeal for calm. As the struggle surged backwards and forwards in the church, some bodies were knocked against the Professor's coffin, which teetered briefly on its supports, then crashed to the ground, the lid springing off and splintering on the stone floor. Ladies screamed and fainted, the pall-bearers shouted in rage, the fighting ceased as suddenly as it had begun. Muttering and fulminating under his breath, the undertaker in his top hat and black gloves lifted the half-emergent corpse of Professor McInnes from the floor and replaced it in the coffin; producing a hammer and nails from his coat-pockets, he set about a rapid and economical repair of the damage and – perhaps because this was a regular occurrence in his experience – soon had everything set to rights once more.

Dr. Wallace, perceiving the situation restored, urged me to play the organ again – "But not that tune," he pleaded. "Play the other one, I beg of you" – to close the service. Unfortunately, Dr. Wallace was unaware that John Flynn had re-entered the church under cover of the disturbance and, as soon as he heard the notes of "The White Cockade", struck up once more with the revolutionary song: it would appear – what was of course quite unknown to me! – that both tunes suit the words of that song in Socialist and Radical circles. Thus it was that the gentle Professor was removed from the church to the rallying-call of the down-trodden and oppressed, "our parting hymn".

*   *   *

Once outside, we discovered that the undertaker had kindly provided a number of black-draped carriages to take mourners to the cemetery; Sir Thomas and I found ourselves space in the first of these, immediately to the rear of the hearse; and we set off. Alas, Professor McInnes' adventures in this world were by no means over; for the undertaker, a man in the stern employment of Mrs. Peter Moir, Senior, Funeral Undertaker, of St. James' Place, had not been given full information, and had mistakenly assumed that gentlemen of the University would always be buried at the South Grange Cemetery, across the Meadows. But on our arrival there, he was greatly enraged to find that the man at the Lodge knew nothing of the proposed burial. We waited a good quarter of an hour while the two of them shouted at each other in increasing anger; great ledgers were adduced as evidence, countered by letters and certificates; until finally our man conceded gracelessly that he was in the wrong, and that the Newington Cemetery at Echo Bank, some distance away on the road to Dalkeith, was the Professor's preferred destination.

Nor was this the final episode.

We rattled eastwards along Grange Road, dodging trams until, reaching Mr. Middlemass' Biscuit Factory at Causewayside, we turned south. Our undertaker was in a great hurry, and whipped the horses on, so that all the carriages following in the cortège were obliged to gallop. Down the cobbles of Causewayside we rushed, parting dogs and bicycles as a mighty steamer parts the waves; we made a sharp turn leftwards at Bright's Crescent, and clattered past the large mansions there; coming out at Mayfield Road, we were obliged to take our lives in our hands and dash straight across, between the on-coming trams which plied between the suburban railway-station and the centre of the city. Into Peel Terrace, then, where we found ourselves in a maze of elegant streets, the very breeding-place of the Merchants and Capitalists of Edinburgh. In appearance, innocent enough: but what heartless Masters of Wage live behind those drawing-room windows, what schemes and plots against the Working Man are hatched in those dining-rooms! We had little time to gaze upon these instructive buildings, for the horses, since they spent their working-days at a solemn pace, were unmanageable as a result of the excitement. Some bolted to the left, up Queen's Crescent, others to the right, down Cobden Crescent; our own horses, with the acquiescence, I suspect, of our young driver, galloped straight forward, down a narrow lane which led to a secluded garden or park behind the confines of the very grandest houses. A number of maid-servants or nannies in uniform grabbed small children from the path of our on-rushing steeds, as we trampled dolls and prams under our hooves; then we emerged into Cobden Crescent from another narrow lane, scarcely avoiding a collision with the carriage which bore the Leibnitzians, their hair flying loose in the wind, shrieking with excitement. With some difficulty, our coachman brought the horses under control as we came upon a jostling mass of carriages negotiating the eastern exit from Queen's Crescent.

But our troubles in the Labyrinth of Capitalism were not yet over. Our undertaker, still in the vanguard, took a premature and false turn down Burgess Terrace and found himself in a quiet dead-end; as we followed him in, in no time at all were we constrained in a narrow street, having no egress, and surrounded by large, imposing houses. We became concerned for the well-being of our undertaker, angry as he already was, for his face turned from red to purple, and he raged and stormed at his unfortunate assistants, with words which were not necessarily seemly for the occasion. At length, some domestic servants appearing in the street to determine the cause of the plebeian uproar, he was advised that he should return the way we had come in, and follow the street out to the main road, then continue southwards for some hundred yards.

This was easier said than done, and it was a good twenty minutes before all the carriages had backed out of the narrow lane and had assembled once more on the Dalkeith Road. Indeed, there was no time to re-constitute the correct order, and we set off in random sequence behind the hearse. Sir Thomas, sensing either a slight to his majesty, or more likely an occasion for sport, bribed our driver with a silver coin (from his Ladies' Fund, I believe) to regain our position at the head of the cortège – at that time we were tenth in line. The passengers in other carriages, finding themselves thus over-hauled, adopted similar measures, and there was a rather tempestuous race down the Dalkeith Road, which took up both sides of the carriage-way, and stretches of the pavement, sending old ladies, errand-boys and carriages scattering, much as the remnants of a weakened army might bolt for cover at the vision of a phalanx of mighty chariots. By the time we reached the entrance to Echo Bank Cemetery, however, our athletic young man had his horses in front, and we veered through the gate-way on two wheels only, to come in just behind the hearse. Behind us, there were numerous collisions, resulting, in one instance, in the spilling of two sets of mourners on to the ground. These victims of adversity were helped up by the customers emerging from the inn nearby, who had burst out, anxious for entertainment.

At the rear of the cemetery, under the trees which over-looked the trickling Pow Burn, we found the Professor's grave opened up and waiting. We understood from the dark looks of the grave-diggers that we were over an hour late, and the grave-diggers anxious for their dinners. We stood at the edge of the secluded plot and paid our last respects as the Professor's slightly damaged coffin was lowered swiftly into the ground. Dr. Wallace muttered some final hasty words and we repaired at a brisk pace, since all stomachs had a fine sense of the lost time, to a reception, arranged by Mrs. Turpie, at the Professor's residence in Upper Gray Street.

*   *   *

We tumbled into the Professor's residence, anxious to be out of the cold, and to see what kind of repast Mrs. Turpie had prepared. Bosman, as on every day and at every hour, made the air filthy with another of his endless cigarettes, which hung from his lower lip as he squinted arrogantly through the spiralling smoke at the world. Ash fell from its tip and left a trail across the carpets. Some of the elderly ladies were discussing the Apocalypse – which, on further invest-igation, turned out to be a debate on the cause of apoplexy, and the likelihood of any surviving husbands of the party to be struck down by such a disease.

And here, amid the cold meats, with the promise of hot lentil soup, succeeded by pots of tea, accompanied by shortbread, Cödel Yagöl first appeared before the members of the Edinburgh Society. It was his finest hour.

Sir Thomas, viewing the assembled mourners from his position of honour at the head of the table, asked me in a whisper if these were those whom I would persuade of the justice of my claims for Volapük. I replied in the affirmative, and he asked me to retire briefly with him. It was the work of moments to assume my cloak, my helmet, my scimitar and my gauntlets, and emerge in all power from the Professor's fine bathroom, coming down upon the funereal feast like an Assyrian upon the fold of the helpless.

"It is time," I cried, as they cowered before me, "for a lesson!"

The women shrieked, the men quaked, all avoided my gaze. Several called out: "It is not time! It is not yet time!" without any real hope in their eyes. I could see through the slits in the helmet that Sir Thomas took full advantage of the chaotic situation to tend to Madame Muriset, the wife of our principal Solresol-ist, whose charms are, indeed, many. Seeing her tremble and wave a fan before her eyes, my travelling companion led her to the open window and was soon, with her flustered acquiescence, engaged in loosening her tight clothing, all the while inquiring politely after her native country, which he loved with *une Grande Amour*, the prospects of her Establishment for the Board and Education of Young Ladies, and the nature of her occasional business in Translation. I chose to ignore this impertinence – as did M. Muriset – and continued.

"You pass before the Hunting Judge, Cödel Yagöl, he who possesses the knowledge of the Language of the Future! Listen to me and understand what I have to tell you! *Cödel Yagöl opükom!* – the Hunting Judge is about to speak!" And, with the entire room in thrall to my words, I engaged them in

Tidüp velid Persons.

First, I refreshed their memory of the Personal pronouns:

Ob, I   **Obs**, we
Ol, you, thou   **Ols**, you in the plural
Om, he   **Oms**, they (masculine, or neuter)
Of, she   **Ofs**, they (feminine)
Os, it, or "something", and **On**, one

At my command, my captive audience desperately shouted out the watch-word OBOLOMOFOSON; and I expressed my satisfaction, by requesting that the soup be served up. As spoons clattered in our bowls, we continued.

The pronoun is united with the verb as a person ending, forming one word. Thus, when the verb is in the FIRST person: **binob**, I am; **pükob**, I speak; **fidobs**, we eat; **lobedobs**, we obey.

For the SECOND person the suffix is **ol**, thou or you (singular); **ols**, you, plural; forming one word. Thus, **binol**, thou art or you are; **pükol**, you speak; **fidols flens**, you, friends, are eating; **lobedols**, you obey.

Note that we may also translate "I am" by **ob binob**, and, "thou art" by **ol binol**; but this repetition of the personal syllable is unusual, and only employed for emphasis or when it is desired to place the subject at a distance from the verb.

And finally, we are reminded that, in the THIRD person, the four pronouns are also suffixed to the verb: thus, **binom**, he is, it is; **dlemof**, she trembles; **kreiofs**, they (the women) cry out; **nifos**, it snows; **sagon**, they say, people say, one says, it is said.

In this instance, even when the subject of the verb is a noun expressed, yet the **om** or **of** must be added: **of** for a feminine subject, **om** for any other. Thus:

> **Vom binof jönik**, the woman is beautiful.
> **Plofed binom nelifik**, the Professor is dead.
> **Dom binom gletik** (not **dom binos gletik**), the house is large.
> **Doms binoms gletik**, the houses are large.
> **Jiflens binofs nebeatik**, the lady-friends are unhappy.

"Now," I demanded of my class, "let us together conjugate the verb, 'I fear', through the persons of the present tense!" I pounded out a rhythm with my sword upon the sideboard, a smart marching pace, and my students chanted eagerly, over and over, to themselves, to each other, so that there could be no doubt about it:

Dledob, I fear	**Dledobs**, we fear
Dledol, thou fearest, you fear	**Dledols**, you fear
Dledom, he fears, it fears	**Dledoms**, they fear
Dledof, she fears	**Dledofs**, they fear
Dledos, it fears	**Dledon**, one fears, people fear

We celebrated our fluency by summoning the cold cuts of ham, beef and pork, garnished with assorted pickles and sauces. I noted that on this occasion, once more, the colouring of the world was black and white. Everything, from the Professor's Persian rug, to the flowers and their vases, to the curtains tied back from the windows – all was black and white, separated only by grey lines. In this world, Cödel Yagöl was lord of the monochrome and held sway over them all; from his wisdom, he taught them some new vocabulary, as follows:

• **Buk**, book	• **Sep**, tomb	• **Kömob**, I come
• **Golob**, I go	• **Givob**, I go	• **Lilob**, I hear
• **Stimob**, I honour	• **Binob**, I am	• **Blinob**, I bring
• **Pükob**, I speak	• **Kreiob**, I cry out	• **Fidob**, I eat
• **Fugob**, I flee	• **Labob**, I have	• **Tidel**, teacher
• **Vom**, woman	• **Fid**, food	• **Valüd**, power

and then sat them down to:

Exercise 6.
I asked them to translate into English, each person, around the table in turn:

- **Binob.**
- **Givol.**
- **Lobedom.**
- **Kreiof.**
- **Golos.**
- **Dledon.**

And, having successfully mastered this – although I noted that Dr. Bosman, in a fit of coughing, had faltered audibly at his turn – I told them to translate into Volapük:

- I speak.
- I obey.
- We go to the tomb.
- I have the power.
- We bring a man to the tomb.
- He brings the food.

I was satisfied with their efforts, and, being satisfied, I commanded that another round of cold meat, with boiled potatoes, be served; it was done.

At around this time, I became aware of another curious phenomenon, which was this: that the little black and white figures who cowered and trembled under the sword of the Hunting Judge, they flickered and darted, with jerky movements, like figures seen in a zoetrope. I blinked and screwed up my eyes, but to no avail – my audience hopped or convulsed as they sat. The whole scene made me, of a sudden, feel nauseous. The only one free of this disturbing movement, and who, incidentally, appeared in natural colours, was Sir Thomas; he, I noted, had made considerable progress in providing Madame Muriset with a good dose of fresh air, to the extent that she was in danger of catching a chill in the chest. Around the table twitched not merely all the active members of The Edinburgh Society for the Propagation of a Universal Language, but also a number of other parties – Dr. Wallace, the Minister; some neighbours, uncertain as to the proprieties of the celebration; the product of Leibnitzians, now subdued; and three confused old ladies, each knitting at very long pieces of wool, with knitting needles which blurred and stopped dead by turns; these three were introduced as sisters of the late Professor. I excused all of the other parties from the next exercise, on the grounds that they had done enough to cover themselves with glory, as initiates. As they passed again from black and white to insignificant grey, I encouraged the others to pay the closest attention to

Exercise 7.

"Dr. Bosman," I turned to him, for I saw that he was trying to make himself invisible behind the ample bosom of Mrs. Keenan. "Perhaps you will translate into English the following?" He obliged, miserably, but efficiently.

- **Labol valüdi.**
- **Pükol.**
- **Golol.**
- **Kömols e fugobs.**
- **Pükobs e lilobs.**

I was pleased with his responses, for he had the makings of a true Volapükist. But I did not tell him this; rather, I commanded him to translate into Volapük:

- He has a tomb.
- You go and I come.
- You obey me.
- He cries out.
- She flees.
- He brings a man to the tomb.

I could see that, after ten minutes of this, Dr. Bosman was on the verge of hysteria. So I thanked him for his efforts, and turned my attention to the two Solresol-ists, M. Coens and M. Muriset. Some months previously, the two Belgian gentlemen had fallen out with each other. The cause of this schism was not publicly known: some said that it arose from a poor translation by M. Muriset of a legal document pertaining to M. Coens' Toilet Water factory in Gilmerton; others surmised an affair between Mme. Muriset – a woman some ten years younger than her husband, and, while not in the first flush of youth, with magnetism powerful enough for the men of Edinburgh – and M. Coens, whose infatuations were common knowledge. M. Coens is at this time besotted with Miss Hepburn, a middle-aged, shrewish teacher of Latin. In earlier months, he had burned with longing at the eyes of Lizzie Forbes. Even, it was said, had Mrs. Keenan fuelled the flames of his ill-disguised ardour, until Mr. Gunn had threatened a good British beating, which threat quickly doused his Continental passions.

At all events, the last two speakers of Solresol – if we can call them speakers, for they had, at their peak, communicated only with whistles, flags and drums – had not spoken to each other in English, French or Solresol for many weeks. The epitaph for Solresol was written on their faces whenever they were obliged to meet.

I thought then to have the pair of them converse in Volapük. If they could not communicate in their chosen language, then the Universal Language should prove its worth as a medium of reconciliation! I provided them with the following modest vocabulary:

- **Selob,** I sell
- **No,** not, no
- **Vin,** wine
- **Kim,** who
- **Stim,** honour

- **Neflen,** enemy
- **Fidob,** I eat
- **Blud,** blood
- **Kusadom,** I accuse
- **Nestim,** dishonour

- **Lemob,** I buy
- **Dlinob,** I drink
- **Kis,** what
- **Vom,** wife
- **Löfob,** I love

and requested that the pudding be served – it was a splendid, large rhubarb tart, served hot with custard – before Messieurs Coens and Muriset proceeded to engage each other in bantering conversation:

Kusadom.
 Kimi kusadol?
  Kusadol nefleni.
 Löfol vomi.
  No löfom vomi!
   Kusadol nefleni.
 Selol stimi.
  No selom stimi!
   Lemob nestimi.
 Binol nefleni.
  Binom nefleni.
   Kusadom nefleni.

And then, in **Exercise 8,**
M. Coens asked M. Muriset to supply the correct verb- and noun-endings in the following phrases:

* **Man löf— vom—.**
* **Neflen— man— giv— mon— vom—.**

And then M. Muriset asked M. Coens to supply the correct verb- and noun-endings in return:

* **Vom— dlin— blud—.**
* **Vom— lem— vin— neflen—.**

Fin tidüpa velid.

Cödel Yagöl epükom! The Hunting Judge has spoken!

What a triumph for Cödel Yagöl and what a victory for Volapük! A miracle, perhaps. There was no doubt but that, as a Universal Language, as a means of communicating where other communication had failed, Volapük had succeeded! I ordered a cessation of the lesson, and the introduction of pots of tea and plates of scones. The rest of the afternoon passed uneventfully, Cödel Yagöl taking his tea and his shortbread like any other man, passing the milk and sugar, in the company of friends. When he asked Mrs. Turpie to pour him another cup, she did so without a shriek. And so, at around four o'clock, Mme. Muriset buttoned herself up, the company dissolved, and its members went home, muttering "*OBOLOMOFOSON*" as they did so.

I found, on returning the regalia and raiment of Cödel Yagöl, that my view of the world was restored once more. All movements became smooth and conjoined, all colouring was natural. The restoration of the tints and speed of the world was, I may say, a considerable relief.

*   *   *

The Scotsman on the following day carried a pair of articles entitled "Drawing-Room Disturbance in Newington" and "The Unusual Funeral of Professor McInnes", the former making mention of events in Upper Gray Street which were as mysterious as they were vague, the latter being based on public knowledge and scandal. I discovered later that Mr. Gunn had stepped directly from the wake to a public-house nearby, had there encountered a writer for the newspaper, and had given him a garbled account of the celebrations of the life of Professor McInnes; the journalist, to his credit, assumed that drink explained most of the unlikely anecdote, but thought to have the story printed nevertheless.

Transactions V: Speaking with Animals

Written in Edinburgh, on 25th March, 1891.

At an early moment in the construction of The Edinburgh Society for the Propagation of a Universal Language, a matter had arisen for debate. I cannot now recall who proposed the motion, but the matter caused considerable discussion. It was this: could a Universal Language be understood by the higher animals, other than Man?

There were, of course, those who violently disagreed with the notion. I was, in fact, one of those. But then I began to reflect on the matter, and considered for myself the wit and wisdom of several species of birds, such as parrots, crows, magpies and mynahs; and the apparent comprehension of sheep-dogs to the spoken commands of their masters; and finally, I suggested at the next meeting of the Society, that an experiment be conducted, under the strictest control of impartial observers, to train a parrot in the Universal Language. The Reverend Goodfellow, Miss Hepburn, and M. Desdemoni were pleased to offer themselves up as Judges in this matter; certainly, I would never expect them to judge in favour of the proposition, if there was the slightest doubt.

Of course, Bosman was determined that I should not, in any way imaginable, steal a march upon him; and proposed a slight alteration to the experiment. Instead of, as was agreed, myself alone purchasing and training a suitable animal, both he and I should train one animal each, mine in Volapük and his in Esperanto, and we would compare the results after three months. Feeling that he had gained some kind of advantage on me, I acquiesced.

*   *   *

In July of last year, therefore, a visit was made to the premises of Mr. James Dewar, Naturalist and Bird-Stuffer, of St. Patrick Square. On his advice, two parrots were purchased, at considerable expense to the funds of the Society (this expenditure having been agreed, against the express wishes of Mr. Gunn, Treasurer, but by the democratic majority of the rest of the membership). Mr. Dewar assured us that the parrots were still young, and had had little opportunity to learn much of the English language, and would therefore be most suitable for our experiment. His claims were soon exposed as blatant untruths as we made our way home, when first Bosman's, and then my, parrot began to subject passers-by to sea-faring oaths and unsuitable language. We arrived home at full tilt, fearing arrest and being hauled before the magistrate for indecent conduct on the public highway.

Over the following few months, we each laboured at our task, myself of teaching my parrot – which I named Henry – the grammar and vocabulary of Volapük; and Bosman in teaching his parrot – which he named Gemmell – the basics of Esperanto. In the early days, progress was not promising, for my bird, despite all use of carrot or stick (or, in this case, being covered up in its cage, as punishment, or given a handful of seeds as reward), persevered with its stevedorean language, and refused to grasp even the basics of numbers, the conjugation of verbs, or simple declension of nouns. I guarded the secret of my lack of progress jealously, as did Bosman. Frequently, I crept down the stair on the tips of my toes, and listened outside the door of Bosman's dwelling-place. But I heard nothing to my advantage. I am sure that Bosman did likewise, for I frequently heard Mrs. Forbes standing in the stair, castigating us both for our "daft" behaviour.

The agreement reached by the Society was that our experiment should run until Christmas, at which time, both birds should be brought before the Society and judged by the three dis-interested parties.

It was in the early part of December that Henry, my bird, finally began to speak in Volapük, thereby confirming my initial conjecture that the Universal Language could have a use outside of Human Society. By the twentieth of that month, I was able to ask it simple questions about the day of the week, the weather and the warmth (or otherwise) of the room; and receive suitable replies.

It was a startling triumph, made all the more pleasurable by the abject failure of Bosman to teach his parrot any Esperanto! At the Christmas meeting of the Society, the two birds were presented and Henry the parrot conversed intelligently with me for over a minute. There was a ripple of applause from the assembled membership, and a look of epiphany passed over Mr. Goodfellow's face. It was then

Bosman's turn: but when he pulled the cover off his parrot's cage, all that he could coax from the beast were the worst oaths, the strongest curses and the most devilish squawks that Miss Hepburn had ever heard. There were shrieks of protest from the floor, and, however hard Bosman tried to pretend that these were words of Esperanto, his demeanour betrayed him. In the contest between us, I had been victorious.

But for the more serious scientific matter, whether I had indeed taught an animal to speak in Volapük, the judges were divided. Miss Hepburn was adamant that I had not, Mr. Desdemoni equally convinced that I had; the Reverend Goodfellow, unwilling to upset either one party or the other, refused to cast a vote either way; and so the matter was left undecided by the Society, although proven to all the scientific minds. It is clear that a well-constructed Universal Language can have an application beyond the fraternity of Nations – it can also bridge the gap between the species, perhaps even between Humanity and any creatures which fly between the stars.

So matters were left. Bosman continued to try to teach his bird Esperanto – but with what success, I am unsure, for he never again discussed it with me. When I left for my professional trip to the North of Scotland, on the nineteenth day of January, I was obliged to leave my parrot, Henry, in the care of Mrs. Forbes, my landlady.

*   *   *

On my return, last week, to Edinburgh, my parrot could speak no more.

Mrs. Forbes, when questioned, was unapologetic. The two birds, she advised me, had, from the very first moment together, shouted and squawked at each other night and day, now in coarse English, now in Volapük, occasionally – if Bosman was to be believed, and Mrs. Forbes did not care whether he spoke the truth or nay – in Esperanto. The noise became unbearable, and the two birds were separated, one in the front room, the other in the kitchen. But this did little to stop their rivalry, and they took to calling out to each other between the rooms, whether or not doors were closed and blankets rolled across to block the gaps.

Finally, Mrs. Forbes could take no more and, one Tuesday morning in early February (when, by my calculations, I was still in Portsoy), she had gathered up the birds which now spoke in tongues, and marched off to the premises of Mr. Dewar, demanding that he exercise that part of his trade which promised a permanent silence. When Mr. Dewar demurred, our irate landlady pointed out to him the sign in his shop-window which advertised "bird and animal stuffing in all its branches". Reluctantly, Mr. Dewar was persuaded to silence the birds in a humane manner, and to stuff and mount them in life-like poses. The two birds were delivered back to our house in Carlung Place at the end of February, and Henry now gazes down at me from the top of my wardrobe. It is my intention, when Volapük has been adopted as the Universal Language, to make a gift of this unique bird to the National Museum in Chambers Street, to commemorate its achievement.

But before Mr. Dewar had carried out his professional duties, he had had the opportunity of hearing Henry speaking fluent Volapük. Indeed, Mr. Dewar reports to me that Henry's last words before falling into an endless sleep were: "*adyö – adelo deilob!!*" (The final words of Bosman's parrot, by contrast, related to the free and easy morals of female Bostonians of the night.) It was this wonder, Mr. Dewar told me yesterday, that had persuaded him to join the Society, and to campaign for the introduction of Volapük as the Universal Language of the future. Thus, my anger and chagrin at losing one speaker of Volapük was counter-balanced by my pleasure at gaining a new recruit to the cause.

Katel Mälid, the Sixth Chapter: The Genders

Preparations for the Annual General Meeting of
The Edinburgh Society for the Propagation of a
Universal Language. Easter Sunday, 1891.

"There needs be at least eleven genders in any worthy Universal Language," stated Sir Thomas.

His remark was sparked, I believe, by the discovery that morning, that Adam and Eve (the mice) had succeeded in producing a second brood of babies, barely eight weeks after their Elgin births. This time, however, a mere ten small mice were born, a matter for concern for Sir Thomas, who wondered if Adam was off his food. My only concern was that the mice – now twenty-four in number – might escape and over-run the building; but Sir Thomas assured me that they were "disciplinarians", these mice, and that I need not fear on that score.

Returning to the matter of genders: I remarked mildly that I considered this number to be excessive. The purity of the Universal Language should not be muddied by the introduction of unnecessary detail. I asked him which genders he had in mind, thinking for myself only of two or three.

Sir Thomas, sitting in my best arm-chair, counted them off on the fingers of his embroidered mittens: "*Balid* – a man; *Telid* – a woman; *Kilid* – a beast; *Folid* – such a thing as is inanimate; *Lulid* – a god; *Mälid* – a goddess . . . " Here he faltered, looking in some confusion at the fingers of his right hand. "That is six – and so it goes on through the other five genders," he added quickly, and turned to toast himself some bread at my smoking fire. "Miss Jamieson of Laurencekirk was most accommodating," he murmured, apparently referring to the mittens, but perhaps reminiscing on something else entirely.

I persisted: "But you said there were eleven genders – have you forgotten the others?" I asked, with some malice in my voice. Here before me sat a man who claimed to know the best way of doing everything, who professed to have all the knowledge required for a Universal Language, who knocked me back at every suggestion, who laughed openly at the logical simplicity of Volapük. And now, for once, I had found a chink in his armour, or a failure of memory.

Sir Thomas sighed. "No," he said. "I am not held captive by Amnesia – I merely succumb to Morpheus." He adopted a whining tone of voice, which did not suit him at all. "I am a venerable old man, you know, and the troubles of recent days have exhausted me . . . " I was expected to believe that his reserves of energy were drained by travel, by the company of many people, by the noises of the city, and by the interminable walking on hard pavement. But I suspected strongly that, if he were truly exhausted, it was from his pursuit of women, his partiality to feasts, and his monstrous appetite for strong drink and argumentation. Already that morning, we had fallen out over a small matter: Sir Thomas had, prying under my mattress in search of spirits, come across a number of small muslin bags, each containing the dried remnants of a week's residue of tea-leaves from my tea-pot. Making much of this discovery, and endeavouring thereby to mock me, he proceeded to throw these bags around the room. I, meanwhile, collected them from the corners into which they were cast and replaced them under the mattress: they were, after all, no concern of his.

I suspected also that his Universal Language had been developed no further than a vague list of wild promises, without force or flesh.

"Well, let me guess," I said. "Five genders in addition? Well, what about . . . an Angel?"

Sir Thomas nodded: "Good, good, yes: an Angel."

"A Devil?"

No, a Devil was simply another Angel. Fallen.

I pondered long and hard, trying to imagine some entity or object or person who was not categorised by any of the seven so far determined. Perhaps a Chimaera, half-man half-beast, such as a Centaur? Yes, that would be acceptable as the eighth gender. A Hermaphrodite? Sir Thomas was shocked at this; he had never heard of such a thing. Did such people exist? I had no personal knowledge to draw on, but I was assured that they did. If so, he demanded to know, which part was woman and which part man? He was unreasonably concerned at the detail. I could not clarify matters, which disappointed him. But, if it were true . . . yes, a Hermaphrodite was admirably suited to the ninth gender.

How about Geldings and *Castrati*, who, having had their gender removed in the most unalterable way, might be said to constitute one of their own? Yes, this was reasonable. The tenth gender was formed by those with a lack-of-gender, those being de-generate.

An hour or so of closely argued discussion and deep reflection did not reveal the eleventh and final gender to either of us. I could tell that Sir Thomas' thoughts were still concentrated on the hermaphrodite. I tested him with all manner of animate objects, but none seemed to fire his enthusiasm: Dragons and Leviathans? – he would not countenance them; Brownies, Goblins and Fairies? – to be categorised with Angels and Devils; Insects, Plants or Fish? – all male or female; the Haggis, and the related sausage-meats of Europe? – arrant folly; Rain, Snow and Sleet? – inanimate; Kings and Queens? (Sir Thomas almost succumbed to this suggestion, but then withdrew his patronage at the last moment – "I have seen the Monarch naked in the flesh," he announced, a statement which caused me grave concern, but I chose not to pursue his claim); Fire, Water, Air and Stone? – beneath his contempt as a proposal; Elderly women of the night? – an interesting suggestion, which had him persuaded for a moment, for he claimed to have seen much of such creatures; but then he charitably decided against – "A woman is always a woman," he preached; and, finally, Witches and Wizards? – he referred me to Fairies and Elves, aforementioned.

It seemed that the eleventh gender would be reserved for some form of life which we had not yet discovered – it would scarcely surprise me to learn that it was some noxious disease, typhus or tuberculosis, or a deadly fungus.

As Sir Thomas spread my jam thickly upon his toast, I asked him to explain to me how the eleven genders would be expressed in his Universal Language. All he could do was repeat the idle boast about the expression of numbers, as he had in Inverkeilor: that each gender could be identified by just one letter attached to the noun or verb it described. "Much like Volapük, then," I suggested. Sir Thomas was having none of that – "Not like Volapük in the least, you neophyte!" he exclaimed. "Mine is thaumacomplexitory and hyperesoteric!"

I was pleased with his answer, for it confirmed to me that his Universal Language was precisely what it should not be – difficult and strewn with obstacles. Volapük, after all, had barely three genders – he, she or it, which are expressed thus:

Tidüp jölid: The Genders.

Om, he (or, it);   **of**, she;   **os**, it.

All nouns are considered as "masculine", unless expressly denoting females. What we call the neuter gender of nouns does not exist in Volapük. Thus **of** is used of female persons or animals; **om** is used, firstly, of males; secondly, of living beings whose sex is disregarded; thirdly, of lifeless or sexless things (it). And **os** is "it", used only when speaking abstractly, where no noun is referred to, as in:

"*It* is stormy weather."

"Will you be an ally? I swear *it*."

When I explained the subtler sub-divisions of the male gender, Sir Thomas bridled up, wroth that a man could be equated to something sexless or something inanimate. "That, precisely, is why the Universal Language needs eleven genders, you obdurate!" he maintained, so agitated that he quit his comfortable seat to march up and down, the better to shout and complain. "You have been supposititious, you knave: eleven are requisite! No, eleven is by far not sufficient! Indeed – we need nineteen, nineteen, damn you to everlasting flames! Nineteen genders, all clearly defined, set down and categorised for simple usage by idiots and professors alike! Let us have Snow and Rain, let us have Fairies and Elves, let us have Kings and Queens – what else was there? Chameleons, indeed, and Salamanders, such as change their form. And Clegs, Slaters and Midges! How many is that?"

I made a rapid calculation and found that we had arrived at sixteen genders, assuming Kings to be separate from Queens. "And the Souls of the Dead!" he proposed, rubbing his wrinkled hands with a great deal of satisfaction. "The Souls of the Departed, Poltergeists, Ghosts, Bogies, Wraiths, Banshees and Succubi – life without life, form without form – they constitute the seventeenth gender!" He fell to reflection for a few minutes, to which I left him as I arranged my own breakfast. As I poured myself a cup of tea, he had hit upon: "Smokies!" I argued with him briefly, but he claimed that a Smokie could not be considered male or female, and so we were left with it.

But we stumbled again at the final hurdle, and no amount of shouted persuasion could shift him to accept any other category or classification of animate or inanimate life as the nineteenth gender.

Our argument made so much noise, I fear, that my neighbour despatched young Lizzie up the stair to see what was amiss, this being a Sunday afternoon and the street and building being otherwise quiet. At her appearance at the door, Sir Thomas was transformed in a moment from cross old tyrant to silky-smooth seducer. Lizzie was enticed in to help him make some more toast, and was soon seated before the fire, listening suspiciously to what I had to say on The Genders.

I continued with the lesson, therefore, anxious to make a good impression on Lizzie, who I knew to be in the Bosmanite camp; but she was young, easily swayed by argument and enthusiasms, and could perhaps be won over.

Ji- is a prefix (English, "she") used to make nouns feminine, when the gender is to be especially pointed out.

Most words, if relating to men, are masculine without any prefix; if relating to animals, the unprefixed word is the common (in a sense, *indifferent*) gender, the name of the male animal has the prefix **om-**, and the name of the female the prefix **ji-**.

Thus, **jeval** means "a horse", undifferentiated as to gender; but **omjeval** specifically means "a stallion"; while **jijeval** specifically refers to "a mare". At the mention of stallions and mares, Sir Thomas leered unpleasantly at young Lizzie, who transfixed him with a look of youthful disgust. I chose to ignore the old man, and hurried ever onwards.

A few words, I said, which are in common currency, are always feminine – such as:

- **mot,** mother (which would otherwise be, **jifat**, female father)
- **vom,** woman, or wife (otherwise, **jiman**, female man)
- **läd,** lady (otherwise, **jisöl**, female "mister, sir")
- **kun,** cow (otherwise, **jixol**, female ox)

All this was too much for Lizzie: "Mr. Justice!" she exclaimed. "Just what do you think you are saying? Do you suppose the female gender to be mere servants of the male, do you think that Man came first and all Women are just . . . slaves?" Her face had flushed red with anger, and she stood up. "What kind of future does that hold for us, if women are to continue to be the mere hangers-on of men? Is this your Equal Society of Nations?"

I was surprised by her violent reaction. I pointed out that most words specifically used for females, in English, were of the same nature: woman, authoress, clerkess, shepherdess, Mistress; except where the word was for an animal, such as: cow, ewe, mare, hen. And that, in those instances where gender was not relevant, the same word could be used to apply to both male and female: cook, weaver, worker.

"Exactly, Mr. Justice!" exclaimed Lizzie, now quite agitated, and marching up and down in my small room, to Sir Thomas' ill-concealed delight. "Exactly so – the English language until now has never given a woman her equal status with a man. It is up to the Universal Language to do that – "

"And Esperanto, precisely, will do that," came a voice from behind us. Surprised, I turned round, and found that viper, Dr. Bosman, lounging in my door-way, a cigarette hanging from his lower lip, as always, while he polished his spectacles, and looked smug. "Forgive my intrusion, Mr. Justice," he went on, breathing smoke into my room, and looking at Lizzie, "but I had stepped out downstairs and heard Lizzie's voice. It seems we are in debate?" He looked from one to the other of us, eyebrows raised, in that calculating, theatrical way he has.

Sir Thomas growled at me, to ask who was the young dog. "This, Sir Thomas, is my neighbour, Dr. Henry Bosman. Sir Thomas – Dr. Bosman, Dr. Bosman – Sir Thomas. Dr. Bosman also holds the post – for the moment – of Chairman of the Edinburgh Society."

"Delighted, I'm sure," said Bosman suavely, stepping over to shake the old man's hand. Having done so, he stepped back, looking puzzled, as if something in the touch had given him pause for thought. However, he turned his attention to Lizzie and myself.

"The matter of gender, eh?" he asked. He extinguished the end of his cigarette in my tea-cup, and proceeded immediately to light up another, whose first fumes he drew in like some opium-addict, eyes closed, hissing. "Of course, our Esperanto, being the language of the future, has no genders for its nouns, and the gender of person is only distinguished in the singular personal pronouns: *li* for 'he', *ŝi* for 'she' and *ĝi* for 'it'. And in the plural, no gender at all – *ili* for 'them'. Simple, but effective, and demonstrably egalitarian, I think you'll agree?"

Sir Thomas was greatly taken aback at this. It was evident that he could not conceive of a language that paid so little attention to gender. He was, for a brief moment, lost for words to express his horror. In the meantime, Bosman pointed out that all nouns would be preceded by *la* for "the", and ended with the suffix *-o*, a rather neat balance – he claimed – between the traditional feminine "la" and the traditional masculine suffix "-o".

"You immature driveller!" exclaimed Sir Thomas, raising himself from his seat. "What vacancy is this? What are your words for a woman, a girl, a wife, female servant, a procuress, a duchess, a . . . a . . . ?" He was suddenly overcome, and had to sit down again. Dr. Bosman expressed a professional interest in him, felt his pulse, and hushed him. Again, I noticed a discomfited expression on his face as he stood up. But it barely interrupted his stride.

"Do not excite yourself, sir," continued Bosman, "for we have as many good words as are needed for everything to do with women, girls, females: all we do is take the root-word – for example: *la ŝafo*, a sheep; and introduce the prefix *vir-* for the male sheep – *la virŝafo*, a ram; and the affix *-in-* to get *la ŝafino*, a ewe. Or *la ĉevalo* – a horse, *la vir ĉevalo*, a stallion and *la ĉevalino*, a mare. What, really, could be simpler?" Bosman looked about him, absolutely convinced that he had won the argument. "The only exceptions to the rule are, of course, in the familial relationships, where a husband is *la edzo* and a wife is *la edzino*, a son is *la filo* and a daughter is *la filino*. As for your other questions, Sir Thomas . . . let me see: *la viro* becomes *la virino*, *la knabo* becomes *la knabino*, *la dino* becomes *la dinino*; *la duco* becomes *la ducino*; and I have really no idea what your other word is, Sir Thomas, and I do not think it appropriate to pursue the matter in the present company." He smirked at Lizzie.

I saw my opening: "So, Dr. Bosman, what you are saying is this: that all nouns can be made either masculine or feminine, by inserting an affix."

"My point precisely, Mr. Justice. I must say that you learn fast, for one who is so entrenched in the past!"

"But," I continued, "am I correct in understanding that the principal exceptions to this rule are all the words for family relation-ships, and above all for man and woman? And that, for the pronouns, the single plural, which you describe as having no gender at all – *ili* – is in fact the masculine plural?"

Bosman nodded languidly, quite blind to the pit opening up before him. He leaned casually against the door-post.

"Which," I pushed home the sword, "would suggest to me, and I am sure would suggest to young Lizzie here, that, in the family and in human relationships, the male has the upper hand and the female is subservient?"

I saw Lizzie looking at Bosman fixedly. Bosman's eyes darted from me to her and back again.

He stood up straight. "Well," he began, "I'm not so sure . . . "

"So the essential difference between Esperanto and Volapük is not so much in the manner in which genders are distinguished, but in the quantity thereof?"

"That is . . . " he faltered, at a loss as to how he should reply.

"Thus," I continued, pressing home my advantage, and noting how Lizzie was deep in thought, with her eyes fixed upon Bosman. "Thus, Esperanto claims to make all things equal in gender, but holds fast to the old regime when it comes to the home and the family, when all its posturings and claims are exposed for all to see. The beauty of Volapük, on the other hand – "

Bosman snorted angrily and rudely. "Beauty, indeed, if such a word – "

I cut him short: "Dr. Bosman, you will have the grace to hear me out. Do not come into my room with your Cape Colony manners and your supercilious arguments! The beauty of Volapük, as I was saying, and its basic honesty, is that the number of words can be greatly reduced by assuming the root-word to be male, unless advised otherwise by one prefix."

"Maybe so, Mr. Justice, maybe so," replied Bosman. "But History alone will tell which of us is right. And I believe that the great movement in Europe, to take up Esperanto at the expense of Volapük, indicates what History thinks of it all, does it not?"

Before I had a chance to reply to this nonsense, there was a sharp rap on the door, and another visitor entered. This was my neighbour, Mrs. Mary Forbes. A lady of some fifty years of age, and thus a contemporary of mine, she was a tall, slim woman. She lived alone, an earlier husband having been abandoned. I have tried to maintain a friendship with her over the years that I have lived in her rented room at the top of the stair; but it has not been easy. Her hair, worn long, was greying, and there was a deep sadness in her brown eyes.

And on this Sunday afternoon, as on many other days, she was angry and upset. "What is this behaviour, Mr. Justice?" she demanded, withering me with her glance. "I expected better of you than these violent arguments and this raising of voices, which is quite unacceptable in my house. And you, too, Dr. Bosman – have you no shame? What example is this to set for my poor Lizzie?"

Embarrassed, I shuffled and stammered, and looked at Bosman, in the hope and expectation of his sudden demise. Out of the corner of my eye, I noticed that Sir Thomas was preparing himself for some kind of assault, with his weapons of charm, upon Mrs. Forbes' defences. Moving adroitly, I managed to upturn him as he came up out of his seat, and sent him sprawling on the hearth-rug; and with a great show of concern, I helped him to his feet, and surreptitiously kicked him backwards into his seat, to all appearances as if I were struggling to support a man with no control over his legs. "Now, sir," I admonished gently. "You just rest and do not upset yourself with that Dr. Bosman. Mrs. Forbes," I turned to her, and was smitten, as many times before, by the anger in her large eyes and the charming downwards curve of her lips. "Mrs. Forbes, I do apologise for this uproar – I feel that Dr. Bosman has excited my old friend too much . . . "

Dr. Bosman also felt it was time for him to defend himself to his landlady. Although he lived within the main door of Mrs. Forbes' dwelling-place, there was no reason to suppose that he thereby held any great advantage over me, who live in the attic-room at the head of the stair. "Mrs. Forbes," he said, turning to her with all that he could muster in the way of charm. "Your daughter and I were just debating with Mr. Justice the nature of gender in the nouns and verbs of the Universal Languages. I fear we were carried away by our excitement, for which I can only apologise."

Mrs. Forbes sighed, and looked for a seat. I made haste to move the mouse-box from the chair by the table, trusting that the inhabitants would not squeak loudly; and she sat down. "And what, precisely, were you all saying about gender, if I might ask?"

"Oh," laughed the reptilian Bosman. "Nothing of great moment, I fear!"

Mrs. Forbes looked sharply at him. "Do not patronise me, sir," she scolded him sternly. "I am not some simpleton to be brushed off!"

Seeing my chance, I intervened quickly: "We were just debating the advantages and disadvantages of recognising or concealing the gender of words, and the nature of gender prefixes and suffixes. Dr. Bosman suggested that gender was not relevant in a language, and I proposed the usual three genders as being necessary for a clear understanding of what is being said or written. My old friend here," I waved at Sir Thomas, who sat in his chair wishing bloody death upon me, "argued for – how many was it, sir? – nineteen? – yes, nineteen genders."

Mrs. Forbes looked at me speculatively. I confess that that look confirmed my fascination for her faded looks and strength of character.

"But what is the good of gender in a language, at all, do you think, Mr. Justice?" she asked me.

The question startled me. "My dear lady," I began. "To begin with we need to distinguish between male, female and inanimate objects . . . "

"To begin with," she interrupted. "I am not your 'dear lady', as you well know, Mr. Justice. And why do we need to make that distinction? Should it not be obvious? A man would be male, a woman, female, and a stone inanimate. A dog would be either male or female, a bee likewise, a bird or a fish, would they not? Is it not always apparent from every sentence what is male and what is female and what is neither? What need do we have of genders in nouns and verbs?"

I could see Bosman nodding sagely, and Lizzie looking at her mother in astonishment – evidently, she knew little of her mother's depth of intelligence.

"The very point, my dear – Mrs. Forbes," I replied, "which we were debating, albeit over-energetically. Perhaps there is a happy medium to be struck – although I suspect my old friend would say otherwise!" Sir Thomas continued to stare me down, and held his tongue.

"But how many times is it necessary to make that distinction?" she persisted. "Would it not be simpler, in those cases when the gender of a person or animal was of importance, to simply introduce some small word to point this out; and at all other times, simply proceed on the basis of gender being unimportant?"

I considered this proposition for a moment, and found it, on the face of things, not unreasonable. But there was something in here which smacked of lumpen Esperantism, and I did not like it one bit. As I did not want to argue with her, I changed tack slightly. "Young Lizzie here, of course," I smiled at her daughter in a manner which I hoped would placate, "was suggesting that the forms of gender which are apparent in nouns in English – and, as I now understand it, in Esperanto – are designed to enslave and imprison the gentler and more beautiful sex!"

Mrs. Forbes snorted. "I know exactly what my daughter's views are, and she does not go far enough, Mr. Justice. How would it be if you gentlemen," she indicated myself and Bosman here, "were to come up with a language in which the male was subservient to the female? H'm? That would be a good step forward for civilised society, would it not?" She smiled in triumph, knowing that neither of us dared to answer. "Now, Lizzie, I think we have chores to do downstairs, have we not, lest our male oppressors go hungry for their supper?"

The lady and the girl departed in spirited manner, leaving Bosman fuming with silent rage, Sir Thomas cursing the pain in his legs, and myself in agony as to whether I had raised, or lowered, myself in the estimation of Mrs. Forbes.

Dr. Bosman was the first to recover his equanimity, and did so with an easy laugh. "Women!" he said. "What do they know?" He lit himself another foul-smelling cigarette, and lit one also for Sir Thomas, who expressed his interest in that filthy habit. I was about to take issue with Bosman, but, on reflection, could not see any purpose in that. I would store that one disparaging word, and the way it was said, in mind, and bring it against him when it most suited the promotion of Volapük, or of undermining his ill-concealed suit of Lizzie Forbes. I wished heartily that the doctor would leave, and take his evil smoke with him; but he seemed quite determined to stay on.

"By the way, Justice," he said airily. "You will be aware that our Annual General Meeting will take place on the very same day as the Census of Scotland?"

I was but dimly aware of this, never having considered it to be of any importance whatsoever. "Of course I am. What of it?" I demanded.

"Just that I am the Census Returns Officer for this district, and I expect you to make a proper return for your guest, if he is staying over next Sunday night?" Bosman waved at Sir Thomas, who snarled in response and spat in the fire.

I assured Bosman that I would do whatever was fitting to do, as a good citizen.

"For if," continued the objectionable young medical man, "I find that you make a false declaration on the Census form, then I will be obliged to report you to the Authorities."

"You can do as you see fit, Mr. Bosman," I replied. "You can do as you see fit. But if you think these threats will assist you to victory at the General Meeting, then you are very much mistaken. And now—" I indicated the door.

Bosman turned easily to leave. "I have my eye on you," he said, winked at me in the most despicable manner, slammed the door and sauntered downstairs whistling a religious tune.

At last silence descended once more over the house and I was left to my thoughts – largely of Mary Forbes – and the occasional angry word which escaped Sir Thomas. At length, however, he laughed and shook his fist at me in what I interpreted to be an amicable fashion. "Young Mrs. Forbes, eh?" he chuckled. "Well, good fortune in your wooing, you simpleton. I wager you'll find her mastery of logic too strong for you to handle. Myself, I enjoy a woman with conversation; but the ones with logic are too hard to chew on!" I found the man's metaphors little to my taste, and asked him never to mention such a painful matter again. Of course, he ignored my request.

*   *   *

At length, at about five o'clock, when we had both dozed awhile, Sir Thomas stirred himself. "Wake up, Mr. Justice, wake up: there is man's work to be done, is there not?"

I had no idea of what it was he spoke, and told him so.

"Our agreement, you addle-bowelled tom-tit!" was his sharp response. "What I came here to do. You want to gain the ascendancy over that young cur, what's his name – Bösemann? So we have work to do, have we not? Tell me about those people who are most likely to be swayed in your favour."

I told off the names to him: there was Bosman, and Lizzie and Issachar Clark, all Esperantists – I did not hold out any great hopes with them. Then there were Walther Coens, and the couple Muriset – all Solresolists, but a broken faction, who were no threat to me. I would expect two to vote in my favour and, because of that, the other would vote against me. Mr. Gunn and Mrs. Keenan might be readily swayed from their position, which was that English was the greatest and simplest Universal Language. The Reverend Goodfellow and Miss Hepburn both defended the dead Classical languages: it might be possible to persuade the former, but I thought it unlikely that the latter would be ousted from her entrenched views. Then there was Louis Desdemoni and John Flynn, both volatile men, who might one day vote in favour and another against – but I knew they could be relied on never to vote for Bosman, for he had frequently and pitilessly mocked them in public gatherings. Which left only the two McKelvies, father and son, who were already in my party, as was Mr. Dewar; Mrs. Turpie whom, since the loss of her Professor, I did not expect to see again; and the unknown quantity represented by Miss Ethelreda Hutchinson, a woman of very rare qualities, who vouched for no single language at all, but for any which communicated best.

"And which of these should we visit, do you consider?" Sir Thomas asked me.

I considered for a few moments, then decided. "My opinion is that the homes of Goodfellow, Gunn, Desdemoni and Miss Hepburn might be our most fertile grounds, Sir Thomas."

"Then let it be so!" he exclaimed, struggling to his feet with a burst of energy.

"What? Before our tea, Sir Thomas?" I remonstrated. "Whatever are you thinking of?"

"Tea? Tea? You can think of your scones and pots of tea at a time like this?" Sir Thomas swiped at me with his omnipresent stick, which I managed to avoid by an agile leap. "This is a moment to strike, the helioprecedentic cavalry-charge, the exploding mortars as they come out from their defences, striking down hill at them from out of the rising sun! Let us strike – now!" He produced once more the costume of Cödel Yagöl, which I put on hastily; then, as I felt the power of the Judiciary flood through my limbs and sharpen my mind, he hustled me towards the door. I carried him down the stairs, for he was unnaturally light.

"My carriage!" he demanded.

Two days earlier, we had discussed how best to get him around the streets of Edinburgh. At length, I had proposed that I purchase or hire, from the local butcher's boy, a hand-barrow normally designated as the conveyance for pounds of mince and Sunday roasts. We negotiated, young William Henderson and I, for a good ten minutes, until terms were agreed for hire. With a liberal sprinkling of sawdust, covered by an old blanket, we covered the worst of the gore of years, and Sir Thomas fitted in to the box as if it were crafted to his own size by some master-carpenter. Henderson and I agreed that this barrow would be left at the foot of our stairs whenever he did not need it for business, and that I would pay him one shilling per hour for each period of use, or sixpence for each half-hour.

It being Easter Sunday, the barrow stood waiting for us. I placed Sir Thomas into the barrow, tucked a blanket around his feet to keep out the worst of the draughts, and set off down to the Meadows, and across them into the centre of our capital city. It was, by then, six o'clock and growing dark. The appearance on the Meadows of Cödel Yagöl seemed not to create any interest; and such passers-by as lifted their eyes from a sad contemplation of their existence, were soon stared down by my gimlet gaze from behind the helmet.

I had expected the world to appear, once more, altered by the mask of Cödel Yagöl. But I was greatly disturbed to see the changes which had been effected on this fateful evening. Which were these: that most figures which flickered in and out of my vision in the gloom, black and white only in colouring, suffered from the strangest co-mingling of limbs, heads, bodies from quite separate species: in short, everyone seemed to be of the eighth gender of Sir Thomas' scheme. Was I wrong, therefore, to limit myself to three genders? Was this person here, with the head of a goat, the body of a hedgehog and the long legs of a frog or toad – was it male or female? And the fast old cat, with the head of a magpie and the many feet of a centipede – a woman? Most disturbing of all, as I passed the junction of the High Street, was a procession of birds, having no legs or tails to speak of, which nevertheless fluttered and swooped down upon St. Giles' Cathedral, to be impaled upon stakes held aloft and driven through their abdomens by a single black bull with eyes that shot forth white fire and smoke.

But each and every one of these nightmares, regardless of their composition, bore a simple label, indicating "Man", "Woman", or "Child", or "Student"; occasionally, there was one labelled "Police-man" or "Soldier".

Mustering my courage, I understood all this to be a trick of the mask, and ignored the on-set of chimaerae. At length, we reached the junction of George Street and Hanover Street, and Sir Thomas expressed his desire to board the cable-tramcar which would take us down the hill. I was pleased with his choice, for my arms grew tired with the constant need to steer and drive the barrow. Never again would I fault a butcher's boy for his lack of energy!

When the tramcar arrived, I placed Sir Thomas aboard, and then clambered up with the barrow. The centaur which oversaw the loading of the car on behalf of the Edinburgh Northern Cable Railway Company looked at me askance and stirred its horns, but I roared at him in Volapük that he should beware of poking his nose into the affairs of others: *"Kautö!"*, I cried, Beware! *"Seilö!"*, Be Silent! I would point out to the student of Volapük that the Imperative and Interjective forms of the verb will be covered later; but I had no time to instruct the tramcar-attendant in the finer points of grammar.

In little over five minutes, our conveyance had rattled down the slopes of Dundas Street, past the junction with Henderson Row, where stand the winding-halls for the cables, and round the corner on to Inverleith Row, travelling on the flat at a more leisurely pace. The smell of the smoke from all the chimneys in Edinburgh appeared to be funnelled into that part of town, and the sour air was difficult to breathe. Another five or ten minutes brought us to the terminus of the tramway, at the junction with Ferry Road. The Reverend Goodfellow, I knew, occupied a house at the head of Wardie Road. The last few yards flew past as Cödel Yagöl wheeled the barrow to its first destination, which we reached at about seven o'clock. I thumped on his door, and a tiny, nervous creature, labelled "House-keeper", opened it cautiously, whiskers twitching.

"Announce to the Reverend Goodfellow," I ordered her, "that the Hunting Judge has come to visit."

A moment later, the Reverend, with the head of a heron and the body of a squirrel, came out into the entrance-hall, smiling nervously and asking us to come into his dining-room, where he was "taking High Tea".

We entered. The Reverend's house-keeper hurriedly set two more places at the table – we were the only others, Goodfellow being a bachelor – and soon we were enjoying a lightly-poached fish with cheese sauce, accompanied by cups of tea and good bread. I tested Goodfellow in the simple numbers of Volapük, and found him wanting. "Oh dear," he stuttered, as, for the fifth time, he confused *fol* and *vel*. "Oh dear, oh dear, oh dear! Whatever will you think of me?"

Cödel Yagöl ordered him to think less of the judgement of others and more of the numbers themselves; and by and by, as the hot scones vanished and the Madeira cake diminished, he managed to make sense of it all.

I congratulated him, but warned him that he followed a very narrow path. "Ah yes, indeed, sir: strait is the gate, is it not?" he twittered, looking at us from one to the other. Finally, I took him by the throat and demanded to know where he stood in the controversy between Volapük and Esperanto? At first, he professed to having no opinion, "being a Classics man myself". But gradually, as his face turned darker and my hand on his throat grew hard, he unburdened himself of the opinion that he much preferred Volapük, "a Universal Language after my own heart!"

Sir Thomas, apparently oblivious to the intellectual struggles taking place, finished off the last of the Dundee cake, brushed the crumbs from his fingers, and proposed that we "secure our next position".

*   *   *

A short trip by hand-barrow brought us to a place where we could catch an omnibus to Leith, where Mr. Gunn resides. Again, the minion of Edinburgh Corporation remonstrated with me for bringing the barrow on board his vehicle; but, although the man was a python, breathing fire, expelling locusts from his satchel, I saw only the label around his neck which declared him to be a "Conductor" and I paid no attention to his protests. Cödel Yagöl travels in his own manner and under his own bye-laws! The only concession I made was to offer the creature two penny-pieces for our fare, and we settled down to enjoy the ride as far as Fort Street, where Mr. Gunn ruled over the life and opinions of Mrs. Keenan.

On this evening, at about half-past eight o'clock, Mr. Gunn had the aspect of a fish with the rear-most quarters of a pig. When he saw Cödel Yagöl at his threshold, he staggered back in horror, throwing his arms before his face. Mrs. Keenan, watching in the shadows in the furry guise of a black-and-white cat, ran on her hind legs to protect him and threw herself in front of her master. But to no avail. Cödel Yagöl swept in over the vestibule, bearing barrow, Sir Thomas, Mrs. Keenan and Mr. Gunn ahead of him. We entered the front-room, where Mr. Gunn had evidently been interrupted in the act of enjoying a wee refreshment, in the company of two Oriental gentlemen. Upon our noisy arrival, the two gentlemen, whose aspects were curiously unaltered through the mask of the Hunting Judge, leaped to their feet and bowed to us.

"Gunn San," asked one of them politely of Mr. Gunn. "This man Samurai?"

Mr. Gunn looked confused. "Samurai, Mr. Kobayashi?"

"Famous noble warrior, Gunn San," elaborated the Oriental gentleman.

Gunn nodded, quite out of his depth, his mouth opening and shutting in a most embarrassing manner.

Gratified to meet a famous noble warrior, Mr. Kobayashi and his friend presented themselves to me.

"We gentlemen from Japan, O famous Samurai. Mr. Kobayashi, Mr. Kumakura. We stay home Gunn San. We visit Scotland to see great new Forth Bridge. Very many Japanese interested in great new Forth Bridge. We build many, many railway in Japan now. We very honoured to meet you." It must be said that Mr. Kumakura seemed less than honoured, for he glared at us fixedly. However, the pair bowed again and retired to a distant corner of the room, where, sitting cross-legged upon the bare boards, they watched us with the greatest of interest. I noticed, after five minutes, that Mr. Kumakura was viciously scribbling down notes in a large black notebook.

Cödel Yagöl ordered Mrs. Keenan to produce two more glasses, and Sir Thomas settled down snugly in a corner beside the blazing fire, taking a glass and the bottle with him. I turned to Mr. Gunn and demanded that he complete

Exercise 9.

using the vocabulary:

Flen, friend	**Bisiedel**, president	**Jeval**, horse
Dog, dog	**Viudel**, widower	**Capel**, Japanese gentleman
Tedel, merchant	**Blod**, brother	**Matel**, husband

he should express in Volapük:

- A lady-friend
- Widow
- Wife
- A female merchant
- A female president
- Japanese lady
- Sister
- Mare
- Bitch

In truth, Gunn's grasp of the fundamentals of Volapük was extremely threadbare, and he needed a great deal of encouragement from the sword of Cödel Yagöl. He was particularly unwilling to admit of the concept of a female merchant or a female president. Struck dumb, Mrs. Keenan could only look on in anguish, yowling and cleaning her whiskers. At length, Mr. Gunn seemed to have passed beyond the point of sensible education, for all that he could muster was a babble of labio-dental noise. As I waited for him to cease his spluttering, my attention was drawn again to his two Japanese lodgers, who, brightly coloured, observed politely.

"Honoured Samurai Shodel," said Mr. Kobayashi, seeing me turn in his direction. "This language you speak, it is language of noble warriors?"

"No," I replied, although greatly tempted to claim otherwise. "This is Volapük, the Universal Language of All Mankind."

Mr. Kumakura scowled, growled and scribbled furiously. It occurred to me of a sudden that here I had an unequalled chance to promote the cause of Volapük in the farthest corners of the Earth. "Would you like to learn this language?" I enquired of the visitors.

Mr. Kobayashi nodded his head vigorously. I suggested to Sir Thomas that he pour my new students another tot of whisky each, which he did with much ill-grace and sideways-glancing at them; this act of internationalist friendship, did, however, improve the aspect of Mr. Kumakura, who downed his glass in one swift movement and held it out for more. Sir Thomas warmed to him immediately. And I began with the declensions of the simplest of nouns.

I thought to take the simplest of words: *dog* and *kat*. We talked of *dog, dogi, doge* and *doga*, of *kat, kati, kate* and *kata*. But, although it was evident that the visitors from Nippon were by no means slow-witted, it took several minutes for them to understand the simplest of words: "dog" and "cat" were not words which readily crossed their lips. Indeed, to help them understand, we had to venture out into Fort Street and track down some representatives of those species (disregarding Mrs. Keenan as unsuitable), before Mr. Kobayashi and Mr. Kumakura fully understood of what we spoke. We returned indoors and the lesson went more smoothly for a time. But it was disconcertingly evident that the common vocabulary of Volapük did not find any echoes at all in the languages of the East. We progressed to *jidog* and *jikat*: once again, the feminine prefix seemed to give them inordinate difficulty, despite "she" being the most natural pronoun in the world.

Following a line of investigation which had now suggested itself to me, I tested them then with the word *lol*, a rose; and was deeply disturbed to hear them both repeat, quite clearly: "*ror*". At the height of my encouragements to "*lol*", and with the whisky-bottle now empty, SirThomas found himself bored with his surroundings, and "roared" back at the two Japanese. Startled at first, then highly amused, Mr. Kumakura stood up to his full height and roared like an ogre, while Mr. Kobayashi giggled hysterically, until the inhabitants of Fort Street began to gather at the windows, pressing their antennae up against the glass, curious to find the cause of the Sabbath commotion.

We parted the best of friends – or "frens", as our Oriental brothers pronounced it – and urged Mr. Gunn to vote in favour of Volapük at the General Meeting; but he seemed to have lost all comprehension. His mouth opened and shut, and his eyes blinked. I confess, I worried for the health of his shipping business on the following day.

*   *   *

Outside in Leith, a drizzle had begun, but CödelYagöl felt it not. The helmet and cloak protected me from the rain, and my gauntlets from the chill. I placed SirThomas in his barrow, and we raced to the foot of Leith Walk and boarded a tramcar, whose horses steamed in the down-pour. Around me, a number of passengers looked from under their twitching horns, then quickly curled up into their shells. The conductor, a large slater, decided not to challenge us, so we passed without incident to the east end of Princes Street, where we disembarked, and mingled with the few bat-headed, snake-tailed, hirsute "Bourgeois" that still wandered the streets. It was very late: the last trams and omnibuses were vanishing from the streets, and the drizzle had turned to a heavy rain.

There was no sense now in visiting Mr. Desdemoni or Miss Hepburn. The weight of Cödel Yagöl became a burden on me; the prolongation of the flickering, grey and black visions of Hell had weighted my head with lead; my arms were weary with the propulsion of SirThomas, now fast asleep in the barrow. It was a long and timeless climb across the Bridges, and then an endless road to Carlung Place.

We reached it after midnight, and I decanted Sir Thomas in the entrance-hall. He woke up, as sprightly as ever a man awoke, and obliged me to help him up the stair. When we gained my door, I was fit to fall over in a faint. Before I could divest myself of the trappings and clothing of power, Sir Thomas lewdly suggested that I keep them on, "and pay court to your lady-love". She would, he assured me with energetic posturing and much obscene mimicry, "Welcome you with open arms! Her heart can be yours this night, Mr. Justice, oh yes, her heart and all else besides, O! Mr. Justice, my adored one, my true love, my gallant!"

But I was exhausted beyond reason, and little tempted by his profane abuse of Mrs. Forbes. I threw off the helmet, the gauntlets and the cloak and fell into a deep, dreamless sleep upon my bed.

Fin tidüpa jölid.

Transactions VI: A New Era

Written in Edinburgh, on 4ᵗʰ April, 1891.

When we awoke this morning, a strong wind rattled the thin panes in my window, and banged doors somewhere down the stair. I felt the cold whistle under my blankets, and penetrate every limb of my body. I dressed quickly, and huddled close to the fire in the grate. Sir Thomas, however, seemed not to notice greatly, and stotted about, looking pleased with himself.

"I wish you a happy New Year!" he shouted to me, as I emerged from my blankets.

My look in response was, I fear, blank, as I had no glimmering of his meaning. This was precisely his intention, and he amused himself for the next few minutes in pointing gleefully at me, wielding his stick, and mocking me by turns. At last, warmed by the pitiful fire, which belched soot and sour smoke at us every time a new gust of wind passed above our heads, I turned on him and demanded to know what was the object of his joke.

"Your ignorance, sir, is demotic! Have you no idea of the nature of the Julian and Gregorian Calendars?"

Suspecting some nonsense or other, I advised him sharply that I had some knowledge of these matters, but that the calendar on the wall, which had kindly been presented to me by Bertram Borthwick & Sons, Butchers and Poulterers, sufficed.

"Listen very carefully, then, you simpleton," I was instructed. "By the recently-introduced Gregorian Calendar, to-day is – as your saussicophile Borthwick will agree – the fourth day of April, in the year 1891."

I gave my agreement, cautiously.

"By the traditional Calendar of Julius Caesar, however, the date is ten days earlier, to wit, the twenty-fifth day of March."

I sighed, for this really had no sense. "As I recall," I muttered, "the Julian Calendar fell out of favour some three hundred years ago. Pope Gregory, I believe, brought about significant changes. Why are you telling me all this now?"

Sir Thomas looked, for a brief moment, like a child who has lost a boiled sweetie; then he raged at me for my ignorance and disrespect for the old traditions. "Not so, gnatonic discreditor!" he cried. "The reforms of Pope Gregory were not adopted in this country with my agreement! Over my disparpled body alone shall they be accepted!"

I passed over this remark, and began to boil the kettle for some tea. I could hear Sir Thomas muttering to himself behind me. Finally he spoke up. "Taking your nonsensical remarks into disregard, you whelp, let me tell you that to-day, being the twenty-fifth of March, is the start of the New Year, by the old Calendars.* And to-day begins the year 1891. I bid you, once more, a happy New Year."

I sighed, wished him likewise for the sake of peace and quiet, and continued at my chore. It was then that I decided that the price I was paying for my success with the Edinburgh Society was too high. Sir Thomas would have to be stopped. He brought only confusion, cloudiness, irrational thought, and the dead-weight of the past, to our revolution of language.

When the tea had been brewed and poured, and Sir Thomas had set himself before the fire, blocking the heat from reaching any other part of the room, or any other occupant of the room, I instructed him, once more, in the days of the week, the months of the year, and the numbers of the years.

Vig labom delis vel.	The week has seven days.
Del binom dil viga.	The day is part of the week.
Düp binom dil dela.	The hour is part of the day.
Mul binom dil yela.	The month is part of the year.

Sir Thomas expressed no interest in these common-places, so I delved into some French Republican facts imparted to us by Mr. Jo and advised him that

Del labom düpis bals.	The day has ten hours.
Del binom dil dekadela.	The day is part of a "decade".
Mul labom dekadelis kil.	The month has three "decades".
Yel labom mulis balsetel e delis lül votik.	
	The year has twelve months and five more days.
Mul at binom "Floréal".	This month is "Floréal".

But, unusually for him, he sat and ignored me, did not rise to the bait which I cast out upon the waters. And for the rest of that day, he chose to say nothing more, celebrating in his own mind, no doubt, the ancient rites of the New Year.

I reflected, however, that Sir Thomas had raised a happy omen for our Annual General Meeting, due to take place to-morrow. Perhaps it would indeed be a great success for the Academy of Volapük, and perhaps – indeed – a new era, not merely a new year, would be ushered in. With that convenient thought, I smiled upon Sir Thomas, passed him another cup of tea, and ignored his cursing.

*   *   *

* Note by the Contributing Editor of Logic:

Sir Thomas is, I am troubled to state, incorrect: I have been put to great pains to confirm the facts. Pope Gregory XIII's Bull of 1582 ordained that ten days be excised that year from the month of October in order to re-align the Calendar correctly with the Seasons. Ten days was the correct interval of correction at that time and were correctly added by the Italians, the French, the Iberians et alia; even in 1652, had Sir Thomas flourished then, the correction would yet have been ten days; but it was not until 1752 that the interval was corrected in Great Britain, by which time the correct correction had grown to eleven days. By the present era, an additional day would have to be added to the correction, now corrected to twelve days. Sir Thomas' "New Year" should therefore have been celebrated correctly on the sixth day of April 1891, not the fourth. He must stand corrected. Mr. Justice's narrative must stand corrected. We must all stand corrected. I have made the correction. We are all, *ergo*, corrected. (FRL)

Katel Velid, the Seventh Chapter:
The Relative Pronoun and the Interrogative

*The Annual General Meeting of The Edinburgh Society for the
Propagation of a Universal Language. 5ᵗʰ April, 1891.*

Del Lulid Folula, Balmil Jöltum Zülsebal.

The day of our Annual General Meeting had arrived. I was prepared,
as much as a modest man can be, for the great occasion. Sunday
(*balüdel*), the fifth day (*del lulid*) of April (*folula*). By whatever
Calendar, the year 1891 (*balmil jöltum zülsebal*). While all around
Edinburgh, there was talk of the Population Census, which had as its
goal the numbering of the peoples, in my head there was only reflection
on the struggle ahead, the need and the desire for Universal Peace,
founded solidly upon Universal Comprehension. Cödel Yagöl had
prepared the ground in some degree, but still I feared that perhaps the
day would not be won for Volapük, or the future salvation of Humanity.

With these thoughts flying through my head like a cloud of bees
upon the lavender, I did not sleep well on the Saturday night. There
was a wild storm blowing outside, and the rain lashed against the
window and upon the roof. A steady drip came from a leak in the
ceiling. From the other side of my room, I could hear Sir Thomas
snoring in his slumbers; in the weeks in which I had known him,
I found that he had never any difficulty in falling asleep, staying
asleep, or, indeed, waking to a hearty breakfast, comprising porridge
with cream, and tea with brandy. Fitfully, I slept, waking finally
towards five o'clock, to lie turning and turning under the blankets. It
was with some relief that I heard seven o'clock strike, the sound
blown from some distant clock-tower by the howling wind; and
dressed.

Within minutes, Sir Thomas also raised himself from the sofa,
where he slept under a huge pile of blankets, and eagerly held out his
hand for some restorative.

I proposed that we begin the day with a review of the Relative Pronouns and the Interrogative form in Volapük.

Sir Thomas barely raised any enthusiasm at my suggestion, but agree to participate in

Tidüp zülid: The Relative Pronoun and the Interrogatives.

The Relative Pronoun – by which we mean the joining word "which", "who" or "what", or, less accurately, "that" – is, in Volapük, simply **kel**. Thus, the phrase "the man who feeds the dog" is rendered **man, kel dogi fidom**; "the woman who speaks to the boy" is **vom, kel pule pükof**.

Like all other nouns, it can be declined: thus, **kel, kela, keli, kele** – which, of which, to which, for which.

As for the Interrogatives, I advised Sir Thomas, as he consumed his seventh cup of tea, liberally dosed with sugar and brandy, and kept as hot as his mouth could tolerate by the proximity of the teapot to the fire – as for the Interrogatives, they are really quite simple:

The Interrogative pronouns are **kim?** (who, masculine), **kif?** (who, feminine) and **kis?** (who or what, neuter). Thus, "who is this man?" is to be translated as **kim binom man?**, "who is this woman?" as **kif binof vom?** "what is that dog?" – **kis binos dog?**

The Interrogative form – asking a question – is, I advised Sir Thomas as we prepared for a short stroll upon the Meadows, almost facile.

"It is, is it?" he responded, giggling unnecessarily.

Ignoring his whimsy, I replied: indeed. In English we change an assertion into a question by changing the order of the words; for example:

I have.	Have I?
He will go.	Will he go?
You have seen.	Have you seen?

But we seldom put a verb before the subject. We use, instead, the emphatic form with *do*:

You go.	Do you go? *instead of Go you?*
He speaks.	Does he speak?

In Volapük the sign of the question is the syllable **li**, generally placed either after or, less commonly, before the verb and joined to it by a hyphen. The accent of the verb is unchanged. **Li** should not be placed after the verb, if this would bring two l's or three consonants together: we prefer **li-binoms?** to **binoms-li?**

Thus:

Man binom gudik,	The man is good:	**Man binom-li gudik?**
Labob,	I have:	**Labob-li?**
Goloms,	We go:	**Li-goloms?**
Logols,	You look:	**Li-golols?**

If the sentence contains an interrogative word, such as – who? which? what? how? when? where? – then the syllable **li** is unnecessary:

Kim binoms mans?   Who are the men?

not

Kim li-binoms mans?

Sir Thomas found all this, I understood from his expression, rather tedious, and was anxious to get out into the bracing air which, perhaps to greet the momentous day of our General Meeting, was whistling over the roof-tops of Edinburgh. Sir Thomas had been twice for a walk on the Meadows, and was much enchanted by the fashions and pretty faces of some of the ladies who took the air there. If the man had been several decades younger, I could have mistaken his keenness to be out under the ravaged trees that morning, as an expression of the sap which, at that season of the year, rises in men in their prime. As it was, I saw only a rather ill-fitting lechery.

At around ten o'clock, we took ourselves down the stairs, past the door of Mrs. Forbes, and found the hand-barrow in its usual place; it was partly filled with rain-water; but I emptied the water, and loaded Sir Thomas in; and we turned from Carlung Place, down Sylvan Place, beside the long wall of the Trades Maiden Hospital – a place that since our arrival, had greatly interested Sir Thomas; he had offered me untold wealth if I were to succeed in gaining him entrance to that refuge of young educated ladies – until we came to Rillbank Crescent and Melville Place. Under the trees, in whose branches the wind whipped and cracked, and threatened us at every moment with a dreadful accident.

I seized the opportunity to set Sir Thomas some exercises, for to examine his newly-acquired knowledge of the Interrogative forms.

He would require the following new words, which he learned before
we had risked our necks in the avoidance of carriages and horses on
Melville Drive.

- **Kikod?** why?
- **Kiplad** or **kiöp?** where?
- **Kipladi?** where, whither (*to* what place)?
- **Kiüp** or **kitim?** when?
- **Liko?** how?

(These are, I should indicate to the keen student, interrogatives
which do not require -**li**.)

And: **stadön**, to be (in a certain state or condition), to do, as in
"how do you do?", "how are you?"

Exercise 10.

- **Liko stadol, o söl!? Stadob gudiko, danob ole.**
- **Li-binol lonedo in zif? No lonedo, gomob bletimo al
  Daisart.**
- **Binom-li Daisart zif jönik? Binom lejönik.**
- Have you seen my wife to-day? No, sir; is she not in the house?
- How is your daughter to-day? Thank you; she is much better.

This was a pleasant enough morning: I was in the civilised city of
Edinburgh, I had a lively expectation of persuading the members of
the Society to adopt Volapük as their chosen Universal Language,
and there was an invigorating breeze. I wheeled Sir Thomas in his
barrow up and down the walks of the Meadows, as we made our
way gradually towards the western end of those Elysian Fields. Sir
Thomas was greatly interested in the great cetacean jaw-bone which
acts as the gateway to Jawbone Walk, and insisted on stopping beside
it to stroke the smooth bone. I advised him that it had been donated
to the Citizens of Edinburgh by the Zetland and Fair Isle Knitters
Association, at the termination of the International Exhibition of
1886. I rather think that Sir Thomas had a vision of the good folk of
Zetland, out in their boats upon the freezing Arctic waters, protected
only by their knitted hats, harpooning behemoths with their knitting-
needles, for he muttered, in a voice almost quietened with admiration,
"So the valour of Scots is not yet moribund?"

Alas, our reveries were rudely interrupted as we gazed up at the Jawbone, by Mr. McBirnie. McBirnie had been, for a brief fortnight last year, an enthusiastic member of the Society; he gave every promise of being a model student and a vociferous proponent of Volapük, until, during a rather pointless debate on the nature of language, instigated by the late Professor McInnes, McBirnie had suddenly assailed me with a hundred questions.

To this day, I have no idea whence these questions came: my initial suspicion had been that this was yet another low intrigue by Bosman; but such a thought had soon been put away, as McBirnie questioned the champion of Esperanto with the same aggression as he used towards me. The questions were too incisive to have sprung from the mind of Mr. Gunn. I can only suppose that McBirnie had thought of them himself – a curious achievement for a currier, whose clothes and home smelled perpetually of the skins of dead animals.

But there he was again, holding his hat firmly upon his head, strolling with a woman, whom I understood to be his wife. Spying me from a distance, he brandished his umbrella and directed his foot-steps towards me, so there was no avoiding the man.

"Have you the answers, then, Mr. Justice?" he enquired, a smile with the character of a sneer upon his lips.

Sir Thomas looked from one to the other, and demanded to know what was afoot. McBirnie introduced himself to the old man, and his wife curtseyed when Sir Thomas informed them of his nobility.

"I asked Mr. Justice, some time ago," explained McBirnie to Sir Thomas, "to explain the descriptive and suggestive power of these new languages. For example, I wished to know a simple witticism, a joke, in Volapük. Or a curse or word used for swearing. Or the ability of his language to pick up the words from fish-wives and make use of them. Could he, I asked him, be sarcastic or ironical, satirical or cutting? Could he recite some poetry in his new language, or com-pose a song? Could he tell me a word, whose very sound would suggest to me a picture of green fields and shady woods, maybe a wee burn running through it?"

During this long-winded, but faithful, re-iteration of his original questions, McBirnie fixed me with a humorous eye, daring me either to deny his assertions or to respond.

Sir Thomas was greatly amused: "Pertinent questions, indeed, Mr.

McBirnie. What a fine-looking wife you have, if I might be so bold?
My compliments, sir! And has Mr. Justice replied to your questions?"

McBirnie shook his head, in pretence of sorrow. "Not one question
could he answer adequately, sir," he stated. "He offered me a poem
written by some madman in Belgium, but even he will admit it had no
resonance."

McBirnie referred to the epic verse by M. Jonquin of Bruges, written
entirely in Volapük, to celebrate the occasion of the Third General
Assembly of 1889; it was entitled *O Flens! O Blods! O Sörs!*, and ran to
sixty-four verses, each of eight lines. As an example of Volapük, it was
almost unparalleled in scope; and yet, as a work of poetic beauty, there
were some doubts even in my mind.

"But Volapük is a young language, which will grow to fit the human
need, Mr. McBirnie," I protested, stung to a response by the supercilious attitude of both the men. "There will be jokes, puns, *bons mots*,
curses and songs. Of course there will! It is a living language and will
be spoken by the accomplished wit, the artist, the drunkard, the
buffoon and the wise-man." Of that, I am sure. For my part, I have sat
up many a night on my travels, trying to compose a jocose phrase, or
a story with a witty twist at the end, such as men can stand up and
deliver at festive occasions. I have tried in vain for many months to
compose a Limerick in my preferred language. On other nights, too, I
have been engaged in the furtherance of Dr. Vallienne's campaign for a
strong body of literature composed in Volapük. I may say, modestly,
that my tale, modelled to some degree on the work of Mr. R. L.
Stevenson, is progressing well, and that I have high hopes of having it
ready for publication for the Fourth General Assembly, due to take
place in Breslau in 1892: it is entitled *Tlät! (Treachery!)* and deals with
the adventures of a young man kidnapped from his home in Borrow-
stounness, and his subsequent rise to fame and fortune after finding
employment in building a railway from Inverness to Ullapool.

I bade Mr. McBirnie a good day, and wheeled Sir Thomas away
from the currier and his wife, as fast as I could manage with dignity.
We arrived home in short time. Sir Thomas was chuckling to himself.
The import of his chatter for the next half-an-hour, was that his own
Universal Language had thirteen different forms of the Facetive, or
Comic, mode; no fewer than eight forms of the Epigrammatic; and –
I believe he was now inventing his categories as we crouched over yet

more tea and brandy – sixteen forms of the Equivocative: each one suited for a particular audience or occasion. My mind bent on the afternoon's proceedings, I paid him little attention.

We lunched lightly on

Exercise 11.

Sevob, I know
Tomob, I torment
Läd, lady
Lömibajeli, umbrella
Kalad, character

* **Sevob mani, kel tomom obi.**
* **Man, keli sevob, tomom obi.**
* **Kif binof läd et, kel labof lömibajeli?**
* I see the man who speaks to the woman. He is my tormentor.
* That woman is the wife of my tormentor.
* Does this lady know the character of her husband?

– came to the *Fin tidüpa zülid,* and then proceeded to our Annual General Meeting.

*   *   *

As we left the house, Bosman and Lizzie Forbes were slightly ahead of us, the former poisoning the fresh air with a cloud of blue smoke. We had not far to go, for I had come to an arrangement with the care-taker of the old stables attached to the big house in Millerfield Place. The house is, I understand, expected to be demolished and replaced with a bright new school for the young citizens of this part of Edinburgh, whose noise will doubtless be a burden upon the ears of all those who live within two hundred yards; or metres.

Mr. John MacDonald, the care-taker, was a native of the Island of Uist in the farthest Hebrides, and a speaker, and great representer of the Gaelic tongue, for which I have no time, it being the dead voice of a pitiful breed in a moribund part of the wider world. Mr. MacDonald could recite for hours – and frequently did – the poems and tales of his people and his ancestors, all in the Gaelic tongue; and to the ear it sounded pleasant enough. But it was quite incomprehensible. I had seen some of it written down, and could make no sense of the pronunciation. This is scarcely a language suited for the new century!

Mr. MacDonald occupied the stables in rather an unofficial capacity, and there was some doubt on whether he would have somewhere to live once the new school was built. For the moment, however, he lived there, in the company of a large number of curious objects, rusting machinery and other vestiges from the International Exhibition of Industry, Science and Art, which was held on the Meadows in 1886. The piles of these objects made it rather difficult to arrange seating and tables for our meeting: spilling out from the corners were the gondolas for fairground-swings; the pillars from the façade of some Ancient Egyptian temple; vast piles of plant-pots, broken and shattered by misuse, water and frost; the image of Queen Victoria painted in bronze at thrice life-size, balanced on top of a collection of stuffed and mounted fish from the North Sea, piles of rusting cogs and ropes covered with tarpaulins; from the ceiling hung artificial jungle-creepers, tangled with fishing nets from the Zetland and Orcadian Isles; and an extraordinary pair of Sheffield steel scissors, some twelve feet in length, which were suspended over the table at which I sat, as if I were the terrible tyrant Damocles: in the strong draughts which assailed the room, the scissors slowly twirled and swung. In amongst all of this, MacDonald had managed to-day to place some two dozen chairs, faced at the front by a solid table with three chairs behind it.

At the stroke of one o'clock, Bosman opened our Second Annual General Meeting with two blows of his mallet upon the table. To our consternation, and that of all those assembled, Mr. MacDonald was at Bosman's side almost immediately, demanding that he should not do that again, for the table was of precious walnut, and, he understood, had once belonged to the King of Spain. He bent his head sideways to the surface, looking for any dents, polished it with a handkerchief, and retreated to his seat at the side of the room, from where he regarded us with a baleful eye.

It was a pleasing attendance: every member of the Society who had paid their annual subscription in full last year, was present – except, of course, for Professor McInnes, who had been unavoidably detained. For the record, I will list them: Mr. Gemmell Justice, *General Secretary*; Dr. Henry Bosman, *Chairman*; Mr. William Gunn, *Treasurer* – these first three constituted the Committee. Then there were the Ordinary Members, in alphabetical order: Mr. Bertram Borthwick (Butcher); Mr. Issachar Clark (Book-shop Clerk); M. Walther Coens (Manufacturer); Mr. Louis Desdemoni (Commercial Traveller); Mr. James Dewar (Naturalist and Bird-Stuffer); Mr. John Easton (Confectioner); Mr. John Flynn (Watchman); Miss Lizzie Forbes (Pupil Teacher); the Reverend Goodfellow (Minister); Miss Lillian Hepburn (School-teacher); Miss Ethelreda Hutchinson (Dress-maker); Mrs. Mary Keenan (House-keeper); Mr. Sutherland Kilpatrick (Bank Clerk); Mr. Archibald McKelvie, father (Stevedore); Mr. Archibald McKelvie, son (Mercantile Clerk); Mr. Thomas McPheely (Waiter); M. Edmond Muriset (School-proprietor); Mme. Virginie Muriset (School-mistress); Mr. William Pheiffer (Iron-moulder); Mrs. Catherine Ramsay (Ham-curer's widow); Mrs. Jemima Turpie (House-keeper); Mr. John Wilson (General Labourer). Also noted in the Minutes were Mr. John Mac-Donald (Watchman), and Sir Thomas Urquhart (retired Colonel) – both non-voting delegates; and Mr. Kobayashi and Mr. Kumakura, whose role as "International Observers" was greatly applauded by all those present, which delighted the Japanese gentlemen to a high degree.

In all, as I noted for the Minute, an attendance of twenty-five members. Bosman then read out the Agenda, or Items for Debate, which I had prepared. But before we could proceed, there was an interruption from the floor; inevitably, it was Mr. Kilpatrick. It should be noted for this History of our Movement and Society, that Mr. Kilpatrick's greatest interest in life is not, by any means, the Universal Language; Mr. Kilpatrick is one who describes himself as a Friend of Mantology and a Consultant in Procedure; by which first epithet, he means that he derives immense satisfaction from methods of taking decisions; and by the second, he represents himself as an expert in all matters relating to the conduct of meetings. It would not be unfair to the man to say that we never saw him from one Annual Meeting to the next; but he was not idle in between times. A large and jolly man, aged about five-and-forty years, with a thick black beard, short legs and a disposition to peer at all around him, he was known to have enrolled himself as an Ordinary Member in a large number of Societies in Edinburgh, from which he derived unsurpassable pleasure and delight, for he was able to attend at least one Annual General Meeting in any given week of the year.

On this occasion, Mr. Kilpatrick wished, "as a Point of Order, Mr. Chairman!" – by which form of words, he knew he weakened the defences of all around him, for very few people knew what he meant by it – to know what Method of Voting would be adopted at this meeting. Indeed, he went so far as to propose a vote on the Method of Voting. Mr. McPheely, whose capacity of practical jokes was second-to-none, egged him on, by enquiring what methods Mr. Kilpatrick might recommend?

Fifteen minutes were now lost as Kilpatrick offered a historical perspective on Methods for Arriving at Decisions; I have them listed here, for I copied them assiduously into the Minutes:

Theomancy, the making of decisions by reference to oracles; Bibliomancy, by reference to the Bible; Psychomancy, by reference to ghosts; Cristallomantia, spirits seen in a magic lens; Sciomancy, shadows; Aeromancy, appearances in the air; Genethliacs, the stars at birth; Meteoromancy, the meteors; Austromancy, the winds; Aruspicy, sacrificial appearances; Hieromancy, the entrails of animals; Anthropomancy, the human entrails (scream from Mrs. Turpie); Ichthyomancy, the entrails of fish; Pyromancy, sacrificial fire; Sideromancy, a red-hot iron; Capnomancy, the smoke from an altar; Myomancy, the scurrying of mice (here, Mr. McPheely regaled the company with a brief rendition of the song "Nancy, oh my Nancy!"); Orniscopy, birds; Alectryomancy, a Cock picking up grains; Ophiomancy, the fishes; Botanomancy, herbs; Hydromancy, water; Pegomancy, fountains; Rhabdomancy, a wand; Crithomancy, the dough of cakes; Aleuromancy, grain or meal; Halomancy, the scattering of salt; Cleromancy, the throw of dice; Belomancy, the flight of arrows; Axiomancy, a balanced hatchet; Coscinomancy, a balanced sieve; Dactyliomancy, a suspended ring; Geomancy, dots drawn at random on paper; Lithomancy, precious stones; Pessomancy (Mr. Easton made a coarse remark at this), by pebbles; Psephomancy, pebbles drawn from a heap; Catoptromancy, mirrors; Tephramancy, writing found in ashes; Oneiromancy, dreams; Palmistry, the hand; Onychomancy, the reflection of the sun's rays in nails; Dactylomancy, finger-rings; Mycomancy, mushrooms; Arithmancy, numbers; Sortilege, the drawing of lots; Stichomancy, random passages in books; Onomancy, the letters forming the name of a person (Mr. McPheely repeated his earlier music-hall witticism, to the great amusement of his friends); Geloscopy, the mode of laughing; Anthroscopy, the face; Gastromancy, ventriloquism; Gyromancy, walking in a circle; Ceromancy, the dropping of melted wax into water; Bletonism, by reference to the currents.

The Chairman decided at length to curtail Mr. Kilpatrick's enthusiasm for forms and procedures, and called the meeting to order. We voted on the Method of Voting and, to Mr. Kilpatrick's obvious disappointment, decided by a majority of twenty-four to one, to vote on all items by the raising of hands (or "manumancy", as Sir Thomas informed us), and to pass motions by a simple majority, since all Members were present. Before Kilpatrick could confound us with some other "Point of Order", we moved to Item *Bal*, which was the election of the Committee. To my gratification, the Members recorded their unanimous confidence in the present Committee, with no changes; and we proceeded to Item *Tel*, which had been put up by Mrs. Keenan, and related to the arrangements for tea-making and the provision of scones for the monthly meetings. Unambiguously, the Society expressed its thanks and satisfaction with the arrangements made in the last year by Mrs. Keenan and Mrs. Turpie, and invited them to continue their invaluable work. Mrs. Turpie burst into floods of tears, and called upon the spirit of Professor McInnes to witness her pride on being re-elected, and was generously comforted by Sir Thomas. My friend had found himself a cushioned seat in the shell of a rickshaw, or Chinese conveyance, which had been abandoned by the Scottish and Shanghai Bank after the great Exhibition, and found its way into Mr. MacDonald's care. The rickshaw was more sheltered from wind than any other seat in the room. Mr. Gunn tried to interest our "International Observers" in this conveyance, but they were polite in their refusal, and expressed a keener interest in the Sheffield scissors, murmuring "Steer" and making careful drawings in their notebooks.

Items *Kil*, *Fol* and *Lul* brought up for discussion: the establishment of a Journal (which was, once more, agreed to be a good thing; but no one offered to act as Editor; and so the idea was, once more, postponed); the establishment of amicable relations with other language societies in Edinburgh (the Italian, French and Icelandic societies had all written to us recently); and the matter of an annual subscription, which was set at six shillings, payable in monthly instalments to Mr. Gunn. Mr. Gunn rubbed his hands with satisfaction.

Items *Mäl*, *Vel* and *Jöl* related to: sixthly, the election of an office-bearer who would formulate a Constitution for the Society – Mr. Kilpatrick was in transports of rapture on being elected, without opposition, to this post; seventhly, the preparation of a Revised Schedule, or Programme, of Education (which was made the responsibility of Miss Hutchinson); and, eighthly, a consideration of the venue for the next Christmas Dinner (Mr. McPheely, again, made his presence known, and recommended the Lofoten Hotel in Jeffrey Street, for he had two acquaintances who worked there, and Mr. McPheely supposed that we might get a discount).

Item *Zül* had been raised by M. Muriset. His motion proposed the "purchase, re-furbishment, and management" of a suitable building in Edinburgh, to be a permanent College for Universal Languages. He argued that it was lacking in dignity for respectable people like himself and his wife, to have to enter the back-rooms of public-bars, billiard-clubs, old stables and front-parlours, to discuss the weighty and spiritual matters of concern. Mme. Muriset nodded in agreement at this, holding her handkerchief to her nose and regarding Mr. MacDonald balefully, blaming him for her manifest humiliation. "Must we continue to enter low buildings with our hats pulled down over our eyes?" demanded M. Muriset. "So that we are not recognised by our neighbours and customers?"There were voices of agreement from our commercial members. It was agreed, by seven votes to four, with fourteen abstaining, that M. and Mme. Muriset, along with Mr. Easton, should draw up a firm proposal, with costs and possible addresses, for the establishment of such a College. With mixed emotions, I voted in favour of the proposal, but cannot feel that we are yet, as a Society, ready for such a heavy financial and intellectual commitment.

And so we passed to item *Bals*, which was the principal item on our Agenda, and one in which I had a great interest.There was to be a debate on the name of the Society, and whether it was time to change it to something more specific. Of course, the question held many layers of significance, and the debate was eagerly awaited; but not until after Mrs. Keenan and Mrs. Turpie, red-eyed and sniffing through a beatific smile, had served up tea and biscuits. For it was, by now, three o'clock.

When, after thirty minutes, Bosman once more called the meeting to order, I noted a challenging look in his eye. He avoided my gaze, and announced the debate on "The name of the Society – should it be changed?" Almost immediately, a number of hands were raised, as members demanded the right to speak. It was decided that those from the floor should make their contributions first, everyone understanding tacitly that the main speeches would be made by myself and Bosman.

It is not strictly relevant to the matter of this Hand-Book what was said from the floor. The contribution of Mr. Borthwick the butcher might be noted, if only for its irrelevant insolence. He asked:

"Should our Society be named the 'Edinburgh Society for the Propagation of a Universal Language'; or perhaps the 'Society for the Propagation of a Universal Language in Edinburgh'; or – " I noticed that he glanced surreptitiously at McPheely, and I wondered whether the two men, great pals, had been preparing this practical joke, "should we name it the 'Society for the Prevention of a Universal Language in Edinburgh'?" There was some embarrassed laughter at this proposal, although there was more than a grain of truth in his witty remarks. The distinction between "Edinburgh Society" and "Society ... in Edinburgh" was – I had to admit – quite neat: was our goal parochial, or was it the goal of a larger international movement? Many is the time when I have inclined to believe that we had bogged the wheels of our movement in the parochial mud. As for his "Prevention", I fear we can thank only the machinations of Bosman and his criminal accomplices for that!

Mr. Gunn, rather against the prevailing mood of the meeting, suggested we change our name to the "Edinburgh Society for Translation of Foreign Tongues into English"; but found not a single backer, except Mrs. Keenan, for his proposal.

Dr. Bosman then took the floor. It is not my task in this Hand-Book and Record of Transactions of the Society, to repeat *verbatim* the arguments which he adduced for the changing of the name to the "Edinburgh Society for the Promotion of Esperanto"! The man made no attempt to disguise his shamelessness; he simply stood before us, advanced spurious arguments such as the reported numbers of people who were adopting Zamenhof's language – reports which I repeatedly challenged, demanding to know the source of his assertions – and the simplicity of Esperanto compared to other languages. In short, the man proposed a *coup*, and the immediate surrendering of the Society, its funds, its history and its integrity, to his farrago of grammar and vocabulary.

But I was confident that the ground-work performed by Cödel Yagöl would shortly prepare a goodly harvest, and stepped forward, at half-past four o'clock, to argue in favour of a minor change to the name, to the "Edinburgh Society for the Propagation of Volapük", it being now the year, the day and the hour for that mature language to take its place in the culture of Scotland and Greater Britain. One or two dissenting voices were heard, in particular from those Members whom Cödel Yagöl had not yet visited: I noted some names for another night's work.

But, just before we could take a vote on the several proposals, Sir Thomas stood up perilously in his rickshaw.

"Let an old soldier be heard!" he shouted. All faces turned to the back of the room, where the cart was propped up against a stuffed Arctic bear. Sir Thomas stood in the body of the carriage, whose hood had long since been devoured and carried off by mice and spiders. In his hands he clutched my scimitar; on his head, he wore my helmet; over his back was draped my cloak; and his hands were encased in my gauntlets. There, for all to see, stood Cödel Yagöl!

"The 'Irksome Judge' appears before you!" cried Sir Thomas, in a voice that demanded to be heard. "You have heard the lesser arguments, from the paltry captains and the sergeants of cowards and poltroons! Now listen to the Condemnatory Colonel, the Gargantuan General, the Irksome Judge!"

There was an absolute silence in the room. It was clear from the expressions on the faces of the members, that the figure was recognised. This was the Judge who descended on their spirit from nowhere and incited them to speak flawlessly in the One Universal Language.

I thought to challenge Sir Thomas for his interruption: he was, after all, no member of the Society. But no words could leave my mouth – my throat was dry.

Sir Thomas spoke, of *his* Universal Language: he called it "The

Jewel". He spoke for over an hour in his description of this marvellous language; I managed to make a record in the Minute of some of the claims he made for it. But, I noted then and I remember now – not once did he utter a single word in the language for which he made so many claims!

"To the end that you may be more enamoured of the Universal Language whereof I am to publish a Grammar and Lexicon," stated Sir Thomas grandly. "I will tell you of some few qualities and advantages peculiar to itself.

"First, there is not a word utterable by the mouth of man which, in this language, has not a peculiar signification by itself.

"This world of words has but two hundred and fifty prime radices upon which the rest are branched so methodically, that he who observes my precepts thereanent shall, at the first hearing of a word, know to what city it belongs and consequently not be ignorant of the general signification thereof, till, after a most exact prying into all its letters, finding the street, lane, house, story and room thereby denotated, he punctually hits upon the very proper thing it represents in its most specifical signification."

There were murmurs at this statement – but whether of confusion or awe, I had no way of telling. Sir Thomas continued with his boasting:

"One word, though but of seven syllables at most, shall comprehend that which no language else in the world is able to express in fewer than four-score and fifteen several words.

"Whilst others have five or six declinable parts of speech at most, it has ten besides the Nominative.

"Instead of two or three numbers, which others have, this will afford you four: to wit, the singular, dual, plural and redual.

"There are nineteen genders, wherein likewise it exceeds all other languages.

"Verbs, mongrels" (by which he meant words formed of elements from different languages, and not Mrs. Keenan's lap-dog), "participles and hybrids have all of them ten Tenses besides the present, which number no language else is able to attain to.

"In lieu of six moods, this one enjoys seven in its conjugable words.

"In this language, the verbs and participles have four voices.

"No other tongue has above eight or nine parts of speech, but this has twelve.

"Every word of this language, declinable or indeclinable, has at least ten several synonyms. Each of these synonyms, in some circumstances of the signification, differs from the rest."

Mr. Gunn, a shallow man, seemed particularly impressed by this proliferation of grammatical confusion, and the sheer quantities involved.

"Each noun thereof or verb may begin or end with a vowel or consonant, as to the peruser shall seem most expedient.

"In this language, the opposite members of a division have usually the same letters in the words which signify them; the initial and final letters being all one with a transmutation only in the middle ones.

"Every word in this language signifies as well backward as forward.

"There is no hexameter, elegiac, sophic, asclepiad, iambic or any other kind of Latin or Greek verse, but I will afford you another in this language of the same sort without a syllable more or less in the one than the other, *spondae* answering to *spondae*, *dactyl* to *dactyl*, *caesure* to *caesure*, and each foot to another with all uniformity imaginable."

The Reverend Goodfellow, a literary man, quietly applauded this outrage.

"What rational logarithms do by writing, this language does by heart, and by adding of letters shall multiply numbers, which is a most exquisite secret.

"In the denomination of the fixed stars by a single word alone, which represents the start, you shall know the magnitude together with the longitude and latitude, both in degrees and minutes, of the star that is expressed by it.

"As for the year of God, the month of that year, week of the month, day of that week, partition of that day, hour of that partition, quarter and half-quarter of the hour, a word of but one syllable in this language will express it all to the full.

"In the matter of colours, we shall learn by words in this language the proportion of light, shadow or darkness commixed in them.

"This language shall be so convenient, that if a General will give new names to his soldiers, he shall be able, at the first hearing of the word that represents the name of a soldier, to know what Brigade, Regiment, Troop, Company, Squadron or Division he is and whether he be of the Cavalry or the Foot, a simple soldier or an officer, or belonging to the artillery or baggage; which device in my opinion is not unuseful for those great captains that would endear themselves in the favour of the soldiery.

"In this language every number, how great soever, may be expressed by a single word.

"No language but this has in its words the whole number of letters, that is ten vowels and five and twenty consonants.

"Of all languages, this is the most compendious in complement and consequently fittest for courtiers and ladies; for writing of missives, letters of state, it has the compactest style; no language in matter of prayer and ejaculation to Almighty God is able, for conciseness of expression, to compare with it."

Again, gentlemanly applause from Mr. Goodfellow.

"In the many thousands of words belonging to this language, there is not a letter which hath not a peculiar signification by itself.

"For pithiness of proverbs, oracles and sentences, no language can parallel with it.

"For the affirmation, negation and infinitation of propositions, it has properties unknown to any other language.

"Negative expressions are more compendiously uttered in this language than in any other in the world.

"The greatest wonder of all is that, of all the languages in the world, it is the easiest to learn, a boy of ten years old being able to attain to the knowledge thereof in three weeks' space."

There were many more claims and wild promises from Sir Thomas, during his oration lasting over one and one-quarter hours. One hundred and thirty-four in all. Many more and wild, also, were the plaudits he received. Finally, as my hand grew tired of transcription, he stated, without any embarrassment:

"Besides these advantages above all other languages, I might have couched thrice as many more of no less consideration than the aforesaid, but these same will suffice to sharpen your longing after the intrinsical and most researched secrets of the new Grammar and Lexicon which I am to evulge."

Outside, dusk was falling. I believe that it is a fair judgement of mine, that none in that room understood even one half of his wild boasting; but this lack of intelligence did not affect their enraptured fascination. Several times during his rhetorical performance, he had stepped down from the rickshaw and walked among the open-mouthed Ordinary

Members of the Society. When he came to his closing remarks, however, he was back in the conveyance, waving his scimitar so that it
caught the light from Mr. MacDonald's lanterns.

"Foot-soldiers of the Edinburgh Society for Ekskubalauron, Also
Known as The Jewel!" he cried. "You have attended to my words.
What say you? Shall it be Esperanto?"

"No!" shouted back almost all of his captive audience.

"Shall it be Solresol?" he continued his interrogation.

"It shall not be Solresol!" they cried, with one voice. M. Coens was
moved to beat out the word "No" on the floor, with the point of his
umbrella, all the while smiling pathetically at Miss Hepburn.

"Should it be Nal Bino, should it be Latin, or Greek, or French, or
English?" he demanded, slashing the air with his sword. The air
whistled.

"No! No, no, no and no!" they cried with a single voice, standing up
from their seats. Our International Delegates joined in the general
enthusiasm, applauding energetically at each shout, beaming. It was
evident that our meeting had captured their lively interest.

Sir Thomas gazed at me, full in the eye, but directed his final
interrogative to his audience. "Will you learn Volapük?"

"No, we will not learn Volapük!" they replied.

*   *   *

I tasted then the bitter dregs of my betrayal. The Contract, which two
men had signed, was torn up and burned before the Public Eye.
Picitob! – I had been deceived! As on many occasions before, I now
beheld the deepest depths of treachery.

Katel Jölid, the Eighth Chapter:
Demonstratives and Possessives

Decisions of the Annual General Meeting of The Edinburgh Society for the Propagation of a Universal Language. 5ᵗʰ April, 1891.

Del Lulid Folula, Balmil Jöltum Zülsebal.

When the acclamation had abated, Mr. Sutherland Kilpatrick called for a vote on the item under discussion. Since a number of proposals had been put forward, I was obliged to put up each in turn and Mr. Kilpatrick counted the hands which were raised in favour. For: the retention of the existing name, no votes; for the insertion of the word "Volapük", two votes – my own and that of the younger McKelvie; for the insertion of the word "Esperanto", one vote – I tasted sweet satisfaction in recording that Lizzie Forbes and Issachar Clark had deserted Bosman; for sundry other proposals, no votes; and for the change of the name to the "Edinburgh Society for Ekskubalauron, Also Known as The Jewel" – by which precious article, the language of Sir Thomas was intended, that language which dares not speak its own words: twenty votes. There were two abstentions, those of Mr. Dewar and Miss Hutchinson.

I was obliged to announce that the name of the Society, henceforward, and until the next Annual General Meeting, or any Extraordinary General Meeting convened by the agreement of at least one half of the registered Members, was agreed and would be noted as such in the Minutes.

In the enthusiasm of the moment, the Reverend Goodfellow stood up and proposed a further vote: that, in recognition of the progress promised by his new Universal Language, Sir Thomas should be provided with a small remuneration, or stipend, for his board and lodging, in order that he should want for nothing. I could see the old man, who had by now removed his helmet, but still stood in cloak and gauntlets, beaming and smirking at this proposal, and bowing. The vote was immediately taken and, once more, it was almost unanimous, the only votes *contra* being that of Miss Hutchinson and those of the entire Committee, Mr. Gunn having a great incapacity to surrender his Treasury for any purpose at all, which was the very reason he had been the popular candidate in the first place. Notwithstanding which objection, the Society proposed to give Sir Thomas the princely sum of three shillings per week, "until such time as the entire Membership of the Society had been fully initiated into the Grammar, Vocabulary and Idiom of The Universal Language".

For a few minutes, the meeting broke up into small groups engaged in excited conversation; under other circumstances, these groups would have been discussing the rules and merits of their own language; now, they stepped up to the rickshaw at the rear of the room and offered their congratulations to The Usurper. To me, their actions appeared as the offering of tribute to a Conqueror; and I am sure that Sir Thomas considered them in the same light.

As I observed the scene before me, and tried to understand the breadth and depth of the treachery, I failed to notice that Dr. Bosman had stood up from his seat, and was making his way through the agitated crowd, to the carriage. It was only when I heard the cries of fear and rage, that I focused my attention on the scene which then unfolded.

Bosman, having arrived at the carriage, in which Sir Thomas stood triumphant, leaped energetically upon it, seized the old man by his arm and, sweeping round with his body, hurled him headlong into the terror-struck crowd below. With a billow of his cloak, and an abrupt exclamation, Sir Thomas disappeared into a press of bodies, several of whom fell down in a clatter, as if they were pins in a bowling-lane. Bosman had not finished, however, for he leaped down after his victim and, after a few moments, I beheld him in the centre of a circle of the members, picking Sir Thomas up by the scruff of his neck and shaking him, much as a dog might shake a rat in its jaws.

Feeling that it was my duty to afford some protection to the old man, despite my outrage at his perfidy, I made my way swiftly to the scene, pushing my way through the throng.

"This man is an imposter!" cried Bosman, white with rage, his Cape accent escaping him in an uncontrolled fit. "Look – he has no life in him, he is not of our world!"

The on-lookers gasped and screamed. "What nonsense is this?" cried Miss Hepburn. "Put the poor gentleman down at once!"

Normally, Miss Hepburn was not a woman that any man would lightly cross, for she was small and steely and her tongue was as sharp as a razor, from whose slight cuts a person would be troubled for days. But Bosman repeated his assertion.

"Madam, I am a doctor, a medical man, a man of science!" he shouted. "I tell you that this man has no pulse, has no beating heart in him: in short, he is dead!"

"You've killed him!" shrieked Mrs. Turpie, prior to fainting.

"Murderer! Assassin!" cried Mr. Borthwick, stepping backwards as rapidly as he could. "Shall I fetch a policeman?"

"Be quiet, you fools!" cried Bosman, in rather an uncharitable manner. "Mr. Justice," he turned to me, still with the limp shape of Sir Thomas dangling from his right hand. "Perhaps you can explain to us who is this man, and how he comes to be here?"

It was unwise to conceal the truth any longer. Honesty was my only card to play. "Well, of course he is dead, Dr. Bosman! It does not take a member of the Royal College of Surgeons to detect that! How could it be otherwise – the old gentleman is almost three hundred years old!"

This statement, not unnaturally, excited a considerable hubbub of argument, outrage and horror; not to say, disbelief.

"This man," I raised my voice above the turmoil, "is known to the world as Sir Thomas Urquhart, loyal to the first King Charles, Scottish soldier, respected Author of 'The Jewel' and inventor of a 'Universal Language', which should be known to all of you. He was born in the year 1611 – and if you imagine for a moment that a man of such age and such distinction could still be alive to-day, then I am sorry for you."

My candid explanation, I fear, did little to calm the stormy waters of the Meeting. Everyone wished to have more details – either about the age of the man, or his works, or the significance of his presence here, or my intentions in introducing him to the Society. Was I a robber of tombs, or a geronticide? Bosman, now that he knew he was justified in his accusations, gazed at the withered sack of skin and bones which he held, with a mixture of shocked fascination and intense medical interest.

I felt no obligation to anyone to go into detail of the Contract agreed between myself and Urquhart: that was a matter between two private individuals. To those who now demanded it, I gave a brief, and perhaps superficial, account of my chance meeting with him in distant Cromarty, and our journey here to Edinburgh, where, as I explained it now, "He wished to study the advances made in the establishment of a Universal Language."

As for the object of our heightened interest, it seemed that all life had been taken from him, like the light from a snuffed candle. I could not tell whether he was alive or dead, attentive to our debate or unconscious; whether Bosman may have killed him, or simply stunned him. And, in any event, I felt no great interest.

With Urquhart unmasked for what he was – a respected corpse – the course of the meeting suddenly veered off in a rather unexpected direction. Mr. Gunn took the floor and called for the immediate "voidment" of the previous two votes; Messrs. McPheely and Borthwick supported him in this; Kilpatrick was enthusiastic, his vista of procedural niceties suddenly opened up to reveal a fertile landscape of options and Constitutional exceptions. For several minutes, there was a violent debate between Gunn and Kilpatrick, until the latter conceded that, while there were no precedents for what Gunn wished to effect, there was nothing in the rules of the Society which would prohibit it; indeed, in Kilpatrick's broad experience, he had come across such matters before – most dramatically, at the Bi-Ennial Congress of the Society of Boot-Closers, and, indeed, at the recent inaugural Conference of the Midwifery Federations of Edinburgh-Shire. With which irrelevant matter, he entertained us for several moments. Having reached agreement that the votes could now be re-taken, the meeting gathered itself, and sat down.

The first item for debate was whether Sir Thomas Urquhart should benefit from the moneys or stipend recently voted to him. There was no one in favour of the motion, not even Goodfellow; all arguments centred around the fact that, if the man was corporeally dead, then he had no real need for food and drink, and he could find accommodation where he wished, without fear of harming his health if that accommodation were damp, draughty or simply louse-ridden. Bosman strongly recommended the church-yard at Greyfriars. When the vote was taken, the original munificence was annulled, and Mr. Gunn expressed his thanks as Treasurer. Urquhart had, in the meantime, been bundled up in his cloak and replaced in the rickshaw.

The second item to which we returned, was the proposal for the name of the Society. And, with Urquhart out of the reckoning, all the bitterness between factions and individuals spilled out, like blood on the floor of a lively abattoir. I had secretly hoped that my appearances as Cödel Yagöl in recent nights would have yielded some return, and that the vote would be swayed in favour of my proposal; but that was not to be. The shock and upheaval caused by the unmasking of Urquhart had liberated all minds from the power of any suggestion.

Thus, the hours moved slowly past, as the battle swung, now one way, now another. The main contenders were Volapük, Esperanto and Solresol, since, in quantity of supporting members, these were the only languages having more than one or two exponents. Solresol dropped out of the contest at around seven o'clock, the bitter rivalry between Coens and Muriset suddenly bursting into the open with an accusation by the latter that the former had made advances towards his wife; an accusation which Coens, gripped by some irrational passion, did not attempt to deny, despite the fact that it was – at least now – not true. Coens laughed in his face, laughed twice, laughed thrice; Muriset interpreted the pattern and the pitch of the repeated "ha!" to be a deadly insult rendered in Solresol, and laid him flat on his back with a single blow of his fist, in the key of "fa". Miss Hepburn struck Muriset with her umbrella, Mme. Muriset struck Miss Hepburn with the flat of her hand, and soon both main advocates were laid low, their women-folk likewise.

By eight o'clock, it became evident that there were three advocated groups within the Society – that in support of Volapük, that in support of Esperanto, and the larger party which wished to have nothing to do with either. At half-past eight, the larger party walked out, leaving – apart from Mr. Kilpatrick, who was, in this environment, as excited as a fish in the spawning grounds – myself, young McKelvie, Bosman, Gunn, Clark, Wilson, McPheely, Desdemoni, and Miss Hutchinson. Also present, but without any voting-rights, were Urquhart, who was detected stirring uneasily in his carriage; and the Gael, MacDonald, who seemed to enjoy the proceedings much as a man would enjoy a melodrama at the theatre, or the declamation of some ancient Ossianic ode.

I sought to bring the light of reason to the debate: I proposed that each of us be given thirty minutes to summarise our arguments in favour of our preferred changes; and then a simple vote be taken. Kilpatrick confirmed that, despite the fact that less than half of the membership were left in attendance, any vote would be binding upon the whole Society, since those who had left had, *de facto* and *in principe*, relinquished their right to a vote on the matter. He cited the recent vote on Constitutional Reform in the United Granton and Newhaven Society of Bell-Hangers and Gas-Fitters, as evidence of this.

Kilpatrick having settled upon the method of Numismancy, we agreed at the toss of a farthing that Bosman should state his case first. It is not my purpose to relate in any detail what arguments he adduced in favour of Esperanto. Suffice it to state that they were arguments which we had heard many times before. They persuaded no one, except perhaps his young acolyte, Issachar Clark, a young man greatly troubled by a skin-rash and incoherence, who fulfils a menial role as clerk in the house of James Thin and Company, on the South Bridge. Clark was smitten with Lizzie Forbes, as were many of the younger males in the Society; but her desertion of Esperanto on this night – arising, I would imagine, from my exposure of Bosman the previous Sunday – seemed not to have cooled his idealism for Esperanto. Every statement by his captain, Bosman, in the allotted thirty minutes was greeted with wild, and solitary, applause from the inexperienced cadet.

When my time came, I decided to make best use of it by conducting a lesson in the Demonstratives and Possessives of Volapük. I felt that we were beyond polemic; and that a practical demonstration of these items of grammar would be indicative of the facility of learning the language in its entirety.

Tidüp balsid – The Demonstratives and the Possessives.

A *demonstrative*, I explained to my students, is an adjective which points out or makes evident; a *possessive* denotes possession.

The Demonstratives, therefore, are the words: "this, that, these, those, itself, the same, such a" – "this man", "that usurper", "those recalcitrants", "such a traitor", "the same tired arguments".

The Possessives are the words: "my, your, his, her" – "Our Society", "His faction", "Her outrage", "My authority", "Their preferred language", and so forth.

I would begin with the

Possessive Pronouns.

The Possessives, "my", "mine", "thy", "thine", etc., may be rendered in two ways:

Firstly, by the genitive (the "of") of the pronoun: thus, **neflen oba**, my enemy (enemy of me); **neflen obas**, our enemy.

Secondly, by the termination **-ik**, forming a possessive adjective: thus, **pük obik**, my language; **püks omsik**, their languages; **pük at binom olik**, this language is yours.

By preference, the second form, the adjectival form, should be used, unless there would be too much repetition of the termination **-ik**.

We can see the ease with which these possessives may be used by engaging in

Exercise 12.

For which the following words are to be learned:

Kopan, a member, companion **Klub**, club   **Glup**, group

- **Klub obsik labom kopanalis telselul.**
- **Kis binom pük ola?**
- **Flen oba löfom pükis obik.**
- **Neflens obik löfoms pükis omsik.**
- My language is Volapük.
- Who is your friend?
- Our enemies are members of that group.

Demonstratives.

If we now pass on to the Demonstratives, I advised my restless audience, the matter is equally simple. The demonstrative pronouns, which are used as adjectives, and also by themselves, are the following:

At, this	**Et**, that
It, -self	**Ot**, same
Ut, that	**Som**, such

We should note, that there are some emphatic forms of these words:

Ät, this very	**Eit**, that very
Iet, own self	**Öt**, just the same
Üt, that very	**Söm**, just such

but I would stress that the emphatic form is rarely used.

> At, this: **flekaden at**, this scimitar; **mens at**, these men; **valüd ät**, this very power.
>
> Et, that: **leluman et**, that scoundrel; **jikompanals eit**, those very female members.
>
> It, -self: **man it**, the man himself ; **häm it**, the helmet itself; **ob it**, I myself; **obs iet**, we, our own selves.
>
> Ot, same: **kon ot**, the same story, **tid öt**, just the same instruction.
>
> Ut, that, before a relative: **man ut, kel vilom binön libik**, that man (or the man) who wishes to be free.
>
> **Som**, such: **dog som**, such a dog; **jidogs söm**, just such bitches.

With this very knowledge, we may proceed to

Exercise 13.

> **Sevob**, I know, am acquainted with (a person)   **Ab**, but **No**, not, no   **Klödob**, I trust

- **Pük at binom pük obsik.**
- **Man et labom flenis kil; löfob flenis ab no mani it**
- **Sevol kopanalis kluba obsik; ob sevob manis ot.**
- This language is ours.
- I do not trust that man. *Etcetera.*

Within my allotted thirty minutes, I had shared with my audience the basic rules governing the Demonstrative and Possessive Pronouns, and I felt that we had made respectable progress. Not one person interrupted. Mr. Kilpatrick then called for a vote. The results were, alas, inconclusive: in favour of no change of name for the Society – the four votes of Gunn, McPheely, Desdemoni, and Miss Hutchinson; in favour of Esperanto – Bosman and Clark; in favour of Volapük – the three votes of myself, Mr. McKelvie, and Mr. Wilson (a silent man, evidently deep of thought); and *in abstentio*, Mr. Kilpatrick, who felt that, in his role as procedural adviser, he could not take sides.

Since it was by now close on ten o'clock, the four members of the "conservative" faction decided that they would surrender any further voting rights, and retire to bed. With Mr. Gunn went our two friends from Japan, who politely stopped to thank me for the "*teat gretik"*: I was so startled by their rapid, although inaccurate, grasp of Volapük, that I could only bow in acknowledgement. It was not until some time later that I realised that they thought they had attended the performance of some Shakespearean drama. Mr. MacDonald, humming a soft tune from the Isles, went around trimming the lamps; looking in on Urquhart, who had disengaged himself from his cloak and gauntlets to nurse a cracked skull; and, by his scowling demeanour, hinting that our welcome could not be extended for much longer.

I consulted with Mr. Kilpatrick asking if, as the faction which had received the greatest number of votes had now left voluntarily, they had thereby relinquished their voting rights; and that I should now be declared the victor? Mr. Kilpatrick wished to consult his notes. While he did so, unfortunately, Wilson also departed, reducing my support to the same numbers as that of the Esperantist Bosman-ites. So that, when Mr. Kilpatrick looked up, having decided in favour of my application, he was obliged to maintain that the vote was once again tied, by virtue of the numbers remaining.

*   *   *

There seemed little point in extending our debate. The Annual General Meeting had, by default, not succeeded in changing the name of the Society, and was unlikely to do so until the next General Meeting. My Contract with Urquhart had, therefore, borne no fruit.

Bosman banged his mallet on the table, and declared the Meeting closed. Mr. MacDonald bounded up in fury, wrestling the mallet from Bosman and flinging it far into a dark corner cluttered with contrivances for cheese-making, before peering and rubbing at his precious table-top. Bosman shrugged, lit another cigarette, and gathered up his papers. Young Clark slipped out of the door. Kilpatrick thanked me for a fascinating evening, "which had laid down great treasures in the store-room of the Science of Dietology"; and departed.

Thinking that I had best take possession of Urquhart, I asked young McKelvie to bundle up my own papers and notes, and made my way to the rickshaw, where I found the old man, moaning in self-pity. The cloak, gauntlets, helmet and scimitar lay scattered about him in the filthy recesses of the old cart. Of a sudden, an irresistible impulse seized me; swiftly I slipped on the cloak, pulled the helmet over my head and the gauntlets over my hands, snatched up the scimitar.

Oh! What a feeling ran through me! This was my power, this was the power itself, *valüd it*! I stood two feet taller, my chest three feet wider, my feet planted four times more firmly on the Earth. I glanced out from the eye-piece and saw both McKelvie and Bosman look up, aghast. I knew what I had to do. Leaping down from the carriage with the agility of a man of twenty, I strode towards Bosman, my scimitar singing through the air.

"*Cödel Yagöl it cödob! At del binom del omik!*" The Hunting Judge himself judges! This day is his day! In such a satisfactory manner, I provided two good examples of the Possessive and the Demonstrative, without being emphatic in the latter. In my vision, the air itself, black and white, narrowed to a mere corridor of light, at the end of which, with no escape, stood Bosman; the label "Defeated Enemy" adhered to his forehead.

"McKelvie!" I commanded. "Take the old man in that cart, and follow me! Do not forget the mice!" McKelvie, rendered mute, did as I ordered.

"Bosman!" I commanded. "Walk before me!" Bosman, rendered mute, did as I ordered. Mr. MacDonald kindly opened the door for us, and we stepped out into the night. The clock struck wildly for the half-hour. The wind which whistled in through the open door caught the gigantic Sheffield scissors, twisted them once, twice, the rope snapped, the blades scythed through the air and impaled themselves, quivering, in the walnut table-top. MacDonald screamed like a banshee, the door slammed shut, and we strode off into the night.

Fin tidüpa balsid.

Katel Zülid, the Ninth Chapter:
The Adverbs and Adjectives

Lasswade, Mid-Lothian. 6th April, 1891.

Jipulaflumatragölöl, Zen-Lodän.
Del 6id Folula, Balmil Jöltum Zülsebal.

The night was dark as we left the Augean Stables of Millerfield behind us; the wind had abated but little, and, although the air was mild, I wrapped my cloak around me more tightly. I had no detailed plan in mind, now that I had Bosman and Urquhart in my power, but my legs felt restless, and I knew I had to leave the paved streets of Edinburgh. I knew of one place where I could find a temporary refuge: the parks of the River Esk in Mid-Lothian beckoned. Keeping my left hand upon Bosman's left shoulder, and my scimitar across his right arm, I marched him towards Causewayside, and then to Minto Street. There was not a soul in sight, the vast majority of citizens being at home, counting themselves for the great Population Census; of which Bosman continually and piteously reminded me as we stepped southwards. "But I must collect the forms to-morrow!" he wailed, as if that small affair could be valued more highly than his life.

Behind us marched young McKelvie, pulling the frail rickshaw along. The combined weight of cart and Urquhart cannot have been very great, the one composed of light wood and paper-thin cloth, the other of brittle bone and dried skin, and not much else. McKelvie was built to the same architecture as his father, a man as wide as he was tall, carved and hardened by years of toil among the cargoes of ships at the quaysides of Leith. The son, although a clerk by trade, was capable of over-turning any obstacle in his path, and the exercise of pulling the cart seemed as nothing to him. He had explained to me that the recent storms at sea had drastically reduced the need for him to turn up to work the following day, and he was eager enough for an evening stroll.

It occurred to me, as we proceeded down the road leading southwards from the metropolis, over-looked by huge, silent houses, that I had never yet taught Bosman two of the simplest words in every-day conversation. I now rectified that omission, by illustrating, with the point of my scimitar as a teaching-aid, the difference between "yes" and "no".

"Dr. Bosman," I began. "The word for 'yes' in Volapük is *si*. Do you understand that?"

Bosman was silent, thinking more, perhaps, of his fate that night.

I was obliged to ask him again – "Do you understand?" – more pressingly.

"*Si, si*, yes, yes!" he squealed, rubbing that part of his anatomy where my scimitar had found redundant flesh.

"Excellent, Dr. Bosman," I applauded him. "And the word for 'no' is simple even for a man of your limited abilities – it is *no*. Do you understand, Dr. Bosman?"

Of course, the man responded "*No, no!*", when what he meant in truth was "*Si, si!*". I had once more to encourage his learning, and this time he received excellent marks.

I advised him further that the word "*no*", when it means "not", is placed next before the verb which is to be denied. Thus "You do not judge", would be: "*No cödol*" – our brief exercise in this was for me to say, "*Cödob, no cödol*" and for Bosman to reply, "*No cödob, cödol*".

"*Lesi!*" I congratulated him, yes indeed! You do not judge, "*Leno*", not at all, not by any means.

With this understanding between us, we came down among the cottages and fields beyond the last mansions of Newington, and pulled up the easy hill to Liberton. Bosman proved to be a great annoyance, complaining at every step of a pain in his leg, coughing with each pull of his cigarette, and repeating endlessly that his civic duties called him back to Edinburgh, for the great work of the Census. To distract him, I decided upon

Tidüp balsebalid – The Adverbs and Adjectives.

An *adverb* is a word added to a verb or adjective to express some modification of the meaning.

An *adjective* is a word added to a noun to qualify it.

Thus, Dr. Bosman, if I call you a base and unworthy man, then "base" and "unworthy" are both adjectives. If I say that that Urquhart has acted treacherously and slyly, then "treacherously" and "slyly" are adverbs.

Let us deal with the adjectives first, for they are simple to form and simple to use.

The Formation of Adjectives.

We have already covered the "ordinal" numerical adjectives, when we earlier discussed The Numbers. To recapitulate, the ordinal numerals, "first", "second", "third", etc., end in **id**. First, **balid**; second, **telid**; tenth, **balsid**; eleventh, **balsebalid**; 377th, **kiltumvelsevelid** – note that, for facility, this may be written down, in a similar way to English, as **377id**.

All other adjectives are formed from nouns simply by adding the ending **-ik**.

Thus:

> **Gud**, goodness　　**Gudik**, good
> **Löf**, love　　**Löfik**, dear　　**Löflik**, lovely
> **Yel**, year　　**Yelik**, pertaining to the year　　**Yelsik**, yearly

You may be sure, then, that any word with the end-syllable **-ik** is an adjective.

As we laboured up Kirk Brae in Liberton, in the midnight hour, I provided my eager pupil with some examples of the Adjective in Volapük:

Anik	Some, any	**Badik**	Bad
Blägik	Black	**Blefik**	Short
Delidik	Dear, expensive	**Gletik**	Great, large
Glünik	Green	**Gudik**	Good
Jilik	Feminine	**Ledik**	Red
Libik	Free	**Lienitik**	Mad
Löfik	Dear, beloved	**Lonedik**	Long
Manik	Masculine	**Mödik**	Many
Nonik	None	**Saunik**	Healthy, well
Smalik	Small, wee	**Valik**	All
Vietik	White	**Yulibik**	Blue

Apart from a few specific cases, an adjective may be "negated", or turned into its opposite, by prefixing it with **ne-**. Thus, the opposite of

mödik (many) is **nemödik** (a few); the opposite of **delidik** (costly) is **nedelidik** (cheap); the opposite of **lienitik** (insane) is **nelienitik**.

Reaching the inn at Liberton, we stopped, for Bosman was weary upon his feet and McKelvie – even he – required to draw breath and to rest his legs and arms. But despite my own exertions, I found no need for recuperation: I strode up and down the cobbles impatiently, firing questions at Bosman, to test and hone his knowledge of adjectives:

Exercise 14.
Translate:

- **Sil binom blägik.**
- **Blud obik binom ledik; blud omik binom yulibik.**
- **Valüd oba binom gletik; valüd ola binom smalik.**
- No, Esperanto is bad!
- Yes, indeed, Volapük is good.
- You are a quick pupil.

I have to report with some heaviness of heart, that the last sentence which I gave Bosman to translate, did not fulfil itself, despite the very strongest (**stenüdik**) encouragement from myself and my scimitar. The man seemed to have lost heart and strength.

It was growing cold, and I wished to reach our destination without delay. I arranged therefore that Bosman should be placed in the rickshaw, to be pulled by an ever-willing McKelvie, and that I should bear Urquhart upon my back, as a man would carry a sack of potatoes. In this case, the sack was almost empty (**ti vagik**), and the burden was light (**leitik**). We proceeded at a good pace, swiftly (**vifiko** – as we shall see) on the windy and dismal road to Lasswade.

The sky was lightly covered with scudding clouds, and the faintest of waning moons occasionally glimmered upon us. As a result, it was very dark for most of our journey, and we were obliged to move more slowly across the open countryside, listening to the wind in the hedges and trees, expecting at any moment to encounter a carriage on the road. I found it easier in my mask, for it seemed to focus the little light that there was, and this allowed me to see through the blackness. But my companion had to walk with great circumspection.

As for adverbs – I advised Bosman, as I resumed my lesson, marching alongside the rickshaw – nothing could be less difficult.

The Formation of Adverbs.

Numeral adverbs, expressing repetition, are formed by adding **na**: thus:

Kilna, three times
Kilidna, the third time

All other adverbs are formed from adjectives, or sometimes from other parts of speech by adding **-o**, corresponding to the English suffix **-ly**. Thus:

Vifik, quick	becomes	**Vifiko**, quickly
Neit, night		**Neitiko**, nocturnally
Gudik, good		**Gudiko**, well
Badik, bad		**Badiko**, badly
Fat, father		**Fatiko**, paternally

I then engaged all three of my travelling-companions in

Exercise 15.

in which we endeavoured to translate back and forth the following phrases:

- **Lenadobs kilna in del, telsebalna in vig.**
- **Buk gudik at tidom volapüki ole balidna.**
- **Düps goloms vifik, e no labobs timi mödik.**
- You write well.
- You speak Volapük badly.
- The Capitalist buys cheap and sells dear.

Archibald McKelvie, breathing heavily as he marched alongside me, did well at these exercises, for he is an intelligent young man, and promises to go far. As for Bosman, he was impotent. Urquhart, somewhat enlivened by the prospect of acquiring greater knowledge, but concealing badly his dislike for any Universal Language other than his own, made a decent fist of the work, as we descended through the fields towards Lasswade. To lighten the atmosphere, I joked that the name "Lasswade", if understood to mean the "place at which the girl crossed the river", might be rendered poetically in Volapük as *"Jipulaflumatragölöl"*, and the broad county of Mid- (or Central-) Lothian might be **"Zen-Lodän"**. McKelvie was faintly amused, Bosman churlish, Urquhart derisive, at this innocent and pleasurable diversion.

By the time we came to the road which led to Loanhead (or *Vegakap*), it was five o'clock in the morning and – had I not had my cloak and gauntlets – I would have been as one in the wastes of the frozen north. Urquhart had contrived to wrap himself in the folds of my cloak, like a louse; Bosman had apparently fallen into a deep sleep. I continued my lesson, then, only with Urquhart and McKelvie.

Adjectival Degrees.

To form the comparative ("more") and superlative ("most") degrees of an adjective, adverb or noun, the suffixes -**um** and -**ün** are used.

> **Gudik,** good   **Gudikum,** better   **Gudikün,** best
> **Gudiko,** well   **Gudikumo,** better, in a better manner
> **Gudiküno,** in the best manner

These endings **um, ün,** may be added even to nouns;

> **Neflenün obik,** my worst enemy.
> **Binom temipelum ka ob,** he is more of a coward than I.

Urquhart was prepared to be questioned on, and excelled in his answers to:

Exercise 16.
Using **Ka,** than   **Äs,** as
     translate:

- **Tlät obik no binom so gletik äs olik: binom smalikum.**
- **Volapük binom pük nefikulikün in vol lölik.**
- You are more cowardly than I.
- I do not know a language which is easier than Volapük.
  Etcetera.

As we finished this exercise, we turned to our left down a dark lane, past a number of large villas, then turned right again through a gateway. A rough roadway led down into the valley, then traversed an expansive park-land. It was the end of the darkest night as we came down the tree-lined lane, and some light was beginning to show in the east, enough only to see the outlines of hill-crest and tree. The branches creaked and rustled in a stiff breeze, and McKelvie's exertions were noisy. After about twenty minutes, stumbling and slipping by turns, we came at last within sight of the grand house of Mavisbank, my goal and retreat. It was time for me to come to the *Fin tidüpa balsebalid.*

*   *   *

Through the eyes of the mask of Cödel Yagöl, I found that the world had taken on disturbing dimensions. Although I knew them to tower tall (*geiliko*) above our heads, the trees were as short (*bapik*) as bushes. The wind flew past in visible streams, as scum on a filthy river. The clouds in the sky passed through my helmet, now clear, now foggy, now damp, now icy. The gates through which we came upon the lane were as boot-scrapers, but the puddles and holes in the road were lakes and pits of unfathomable depth. When we came upon the house of Mavisbank, it seemed only as large as a small cottage, for all its elegance. But the words "Large House" were clearly chiselled upon its portico, so there could be no mistake. All these unaccustomed sights tore at my senses, and I found myself fallen upon the ground, crushing Urquhart under my body. With a great deal of kicking and complaining from him, and with the able assistance of McKelvie, who rushed to our aid, I was able to sit up once more. I removed the helmet, and snatched at my breath, waiting until the world returned to its usual dimensions and perspective, a process that lasted until the sun came up. As it did so, the wind calmed and fell of a sudden, and a great peace spread over the park.

Such a plan as I had for our retreat from the world, centred around one of the men who plied their trade within the walls of Mavisbank Private Lunatic Asylum. By good fortune, as the light came up from behind the hill above Lasswade, I saw my friend, Mr. William Deans, emerging from the kitchens of the grand house, yawning and stretching himself.

"Mr. Deans!" I called out. The man looked up, surprised. It was not difficult to find us, as we stood before the house, for our breath billowed out like steam. He came up close, suspicious. Then he greeted us – not, at first, with any great enthusiasm.

"Why, it is Mr. Justice, is it not?" he said. "I did not recognise you in that cloak . . . " He looked at me dubiously, as I stood there with my sword and gauntlets, the cloak wrapped around me. On noticing the horrible face of Urquhart peering from the lower folds of my cloak, Mr. Deans drew back, startled. "What – in the name of the Wee Man?!" he exclaimed.

I made the necessary introductions of Urquhart, McKelvie, and Bosman. The last-named, whom Deans recognised, appeared to be frozen like a statue in the Scottish and Shanghai Bank's muddy rickshaw; indeed, his cheeks were white and his lips were almost blue. Mr. Deans, being of a generous nature, suggested that it might prove beneficial to Dr. Bosman if we were to carry him inside and place him before the kitchen fire. Urquhart was greatly in favour of this move. We thereupon abandoned the rickshaw, Deans and McKelvie took Bosman between them and carried him in to the side-building which housed the kitchen; I followed, and Urquhart struggled on behind, wheezing and complaining: I cared not.

*   *   *

So dawned the sixth day of April. After two hours, during which he lay limply in a seat hard up against the kitchen-range, while all around him the cook and her hand-maidens scurried and clattered, Bosman finally came to life again. His lips were the last extremities to recover their strength, and for over twenty minutes he sat, dazed, chattering dentilingual and fricative nonsense – which nonsense was Esperanto, as I took the opportunity to advise Mrs. Kirkaldy, the cook. She shook her head in concern, tutted severally, and continued with the preparation of breakfast for the Residents.

I should explain here that Mr. Deans was once a vigorous member of our Society, and a lover of Volapük; but had moved away from Edinburgh in the summer months of 1890, to take up the responsible position of Chief Attendant at Mavisbank. He was a man of about thirty-five years of age, strong, thoughtful, compassionate. I had been sorry to see him leave, but wished him well, and encouraged him to establish classes in Volapük in his new place of work. A letter or two had passed between us since then, but, as is often the way with such things, our mutual promises to correspond regularly soon fell by the wayside of life. It seemed, however, that the superintendent of the Lunatic Asylum was an enlightened man, and had promoted "sociable meetings" of the Residents, had provided carriages for outings to local beauty-spots, maintained a tennis-ground and a short golfing-place; and had, more importantly, encouraged the "frequent delivery of lectures on interesting subjects" – the whole Programme designed to stimulate the senses and the intellect, and encourage the Residents to acceptable behaviour. Mr. Deans had offered to deliver a course of lectures in Volapük; and these, he advised me, had been well-received, to the extent that several of the Residents now greeted each other each morning in Volapük – a gratifying phenomenon which I soon witnessed with my own eyes.

Once our breakfast was done, McKelvie advised me that he must return to take up his work, since, with the passing of the storm, ships could now be expected to load and unload. I gave him some money for the fare on the train which would leave Polton shortly, and sent him on his way; it would not take long, with the efficiency of our railway companies, for him to reach Hardengreen, and change to a train which would transport him to Waverley within thirty minutes; and thence to Leith, where he worked.

After McKelvie had departed, Mr. Deans and one of his assistants returned from upstairs, and took charge of Dr. Bosman. I had explained, as briefly as possible, that Bosman was suffering from Nervous Exhaustion, and was delusional in imagining that Esperanto could hold sway; Mr. Deans nodded sagely, as soon as I mentioned this detail. I accompanied Bosman, lest there be any unpleasant scene. We found him a bed in a large, airy room, which looked out over the park-land and the short canal which lay to the east of the house, and which was now illuminated by strong sun-light. A man in night-attire stepped strangely in the centre of the room, lifting his knees and feet high, smiling to himself, then placing his feet softly upon the floor at each step; with this exaggerated gait, he never ceased to walk up and down. Two of the beds were occupied by men who gazed upon the new arrival with the very liveliest interest.

"Why!" exclaimed one. "It is Dr. Bosman, is it not? Have you come to join us, old chap?"

Bosman, his wits quite entangled after the journey and the night, gazed around him in wonder. Gradually, some recognition stole across his features. "Heavens above!" he exclaimed. "If it isn't Willie Moore!" He looked at the other two gentlemen. "And Mr. Oliver! And Bob Pringle too!"

The man named Moore laughed heartily: "Yes, Henry: all medical men together again, eh? Is that not right, Bob?" Mr. Oliver looked sourly at his interrogator, expelled wind, and slipped his night-cap over his face. Mr. Pringle simply nodded energetically, and waved at Bosman, never ceasing his curious stepping.

I could see Bosman's face turn white again, the colour only recently having returned. The thoughts which crossed his mind were only too visible for anyone to see. "But," he muttered hesitantly, "were you not sent to an Asylum, to recover your nerves, Mr. Moore?" His eyes darted back and forward. "And Bob, too, after the affair of the stolen – ?"

Mr. Moore guffawed, and clapped his hands loudly. "Got it in one, Henry – what a fast fellow you are, to be sure! Bob Pringle and his wild purchases, eh? We won't forget the look on the jeweller's face when Bob asked to buy fifty of his best gold watches! What a day, what a day! And now you too, eh? Well, there's no accounting for a healthy mind, is that not right, Pringle?

"But what are you in for, Bosman?" Moore continued, a tone of deep interest in his voice. "Moral causes, I hazard. Would it be domestic trouble, or religious excitement, maybe mental anxiety and worry, or over-work?" He looked sceptically at the newcomer. "No? Perhaps a love-affair, then? You can tell us in complete confidence, old fellow!"

But Bosman sat miserably on the edge of a bed and said nothing.

Mr. Oliver sat up, revealed an eye under his night-cap. "You're a fool, Moore, and do not forget it. The causes of this man's melancholia are purely physical: I would judge—" he looked Bosman over, expertly. "I would judge a critical combination of intemperance in drink, self-abuse, sunstroke, epilepsy, and some sexual excess. What do you think, Pringle?"

To spare Dr. Bosman the shame of this curious diagnosis, Mr. Deans asked him if he would be so good as to stop a moment and sign a document; Dr. Bosman expressed no interest in the contents when asked to oblige, and dully signed the certificate which surrendered himself into the care of the Mavisbank Asylum.

Then, taking advantage of Bosman's temporary state of shock, Mr. Deans eased the exhausted Esperantist into the spare bed, and tucked the sheets in tightly. And we left him to the diagnoses of his newly-rediscovered colleagues and fellow-students.

Mr. Deans introduced me to Miss Davidson, the Matron of the establishment, a great admirer of Mr. Deans. Miss Davidson, it appeared, was only at Mavisbank for a short time, until a new matron was appointed; the previous incumbent having run off at Candlemas with Mr. Gordon, the disgraced previous Chief Attendant. For some reason, the Medical Superintendent, Dr. Keay, was indisposed; but the Proprietor looked in occasionally. And for just now, Miss Davidson and Mr. Deans ran the place between them, and – from all appearances – made a very respectable job of it.

Miss Davidson took us on a tour of the many rooms in that mansion, and introduced us to some of the Residents. "Forty-five, all told, Mr. Justice," she announced proudly. "And all as fit as fiddles, thanks to the good country air! The air, and, of course," she added with the air of one who had been asked to sell me something, "the moral management of our patients. There is no coercion and no undue medication here, Mr. Justice; a fact of which we are very proud! Moral management is the key."

Each one of these morally-managed fit fiddles had their own interest, and Miss Davidson was good enough, on her short tour of the premises, to furnish me with a short portrait of every man and woman, from the ancient Dr. Lyon, to the fresh young Miss Rose. Here was Margaret Forrest, widow of an Edinburgh clergyman, who delighted in reciting the brief, but illuminating verse of Angelus Silesius. Next to her, Phoebe Duncan, who made a study of caterpillars. In another room sat John Glegg, the Aberdeen druggist, who was interested in toadstools. Next door to him, Professor Cordiner, who was astonished at the magnitude of Urquhart's skull, but whose ability to concentrate for any length of time seemed greatly suspect; and soon found that the paucity of his breakfast was of far greater moment; a matter about which he argued long and loud with his colleagues Dr. Chartres and Dr. Lyon. Kept slightly apart from the other ladies, in a room at the end of a corridor, and with a view to the low hill to the rear of the house, lived Mrs. Bews, whose life as a manufacturer's wife in Glasgow had so excited her mind that she spent the nights in whistling, clapping, dancing, singing and laughing; and the days in breaking furniture, yelling, tearing her clothes, driven by an internal force so great that she could not resist it for even one silent minute.

Naturally, the Residents were strictly segregated as to sex, with the men living in the southern wing of the building, and the women in the northern wing; in the central part of the house were the "common rooms", where, during the day, all the Residents might mingle and converse, so long as they retained some social skills.

Sir Thomas Urquhart, who accompanied us on this tour, was pleased to be introduced to Mrs. Matilda Bentzen, late of Glasgow, whose attractions were two-fold: firstly, she had discovered the language of the Little People, and was even now working on a Grammar and Syntactical Study of the same; more excitingly for the assembled company, she had evidence that she was a distant kinswoman of Urquhart. This revelation she made immediately upon introduction. Urquhart was doubtful of this claim, and advised her that he could trace his ancestry back, through a hundred and fifty-three generations, to Adam; whereupon, Mrs. Bentzen whipped out a document from her bosom, on which (the document) it was clearly proven that her own ancestry went back, also over a hundred and fifty-three generations, to Eve. This was an extraordinary co-incidence, which amazed all who witnessed it; I have therefore taken the trouble to reproduce here Mrs. Bentzen's genealogy, which she and Urquhart discussed rapturously for the remainder of the day.

Mrs. Matilda Bentzen's Antecedents, to the 153rd Generation

1	Eve	15	Aholibamah	29	Tiye		
2	Shifkah	16	Hagar	30	Berenice		
3	Zillah	17	Nut	31	Cleopatra		
4	Naamah	18	Isis	32	Olympias		
5	Sarai	19	Thoueris	33	Hypermnestra		
6	Milcah	20	Ophet	34	Laodice		
7	Rebekah	21	Nephthys	35	Eurydice		
8	Keturah	22	Neith	36	Erytheia		
9	Mahalath	23	Selket	37	Iphigenia		
10	Rachel	24	Hathor	38	Persephone		
11	Leah	25	Tefnuth	39	Agave		
12	Bilhah	26	Arsinoe	40	Empusa		
13	Zibeon	27	Hetepheres	41	Erigone		
14	Anah	28	Artatama	42	Omphale		

43 Asterope	81 Frithugyth	116 Jeanne
44 Themis	82 Waerburh	117 Marie
45 Cassandra	83 Eadburh	118 Mathilde
46 Helen	84 Aethelswith	119 Christina
47 Polyxena	85 Emma	120 Chretienne
48 Andromache	86 Hilda	121 Yseut
49 Jocasta	87 Helga Njalsdottir	122 Heloise
50 Demonessa	88 Thorhalla Asgrimdottir	123 Therese
51 Cybele	89 Thorkatla Gizursdottir	124 Blanchefleur
52 Sybil	90 Unn Mordsdottir	125 Louise
53 Syrinx	91 Hildigunn	126 Marianne
54 Penelope	Gunnarsdottir	127 Isabelle
55 Pudicitia	92 Gudrun Egilsdottir	128 Hortense
56 Lamia	93 Gunnhild Hrutsdottir	129 Eloise
57 Juno	94 Hallgerd	130 Anne-Marie
58 Dido	Gudrunnsdottir	131 Mary-Ann
59 Tanaquil	95 Rannveig Sigfusdottir	132 Annabella
60 Nortia	96 Astrid Bjornsdottir	133 Margaret
61 Lavinia	97 Thorhild Olafsdottir	134 Mhairi
62 Agrippina	98 Hrodny Herjolfsdottir	135 Marjory
63 Agatha	99 Thorgerd Glumsdottir	136 Ann
64 Lucretia	100 Hallbera Hroaldsdottir	137 Meg
65 Tullia	101 Berthora	138 Flora
66 Verginia	Hoskuldsdottir	139 Maggie
67 Camilla	102 Thora Olafsdottir	140 Marianne
68 Estella	103 Gudrun	141 Jehan
69 Aethelthryth	104 Ulrike	142 Elizabeth
70 Seaxburh	105 Frieda	143 Marjorie
71 Cyneburh	106 Hildegard	144 Mary
72 Cyneswith	107 Elfriede	145 Catriona
73 Eanfled	108 Brunnhilde	146 Lizzie
74 Osthryth	109 Bertha	147 Margaret
75 Aethelflaed	110 Hildebrunn	148 Mary
76 Aelfwynn	111 Arnima	149 Catherine
77 Aelfgifu	112 Minnehold	150 Mary
78 Aethelburh	113 Kriemhild	151 Agnes
79 Cwenburh	114 Ute	152 Georgina
80 Cuthburh	115 Judith	153 Bella

It would seem that the respective families of Urquhart and Bentzen had divided as early as the second generation, when two grand-daughters of Eve went their separate ways in the world, losing the One Language of Babel at the fifteenth or sixteenth generation; Mrs. Bentzen's family passing through Judaea, Egypt, Greece, the Roman Empire, Saxon Britain, Iceland, Germany, France and Scotland; Urquhart's family following a similar path, but skipping over Greece, and remaining in Italy after the Romans, before arrival in Scotland. How wonderful, then, and how unlikely, to find their descendants re-united after so many thousand years!

*   *   *

Mr. Deans was kind enough to offer me a bed in his quarters, for I was greatly exhausted by my endeavours and victory at the Annual General Meeting of the Society, and by our forced-march across the blustery plains of Mid-Lothian. At about ten o'clock in the morning, therefore, after writing some notes for the Society, I laid me down to rest, and did not awaken until, at mid-day, the Catastrophe of Dr. Bosman burst in upon my dreams.

Transactions VII: The Sylvan Language

Written on 6th April, 1891, at Mavisbank.

Through the intermediacy of Urquhart, Mrs. Bentzen has provided me with her notes on the language of Little People. By this, she does not refer to children, or those of a height below the medical average; but rather the Elves, the Fairies, the Dwarves, the Leprechauns and so on, those who inhabit, if we accept certain folk-tales, the woods and forests, the water-sides and the streams.

I examined Mrs. Bentzen's rather indisciplined papers, which covered both grammar and vocabulary, not out of any belief that the representatives of Urquhart's fifteenth gender actually exist, nor out of any credulousness such as was shown by the reverend gentleman in Newburgh; but purely from a scientific point of view. Was there anything in here which would either strengthen my belief in the supremacy of Volapük; or was there anything here which I could suggest to the Academy as a further improvement to the already-solid rules of Syntax?

Her notes, as I say, were difficult of comprehension; but they had the great merit of being short. So that it took me barely forty minutes to establish that the language ("Sylvano") could be classified as a dialect of Esperanto, so crude and simplistic it was. Mrs. Bentzen had, despite her claims to the contrary, set out no Rules of Grammar. But my analysis was swift and incisive. Interestingly, there was but one Gender, one form of the Verb, and a single case of the Noun. The nouns all ended in vowels, the adjectives in labial consonants (m, p or b), the verbs in fricatives (f, v or ph). In short, the whole thing was a mess. How the Little People could ever begin to understand each other, unless some Magic was involved, remained unexplained. I shook my head in despair. And also in anger – for this "Sylvano" language was obviously invented – it was spoken by no one, it served for nothing, it was a mere fancy!

Perhaps it was my exhaustion, and the lack of sleep from the preceding night, and the weight of expectation with which I had lived for several days and nights past: but I could not get out of my mind the clear relationship between Esperanto and Sylvano. Which one, asked my troubled mind, was the daughter of the other – was Esperanto the work of a man who had listened to the Polish Fairies; or did Sylvano develop after the Little People had spirited away some student of Esperanto?

Further, was there a similar relationship between, for example, the "one language and one tongue" of the sons of Noah, and the speech of the Lord, when he decided to "confound the language"? Or between the many tongues which existed after Babel, and the "one language"? Was one a mis-heard, dimly-remembered, and mis-understood form of the other? Was the movement for a new Universal Language simply circling back on an ancient tongue from many thousands of years ago; or was the tendency a dialectical one, to confound the many tongues of To-day with a new and higher tongue for To-morrow?

With these thoughts, which I set down for future consideration and clarification, running through my mind, I slept for an hour or two in Mavisbank.

Katel Balsid, the Tenth Chapter:
The Infinitive, the Participle, and the Tenses

Mavisbank, Mid-Lothian. 6ᵗʰ April, 1891.

"Binobön u no binobön."

Dr. Bosman had, since his arrival, been greatly agitated. No amount of soothing talk from his fellow-students and practitioners of medicine could calm him, no amount of straight exhortation from Mr. Deans and his fellows, or Miss Davidson. The root cause of his unease was of course the Population Census. Dr. Bosman had, some time ago, contracted with the civil authority to distribute, explain, collect, and collate the forms from the Census. The first two items of responsibility had been dealt with adequately, as I knew, having had him smoking a cigarette at my door for a good fifteen minutes one evening, while he explained the simple form to me in the greatest detail, advising me sternly of the penalties for not complying with the Census, and the likelihood of public shame, financial penalty, and loss of liberty that would unavoidably ensue should I ignore his advice. The last two items, however, were not within his power, as long as he lay resting on a bed in Mavisbank.

But Mr. Deans was immovable, adamant that the doctor should stay and rest, for the good of his nervous system, which – surely he would be the first to admit? – had been under great stress in recent days, and was in danger of collapse. This medical advice seemed to make matters only worse for Bosman, and he began to shout and howl, as one demented, begging, demanding, threatening, pleading. To no avail. His friends, Mr. Pringle, Mr. Oliver and Mr. Moore, were in heated debate over a number of interesting medical procedures, which, they felt, might alleviate Bosman's condition. Smoke, as from a funeral pyre, emerged from their room as they puffed at cigarettes and debated the possible treatments. Some of the proposals involved the injection of various unusual substances into his veins; others involved cups and the letting of blood; those favoured by Mr. Oliver tended to revolve around the "epiclonos" which was, as all medical scientists knew, the centre of all physical and mental exhaustion, and required to be carefully excised – "but I warn you, it will not be pretty!" Mr. Moore's solutions tended to the uric.

But at last, towards noon, both his fellows and his attendants had had enough. Mr. Deans called in on me. I was already awake, since Bosman's crescendo of complaint had entered into my slumbers and called me out.

"What shall we do, Mr. Justice?" he wanted to know. "We cannot let him return to Edinburgh in that condition; nor can we let him suffer."

I knew that I would have very little influence over Bosman, but agreed to come and speak to him. We made our way back to "the Doctors' Room", whose door-way was thronged about by interested on-lookers, by those who cried "Shame!", and by those animated by spectacle. (It should be noted that Urquhart was not among those present, perhaps because he was discussing genealogical matters in private with Mrs. Bentzen.) Mr. Deans politely requested passage, and we pushed through into the haze of smoke. We found Dr. Bosman in tears upon his bed, his hair, matted with sweat, sticking out like rain-soaked straw. One of the attendants sat by him, patting his shoulder, and looking reproachfully at Mr. Oliver.

For some minutes, we puzzled over what we had to do. And then Mr. Deans received a flash of inspiration.

"Mr. Downie!" he cried, leaping to his feet. "Of course!" He hastened from the room, shouting out the man's name. Mr. Downie was apparently not far off, for, within a minute, Deans returned, gripping by the elbow a tall, thin gentleman, of about my own age, wearing a monocle. We were introduced: Alexander Downie, employed as a Clerk at Her Majesty's General Register House in Edinburgh, and present at Mavisbank only for a brief period while he recovered from the rather unforeseen elopement of his wife with a maker of lamp-shades from Alloa. He was a quiet, polite fellow, and seemed to bear the devastating scene of Dr. Bosman's troubles with equanimity.

We set out the situation to Mr. Downie as lucidly as we could; explaining that Dr. Bosman was suffering from an extended illness of the nervous system, that he could not be allowed to leave for several days, that his civic duties required him, nevertheless, to be in

Edinburgh that very day. Mr. Downie took it all in, nodded at every point, and then said shortly:

"In the case referred to, understood, my obligation clear, no apologies required: deputise for Dr. Bosman. Depart when?"

Arrangements were soon made; Mr. Downie sat down with Dr. Bosman and discussed the responsibilities in some detail. If I had not known the man to be a Resident, I would have imagined Mr. Downie to be the most skilled doctor of nervous diseases in the whole place. In less time than it took for the room to be cleared of speculative by-standers and fascinated spectators, Dr. Bosman had been placated, and was deep in serious and enthusiastic debate with his new-found deputy. He could not have hoped to find a better man for the task in hand. Bosman had with him a list of the streets and houses which had to be visited, and the instructions for dealing with recalcitrant house-holders.

Downie, for the benefit of those who still remained in the room, explained that, according to the stipulations for the Census, "enumerators, active persons of intelligence. Read, write well. Arithmetic knowledge. Neither infirm, nor weak in body. Eighteen, not younger, sixty-five, not older. Orderly, respectable, strictest probity and propriety. Goodwill of inhabitants required. Myself, Dr. Bosman, both suited. Apologies. Settled?"

It was, indeed, soon settled; and Dr. Bosman fell back, smiling, exhausted, into a slumber that was to endure – as I learned later – for four-and-twenty hours.

*   *   *

It was Mr. Downie's suggestion that I accompany him into Edinburgh, being a "local" citizen, and, in some indefinable way, the cause of Dr. Bosman's temporary incapacity. I was, at first, a little reluctant to undertake this journey with a man I did not know and who, for all that I could determine, might at any moment turn violent, or run off. His manner of speech alarmed me, being bereft, it seemed, of most verbs, many pronouns, and all the conjunctions. Mr. Deans re-assured me on this point: "Mr. Downie is neither an Idiot, an Imbecile, or even a Lunatic, Mr. Justice." I understood these terms to be categorisations for various forms of madness, and, at my request, Mr. Deans explained – an "idiot" was someone incapable of attending to their own personal needs, who needed assistance for the most basic bodily functions; an "imbecile" could help themselves at the simplest tasks, but had only a limited grasp of ideas; a "lunatic" was someone who had periods of lucidity, but was frequently gripped by fantastic notions. Mr. Downie fitted into none of these categories; I could think of large numbers of my acquaintances who might easily fall into the second and third categories – but it was not the occasion to dwell on this thought; it was a moment for decisive action.

There was one further matter which gave me pause for thought and hesitation. Dr. Bosman's responsibility during the Census was precisely for those streets and buildings in which I was known. I did not, at this time, wish to face questions from neighbours on the whereabouts of Dr. Bosman. I thought it best, therefore, if I were to place myself in a disguise, which would not excite comment. The clothing of Cödel Yagöl was, for this occasion, not entirely suitable, since it tended to terrify and to enslave, rather than to inspire confidence in those who beheld it; it might also encourage me to acts which were incompatible with the civic duties with which we had been entrusted. I asked myself the question: if I were a simple householder, would I wish for the names, ages and occupations of my family to be entrusted to a man who knocked at my door, and bore a helmet and scimitar? My answer was in the negative.

Mr. Downie proved to be a man of considerable ingenuity; I felt that he was wasted, scribbling away at the ledgers in Register House – here was a man who could make his fortune in criminal activity or in the leadership of some revolutionary movement! He proposed that I travel into Edinburgh with him, as his wife. I looked at him askance, but there seemed no base motive to his proposal; and not a trace of a smile, nor of mockery. We experimented, therefore, with some clothes lent to me by a young nurse, Eliza Ferguson, who was, in build, almost the same as myself. Eliza and one of her colleagues had me dressed up in no time, and were soon giggling and gasping at the transformation. Eliza herself hugged me briefly in her excitement. I looked at myself in the mirror: apart from a darkness about the jowls, which was swiftly resolved by the application of a razor by one of Mr. Deans' skilful colleagues, and a certain stockiness about the upper body, I could pass as a reasonably handsome woman, a fit wife for Mr. Downie.

*   *   *

We set off down the lane towards Polton, and waited for the train due at two o'clock, which would take us into Edinburgh, after a delay at Eskbank, within the hour. Mr. Downie had in his bag, embossed with an official crest, all the documents which would prove necessary for the duties we were about to undertake.

As we waited at Polton, I discovered to my great surprise that Mr. Downie had once been a keen student of Volapük! He had attended eagerly the classes which Mr. Deans, in his wisdom, continued to offer to all those who came through the handsome portals of Mavisbank House. The absent superintendent of Mavisbank had made the discovery that the effort of acquiring the basic rules of grammar of Volapük exerted a calming influence on most people who had been troubled by nervous ailments, or terrible shocks to their constitution. This was not an attribute of Volapük which I had yet discovered, or one which had appeared in the *Volapükabled Zenodik*, the central organ of the movement. I resolved to study this matter on my return to Mavisbank. At any rate, Mr. Downie was greatly interested in the forms taken by the Verb, and asked me, very apologetically, if I would elaborate on them. I was pleased to oblige. I settled my skirts and engaged in

Tidüp balsetelid – The Infinitive, the Participle, and the Tenses. You should know, I began, that the Infinitive is the form which expresses the verb without reference to person, time or number: it is simply "to" – "to break", "to travel", "to learn". The Participle is the non-finite form of a verb used to form compound tenses (for example, the word "broken" in "had broken") or adjectives ("breaking"). And finally, the Tense is the form of a verb to indicate the time of action – "breaks" *or* "is breaking", "was breaking", "broke" *or* "has broken", "had broken", "will break", "will have broken".

Mr. Downie understood this much – it was, after all, the stuff which children learn in their first year of schooling.

The train for Eskbank having arrived, we boarded, and I instructed Mr. Downie in

The Infinitive.
The Infinitive mood, or verb-noun, has the ending **-ön**. It is usually, though not always, preceded in English by "to". In Volapük, there are various tenses of the Infinitive, indicating a point in time:

- **Blekön,** to break (Present Tense)
- **Eblekön,** to have broken (Past, or Perfect, Tense)
- **Oblekön,** to be about to break (Future Tense)
- **Ublekön,** to be about to have broken (Future Perfect Tense)

The Infinitive can also be used as a noun:

- **Blig dunön binos gälik,** to do one's duty is pleasurable.
- **Tävön binos gälik,** travelling is pleasurable.

(Notice that the neuter-impersonal verb, **binos,** is used with the Infinitive as subject.)

- **Vilob yufön mani at,** I wish to help this man.
- **Binön u no binön,** to be or not to be.

The verbs "may", "can", "must" (called by some Grammarians, "auxiliaries of the potential mood", having possibility, but not reality – as with Life), "let", "dare", etc., have no "to" after them in English, notwithstanding which, the verb following them is in the Infinitive.

- **Mutön,** to "must"
- **Dalön,** to "may"
- **Letön,** to "let", allow
- **Kanön,** to "can"
- **Vilön,** to wish, "will"
- **Sötön,** to "ought", "should"

Thus:

- **Mutob pükön,** I must speak (I am obliged to speak).
- **Dalob sagön,** I may say (I am permitted to say).
- **Letom mani golön,** he lets the man go; he allows the man to go.
- **Kanob blig dunön,** I can do my duty.
- **Sötob blig dunön,** I ought to do my duty.

Mr. Downie apologised for having some trouble with this, but only because it was his general habit not to use the word "to" before the Infinitive. We allowed his weakness, and moved on.

The English verb-noun ending in "-ing" must be translated by the Infinitive.

- **Tikön zesüdos al lifön,** thinking is necessary for living.

It is permitted to insert the personal pronouns before the ending **-ön** in order to indicate, or stress, the subject.

- **Binobön u ne binobön!** [for me] to be or not to be!

Which is, of course, quite distinct from

- **Binolön u ne binolön!** [for you] to be or not to be!
- **Binofön u ne binofön!** [for her] to be or not to be!

There was not time, as we changed to the Edinburgh train at Eskbank, to engage in the exercise, but I have provided it here for those who wish to exert their minds in the frequent use of the Infinitive.

Exercise 17.

- **Löfob bligi tunön.**
- **Kim kanom numön stelis sila u tofis mela?**
- **Binob in vol al tikön, no al pledön.**
- **Sötol studön volapüki al kanön pükön ko nets valik.**
- To travel is better than to arrive.
- We ought to travel by train if we can buy a ticket.
- It is better to have loved and lost, than not to have loved.

The main topics of our discussions in the train which took us into Waverley Station, were the Participle, and the Tenses of the Verb.

The Participle.
I explained to Mr. Downie, who seemed to have this knowledge already, that the participle is a verb-adjective. Its ending in Volapük is **-öl**, corresponding to "-ing" or "-ed", or similar. It may be in the Active or Passive Voice, and in any tense, the Present, Perfect and Future being the most common.

- **Bleköl**, breaking
- **Ebleköl**, having broken
- **Obleköl**, about to break, being about to break

The participle is most useful in such phrases as "his courage is breaking", "having won a victory" and so on. I did not deem it necessary to exercise my new companion in this knowledge, so, pausing only to adjust my many skirts, which had become entangled in my boot-laces, I proceed to set forth the grammatical rules for

The Tenses.

Each of the tenses has one of the vowels as its peculiar sign: **a, ä, e, i, o, u**; to correspond to the:

Present Tense	a	For example, "We collect."
Past (or Imperfect)	ä	"We were collecting."
Perfect	e	"We have collected."
Past-Perfect (or Pluperfect)	i	"We had collected."
Future	o	"We will collect."
Future Perfect	u	"We will have collected."

These vowels, when prefixed to the verb, are called tense-signs or *augments*.

The present-sign, **a**, is usually omitted. Thus:

- **binob,** I am (less commonly, **abinob**)
- **äbinob,** I was
- **äbinol,** you were
- **ebinom,** he has been
- **ibinof,** she had been
- **obinos,** it will be
- **ubinon,** one will have been

In English, most of the tenses are expressed by using the auxiliary verbs, "have", "shall" and "will"; but in Volapük there are no such auxiliaries, the verb-form consisting of a single word, with prefix.

In passing, we should note that the word "do" is used in English as an auxiliary denoting emphasis, as, "I do believe." In Volapük, this cannot be translated otherwise than "I believe."

The same tense-signs, **a, ä, e, i, o, u,** are used with some words other than verbs, when time is specifically to be distinguished. In this way:

- **Adelo,** to-day
- **Ädelo,** yesterday
- **Odelo,** to-morrow
- **Udelo,** the day-after-tomorrow
- **Amulo,** this month
- **Omulo, uyelo,** etc.   next month, the year-after-next, etc.

Exercise 18.

I asked Mr. Downie, as our carriage passed into the shadow of Arthur's Seat, to put the following words into all their tenses, giving the meaning of each:

- **Kusadob**
- **Kautol**
- **Ketom**
- **Libof**
- **Lömibos**
- **Dugon**
- **Vikobs**
- **Lugols**
- **Netegoms**

And then I asked him to translate into Volapük:

- I have been the best, I was better yesterday, I am good to-day, I will be worse to-morrow.

Apart from some elementary mistakes in the last question that I set him, he was as good a pupil as I had come across in many a long day. I congratulated him; in return, and to my initial anxiety, he laid his hand upon my knee and smiled. Our train rattled across the points underneath the Calton Hill, and we had arrived at Waverley Station. *Fin tidüpa balsetelid.*

*   *   *

The district which was the responsibility of Dr. Bosman was that bounded by Marchmont Crescent in the west, to Sciennes in the east, by Carlung Place in the south, to Melville Terrace in the north. It included Gladstone Terrace, Rillbank Crescent, Roseneath Place and Millerfield Place: containing perhaps two hundred house-holds in all, a figure daunting enough in itself, but, as Mr. Downie explained to me, scarcely a large number for an Enumerator, as Dr. Bosman – and now ourselves – was entitled. Mr. Downie proved to be a veritable fountain of information on the matter of enumerators, and the duties they were asked to perform. It seems that an enumerator would be paid a sum of money – one guinea fixed, plus 2/6*d.* for every 100 persons above 400; and 6*d.* per mile above the first 5 miles travelled, both when distributing and collecting schedules. He would be supplied with a sheaf of house-hold schedules (or "papers"), an Enumerator's Book, instructions and a memorandum, or common-place, book. The size of an enumerator's district could be as many as 1,500 people, and a total of two hundred or more house-holds was not considered an excessive responsibility.

It was the duty of the "head of a house-hold" to complete the forms handed out, and, under pain of a fine or imprisonment, was obliged to do it accurately. It is a signal condemnation of the trust in which our Government is held, that the poorer people often refuse to have any information at all recorded on paper, until it has been explained to them, very carefully, and with reference to oaths and the Bible, that there is nothing to pay: this is not a tax, nor the prelude to a tax.

Mr. Downie explained that the Census was held in March or April simply to avoid the worst of any seasonal migration of labour. "But," said he, verbosely, "inconvenient schedule, April. Army pensioners, quarterly pensions. Festive mood, contiguous days. Army pensioners not in residence. Not traced. Maybe in ditch, under hedge. Uncommonly bad thing. Apologies." He shook his head; whether at the moral depravity of Army Pensioners, or the ill-conceived time-table of the Pensions Board, I could not tell.

Having reached our "district" at around four o'clock, I was prepared to take a cup of tea. Mr. Downie frowned at this proposal: "Apologies. Our duty not light, regrettably, Mrs. Downie. Before us great responsibilities, behoves us, commence without delay." I yielded to his authority in this matter, and we began to knock on doors.

It seemed that our stratagem of substitution and disguise was successful. Mr. Downie had every appearance of a strict enumerator, and I, as his wife, lent some air of gentility to the whole proceedings, so that, when a woman or child answered our knock upon the door, we rarely un-earthed anyone who did not meekly yield up the requisite form to the enumerator. It is well that we were acting under the seal of Official Approval, else the blind trust placed in us by the citizens were sadly mis-placed!

We divided our responsibilities thus: Mr. Downie would knock and explain his mission. On receipt of the Census form, he would ensure that it was duly completed and signed, and that the information contained thereon bore some credibility; he would then tick that house-hold on his list as "visited", pass the form to me for placing in his official satchel, with the gold-stamped initials "GROS", and we would proceed to the next door. At times, the form would not have been filled in properly; or had not been filled in at all; in one house, we found that "the dog had eaten it" – which did nothing to interrupt our progress, for Bosman had supplied us with a number of blank forms to deal with just such canine proclivities.

In those instances where information had to be checked, corrected, or gleaned verbally, we would enter the house, sit down at a table, and, while I grimaced at the children, Downie would transcribe the details on to the form. All passed without discovery. There were a few house-holds in which I found familiar faces, and I took care to stand in the shadow, or to keep a handkerchief pressed to my lips, to avoid detection.

Those house-holds where we had difficulties were divided into two categories: firstly, where the house-holder placed a different interpretation upon the questions than any sane person might; and secondly, where the house-holder had completed the details in mischievous manner. Mr. Downie was very strict on both accounts.

As we passed down the streets, we found ourselves the centre of attraction to an ever-growing gang of small children, who, having easily determined who we might be, set up a chant: "Census Dame, Census Man, Far frae Hame, and Doon the Pan!"; which chant we contrived to ignore, although I itched to smack them about the head. Their chant preceded us, and had at least the advantage that house-holders had their forms ready when we knocked.

We came to a house on Argyle Place, where it was evident that the servant-girl had completed the form, in the absence of the house-holder or his wife. What was clear to us was that she had presented herself on the form as the "Head of Family", and her employers as her servants: the question, "Relation to Head of Family", was filled in, for all excepting herself, as "Servant" or "Skivvy", or "Thankless Drudge". For herself, "Condition as to Marriage" was "Hopeful, James Scott being willing". Under the same column, a son, James, had been identified, as "Changeling". The "Age" of the true lady of the house was given as "Crabbit" and that of the master, as "Almost dead". But she had excelled herself in response to the question, "Whether (1) Deaf and Dumb (2) Blind (3) Lunatic, Imbecile or Idiot": for Mr. C—, she had put, "Eunuch"; for Mrs. C—, "Drunkard"; and for a Miss C—, who may have been the family's daughter, "Turnip-head". On reading this, Mr. Downie sighed and pointed out that he felt that these entries were not quite correct. The girl was, at first, brazen about the matter, insisting that what she had put down was entirely correct, and who was he to question her like that? At length, however, she burst into angry tears and confessed all; the family was away in London on some trip, and the girl had been left to look after things; she had meant no harm. The matter was soon rectified.

After six o'clock, the men of the houses we visited began to arrive home, and we had dealings with one who, sympathetically to me, denounced the whole proceeding as an attempt by "The Government" to enslave the country's free citizens, and to gather information which would further curtail the liberties of young and old alike. He refused to confirm his name, although it was down on our list as Mr. Morrison; he refused to provide any details of how many people were in his house on the night of the fifth of April; he refused, also, to return the blank form. Mr. Downie spent some time in argument with him, warning him of a stiff fine. The man stood firm, and finally slammed the door in our faces.

On our final call, we came across Mr. McBirnie. Without a word, he handed over the form, looking at me askance, as if struggling to find recognition. Meanwhile, Mr. Downie examined the form, and pursed his lips.

"Apologies. Your form, Mr. McBirnie," he remarked. "Forty-seven people, your house-hold?"

McBirnie neither confirmed nor denied this. "What of it?" he demanded.

"Unusually large number, small residence. Your house, thirty-three rooms, one or more windows. Neighbour down-stairs, Mrs. Finlay, only two rooms, one or more windows. Curious building. Might enquire, answers all veracious? Apologies."

"I have no control over what Mrs. Finlay puts on her form, sir," replied McBirnie, with no concessions, and no further explanation. Downie passed the form over to me. I could see that every available space had been completed, with people whose surnames were McBirnie, others who were of a different family. I noticed, here and there, some familiar names: Karl Marx ("Profession or Occupation": "Dialectician"), Frederick Engels ("Revolutionary"), Ferdinand Lassalle, Pierre Proudhon, Karl Kautsky, and so on; there was Thomas More, Gerrard Winstanley, Fergus O'Connor; Robespierre, Danton, even a man named Robert Owen, had all stayed the night at McBirnie's surprisingly capacious third-floor residence.

But we let the matter go. It was late, we were both tired. We bade McBirnie a pleasant evening, and retired to Number 8, Carlung Place. A good three-quarters of our forms had by then been collected.

As we passed the entrance to Mrs. Forbes' house, I thought it best to advise her that her lodger, Dr. Bosman, had been incapacitated and was now resting for a few days with a friend. In such familiar surroundings, I forgot for the instant that I was now dressed as a nurse, and was unprepared for the startled look of horror which was on her face when, having answered to my knock, she heard my voice issue from the feminine façade. But there was little I could do to salvage any dignity from the situation; I gave her my message, turned, and fled up the stairs to my own room, with Mr. Downie in hot pursuit. As I turned the key in the lock of my door, I could hear exclamations and laughter from the floor below. Unless I could invent a plausible explanation, I had, in one moment, destroyed any residue of respect between myself and that lady.

We dined rather poorly, on potatoes. Mr. Downie did not seem to mind, being of an even temper, and pleased to be out in the world again. He debated with me how the entries of Dr. Bosman and myself should appear in the Census, both of us being "on the road", if he understood correctly. "Such cases," he explained, tersely. "Duty of enumerator, all roofless persons in district, enumerate certainly, determine name, age, gender, occupation, provenance." This, I suggested, seemed rather more simple to propose, than to execute? Mr. Downie agreed. Bosman and I were, by the letter of the law, vagrants at the time of the Census, for we could neither be counted at Carlung Place, nor at Mavisbank House. Someone, in the neighbourhood of Liberton, ought to have been informed of our passage, and recorded us as living "in rickshaw", or similar. I considered this proposal to be impractical at such a late stage of the proceedings. Downie sensibly concurred, and it was agreed that we should add Bosman to the form returned by Mrs. Forbes, and that I return my own one, as if I had been "at home".

When this was settled, I was overcome by a fit of camaraderie, in which I confessed to Mr. Downie that, for more than twenty years, Mrs. Forbes and I had once lived as man and wife. We had raised three children, and the son of another family. All our children except Lizzie, my daughter, have now left home. But as the years of our marriage went by, my relations with my wife grew ever-more strained. Perhaps it was my long and frequent absences from home which caused this; she rarely found it easy to welcome me back, I was always a visitor. I never understood fully in what way I offended her; but it was clear that my presence at home was commonly an annoyance, rather than a pleasure. And my growing interest in the Universal Language appeared to widen the gulf of silence between us. On my enthusiastic return from Paris, eighteen months ago, we finally ceased to have an understanding, and I was obliged to take up residence in the attic-bedroom in our building; while my wife Mary reverted to her maiden surname, and treated me simply as her lodger. Since when, we have lived in this arrangement, respectably enough, no more than that.

As I related these facts, I observed that Mr. Downie's placid demeanour fell away, revealing agitation and worry to a strong degree. Finally he began to walk up and down the floor in a hurried manner, muttering at the lamp-shade. Too late, I remembered the poor man's own domestic dis-arrangement, and deftly turned the subject to less marital matters, until he calmed himself again.

The remainder of the evening, which I might have preferred to spend in a thorough revision of Mr. Downie's knowledge of the Past Tenses, was whiled away with some of his critical reminiscences of the enumerators from the previous Census, in 1881. It appeared that Enumerators were no different from other mortals, that they were subject to the same whims and passions as their fellow-men. From those with a criminal character, who completed bogus forms, thereby to push the numbers of the population within their district in excess of four hundred, in order to line their pockets; over those whose power of arithmetic and spelling was wanting; and those whose only reason for volunteering for the duties was to find out more about their neighbours, and, where possible, to pass moral judgement on them, annotating the factual return with comments of their own ("Pro-fession – Butcher" would be elided and replaced with "Profession – extortioner and bully, gives no credit", for example; "Condition as to

Marriage – Unmarried" might become "Woman of easy virtue – why not ask Mr. McNab!!"; and so on); to those whose splenetic feelings towards their temporary employers knew no bounds.

An enlightening hour was spent in this way, before we retired to bed. It was with a feeling of some disquiet, that I noticed Mr. Downie's wistful looks as I divested myself of Eliza's clothes; but I chose not to remark on this, and the incident passed.

I found it difficult to get to sleep that night, and found myself considering the Past, the Present and the Future of The Edinburgh Society for the Propagation of a Universal Language. It was certain that, in its brief history to date, there had been many events of note, but that the Society had largely been strengthened by the debates, rather than weakened by them. Indeed, I now gave consideration to the thought that it was only my attempted imposition of Volapük – or Bosman's attempt to impose Esperanto – which had disrupted our relatively comradely habits, and threatened, for the future, to create faction and strife. Was the Past Perfect or Imperfect? Was the Future, the Future Perfect? Was the Future only secure if, in the Present as in the Past, I permitted the parallel development of Solresol, Esperanto, Nal Bino, and other absurdities? Or was it more likely that the Future would be the Perfect, if I struggled steadfastly to make Volapük the only permitted Universal Language?

These were deep and weighty matters, and I found no answer in the dark night. I comforted myself by taking the verb "to question" (*säkön*) through all of its cases and tenses:

Present: *Säkob, säkol, säkom, säkof, säkos, säkon, säkobs, säkols, säkoms, säkofs.*

Imperfect: *Äsäkob, äsäkol, äsäkom, äsäkof, äsäkos, äsäkon, äsäkobs, äsäkols, äsäkoms, äsäkofs.*

Perfect: *Esäkob, esäkol, esäkom, esäkof, esäkos, esäkon, esäkobs, esäkols, esäkoms, esäkofs.*

Pluperfect: *Isäkob, isäkol, isäkom, isäkof, isäkos, isäkon, isäkobs, isäkols, isäkoms, isäkofs.*

Future: *Osäkob, osäkol, osäkom, osäkof, osäkos, osäkon, osäkobs, osäkols, osäkoms, osäkofs.*

Future Perfect: *Usäkob, usäkol, usäkom, usäkof, usäkos, usäkon, usäkobs, usäkols, usäkoms, usäkofs.*

This whispered incantation disturbed Mr. Downie in his sleep; he did not wake, but mumbled "Goodness' sake, apologies, quiet, work, concentrate, decorum . . . "; and so I desisted for the present, and passed, perfectly, to sleep.

*   *   *

On the following morning, being the Tuesday after the Census, Mr. Downie and I were out in the district early, fulfilling our obligations. We managed to collect all the remaining forms without new incident, and had it all done by late morning. I chose not to appear at Mrs. Forbes' door that morning, and left Downie to collect her form, to which we subsequently added the name and particulars of Dr. Bosman. My own form was the last to be surrendered, and I did so with some ceremony, over the threshold of my rooms. Rubbing his hands with satisfaction, Mr. Downie proposed that, before returning with our forms to Mavisbank, we should celebrate our success with "brewery ale, convivial celebration". I am by no means a supporter of the Temperance Movement, but I hesitated, knowing that a drink of beer at that hour of the day would cause me illness. However, it seemed churlish to deny the man, so we took ourselves, with all our papers in Downie's official satchel, to the public-room at the Borough-lough Brewery, just across the Meadows. To see Mr. Downie's manifest enjoyment of his refreshment, was refreshment in itself for me, and I limited myself to a small glass.

It was then that an unfortunate incident occurred, which was to have serious consequences for the Civil Governance of the Kingdom.

The public-room was much frequented by individuals from the University; at twelve o'clock, the door was thrust open suddenly, and a crowd of noisy men burst in, talking and shouting excitedly in some foreign language. The throng resolved itself around a table nearby, and I realised, to my chagrin, that this was none other than the Leibnitzian faction, thurifers of the late Professor McInnes. Dressed though I was in Eliza's clothing, I turned my head sharply away from them, and hid my face. Alas! One of the band, more forward than the rest, stepped up to our table and offered to buy me a small drink, "if I would come and sit on his 78". Mr. Downie, who may have led a sheltered life, was astonished and struck dumb. As for myself, I managed to squeak out some deprecating words, and rose to go. But my ardent admirer was not to be so easily thwarted, and stood glaring down at Downie, demanding to know why he should not speak to "the lady". Was he not good enough for her? Downie, to his credit, explained that I was his wife, and that he would thank the gentleman to let us pass. The gentleman was not to be swayed: "Then, by 5,300, I'll fight you for her, you 307!" I did not realise that the Leibnitzians had so much passion enclosed within, and vowed never to let them near the Society, when my routine was once more established.

Such thoughts were, however, short-lived, as the Leibnitzians, in a body, stood up and, throwing over chairs and tables, charged down Downie and the two bar-tenders who were trying to intervene on our behalf. As for myself, I saw no point in keeping up the pretence, and threw myself into the fray, pulling back the Leibnitzians by their hair, dislodging their spectacles, throttling them with their neck-ties. But we were out-numbered by the numerologists.

In minutes, the battle was over. Our assailants, with whoops of delight, retreated through the door, and were heard passing up Buccleuch Street, ringing the door-bells of houses numbered prime, over-setting bicycles in contempt for their "double zeroity", and scaring horses, as they went. The battle was over – but at what cost!

*   *   *

For Mr. Downie's satchel had been torn open in the brawl, all the papers and forms had spilled out; some were ripped to shreds, others soaked in beer, others still covered in blood from ruptured noses and scraped knuckles! Barely a hand-full were still in good condition. The Census was destroyed!

Transactions VIII: The Leibnitzian Scheme

Written first on 2nd March, 1891, at Fettercairn, and Brought Now to the Public Attention as a Consequence of Recent Events.

Before I outline some of the main points of the "Leibnitzian Scheme", I should briefly summarise the nature of "philosophical" languages. These are languages which are constructed upon philosophical principles, that try to apply the power of the Human Mind, to seeking out the relationship between Ideas; and, from there, the relationship between words. Many memorable spirits have worked tirelessly at the problem of a Universal Language. Great work was undertaken in the seventeenth century by men such as Dalgarno and Wilkins, and this work has been continued by many of the keenest minds since then – amongst whom stand tall the German philosopher and mathematician Leibnitz, and our own Mr. Roget.

Some philosophers took an Analytic approach – which is to say that they understood the structure of a Perfect Language to be based around a small number of root-words, which would be joined together until more and more complex ideas could be expressed. The sequence, "boat", "fishing-boat", "herring fishing-boat", "herring fishing-boat net" – is an example of the how the radical might develop into a complex concept.

Other philosophers decided on an Encyclopaedic approach – which is to say that the root-words would be based around a system of classification and logic. This, inevitably, would mean a large number of root-words, since – as anyone can see for themselves by opening one of Mr. Roget's works – there are many dozen classifications. One such encyclopaedic scheme was:

The Leibnitzian Scheme:
Leibnitz developed a scheme which is represented by Professor McInnes of the University of Edinburgh, and a tiny sect of his adherents. The essence of the Leibnitzian scheme was that every "prime number" would be associated with a single philosophical

classification or category. There would be a finite number of these categories, which might range from the higher categories (Abstract Relations, Space, the Material World, the Intellect, Volition, and Sentient or Moral Powers) to the lower ones (for example, Light, Sound, or Emotions and Passions). Any single thing, idea or concept could be traced back to any simple or complex combination of categories; and Leibnitz proposed that this "combination" would be pinned down by the multiplication of the certain numbers associated with those categories.

I am no mathematician, but I understand at least that there are numbers known as "prime", which are those that can be divided only by themselves and a single unit, and by no other numbers. Thus, 1, 2, 3, 5, 7, 11 and so on are said to be "prime". Larger numbers, such as 137 and 257, are also "prime", but I was advised by Professor McInnes that, the greater the number, the smaller the likelihood of it being "prime".

Now, Leibnitz determined that any number of philosophical concepts could be allocated to these prime numbers. Thus "man" could be represented by the number 7, "idea" by the number 17, "correspondence" by the number 137, "hat" by the number 661, and so on. (I give these merely as examples plucked out of the air, for McInnes has never produced any schema for vocabulary based on Leibnitz' own musings on the matter – in all of his dealings, McInnes is a true mathematician and cannot be specific about anything. Even his radical re-development of the roster for tea-making at the monthly meetings of the Society were untainted by any hard-and-fast list of names, so that it fell to Mrs. Keenan and Mrs. Turpie to continue to make the tea, in their uncommonly noisy manner.) Following Leibnitz, then, the word for a man in the employment of the General Post Office would be the product of multiplying the numbers 7 and 137 (959); similarly, a philosopher would be the number 119 (7 times 17); a scientific paper would be 2,329 (17 times 137); and a postman's hat, the number 633,899.

Developing on this basis, Leibnitz would take the simple vowels to represent the units of 1, 10, 100, 1,000 and 10,000 respectively; and the first unique consonants to represent the integers 1 to 9 respectively – as in the following table:

Units		Integers	
1	a	1	b
10	e	2	c
100	i	3	d
1,000	o	4	f
10,000	u	5	g
		6	h
		7	l
		8	m
		9	n

All that was then required was to translate the numbers produced from the multiplication of our primes, and convert them into sounds. 959 would thus be "ni ge na"; 119 would be "bi be na"; and our scientific paper would be "co di ce na". The beauty of this scheme meant that 119 could also be "na be bi", or indeed "be na bi", for there was no mistaking the prefixes and suffixes.

On hearing this for the first time, young Issachar Clark, a foolish and vapid youth, pondered a moment. "Then the number 66,666," he speculated, "would be '*hu ho hi he ha*'?" The Professor, innocently encouraged, agreed that this was so; whereupon Clark, inflamed, perhaps, by the depth of his own wit, broke out into a wearisome and repeated series of the numbers 600 and 6, until I was obliged to call for order, and request that Bosman remove the youth from the meeting until he had recovered some sobriety.

I rather upset the Professor on another occasion, by questioning him closely on the translation of the larger numbers, such as the "tens of millions"; for, although I know little of the higher mathematics, it is certain that the more complex philosophical entities, such as Mrs. Keenan's bulging-eyed terrier, would result in very large numerical products. McInnes had no answer to this immediately, but I understand that he was keen to start work on the problem. Mrs. Keenan felt obliged to point out forcefully that her terrier was named Charlotte, after some minor member of the Royal Family: "This dog is not a number!" she exclaimed, driven almost to tears; which stupidity made me despair of our Society.

I would add that a young teacher at the University, a rather abrasive Londoner named Albert Benham, was of a mind that Leibnitz' philosophical schema might work, if only the numbers were not converted back into sounds. He envisaged some nebulous language of his own, where people would simply pass numbers to each other. His lecture before the Society on this subject had the interesting numerical effect of reducing the audience from fifteen to two. Last Christmas Eve, at our Annual Dinner, he tested us with a witticism during our post-prandial hour of charades and amusements – I believe that the joke was "6,783 and 3,262,623: 71!" No one laughed, excepting Benham himself, and he ranted against us for several minutes; and then resigned from the Society.

Of course, the great problem with this System of Language is that no philosophical categorisation is, by itself, free from variability: for example, the whale might change from a "fish" to a "mammal"; and who is to say whether God might not, under certain social circumstances, migrate from "religion" to "utility"? And where to-day we might categorise light as a "sensation", who can say what it might be shown to be, in ten, a hundred, or a thousand years?

This problem is the Achilles Heel of the Leibnitzian scheme. For no sooner has a philosopher or linguist classified a concept and word under one category, than a rival philosopher will jump up to claim that it should be classified under a quite different category. Thus, in London, "The Society of Leibnitzians" had, over the course of the years, subdivided into many different parties, or factions: "The Leibnitzian Society"; "The Categorical Leibnitzians"; "The Encyclopaedic Leibnitzians"; "The Leibnitzian Society (Classified)"; "The Society of Leibnitzians (Classified and Categorical)"; "The Categorical Society"; "The Analytical Leibnitzians"; "People's Commune of Leibnitzians (Analytic/Categoric)"; "The Categorical Encyclopaedists (Leibnitzian)"; "The Working Men's Categorical Club"; and many others, each having a small prime number of members. I understand, from a complaint voiced to me by Mrs. Keenan, that Professor McInnes had his own troubles in this respect, even in Edinburgh; but I am not party to the factions which may have arisen here.

Katel Balsebalid, the Eleventh Chapter:
The Imperative, Jussive and Optative

"Lit binomöz!"

For a few moments, we stood there, surveying the detritus of the Leibnitzian barbarism. It was indeed a dispiriting sight.

Mr. Downie, who, until that moment, had been the calmest of men, the most unperturbed, suddenly delivered himself of a prolonged howl, which shook the glasses on the bar, and had our bar-keepers clutching their ears.

"Hey!" shouted one of them. "Any more of that and you're out!" The man obviously had no sympathetic spirit. It was, in any case, useless for anyone to try to reason with Mr. Downie, who now began to smite his forehead against the wall, and wail "*epölüdob!*" I understood his despair, but it seemed to me that it had been compounded by a memory of his other recent loss. Recalling that I was still in the guise of Mrs. Downie, I proceeded busily to collect all the forms, and made shift to sort them – those which were destroyed utterly, those which were soaked with beer, or gore, and illegible, those soaked but barely legible, those torn, and – last and smallest of all – a pile of those forms which were either unharmed, or merely sorely crumpled. The worst of them, illegible and lost to posterity, I bundled into a soggy and stinking roll, and pushed into my skirts; the remainder were straightened out as best I could manage and thrust back into Mr. Downie's satchel. My fellow enumerator, all this time, stood beside the wall, rocking back and forth, moaning and perceptibly shrinking in upon himself.

When all was ready, and after one last look under the chairs and tables, now restored to their previous positions, I took Downie by the arm, and we stepped out into the strong mid-day sun-shine. We stood outside, staring out over the peaceful bowling-green and its companion quoiting-ground, and determined what we should do next. Or, to be more exact: Downie sprawled himself upon the ground, plucking at his clothes, sobbing uncontrollably, "Apologies. Despair, or Loss, or Banishment to Dumfries!"; while I considered our course of action. My thoughts were interrupted by the arrival of a stern constable, who demanded to know if Downie were drunk and incapable; and it took some fine acting on my part to persuade the policeman that Mr. Downie was a patient at an Institution, and that I was his nurse, and that we were only out for some fresh air. The man advised us that we could not make that kind of noise here, and advised me to get Downie back to his bed – "or there will be trouble, miss" – before pacing onwards.

Unbidden, I reflected grammatically on the policeman's manner of ordering us to be on our way, and considered for myself (for Downie was not in a receptive mood):

Tidüp balsekilid – The Imperative, Jussive and Optative.
The Imperative is the commanding-form of a verb: "move along!", "leave this place!" or "learn Volapük!" But it is less well-known, even among students of any Universal Language, that there are three forms of the Imperative:

> The Imperative – expressive of command, advice or request.
> The Jussive – expressing a direct order.
> The Optative – expressing a desire or wish.

Examples of this in our policeman's words were: "Get the man back to his bed!" – which expressed the Imperative; "Be away from here before I return!" – which expressed the Jussive; and "Please consider where you are!" – which was the Optative.

In Volapük, the various forms of the Imperative are expressed by different suffixes, following the person-ending of a verb. The ending of the simple Imperative is **-öd**:

- **Gololöd!**   Go! (to one person)
- **Gololsöd!**   Go! (to more than one person)
- **Lit binomöd!**   Let there be light! (Be light!)

The courteous or softened form of the Optative ends a verb in **-ös**:

- **Gololös!**   Please go! (to one person)
- **Gololsös!**   Please go! (to more than one person)
- **Lit binomös!**   I request that there be light!

and the Jussive, the harsh form, ends in **-öz**:

- **Gololöz!**   Begone! (to one person)
- **Gololsöz!**   Begone! (to more than one person)
- **Lit binomöz!**   Light!

It was imperative that we return to Mavisbank, as soon as possible; firstly, because poor Mr. Downie needed Moral Management of the most urgent kind; secondly, because the great maw of the Dragon of Government required to be fed with the names and numbers of its servants; and thirdly, because the dresses and petticoats kindly loaned to me by Miss Eliza Ferguson were draughty, and I was in danger of catching a fever from the breezes which swept the Meadows of Edinburgh.

I turned to Mr. Downie and provided him with some examples of the three Imperative forms, which now constitute, for my Readers only,

Exercise 19.

- **Golobsös al stejen.**
- **Takolös dlenön.**
- **Takolöd böseti!**
- **Polel ogekomom – standolöz!**
- Make haste, for the policeman is angry!
- Please take this bag and run!
- Be a man, you weakest of persons!

And, when Mr. Downie finally understood my commands and allowed himself to be dragged off in the direction of the railway-station, we had reached the *Fin tidüpa balsekilid.*

*   *   *

Our journey back to Mavisbank was not one on which I care to reflect. Mr. Downie found it almost impossible to will one foot in front of another, and I continually had to issue Jussives and Optatives, in equal measure, to drive him back to the station. On the way, because of the man's tendency to stand thrusting his fists at the uncaring heavens and to howl his misery, we were several times apprehended by policemen and other uniformed agents, whose Imperatives did little to help matters. Once at Waverley, we found our train. I bundled Downie aboard an empty carriage, from which, as he chose, he could give full voice to his despair. I could no longer determine, nor did I greatly care, whether he was enraged at the loss of his wife or the loss of the Census forms, or just the Loss, Generally and Universally, of Everything. We howled and stamped our feet and apologised all the way to Eskbank – fortuitously, we howled most as we pulled in at the intervening stations, and thereby ensured that no other passenger would join us. At Eskbank, where we had to change to the local train, the people of Mid-Lothian are manifestly quite accustomed to disrupted fellow-passengers: they sat down equably, chatted amongst themselves, and nodded amicably at me, his nurse, as we careered beside the river to Polton.

The short walk from Polton Station to Mavisbank took but a few minutes, and, in the middle of the afternoon, we were safely back at our grand refuge. I should perhaps, for the sake of a little respite in these adventures, describe to you the House and its policies.

The House lies in a flat bay of land, backed to the west by a low hill surmounted by a copse of trees; in front of the House stretches a long and broad valley, bordered on the south by the fast-flowing River Esk and, beyond that, the ridge of a hill, and on the north, by another ridge. In this valley stand pleasant clumps of trees, and a long pond, or canal, is not far off. The House itself is elegant, having been erected almost three centuries previously, by a man named Adam – not, I should stress, any ancestor of Urquhart or Mrs. Bentzen; nor, indeed, any mouse. There is a square central building, flanked by two wings which stretch forward to either side, thereby creating a courtyard not quite enclosed. The gentlemen Residents occupy the southern wing and the ladies the northern wing. To the south, a pleasant wee fountain plays. To the northern side stands another building, which houses the stables, and various apartments for laundry and so on. Some way off, near the river, lies the circular, and vast, kitchen-garden, in which many of the Residents spend the daylight hours. Pleasant walks and drives cross the park-land, and there are drive-ways to no fewer than three gates – one in the east, one to the north, debouching into Loanhead, and one to the south-west, leading past the walled garden to the bridge that takes one to Polton Station. Up that road, Mr. Downie and I did come.

Mr. Deans and his colleagues quickly took Mr. Downie into their care, while I sought out Bosman and explained the nature of the catastrophe. To my very great surprise, he merely shrugged his shoulders and declared that, "we should do what we can"; a sentiment which I found calm and level-headed, a feature of the man that I had never expected: perhaps his few hours at Mavisbank would eventually wean him from the inanities of Esperanto and bring him back to Volapük? I was able, for the first time in almost two years, to sit with Bosman, without argument, and elaborate a plan of action. Which was this:

That we would gather those fellow-residents as were willing to assist, and ask them to complete new forms to replace those which had been destroyed. The forms would simply be blank pieces of paper, but Dr. Bosman would prompt on the details which had to be supplied. All that was necessary, he explained to me, was for him to collate the completed forms into his Enumerator's Book, which he would return, within a fortnight, to the District Registrar in Edinburgh. The original forms would also have to be returned, for checking, but Bosman surmised that a further, reasonable, accident could befall them, which would allay any suspicions.

The plan seemed full of promise, and we spoke with Mr. Deans, who agreed to arrange enough of the Residents to help us, and a room where we could manage and collect the work that was to be done. He was optimistic that all of the Residents, excepting two Imbeciles and one Idiot, could assist. There were, in addition to that, myself, Bosman and Urquhart. And, since the Residents would, by and large, be occupied, Mr. Deans and Miss Davidson kindly offered the assistance of their staff – a further dozen assorted attendants, nurses, table-maids and laundresses. In all, we might recruit the assistance of almost sixty people: with that, we might retrieve the Census of every citizen of Edinburgh, had it been lost to the predations of a battalion of numerologists!

The work was to be done on the morrow, Wednesday, for it was too late in the day to begin. Word was put round the rooms, and the House began to hum with the excitement promised for the following day. Even Urquhart, who had begun coaching Mrs. Bentzen to prepare a complete genealogy of her paternity, starting at Adam, was moved to voice some enthusiasm, infected, no doubt, by the general air of sanguinity.

In preparation for the great day's work ahead, Miss Davidson proudly offered to show me the Census Return which had been prepared, by herself, for all the Residents and servants of the Asylum. There were eighty-one people in all, divided as follows:

Matron and nurses		- *mäl*
Chief Attendant and staff		- *lul*
Cook and kitchen-staff		- *jöl*
Gardeners, lodge-keeper etc.		- *balsevel*
Residents		- *folselul*
Of whom,	Lunatics	- *kilselul*
	Imbeciles	- *tel*
	Idiots	- *bal*
	"Resting"	- *vel*

My eager examination of the details which Miss Davidson had so accurately completed, was interrupted by the arrival at the portals of Mavisbank House of Mr. William Gourlay, to collect these same Census forms. He was a nervous man, and seemed eager to push the forms into his case and be off, perhaps imagining that he would be attacked by slavering mad-men or witches screaming wild curses. The sight of Urquhart, who was stotting around the entrance-hall at that very moment, in high good humour and declaiming the various persons and tenses of the verb *lugön* – to lie, impart falsehoods – to an enchanted Mrs. Bentzen, very likely confirmed Mr. Gourlay's belief on that account.

We had an excellent supper at eight o'clock sharp, and rested well, and in the short time which Mr. Deans had after completing his duties, he quizzed me on the latest developments in Volapük. For my part, I congratulated him on his efforts to ensure that all Residents had a grounding in our Universal Language; he was modest enough in reply, stating that it was his opinion that the study of grammar was a great aid in calming people of a nervous disposition. An examination of the rules for declensions and cases required a discipline of mind which often and gradually led to a cure. I reflected on this for some time, since I had never considered that Volapük might act as a sedative to troubled minds; indeed, my experience had been quite the opposite to that, as the events of our recent Annual General Meeting had shown; and my students in Dysart, Newburgh, Peterhead, Macduff

and beyond, had scarcely been even-tempered or profitably intro-
spective, as a result of learning the basic rules of grammar. Perhaps, I
asked aloud, as we lay in the darkness, perhaps Volapük has a
soothing effect only on troubled minds, and the reverse effect on
minds untouched by Melancholia? Mr. Deans mumbled that this
was possible, and I was left alone to ponder the consequences of this
thought. Which I did until some distant clock-tower, in the world
outside, struck two, after which I slipped into a slumber.

*   *   *

The day of our venture dawned bright and fair, although there was a
touch of frost upon the ground outside. Once breakfast had been
served at nine o'clock, we gathered all of our volunteers in the
drawing-room of the House. Many of the Residents chose not to look
at each other or at us, but at the drawing-room ceiling, which was
made up of many magnificent blue panels of abstract design: it was as
a picture of Heaven. To this distracted throng, we explained the
purpose of the exercise. Which was to retrieve the information for the
Census of that part of Sciennes in Edinburgh, which had been lost in
an accident. Several people were curious as to the nature of the
accident, in particular Miss Wright and Mrs. Arthur, two gentle-
women of private means, whose imaginations were as unplumbed as
they were fecund, on the matter of "accidents". It took some persuasive talk to move on from this the discussion, for their suppositions
on malicious Acts of God, eruptions of the bubbling tar of Hell from
the sewers, fiery clouds of snarling demons, vats of vitriol, and self-
multiplying eyes, were of the greatest interest to many other Residents;
and there was a danger, in this distraction, of the aim and purpose of
the day being lost.

Apart from these interested parties, there were others in the room
whose daily routine was turned upside-down by our proposal; who,
wishing to spend their hours at the usual pastimes of embroidery or
the writing of letters, or in gardening and the care of sundry rabbits
and chickens, expressed their discontent in no uncertain terms at the
prospect of this unusual and unexpected chore that we proposed.

With considerable effort then, Dr. Bosman and I explained
adequately what had to be done; and the Residents, attendants and
nurses were provided with paper and pencils, along with as many of

the damaged Census forms as seemed fit; and were dispatched again to their day-rooms, there to labour diligently at their task. Each person had two or three house-holds to attend to; each attendant or nurse had four or five Residents to supervise, along with a short list of the house-numbers which required a Return. Bosman and I, along with Mr. Downie, who had greatly recovered his mind, thanks – I have no doubt – to an intense study of the Interrogative form; the three of us patrolled the rooms, issuing advice, checking verisimilitude, gathering up attempts which had failed, or were not suitable, encouraging, always using the Optative.

We came across Urquhart and Mrs. Bentzen, who had recruited into their cabal Mr. Adam Gordon, sheep-farmer of Banff-Shire with a great desire to raise his social standing; the three of them were excitedly engrossed in recording the full occupancy of Mr. Miller's house, which I knew to be entirely empty on the night in question, but had sufficient rooms to house perhaps one fifth of Urquhart's male pre-decessors. These rooms, however, were becoming over-crowded, as mediaeval ancestors of Mrs. Bentzen jostled elbow-to-elbow with Mr. Gordon's Regency fore-bears, while a "syndyasmion" of Ancient Greeks stumbled over each other on the upper floors. There seemed little point in directing the energies of these people to something less imaginative; so we passed on.

"Shall we include the guardian angels of these people?" was not a question I was readily permitted to ignore. It came from a retired Perth-Shire merchant, Mr. Black, who urged an answer to this. Ill-advisedly, I asked him what kinds of angels he had in mind? "The rabbits, of course. And the pigs, also." Startled, I asked him whether these angels had wings? Mr. Black looked at me as if I were an imbecile: "Surely – what else would they have, you ignorant townie?" I realised that the man meant no harm and promised to take advice on the matter from Dr. Bosman and Mr. Downie, once I had met up with them on our tour. Mr. Black was impatient, and insisted that he judged it best that the angels be recorded; but should he record "Guardian Angel" as a "Profession or Occupation", or as "Relation to Head of Family"; "Or should it be 'Condition as to Marriage', Mr. Justice? And is an Angel an 'Employer', or 'Employed', or 'Neither Employer Nor Employed, But Working On Own Account'? These questions are by no means clearly set out!" I hastened from the room, promising to consult with Mr. Downie as soon as I could find him.

The medical friends of Dr. Bosman were hard at their task. We had passed to them some of the original forms which had suffered from the stains of blood, a sight to which they would be readily accustomed, asking them to simply transcribe the details. Mr. Oliver, however, was outraged at the scandalous replies which had been given. "What manner of man," he demanded to know, "lives with six children, a wife, his mother, a brother-in-law, a servant, and two lodgers, in a house which barely has two rooms?" I tried to persuade him that a great many of our citizens lived in such conditions, or worse, and that this form merely described an unpleasant truth. But Oliver, who was possessed of a mis-placed sense of social justice, was having none of it. At the stroke of his pen, he gave the family another five good-sized rooms, having one or more windows; evicted the lodgers; and brought some comfort to the declining years of the house-holder's widowed mother, by resurrecting her late husband.

In various other bedrooms and communal apartments, we distributed blank forms. The Residents were each in their way of great interest to Alienism: Miss Dalton, a tall young lady of many natural charms, had to be distracted from her usual task of arguing with her right leg, in which pursuit she frequently exposed that limb to an immodest degree; fortunately, even Dr. Bosman had the good manners and courtesy to turn away when her shin was thus exposed. The gist of the young lady's difference of opinion with her leg appeared to be the latter's easy acquisition of knowledge of every type, which contrasted unflatteringly with Miss Dalton's own slowness of wit. Sensibly, we gave Miss Dalton a little-used building in Sylvan Place; she and her leg retired to debate the matter at some length.

Mrs. Forrest, a clergyman's widow of perhaps thirty years of age, had strong reason to believe that a particular resident of the New Town of Edinburgh was watching her innermost thoughts and secret desires. She named Mr. T— of Queen Street as the culprit, and advised anyone who would listen that she knew he had an Apparatus in his cellar which communicated, through secret passages beneath the earth, "such as I can easily show you!", with the cellars of Mavisbank House itself; and from there, through the stair-rods, into Mrs. Forrest's mind. Continually, she shook her head so as "to make the picture unclear" and thereby thwart the unspeakable Mr. T—. She avoided at all costs any proximity to the lower floors of Mavisbank, preferring to take the air, once a day, on the roof, behind its elegant stone balustrades. To Mrs. Forrest went a suspicious building in Sciennes.

In the men's apartments, we came across young Mr. Christie, who paced up and down in despair, clutching his hair as though he would tear it off. Mr. Todd, who accompanied me at that time, explained that some malevolent had switched Mr. Christie's head, after a rather inebriated night in the Assembly Rooms, with the head of someone "far cleverer". It was quite clear to me that, if this had indeed been the case, then the present owner of Mr. Christie's original head had made a very poor trade. Mr. Christie's overweening idea was that, because of this new head, he now suffered from "the Beguiling Disease of the Learned"; and he was in Mavisbank only until he was cured of that; or received his old head back. Pending this resolution, Mr. Christie was entrusted with a house of many rooms in Argyle Place.

Finally, we came across Miss Pailes, who, according to Mr. Deans, had been a promising student of Volapük. I was eager to meet Miss Pailes, but was alarmed to find that, in answer to any question posed, she would only say "*epükob*". After several fruitless attempts to strike up a sensible conversation, I handed her a pile of forms for three tenement buildings in Roseneath Terrace; to which she said, simply, "*opükobös*".

There was one lump of beer-sodden relics, those I had brought home concealed in my skirts, which had to be prised apart gently, so that we might make sense of them. Delicate work, which we had allotted to a reclusive collection of widows, seven in all, occupying an airy withdrawing-room in the north wing of the House. Because of the stench of stale beer, the ladies threw wide the windows of their room; then set to with energy. When we paid them a return visit later in the day, we found that they had managed to detach all the forms with exquisite care, almost as if they had been used to such a task all their lives. Unfortunately, every single form was quite illegible. A minute examination of the papers, conducted through a strong magnifying-glass by Mr. Glegg, the Aberdonian druggist, revealed some salient details, which allowed us to determine the addresses. From there, it was an easy matter for the widows to create happy house-holds; in which the house-holder was either dead, but had left his widow with a sound financial pension; or was present, and employed in a good and respectable profession; or had taken in his dear, old, widowed mother-in-law. I began to scent a rising tide of emotions as the ladies settled in to their tasks, and quickly vacated the room, leaving them in the care of the nurse, Mrs. Miller, herself a native of Newington, and particularly qualified to advise the ladies on the house-holds of that district.

The day went well. With a break for dinner at two o'clock, and a nap which all Residents were obliged to take for one hour in the day, we managed to complete all of the forms by the time cups of tea were served at five o'clock. It was perhaps well that the Proprietor of the Asylum, who lived in a great house in Edinburgh, had little interest in surveying his property with any regularity, for he might have debated with us the disruption caused to the routine of his paying guests. Miss Davidson and Mr. Deans took a very pragmatic view – that, if the Residents were happy and occupied, then there was no reason to curtail this unusual activity. Even Mrs. Kirkaldy, Kitchen Goddess, had no complaints, for the industry of the Residents had greatly diminished the number of "inappropriate" calls on her time for cups of tea; and, at dinner-time, and again at supper-time, everyone who had so laboured during the day had found a considerable and appreciative appetite.

Dr. Bosman, Mr. Downie and I then made a final round of the House, gathering up all of the documents, both old and improved; the former we consigned to the furnace which heated the water for the House; the latter we took into safe-keeping, for Dr. Bosman to begin to copy into his Enumerator's Book on the following day. (This book itself had not emerged unscathed from the Borough-lough Brewery Adventure, being spattered with the stains of beer and blood both; but some careful surgery by Mr. Pringle and his medical-bag, followed up by tender nursing from my friend Eliza, whose skirts I had been advised to continue wearing; soon had the book at the peak of health again.)

Solely in pursuit of academic advancement, I sat down to read through the new forms, for one of my special duties as a member of the *Volapükaklub Dugöfik*, apart from the literary obligations, was to record the names of professions and occupations, render them into

Volapük, and contact Paris with the results. You will recall similar duties being performed at Newburgh, where we discussed the "Derivation of Words", in respect of the machinery of industry. I made a list, from just the first pile of forms, of the following trades, occupations and professions, and began to work my way through them:

- Annuitant
- Bank-Agent
- Bar-maid
- Bleacher
- Book-Folder
- Boot and Shoe Machinist
- Boot-Closer Wife
- Clothier
- Confectioner
- Cook (Out of Employment)
- Coppersmith
- Daughter of Officer, Inland Revenue & Excise
- Dress-Maker
- Druggist's Assistant
- Engine Fitter
- Fallen Woman
- Forewoman, Chocolate Covering
- Fugitive Democrat
- General Dealer's Daughter
- General Drudge
- Generally Useful
- Groom's Wife
- Gutter
- House Carpenter
- Housemaid
- Idle-seater
- Jack-of-All-Trades
- Joiner's Machine-Man
- Laundress
- Laundress (Employing Six Women & Four Girls)
- Law Apprentice
- Life Insurance Agent
- Living on Private Means
- Lodging House-Keeper
- Mantle-Maker
- Midwife
- Milliner
- Paper-Worker
- Private Watchman
- Rag-Store Worker
- Scholar
- Shop-keeper, Fancy Goods
- Sick-Nurse
- Steam-Loom Weaver
- Surgeon's Wife
- Teacher
- Thread-Baller
- Tobacco Twister
- Unemployed Domestic Servant
- Warehouse Machinist
- Warehouse Woman
- Washerwoman

Here were some occupations which defied my analysis completely – I could not begin to imagine the skills of the people, their hours of work, the dangers they faced – and there was no prospect of translation; for some occupations, the simple words of Volapük could not do any justice; and the debilitating events of the past few days soon laid their heavy hand upon me. So that I succeeded in translating only a few; the eager student should use this as their Exercise 20; any and all answers to this exercise should be forwarded to the Author, for consideration by the *Volapükaklub Dugöfik*. Thus, with tired legs and red-rimmed eyes, I took myself to our room, which was adjacent to that of the Medical Residents, removed my many dresses, and retired to bed.

There I dreamed of bodice-makers and dry-salters, of esparto-weavers and stay-makers, of endless queues of spaiver-repairers and silk-winders and saufey-agents and surgical catgut trimmers, all clamouring to be recorded, all demanding a title for themselves in Volapük, and myself unable to satisfy even one of them. I awoke in a sweat, my blankets tight around my throat, knowing not what hour or what day it was. I sat up with a gasp. Mr. Deans called out softly to me, "Are you right, Mr. Justice? You have had a night-fright, I think?" I muttered something, and he soon fell back to sleep. For my part, I set my mind once more at ease, by working on a paper which was vital for the illumination of the Society.

Transactions IX: Sir Thomas Urquhart

Written late in the night of 7th April, 1891, at Mavisbank.

I was not greatly surprised to learn, at the Annual General Meeting of The Edinburgh Society for the Propagation of a Universal Language, that none had heard of Sir Thomas Urquhart, and that they were ignorant as to the year of his naturally-occurring death; for my fellow-members are, by and large, unencumbered by historical perspective, preferring the Present to the Past. First among these blinkered charlatans is, of course, Dr. Henry Bosman, his ignorance closely rivalled by that of Mr. Gunn.

So, for the continued education and further enlightenment of the members of the Edinburgh Society, I feel obliged to set down a brief sketch of the aberrant life, and richly verbose works, of Sir Thomas Urquhart.

He was born in 1611; he died in 1660. Between his birth and his death, he lived as an idle Gentleman, being the heir to the lands of Cromarty in the north of Scotland. As a young man, he fought for the King against the Covenanters of Scotland; and should thereby earn the undying contempt of the Common Man. For all his life, he was an unrepentant Royalist and Episcopalian. While he was yet young, his father fell into serious debt with his neighbours, among whom were Mr. Cuthbert of Draikies and Mr. Leslie of Findrassie; and, despite Thomas' unlawful imprisonment of his father, to stem the rising tide of debt, it appears that the family never regained its former possessions or stature thereafter.

During the Civil War in Britain, Urquhart fought on the side of the King; after the very laudable execution of King Charles I in 1649, Urquhart, together with his deluded friends, attempted an uprising in Inverness-Shire, but was roundly defeated by May of that year; and, as a result of further ill-conceived campaigns in the army of the younger Charles, found himself captured after the Battle of Worcester in September 1651.

During his captivity, Urquhart found little else to do but write: he undertook translations of "Gargantua", "Pantagruel" and "The Third

Book" by the eloquently uncouth French writer, François Rabelais; and these were published in 1653. It must grudgingly be admitted that these translations were faultless – Urquhart's linguistic skills cannot be doubted. In 1652, in an attempt to persuade the Commonwealth that he should have lands and wealth restored to him, he elaborated his thoughts for a useful and revolutionary Universal Language, as a contribution to Parliamentary Knowledge. In the year 1652, he published *Pantochronacon*, or *Promptuary of All Time*; later that same year, *Ekskubalauron*, or *Gold Extracted from the Dunghill*, and in 1653, *Logopandecteision* or *A Composite Treatise of Language*. But what these works demonstrated, as I have since discovered to my personal cost, is that Urquhart was a champion of the English Language, not the Universal; of the Classical Languages, not the Modern; a Vocabularian of the Learned, not of the Landless and Luckless. Despite his many thousands of words in these books, he did not once develop the Rules, the Grammar, the Syntax, nor the Vocabulary for his Universal Language.

But his attempts to avoid just retribution for his past loyalties were finally in vain, for he was exiled shortly afterwards to the Netherlands, dying there in 1660, in a fit of excessive amusement after hearing of the ill-advised restoration of Charles II to the throne.

This, alas, was the man on whom, quite without intention, I stumbled that inclement night in Cromarty, amidst the ruins that remained of his family estates. At first I judged it to be an opportune and fortuitous meeting, one that promised the recruitment to my cause of the weighty inspiration of a great and admired intellect. But, no sooner had we set out southwards on our journey, than I began to realise that the dead-weight of this man's past prevents him from having a clear view of the present. Being dead has not in the least improved his attitude to the gentler sex, nor his aristocratic attitude to learning, nor his profligacy with money. His extreme age cannot excuse his vices. Urquhart is, in short, a disreputable man, who, despite his contribution to Learning, has long out-lived his usefulness to the Common Good.

Katel Balsetelid, the Twelfth Chapter:
The Conditional, the Conjunctive and the Potential

"Pölüdobsöx"

Just as soon as the Residents had been served, and had variously consumed, their breakfasts, Bosman arranged himself for work. In the first instance, this required the removal of his person from the vicinity of his erstwhile colleagues Messrs. Oliver, Pringle and Moore. "There must be no juvenile interruption to the work of the State," he declaimed, rather fatuously given the criminal nature of what he was about to engage in. A small room was found for him, sequestered in a quiet corner of the central building, and here, with the piles of paper and with his pen, with his ink-bottle and with his empty Census Book, with an immense pile of cigarettes and a bucket for their ashes, he began on his great work. Thinking to extend an olive-branch, after all that we had passed through together, I tracked him down towards ten o'clock, and suggested that I might help him. "No, sir!" was the flat answer. Perhaps I could read out the names from each sheet, to facilitate their transcription in to the record? "No, sir!" was again the uncompromising response, as one might have expected from an Esperantist. Could I fill his pen, replenish his store of cigarettes, or procure him a cup of tea? "No, sir, you shall do no such thing!" exclaimed Bosman. "Have you not done enough to me, that you hound me thus?"

Seeing that there was little I could do, I closed the door to his small office, and marked it with white chalk, a cross, being the simplest sign that people should avoid it. Unfortunately, this had the effect of attracting the attention of a number of individuals, clergymen and lay-persons alike, who stood before the door and speculated on the nature of the prohibition. Within a minute, Bosman had burst from the room like a jack-in-the-box, pouring foul smoke upon the people without, denounced the speculators as a "band of imbeciles", and demanding that they pass on their way. All bar the Reverend Thomson did so, this gentleman arguing with Bosman that "he should know better" – the term "imbecile" not applying to Respectable Lunatics, of whatever gender. A struggle then ensued, as Bosman advanced, fists flying, and it was only the forceful and calm intervention of Mr. Deans and his colleagues, bundling the Reverend away, that prevented blood-shed. I crept up to Bosman's closed door, and could hear him muttering and coughing quietly inside; but thought it best not to disturb him, and went about my business.

I came across Mr. Downie in one of the several corridors of the House. He seemed to have recovered fully from the excitements and upsets of the previous two days. But, when I asked him if he wished to assist Bosman's efforts, he became agitated, pulled his hair into vertiginous strands, and began to stammer. "Inappropriate . . . apologies . . . a servant of . . . inappropriate . . . my standing . . . " he repeated, over and over, failing completely and ungrammatically to complete his sentences.

Finding myself idle, I took myself down to see Mrs. Kirkaldy, the cook, and spent a pleasant morning sampling the various pots and oven-bound trays which she supervised. I had noticed from the Census forms for Mavisbank, that she claimed to speak the Gaelic tongue; and I asked her about this as, for a respite at eleven o'clock, we settled down to a large pot of tea and a pile of shortbread which could have fed all of the linguists in Babel. She was kind enough to provide me with some phrases in the Gaelic tongue, which I scribbled down, in the hope of rendering either into English or, more directly, into Volapük. I was curious that a woman born in Perth-Shire only forty years previously, should still have the Gaelic; but she advised me that she had it from her parents. "Why, Mr. Justice!" she exclaimed. "Even Miss Davidson, who is a native of Roxburgh-Shire, has the Gaelic, and she just as old as myself! It would only be in the great cities that the English has made its mark." I found this to be a curious remark, betraying a rather rusticated view of life in our cities, but I let it pass.

When Mrs. Kirkaldy went back to beating her pan lids and shrieking at her army of kitchen-maids, I sat in a corner of the warm kitchen and considered more deeply the questions of the Census – "Gaelic or G. & E.", it asked baldly. But why should we only be interested in whether a person had the Gaelic or English – why not, for example, Manx, Erse, French, German, Swedish, Volapük – good heavens! why not, indeed, Esperanto? What about those who had neither English or Gaelic?

What a fine picture of the Nation would be revealed if such questions were asked, up and down the land. When the number of tongues which are spoken within the shores became known, then people would understand the desperate need for a Common Language. Perhaps – and it was too late for this now, but perhaps ten years hence – all of the questions which appear on the Census might be asked, and answered in – Volapük. There would be no room for doubt, no latitude for prevarication, no possible mis-interpretation.

As thus my thoughts on Volapük and the recent Census developed, so did my appetite for dinner. The tumult in the kitchen increased dramatically as we approached the climactic dinner-hour of two o'clock. Not wishing to venture out towards the door; for that would involve considerable danger of entanglement with one of the dervishes who now flew back and forth between range and sink and cupboards, carrying sizzling pans of fat, kettles of boiling water, and great arms-full of greens; I withdrew further into my corner and considered my position. Fortunately, I did not have to spend a great deal of my valuable time on this question, for the dinner-bell was rung, and I was invited to eat.

We congregated around a number of tables in the main room of the House. Bosman, at the call of the bell, had emerged from his cell and looked considerably the worse for his experience. His eyes were wild, and his hair dishevelled, and he had no fewer than two cigarettes blazing, one in each hand, which he applied alternately to his mouth. His tie was loosened, and – all in all – his appearance excited the distaste of a large number of the Residents. I decided to shun him, and sat down at a table occupied by a number of females, including a tall and stately-looking woman. We introduced ourselves. The lady who had attracted my attention was Miss Elizabeth Smyth; her accent betrayed her Irish origins, even before she launched into an exact definition of her age ("fifty-seven"), her place of birth ("Cork"), her marital status ("single, like Judith" – a remark which she gave me little time to consider), and her interests, the numbering of which lasted through the serving, supping and removal of the broth, and which evidently included most of the interests of Mankind. It was evident that *à-la-mode* fashion was not, however, one of her interests: she was arrayed in a pair of trousers which had clearly been filched from a male of considerable proportions, a tight waistcoat with a gold chain, cravat and – although her female companions demanded that she remove it at the dinner-table – a sturdy bowler-hat of grey felt. In short, she was dressed rather handsomely as a man. Her voice was strong, and her opinions stronger. She demanded to know my business in "her" house, and where I slept, and whether I meant to stay for very long – "If you do, I will demand tribute," she insisted, fumbling under the table at my skirt, gripping my thigh firmly and rather impertinently. I answered as best I could, aware of the potential pitfalls of a mis-directed response. When she learned that I was, by trade, a repairer of organs, she vowed eternal friendship, "and I don't care who knows it, Mrs. Mitchell!" she bellowed at a small, timid woman, who formed one of our party. Mrs. Mitchell nodded her head vigorously, and bent her head over her scrambled eggs. Miss Smyth refused the eggs, denouncing the serving-girl for her boldness – "I have no wish to be turned into a chicken, young woman!" she proclaimed grandly – and demanded potatoes instead.

*   *   *

When our dinner was over, Miss Smyth insisted that we take a quiet stroll in the policies of Mavisbank, so that she could learn all about me. The stroll which I was promised was far from quiet, for my companion grabbed my hand, then set off at a roaring pace, her trousers and coat, my skirts and shawl, flapping in the breeze. We made for the river. Within the first two hundred yards, I had yielded up all the information which was mine to give about my life and my hopes. Very swiftly, therefore, we came to Volapük and the Universal Languages. To my chagrin, Miss Smyth had a very poor estimate of any Universal Language.

"There's no such thing, Mr. Justice," was her stated opinion. "Rubbish! You cannot just sweep away the languages of the world and replace them with one!"

I begged to differ with her.

"Are you a Revolutionary?" she demanded outright, stopping to examine me carefully. "Out with it!"

I was not sure whether to answer as I thought she might like, or whether to answer as I thought I might like. I could certainly not find an accurate answer. "Yes, I think I am," I confessed. "Or was, perhaps. I am no longer sure." And, in truth, after the events of the past week, I could no longer tell whether what I had desired over the years – which was now partly achieved – was the right thing for which to strive.

"Was, is, will be," was her assessment. "Never mind! I like a revolutionary, Mr. Justice. There are not enough of them about. Yes, not even of those who would conceal it. So," she continued, striding out across the water-meadow down by the River Esk, "you would impose one language over all others? Does that not strike you as an oppression?"

I thought that it did not, as long as all men and women were in favour of it.

"Tell me about your Volapük, then, Mr. Justice. I have heard that Mr. Deans is a keen advocate, but never thought to listen to what he had to say. Tell me about its words, its vocabulary. Is it French, English, German, Spanish?"

"For the most part," I replied, "it is based on English words, with a sprinkling of German and French, but—"

Miss Smyth interrupted me with an explosive snort. "There you have it – you propose to impose a language which is based on the words of a nation of oppressors! What manner of revolution is that, Mr. Justice? What about the Indians, the Africans, the Chinese, all those people of the South Sea Islands, who have never heard a word of English, or French, or German in their lives? How will they learn your Universal Language?"

This was not a question to which I had a ready answer; and I certainly could not provide one now, as we reached a bend in the river under the brow of the hill, beyond which, so I was advised by my guide, lay the Garden of Earthly Delights, known by mere sinners under the appellation "Lasswade".

"Mr. Justice," she said, seating herself on a bench which overlooked the busy river, "I do not think you are an innocent. But consider this. Sit down, man!" she ordered, and made a lunge for my arm, to pull me beside her; having succeeded, she wrapped her right arm around my left one, and held on tightly. "Consider the language of the Gaels. It was once, I believe, the *lingua franca* of much of Scotland, and easily understood in Wales, Ireland, Cornwall and other places too. But, with the encroachment of soldiers, and then of industry and commerce into even the most backward of places, the old language is being pushed out and replaced. That is ever the way

– where armies march, a foreign language will follow. The Romans brought Latin, the Saxons brought German, the Normans brought French, each language imposed by the sword. No doubt the British Empire is bringing English to the wildest territories of Canada, Africa and India, extinguishing the native tongues and native lives as it goes."

I took issue with this. "But here is one thing which will distinguish Volapük from any other language: that it would not be brought in the baggage-train of a conquering army of warriors, but rather as the herald and advance-guard of peaceful Democrats and Socialists!"

"Piss, Mr. Justice! Piss and pass the pail!" Miss Smyth slapped my thigh, quite strongly, and paid no attention to my protest. "What nonsense! Democrats and Socialists do not go around imposing the language of Empires upon other nations. Do they?"

I supposed that they did not, and attempted to divert her attention by asking her if she could explain to me the difficulties of the grammar of Gaelic. What were the Cases and the Tenses and the Declensions? What of the Persons and the Genders? Did Gaelic and the ancient languages even possess such concepts, in the same way as Latin or Volapük? She had no idea, expressed her view that it was below her station to consider the matter; and continued her previous argument.

"Tell me: when did a language ever come in advance of a conqueror? When?" She gave me a firm shake, which rattled my teeth. "A new language may come after an invasion, or after a revolution, perhaps. But a new government, or new era, will never arise from a new language. You see the arse, Mr. Justice, before you see the face!"

I confess that Miss Smyth asked questions which had occasionally come at me in the early hours of a sleepless night. I had always comforted myself with the thought that the vocabulary would "sort itself out" as nations settled down to fraternal co-operation and peaceful relations. But, as Miss Smyth said, it all had to begin somewhere. And why should it begin with the language of con–querors?

As she rattled on in this vein, I scarcely listened to her. Instead, I began to reflect on the very purpose and inner life of Language. Why choose one word in preference to another – why "dog" and not "*hund*" nor "*chien*" nor "*perro*", nor all the many words for the domesticated canine, surely a creature whose name changes in a hundred different languages? My brief encounter with Mr. Kobayashi had already suggested a problem in this respect. And in a country whose citizens display dozens of types of insanity and nervous illness, perhaps there are dozens of words for "mad", each word distinguishing the ailment as something useful or to be avoided, something morbid or benign, and penetrating to its inner workings. One word for "madness" in a Universal Language just would not suffice in that country; of course, there might only be a single, unvarying, word for "sanity" in that same country; but that is no compensation. And would one word for "October", in a French Republican country or an Antipodean colony or in the language of Friockheim, contain sufficient meaning, if reduced to "the tenth month"? For the Republican, a time of vintage; for the New Zealander, sowing-time; for the man of Angus, the early blasts of winter. If a Universal Language failed to provide sufficient variations in its vocabulary, to reflect the shades of meaning, then the language of such countries would be all the poorer. And the World, too, as a result, for are not the riches of the world the accumulations of wealth of all its nations?

I was jerked from my consideration of the Philosophy of Language by another stinging blow to the thigh, as Miss Smyth brought me back to a state of attentiveness.

"You are not even listening to me, sir!" she exclaimed. "Do you really care about what happens to the speech of Hindoos, of Mussulmen, of Eskimos and Bushmen? Do you care about the fate of Gaelic? Do you care that, in your life-time, it may be thoroughly extinguished in your native land, and replaced with the English?"

"Or with Volapük?" I hazarded.

"Piss and pass the pail! Nonsense, man, and you know it!" The woman rounded on me and held my arm in a vice-like grip. "Language, sir, is a means of Rule, an instrument of Power, a weapon of Oppression, and don't you think for one moment that it is anything else! The language which must be spoken is the language of the King, the Government; those who cannot speak it will be the losers. By using every shade and nuance of language, the rulers can shut out the people from understanding and debate. The longer the word, the longer the weapon of oppression!"

I found the courage to protest: "But Volapük is designed precisely to put paid to the oppression of archaic language and the oppression of language: its vocabulary is designed to be simple!"

"Simple for whom, Mr. Justice?" asked Miss Smyth, relaxing her grip a little, but hooking her boots round the back of my ankles so that I might not flee. "Simple for whom? The speakers of English and German, maybe. But not the greater part of the creatures that walk on two legs upon this earth. Not them!"

We sat in silence for several minutes, Miss Smyth slipping into a heavy-breathed distraction. Suddenly, she turned to me: "Come with me, I believe we have severe business to transact, you in your skirts and I in my trousers. Severe business indeed, oh yes!" She dragged me by the arm, striding at a great speed towards the House. Fortunately for my honour, and perhaps for the preservation of my physical well-being, we were intercepted as we reached the portals of the residence, by the nurses Miss Ferguson and Miss McGarrie, two young ladies who prised me away from Miss Smyth, and suggested she have a rest. Protesting that she needed no rest, merely a "lengthy discussion on some matters of importance with this virile and potent philosopher", she was nevertheless led away to her room, leaving me sweating from the haste of our return, and confused as to the nature of Universal Language. I reminded myself that I was as sane as any man in Scotland, and that Miss Smyth was a lunatic; but somehow these classifications of illness and health were not tangible in this week of my life.

I spent the remainder of the day sitting by the splashing fountain, in consideration of the complexities of the languages of other nations and the austere simplicity of Volapük. I had, in recent days, been questioned on whether Volapük could adequately reflect poetry or humour. I had been asked whether even the Universal Language might not be just another sword wielded by the old oppressors of Europe. I had now to ask myself whether all that a man or woman might wish to do with words was capable of expression in a single language alone. And finally, as the day drew to a chilly close, I had to choose between a light supper of herring and potatoes, or a heavier meal of beef. I chose the lighter meal, for we were promised that evening the "Weekly Dance", an event which inspired the greatest excitement among the Residents, and which could not be enjoyed after too heavy a meal.

At nine o'clock, we assembled in our finery, a more dazzling collection of the cream of society, perhaps, than had been seen for years in that valley. Mrs. Bentzen was to play the piano, accompanied by a rather disreputable fiddler of Loanhead. Dr. Bosman had been persuaded to brush his hair, and to put by, for a moment, his infernal cigarettes. Urquhart was, as one might have expected, gregarious to a fault; but it must be admitted that his elegance of foot in the dances was very fine. Miss Smyth insisted on partnering me several times, using the opportunity to issue outrageous promises of an "earnest debate" in my ear. A great deal of sweat and heat was expended over the course of fifty minutes, Mrs. Bentzen and her wild-eyed accompanist struck many wrong notes; and all, except for Mr. Cordiner, who took exception to the loudness, were delighted. Then we washed, and retired to bed.

*   *   *

On the following day, which was a Thursday, I offered my services once more to Bosman, who, once more, was as rude as any Esperantist could be, blowing the smoke from his cigarette in my eyes, and slamming in my face the door of his small room. Before he did so, however, I had time to notice that he was not a tidy man – papers were strewn about all over the floor, crumpled pages torn from his ledger, stained with great blots of ink, lay in piles, and the receptacle for ashes over-flowed already with the ends of cigarettes and used matches. The air stank horribly, since the tiny sky-light which afforded illumination was tightly closed. As they passed, Residents recoiled from the miasma which leaked from the room, and they voiced their undisguised outrage.

Rejected by Bosman, I was left alone. I made sure not to stray into the path of Miss Smyth. But I need not have worried: turning a corner, I was knocked abruptly to one side as she came from the opposite direction at great velocity and mass. She gave me barely a glance, shouted "Piss and pass the pail, Mr. Volapük!" over her shoulder, and hastened off, her hob-nailed boots tapping powerfully on the wooden floor, in severe philosophical pursuit – as it seemed to me – of the retired Aberdonian apothecary, Mr. Glegg.

It was on this morning that I began to take stock of my situation. I was in no easy position, thanks to Bosman's foolishness, and the breach of contract by Urquhart. I had been obliged to interpret the

Standing Orders of the Edinburgh Society in a way which could –
by adversaries – be debated in the Courts; I had been forced to
masquerade as a woman, and take part in an action which – although,
in logic, to the advantage of the Government of Great Britain – might
be understood wrongly by the agents of that same Government;
and now was associated with an enterprise which might qualify Mr.
Downie and Dr. Bosman for transportation to the Colonies or hard
labour in Peterhead. It was not an easy position in which to find
myself. As if that were not enough, my obligations were to my trade as
much as to the propagation of Volapük, and I was contracted to
appear in Fern in Forfar-Shire, on the Monday following, and subsequently in the towns of Tannadice, Kirriemuir, Meigle and Alyth
before the end of the month. And I was no Mr. Carnegie who might
sustain himself from accumulated riches for some adventure in Mid-
Lothian! Thus, it was my duty to bring these present matters to a safe
conclusion, and return to my life.

Many of these thoughts passed through my mind as I stood gazing
out upon the park of the House, with its vista of grass and lake and
woodland, and its old tower a graceful sentinel at the top of the hill far
in the distance.

A familiar voice roused me from my ruminations.

"*Memento mori*, Mr. Justice, *memento mori!*" I received a sharp poke
on the back from some pointed object, and knew, before I turned
round, that I was in the presence of Urquhart. I looked at him coolly.

"You have abandoned your research into genealogy, then?" I
enquired, as frostily as I could.

He giggled, and scratched at the tufts of hair on his chin. "I have
abandoned Mistress Bentzen in contemplation of the many Houses of
Attica, so that she might consider the most favourable lineage for her
friend Mrs. French. Mrs. French is drollastic." He looked me up and
down. "But you, sir, you have surely alternated your appearance?" He
leered at me. "Alas, my heart is for another, else I might take you for a
fair maid to woo, in some secluded bower!"

I turned my back on this old fool, and determined to be away into
Edinburgh as soon as I could arrange it.

"Ah, a demure woman – a stirring sight!" he exclaimed, determined
to provoke me with his ill-mannered attentions. I rounded on him,
catching him by surprise and over-throwing him completely. He lay

on the floor, whimpering that an old man should not be treated in this way.

"Old?" I exclaimed. "Old? You are not old, you are DEAD, Urquhart, quite dead!"

"Dead, mayhap, but not as dead as you, I'll wager, Mr. Justice. Who, after all, will memorialise you when you have traversed the Styx? Who, when you are as desiccate and climacteric as I am, will irrupt into your tomb and subscribe their name to a contract such as ours?" Urquhart looked at me, with a sneer upon his cracked lips.

I was wrath. "A contract – yes, Urquhart, I'm glad that you mention that; for you have cheaply and with no honour – you have broken our contract, have you not? A contract is a contract, is it not?"

Urquhart looked at me from the floor, with hurt in his eyes and the hint of a pout to his horrible lips. At length, seeing that he would get no sympathy from me, he struggled to his feet, and dusted himself down.

"I can take a beating from a bawd," he declared. "Your complaint, sir, that I have broken a contract: let yourself be reminded, you Surquedist, that our contract was founded on *Verständnis* and on *agréments*! A contract, sir, is a contract, and a whole host of other words besides! And, in any event, contracts are made to be broken, else why should we need contracts?" I let these sophisms pass me by, for they deserved only my contempt. Recognising that he made no good impression on me, he shrugged his shoulders.

"Perhaps I can make recompense by writing some song or poem, or epic tale in verse, in any language of your choosing? French? Spanish? German? Italian? I can do them all."

I thought that I could get rid of him, and nodded. Enthusiastically, he hobbled round me, leaning on his stick.

"A romance of Tristan and Iseult? A tale of unfortunate woe like that of the young lord, Syphilis? Of knights and chivalry, a tale of the Count of Berlichingen? What will you have, Mr. Justice – I can do them all, and you will be as if transported!"

I did not doubt it. But I asked him only for a short verse in Volapük, "the Universal Language". Five lines only, in the Limerick style. Urquhart claimed not to have heard of a Limerick, so I repeated an innocent one which I had heard on my travels in the northern counties:

> "There was a young dame of Fortrose,

In whose shoes there never were bows;
For whenever she bent o'er,
Her corsage hid the floor,
And shut off the view to her toes."

I watched Urquhart listen very carefully to this, and was astonished when I did not hear him laugh or giggle, nor saw any knowing smile illuminate his leathery face. Instead, he thought for several seconds, then stated:

"A Limerick, then, consistent of five lines, rhyming *a-a-b-b-a*; the dominant metre is anapaestic, with two feet in the third and fourth lines, and three feet in the remainder. Am I correct?"

I had no idea whether he was correct or not, having little grounding in the analysis of metre. I was merely astonished at his erudition. And disappointed the next moment, when he howled with laughter, and smacked me right and left across my unprotected ankles with his stick.

"Oh, you fell for my dissembling, Mr. Justice!" he roared. "Anapaestic metre! When you thought I would perchance be aroused by the thaumatics of some wench's corsage? But wait! I will oblige you:

"When I was last in Culbokie,
I offered two maidens – "

"Stop!" I chastised him. "No more! Do as you have promised, do it in Volapük, and leave me alone until you are done!"

"Oh, but you would not let an old gentleman sit alone in this house of Bedlam," he whined, twisting the cloth of my skirts in his bony hand. "It is not safe for me here! Surely you can trust me to keep my word, if I promise not to disturb the profound waters of your deliberations?"

I thought I detected sarcasm in his voice, but could find none in his watery eyes; so I yielded and told him he could accompany me. In some petty fit of remorse, he handed me the cloak of CödelYagöl, which, in a magnanimous fit of forgiveness, I pulled around my shoulders. We set off. As we came down the stair-case, I could hear Urquhart's stick already beating out the metre of the Limerick, doubtless anapaestic, accompanied by mumbled words of Volapük.

When we came out into the cool Spring air, I was startled to find that the landscape had changed subtly. The lake, or pond, which lay some hundred yards from the front of the House, had been transformed into a long and narrow waterway, something akin to a canal or one of those formal basins which I had seen on my travels in France. It was flanked on both sides by willow-trees. Urquhart and I walked down a long straight road which led to the near end of this stretch of water. When we arrived at the edge, which was built solidly of brick-work, we found that a number of flat-bottomed boats were tied to posts there.

"This reminds me sorely of the Italian palaces," said Urquhart with a sigh, which appeared for once not designed to evoke my sympathies. "Will you take me upon the waters?" he asked me, as near to meek as I had yet seen him. In return for meeting his request, I advised Urquhart that I would engage him in

Tidüp balsefolid – The Conditional, Conjunctive and Potential. He nodded courteously, but I very much doubted whether he listened to anything I had to teach him. And so we set out upon the endless stretch of water, in that morning as calm as a mirror, and as long as any man might want it to be. As we sailed peacefully among the weeds and the ducks, I instructed Urquhart.

The Conditional mood expresses something not as actually occurring, but as what "would" or "might" be, under a certain supposition. The Conjunctive is the mood which expresses this supposition, preceded by **if**, "if". Thus, in the phrase, "if I were alone, I would be happy", the Conjunctive is "if I were", and the Conditional "I would be". If The Edinburgh Society for the Propagation of a Universal Language were composed of honest students and not of gossips, wastrels and traitors, then the cause of Volapük would be won.

Additionally, there is the Potential mood, which is expressed in the phrase "might possibly" – "I might possibly return to my former life".

The life of most men and women is but a lengthy passage of Conditional, Conjunctive and Potential moods, sprinkled here and there with the Perfect and the Pluperfect tenses. Just consider the Annual General Meeting, and how the Ship of Potentiality broke open upon the Reefs of Actuality.

Each of these three moods is expressed by different verb-endings in Volapük:

- The Conditional mood places a suffix of **-öv** at the end of the imperfect or pluperfect form of the verb.

* The Conjunctive mood places a suffix of **-la** at the end of the same tense of the verb. Pay attention: not **-li**, which is the Interrogative form, as you will recall from Lesson Nine, but **-la**.
* The Potential mood takes a suffix of **-öx**, usually to the present tense.

Thus:

* "If I were alone, I would be happy", is translated
  if äbinob-la soalik, äbinoböv beatik.
* "I would have been happy, if I had been alone", becomes
  ibinoböv beatik, if ibinob-la soalik.
* "I might possibly be happy, if I were alone", becomes
  binoböx beatik, if binob-la soalik.

As our lesson progressed, so our small boat glided easily and smoothly across the water, creating barely a ripple behind us. To drive the boat forward, I was obliged to stand on a small platform at the rear, holding a long wooden pole, which I drove into the mud periodically, and effected a thrust forwards. Urquhart, meanwhile, was perched on a rather narrow seat at my feet, trailing his fingers in the passing water, and, for once, quite silent.

At the far, or eastern, end of the water-way, we ran aground among reeds, chasing ducks out into the open. We had stuck fast upon some sort of mud-bank, barely twenty feet short of our goal, and I was obliged to ask Urquhart to step into the water to push us free. Which, of course, he refused to do, claiming that it was neither right nor proper for a gentleman of his years and honour to become irriguous. I asked him if he thought he would catch a fever and die? To which he gave no direct response, preferring rather to exercise his mastery of the Conjunctive and Conditional in a loud voice, with his hands clamped over his ears: "*if äbinob-la vatik, ädeiloböv*, if I were to get wet, I would die; *äbinoböv nevatik, if äblibob-la in bot*, I would be dry, if I stayed in the boat". I suggested to him that the Potential mood might be employed, were he not to do as I asked (*falolöx*, you might possibly fall in), but it did not shift him from his seat, where he remained, gripping the sides of the boat as I struggled to free it from the mud.

After several minutes of this, I stopped my struggles, and sat down on my platform. It was a fine day, and, although the mists of the morning had not yet cleared from the valley, still obscuring the tops of the trees around and all but the highest part of the House, several hundred yards to the west, the sun bathed this end of the canal and made us warm. I insisted that Urquhart, if he was unwilling to assist our release, should at least undertake

Exercise 21.
- **Älöfoböv mani at, if äbinom-la nestupikum.**
- **If no äbinos-la so pöligik, älöfoböv gegolön domi obik in zif.**
- **Pölüdobsöx.**
- This book would be useful to you if you should wish to study the language of Volapük.
- If you had helped, I would have forgiven you.

in which, as usual, he proved himself quite capable.

* * *

I found that, under the warm sun and sedated by the soothing sound of the tiny ripples in the lake and the arguing of the ducks, I had fallen asleep; and was quite startled to receive a poke in the leg from Urquhart, summoning me back to consciousness.

"Yonder," he said, pointing in the direction of the bank. "A young gentleman desirous of conversation."

I looked over and saw a tall man, dressed in a white suit, whom I recognised dimly as one of the Residents.

"Ahoy, there!" he was shouting, as if we were sailors upon the Main, and he the Commodore of a naval frigate. "Are you in need of assistance?"

I confessed that we were; immediately, the man removed his boots, rolled up the ends of his trousers above his knees, and waded into the water, which barely topped his shins. Within a moment, he had given us a mighty push, and we were free from the shallows, and adrift again upon the lake. I managed to turn the boat so that, once more, we faced the House. I thanked our rescuer, who introduced himself as Mr. Burnie, some-time Architect, Surveyor and Innovator, of Edinburgh.

As we accompanied each other along the canal, Urquhart and I on our shallow boat, Mr. Burnie wading through the water, carrying his boots and socks in the left hand, with his hat held on his head by his right, lest it fall into the water, we conversed on matters of common interest. It seems that Mr. Burnie had spent the early hours of the morning tramping around the grounds, increasing his collection of horse-shoes. "I have many of them, madam, which you may verify for yourself, should you choose to come to my room. I have them from all across the land – the greatly-coveted Ayr-Shire horse-shoe, the 'Proud Argyll', the crude Wigtown-Shire plough-shoe, even the rare Rothesay Fifteen-Nail Special!" He looked at me in triumph, and I expressed some words of uneasy admiration. "And from these parts, of course, I have the brass shoes favoured by the men of the powder-mills. Two hundred and seventy-three shoes I have in all, madam, polished and labelled, every one. But," he went on, abruptly changing tack, "what of the doo-cot, up yonder?" He risked a tumble into the water by turning back to face the direction from which he approached us, and waved grandly towards the squat tower on the high horizon, walking backwards the while. "A clever design, madam, and most elegant. The work of William Adam himself, if I might risk a con-jecture." We regarded it in all its fine points. "Simplicity, rusticity, elegance of an under-stated nature, a doo-cot of considerable majesty, in my professional opinion." He turned back to us and laid a hand upon the sleeve of my gown. "But it is not that I wished to show you, madam. I believe I have an invention which may help you."

I was greatly surprised at this suggestion, having had no dealings with the man, and unclear as to what invention might be of use to me. One which would facilitate my easy departure from Mavisbank would have been welcome, but I fancied that this was not what he had in mind. I halted my poling, and we glided to a halt at the mid-point of the canal. Mr. Burnie looked around himself vaguely, and proposed that we "cast anchor" by the northern bank, which we duly did, with some difficulty in navigation, in which matter Urquhart proved him-self entirely unhelpful.

"I have, sir and madam," whispered Mr. Burnie confidentially, once we were safely wedged in mud at the side of the canal, and he himself was seated comfortably upon the stump of a tree, "I have plans of an advanced nature for an engine which will translate from one language into another. I call it 'Burnie's Beneficial Translating Engine' or the

'Metamorphologikon', and—"

I begged to interrupt him. "Mr. Burnie, I fear that I have no great interest in a machine which translates, for my goal is far higher than that – it is to do away entirely with the need for anyone – or anything – to translate from one language to another. You should know that the Universal Language will be spoken by all, in a day not too far removed in the Future."

Mr. Burnie looked at me knowingly. "But you will concede, Mrs. Justice, that, until that day dawns, it would be most useful to be able to translate from – let us say – French into Volapük, or English into Volapük, and from Volapük into Chinese, or Volapük into Croatian? Thereby allowing a man to translate from English into Croatian?"

I conceded his point, not wishing to seem churlish.

"Well, then," he continued, reaching into his coat-pocket and extracting a large wad of crumpled papers, which he spread out on his knees; licking the tips of his fingers, he turned the papers one by one, to show me that they were entirely covered in sketches, drawings, mathematical calculations, long passages, and other signifying marks. He thumbed his way thus through some fifty or sixty pages, in silence, and then, looking at me slyly and winking, he pushed the whole bundle back into his pocket.

"That, madam, is the entirety of Burnie's Beneficial Translating Engine or Metamorphologikon, for which I will take out a patent next month, and the peoples of the world will see then how their communicating is facilitated. There will be a Metamorphologikon in every hall of Government, and one in every large Stock Exchange or Bourse. People will speak unto People, Man unto Man, and each will be understood by everyone. Perhaps," he glanced at me in what I perceived to be a crafty manner, "perhaps the Volapük Academy might wish to purchase one or two exemplars?"

I prevaricated on this proposal, indicating that I would need to be shown how it worked. I did not discount the suggestion, however, since the machine, if it functioned, might yet prove of value, and, if that were the case, I would wish to be its Proposer in the International Movement.

"How it works, madam?" asked Mr. Burnie, scratching his chin. "My, but you are a cautious negotiator, to be sure!" He brightened up. "But I admire caution. After all, you scarcely know me, nor yet my reputation as an Innovator. I will therefore give you an outline of how it might work:

"First of all, the Metamorphologikon will be no bigger than a large type-writer. It will work simply by relating two separate batteries, or 'linguapiles'. Each battery will contain the basic rules of grammar and a basic vocabulary for any one language which might be translated. Then – one simply pulls out two levers, corresponding to the languages to be put in and to be put out; uses the keys to form the word which is to be translated; engages the power of the electrical mechanisms; and – hoorah! – the translation will immediately appear on a roll of paper which has previously been inserted! Then one forms the next word with the keys, and the same will happen. And so on, until all words have been formed, and translated. Astounding, but nevertheless efficient! I hazard that one might translate – oh, let us say? Herr Schiller's *Die Räuber* – in less than a day!"

Mr. Burnie looked at me, bursting with pride, and continued.

"And, madam, you will be pleased to know that the Metamorph-ologikon will be furnished with a patented Moral Manager. This device, whose secret is known only to me, fits in amongst the cogs and keys, and deflects any improprieties of translation. For example, you might be aware of the great poet Virgil, and be acquainted with his 'Eclogues'? If so, you will be familiar with one of these, the young gentleman Corydon burns with passion for – ahem! – a young man named Alexis. '*Corydon ardebat Alexin*' runs the verse. Now, with the patent Moral Manager engaged, this passage will be translated as 'Young Corydon for fair Alice burn'd' – which, as I am sure you will concede, is both a pretty translation and a moral one!"

He was jumping up and down with enthusiasm, clapping his hands. I had scarcely the heart to suggest that his view of the complexities of translation was childish in the extreme. He leaned forward and grabbed me excitedly, placing the stability of our craft in very con-siderable danger. "Perhaps we could sit this very afternoon, madam, and I will give you a practical demonstration?"

"A practical demonstration, Mr. Burnie?" I was startled – had he already constructed a machine such as he described?

"Only of the principles, naturally," he explained. "We can elaborate the rules of grammar for Volapük, perhaps, and I could demonstrate just how simple it might be?" The enthusiasm of the young man was persuasive, although Urquhart took no pains to conceal his opinion that the man was a gull and a gudgeon, and not admissible company for Universal Linguists. At my suggestion alone, however, we agreed to meet after dinner, and discuss Mr. Burnie's proposal.

*   *   *

At three o'clock, therefore, the architect and I convened; for our meeting-place, we had decided upon the grand flight of steps which leads into the walled garden belonging to the House, down the hill near the river. Here, we had the warmth of the sun upon our heads and shelter from the wind – which proved to be essential, as Mr. Burnie had brought along a pile of paper on which to write his notes, and I had brought the papers on which this very Hand-Book is being written, for I would need to refer Mr. Burnie to the simple Rules of Grammar contained therein. Urquhart had accompanied me, but was soon dozing in the warmth of the sun, stretched out like an old goat on the broad stone steps.

Within a short space of time, I had convinced Mr. Burnie that the grammar of Volapük was so logically and philosophically constructed that it was an easy matter to identify the persons and moods and tenses of a verb; and simple, too, to discern the cases of a Noun. After barely half-an-hour had passed, Mr. Burnie was, under my mature instruction, chanting out the mnemonic with the practised ease of any one of my students. Feverishly, he began to scribble down notes; shortly thereafter, I obtained a copy of these notes, and will take the liberty of presenting an edited version thereof at the end of this present volume, as a "Synopsis of Inflections", which sets out, very simply, all the possible prefixes and suffixes for any verb or noun.

By the end of the first hour, the Innovator was ablaze with enthusiasm. "Why, Mrs. Justice!" he exclaimed, jumping up and scattering his notes among the early cabbages in the beds below us. "I believe this is the most practical of all possible languages! How easy it will be to teach this language to the Metamorphologikon! All we need do is to identify the prefixes or suffixes to a word, and we are more than half-way to a translation!" He ran about, collecting up his notes, ascended the steps to where I sat, and, pen poised, enquired after "the basic vocabulary".

I obliged by briefly summarising my standard Lesson Four. But I regret to say that the succeeding half-hour dampened Mr. Burnie's enthusiasm to such an extent that, after ten minutes, his face fell; after twenty, his pen drooped in despair; after thirty, he paced about in the afternoon sun, amongst the potatoes and root-crops, biting his lower lip, his brow creased deeply in an effort of thought. Finally, he broke out:

"But this is an outrage, Mrs. Justice! How can the vocabulary be so complex, and yet the grammar so simple? There are no rules here, just words ransacked at random from the treasury of nations! And to turn the word 'rose' into '*lol*' defies my understanding!" He forgot himself so far as to poke me in the chest, demanding an answer. "What do you mean by it?" he demanded. "What do you mean by it, madam? Do you not realise that this complexity will ruin my most extraordinary invention? If my patent fails because of you, then, my good woman, you will feel my wrath!"

I remonstrated with him, trying to convince him that it was not my blame if his Invention failed to take into account the rich diversity of words in any language, not just Volapük. But he was not in a mood for compromise.

"You shall hear from me, Mrs. Justice, you scheming woman, you and your decrepit Lothario! I will never accept this affront to my intellect!" Angrily, he thrust all of his notes concerning the Meta-morphologikon into my hands, and stalked away up the path which led to the House, shouting to himself as he went. For the scientific purpose of this Hand-Book, I have analysed and explained these papers as best I can in the Transaction which follows.

This final disturbance woke Urquhart and he giggled idiotically. "It might perhaps have been such a triumph, Mrs. Justice, if only it were neither Conditional nor Potential!" I said nothing, and left him in the garden, to whine and lament, and find his own way up the hill.

Fin tidüpa balsefolid.

Transactions X: The Metamorphologikon

Written on 9th April, 1891, at Mavisbank, Describing,
for the first time, and in simple terms, Mr. Burnie's
Beneficial Translating Engine or Metamorphologikon.

The following description of a Translating Engine, or Machine, which will be patented by Mr. Burnie of Edinburgh, is offered for a scholarly debate amongst people interested in the Universal Language, and the transition of communication from a multitude of languages to a single human language. We do not claim that such a machine does, or can, exist: simply that an idea has been elaborated for such a machine.

The Metamorphologikon, or engine for changing one language into another, is, in outward appearance, very similar to a mechanical "type-writer". At the front, there are keys, such as one might encounter on one of those writing-machines, square in shape and black. There are three rows of keys in a pyramidal shape: the top-most row contains nine keys; the middle row, eighteen; the bottom row, thirty-six, each with one letter of the alphabet, or an integer, painted on it. On the black metal panel above the top-most row of keys, a score or more of brass handles, in appearance and function much like organ-stops, are displayed, each being engraved with the name of one language: thus, one will be the handle for "English", another for "Volapük", yet another for "Chinese".

At the side of the machine, a number of large levers, made in silver metal, of various shapes and sundry dimensions; some of which have a known function, others of which are for a purpose as yet unclear.

Stretching behind the front of the machine, to a distance of some six feet – for it is an elongated type-writer indeed – is the body of the machinery. The workings comprise the following parts, moving from front to back of the machine: dozens of strong wires, which connect the keys at the front to a rank of magnets; some thirty sets of strong magnets linked to electrical batteries, which form the fundament or basis of the entire machine; from the magnets, more wires attached to several linked cogs, gears and wheels, all of steel, which connect also with each other; an array of levers, each embossed with letters or words; a large brass roller, around which paper may be wound; finally, a large vane, or windmill-sail, which perpetually circles over the whole device, cooling the air. The whole is covered in clear glass so that the mechanisms contained therein may be observed.

To translate a word or phrase from one language into another, the procedure is as follows:

Firstly, one selects the language *from* which the translation is to be made, by pulling on one of the brass handles at the front – for example, the one marked "English". This engages one of the magnets, which begins to hum with power from its associated battery. One of the wheels will begin to spin.

Secondly, one selects the language *into* which the translation is to be made, by pulling a second lever – for example, the one marked "Volapük". This will engage a second magnet and its battery. A second wheel will spin.

Thirdly, one engages one or more gears, by pulling on one of the levers at the side of the machine; these activated gears will connect the two spinning wheels; and the cooling-fan will begin to turn.

The machine is now ready to operate.

Fourthly, one uses the rows of keys to enter a word. This is achieved as follows: one presses one or more keys on the top row, to indicate that the word is a noun, a verb, an adjective, etc; one presses one or more keys from the middle row, to indicate the case of the noun, or the person of the verb, the mood and the tense, as appropriate. Then, one presses a combination of keys from the bottom row, which simply spells the letters of the word. When the word has been fully entered, one pulls another lever at the side, and the machine will use the wheels and cogs to recognise the word and to translate it.

Fifthly, when the word has thus been translated, the machine will type it out on the roll of paper conveniently placed at the rear of the machine. The next word may then be entered.

Mr. Burnie's notes on this interesting engine explain other levers whose function is sometimes clear, sometimes obscure. He has already described to me a "Moral Manager", whose function is to amend the translation in order to preserve decency. On his diagrams, the "Moral Manager" is shown as a large knob, six or seven inches in length, which protrudes at an angle of some seventy degrees from the vertical at the side of the machine, and which is activated by sliding it up and down, in a manner we find distasteful. But there are other items which are labelled, but not, unfortunately, annotated: the "Eudiometer", for example, whose scientific meaning is understood, but whose purpose in this machine is unclear – it may be related to a collection of stoppered flasks which are enclosed below the batteries in the centre of the machine, clearly marked as containing "Emancipated Suction Fluid" and "Virile Vitriol". Then there is the "Quodlibet Variator" lever; and the "Pleiomerous Comb", a fine mesh suspended just behind the wheels, and related in some utilitarian way to the typing-device.

However, the purpose of this Transactional Note is not to speculate on the exact nature of the various parts of Mr. Burnie's Engine; but to commence a debate on whether such a machine, or a similar one, could be built, taking into account the complexities of the grammars and vocabularies of the world's most common languages. Could one make a machine which would translate Shakespeare into Oordoo, or Rabelais into Gaelic?

We are sceptical.

Katel Balsekilid, the Thirteenth Chapter:
The Passive and the Reflexive Voices

"Penetegobs!"

I spent the evening of Thursday, the ninth of April, in "writing up" my notes for these lessons, and preparing myself for the following day, on which we designed to return the completed Enumerator's Book to the Authorities in Edinburgh.

I had little opportunity to talk to Bosman; the man seemed to have suffered greatly for his cause, for, when I knocked on the door of his cupboard late in the day, he emerged and pushed past me without a word, filthy with ash from cigarettes, eyes red-rimmed and blood-shot. Miss Smyth came across him a few moments later, wandering aimlessly in front of the House, feverishly smoking and muttering to himself. With her accustomed sense of purpose, she took hold of him and led him off, despite his protests, for "a short discussion and a good bath". When I met him, an hour later, he seemed much cleaner, but uncharacteristically emptied of spirit.

In that intervening hour, I took the opportunity, with Mr. Downie and Urquhart, to examine the Enumerator's Book, which Bosman had completed. It was, if the truth were told, a fine piece of pen-manship. Every entry, however odd and unlikely, had been faithfully transcribed from the papers which our friends in Mavisbank had completed; all the entries had been made exactly in the order which would have prevailed, had Bosman collected those papers himself from the residents of his district. Mr. Downie was greatly admiring of the completed work, and spent several minutes, awe-struck, turning over the few pages, back and forward, making appreciative noises and nodding sagely.

I noted some of the entries on the pages: the immediate family of Napoleon Bonaparte now resided at Number 3, Sylvan Place; a house in Argyle Place was fully occupied by no fewer than seven-and-thirty descendants of the German mystic, Angelus Silesius; in Millbank Terrace, we had a coven of seven Necromancers, and a nest of blood-suckers, not to mention three men with the identical name of John Bews, who, while not "deaf or dumb or blind", nevertheless suffered from being "unsatisfactory", a "milk-sop", and incapacitated by "a surfeit of pleasuring"; in my own building, at Number 8, Carlung Place, I discovered a neighbour whom I had never met, whose main occupation seemed to be that of "dinner-companion to Duke Humphrey". Elsewhere in the district lived unfortunate females who had "succumbed to sexual accident", or gentlemen "exhausted by melancholia". Similar entries were carefully copied across from all the papers into Dr. Bosman's book. I felt some mis-giving on this account, that perhaps we would be discovered. But Mr. Downie thought it "admirable, splendid, indeed", and fore-saw no problems. In a positive spirit, he pointed out that some of the entries were even quite factual – my own, for example, and Dr. Bosman's, along with Mrs. Forbes and her daughter.

"Census legible, signed for, Justice," he explained expansively. "Sufficiency, nothing more requisite. Registrar no opportunity, examine details. Over-whelming numbers submitted."

This explanation did indeed seem reasonable. Nevertheless, I did wonder whether the inaccuracy of some of the entries might not seem so obvious that even the most distracted eye might notice. I suggested this to Mr. Downie.

"Apologies. Excessive worry!" he laughed, again the care-free man I had dealt with in Edinburgh. "Details not important, Census; Census takes place, important!"

I must have looked puzzled, for he went on to divulge to me that, when the Romans took a Census of the people of Palestine nineteen hundred years ago, they were not concerned about who lived where, or whether they spoke Latin or Hebrew, or what they did for a living: it was enough that the people realised that they had to move about the land at the whim of the Roman government. "Same applies, Justice, see?" I confess that it was no clearer to me then than before, but I let it pass. At that moment, in any case, Bosman came back from his bath, and silently took possession of all the materials, ushering us from the room, and locking it very deliberately behind him: "That Book is the property of Her Majesty's Government," he stated sententiously, "and I am responsible for it until it is handed over to the Authorities to-morrow."

After supper, we laid our plans for the following day. It was agreed
that Dr. Bosman should submit all the papers to Mr. Henry Murray,
the District Registrar for Newington, in Edinburgh, as if all was in
order; but that both Mr. Downie and I should accompany him, to
ensure that no harm should befall him, and that no repercussions
should fall upon any of those involved in the collection of the information so documented. Mr. Deans and Urquhart attended this discussion; the latter expressed a keen desire to return to the capital city,
but it was agreed that his presence would scarcely be helpful, and would
be only a guarantee for attracting unwanted attention. He grumbled
and cursed for a few minutes, but when I called him to reason, he fell
off his chair as if struck by a thuggee, and lapsed into a sulk.

Mr. Deans knew the times of the trains for Edinburgh: one would
leave Polton Station at half-past eight, and reach Eskbank at seventeen
minutes to the hour; with great efficiency, the Railway Company had
ordained that a train leave Eskbank for Edinburgh exactly one minute
later, and we would be at the main station in Edinburgh after barely
twenty-eight minutes, at twelve minutes past nine. If we then amused
ourselves for a time, and entered the Registry Office at five minutes
before one o'clock, just before the clerks and District Registrar went
for their dinner, then we could be away and back to Mid-Lothian, on
the twenty-to-two train for Eskbank. Mr. Deans apologised that the
Railway Company's time-table meant that we would have to cool our
heels in Eskbank for two hours or more, the next train for Polton being
at twenty-eight minutes past four. It was my view that, rather than wait
uselessly, we should simply walk from Eskbank, a matter of a few
miles. Of course, Dr. Bosman made a fuss about that, but I ignored
him. Urquhart brightened up when he realised that, by not joining us,
he was saving himself a considerable walk; and proceeded to mock
Bosman for his want of youthful energy, listing his many great forced
marches at the age of forty and invoking the names of the great
Scottish soldiers (amongst whom were: "Sir Andrew Gary, Sir John
Seatoun, Sir John Fulerton, the Earl of Irvin, Colonel Erskin, Colonel
Andrew Linsay, Colonel John Kinindmond, Colonel William Kinindmond, besides a great many other Scots of their charge, condition and
quality") whose feats of endurance far exceeded our mean journey
into Edinburgh and a "paltry pedical league".

Bosman, however, whose spirit had all but been extinguished by the events of the past week and the ministrations, perhaps, of Miss Smyth, simply closed his eyes and sat back in his seat, surrounding himself with his foul smoke, until Urquhart had rounded off his tirade. At which time, we retired to bed, leaving Urquhart in the company of a good half-dozen female admirers; to whom he was teaching a game of cards in which the forfeits and favours excited much giggling and the arching of eyebrows.

*   *   *

Friday, the tenth of April, dawned blustery. Showers of rain broke over the House. We were up early, and had broken our fast before eight o'clock. I chose to cast off my feminine attire for this journey, considering that it would ill-suit us to attract attention in this venture. But, in order to ensure that Bosman did nothing rash which might imperil us all, I had looked out the garb of Cödel Yagöl, cloak, gauntlets, and helmet; in order to remain *incognito*, I concealed the Scimitar of Justice underneath the cloak. Mr. Downie and Dr. Bosman dressed themselves sensibly in overcoats, the papers were packed into Mr. Downie's document-case. And we set off, down the road past the walled garden, and out into the lane which led over the river to the station.

As before, I found that the mask rendered the world about me in black and white. The very faces of the men who waited for the train at Polton flickered before me, making my stomach turn over, and I found it difficult to tell whether they looked at us askance, or simply watched us as any passenger might watch his fellows on a tedious journey by train. At half-past eight precisely, the guard waved his flag and we rattled off down the bank of the River Esk, crossed it and came in past the steaming paper-mill at Lasswade, where two gentlemen, gagged and bound for Edinburgh, joined our carriage; and then once more across the river, through the tunnel, to Broomieknowe, and shortly afterwards to Eskbank.

During our rush from one train to another, Urquhart dropped the document-case, and I dropped the scimitar. Mr. Downie tutted in exasperation while we retrieved these important objects, and the guard whistled angrily as we leaped aboard the Edinburgh train. The countryside flashed past, black upon black. I examined my scimitar; it had suffered no damage; but I was interested to note that several fellow-travellers seemed to recoil from my presence as I made the blade whistle through the air, narrowly missing Bosman's hat and cigarette. I amused myself later by preventing him from lighting another cigarette, in cutting the match from his shaking hand, time after time; while simultaneously educating all those in our compartment on the simple numbers of Volapük, *bal, tel, kil, fol, lul, mäl, vel, jöl, zül*, which they repeated avidly until we pulled in to Waverley Station, exactly on time.

It was now a question of how we should occupy ourselves for three and one-half hours. For Mr. Downie's plan had determined that, in order to avoid any unwelcome examination of Dr. Bosman's handiwork by a receiving official at the District Registry Office in Hope Park Terrace, he should submit the records just as the official was thinking of his dinner, and be long gone by the time he returned, full of mince and tatties, an hour later. It seemed a plan without flaw, and there was no reason to stray from it. But what were we to do? We were, all three, unused to strolling at a leisurely pace in our own hometown at such an hour on a day of work; and felt uncomfortable doing so. For no good reason, we felt that we were the subject of the closest attention of every soberly-dressed banker, every constable, matron and carriage-driver, as we came up on to the noisy and crowded thoroughfare of Princes Street.

I proposed that we cross the North Bridge and make our way to quieter streets, the Cowgate or Grassmarket. Accordingly we did so. As we crossed above the railway, a bitter east wind caught and buffeted us. My mask was all but torn from my head, but I clutched at it and saved it. I noticed then a strange phenomenon: that the tenements and grander buildings which over-looked Waverley had greatly increased in height, floor upon floor of windows, towering into the very heavens. From every window, it seemed that a sinner looked out, eyes on fire, black flames licking from the sockets, as each one spoke in tongues which none other could comprehend. The grand Bank of Scotland was placed high on a rock that itself mounted some hundreds of feet into the air. Around its base were set small towers, moats and defensive walls; above these rose great walls, perforated by windows and studded with balconies, from which a man might fall and be crushed by the sheer weight of gravity; above these again, high above us all, and as if carved from the living rock, a huge building arose, some fourteen storeys in all, ledge after ledge, window after window;

surmounted at last by an elegant portico, wherein the pillars and the masonry were of the very finest design, and the windows thereof were wide; at the very top, hundreds of dizzying feet above us, a mountain of caves, which slaves had excavated with picks and hammers and shovels, each window a black cavern-entrance, some twenty feet across and some fifty feet in height, an entrance into unknown halls of richness and depravity. At these windows, gentlemen shrieked in agony as coins of every denomination cascaded from their mouths, the explosive force ripping out the very innards and bowels of these men, and spilling them far over the railway-lines laid out below.

I considered this sight unusual.

As I looked further afield, I could see that the hill of Calton was topped by a castle with many turrets, each one the prison of a Bavarian king, or the tower of a lovelorn princess, whose grey hair tumbled down, fifty, one hundred feet into the breeze below. A forest of black trees crept slowly up the flanks of the hill, threatening to overwhelm all the buildings thereon. The monument to Sir Walter Scott, over to the west, was crumbling from its base, no more the elegant carvings, now just a slowly shifting pile of rubble, which desperate men tried to prop up as it sank.

I did not tell my friends what I saw there. For they would likely not believe me; or, worse, they would be struck by panic, and either Downie or Bosman would undertake some foolish action which would expose us all to the full force of the Law. It was I, Cödel Yagöl, who had to retain a grasp upon reality, and ensure that we did not stray from our intent.

We reached the High Street, and then took a narrow road down to the Cowgate, where, in the very ditches and underbelly of the metropolis, we could feel safe. Our appearance seemed to attract no unwelcome attention, and policemen were few and far between. Above our heads, the bustle of South Bridge and then of George the Fourth Bridge, the great cliffs of the old town towering above us; from the heavens came the cries of gulls against a sky now white, now black. No sun-light reached into those depths, where, like three warriors of Greek legend, we strolled amongst dragons, and serpents, and old women with missing teeth. But I noticed that every wall, every brick, every stone, had been painted in the style of the Dutch painters of old, with landscapes of lake and mountain and hill, every scene filled with peasants and sheep and cows, shepherds, pig-swains, skaters and angels. The scale and scope of these paintings was beyond my comprehension.

We saw daylight ahead of us, in the Grassmarket, as if at the end of a long tunnel. But Mr. Downie was greatly attracted by a building to our left, which bore a label proclaiming itself to be the "Magdalen Chapel". I had never seen this place before – indeed, I had not noticed it even as we walked past now – and neither had my companions; but its very seclusion seemed to offer some sanctuary. We effected an entry, and found ourselves in a square, high-ceilinged room, panelled in dark wood, and with the air and scent of an old church. Along one wall were the names of men long-dead, smiths and masters of metal, "peutherers" and saddlers, whose money had built this place. It was very quiet, the sounds of the streets around and above closed out, leaving only the odd creak of cold wood, and the scratch of a mouse.

Since it was barely ten o'clock, I decided to while away the time with a lesson in Volapük, which would pleasantly pass two hours and keep our minds engaged. I therefore took my place in a splendid old chair, or throne, which stood in one corner of the room, up on a low balcony, and proceeded to teach my students

Tidüp balselulid – The Passive and Reflexive Voices.

The Passive Voice – the person is being acted on by, or subjected to, another party.
The Reflexive Voice – indicating that the action turns back on the person.

Thus, "You are being taught" is in the Passive Voice, since it is not you two who are conducting the lesson, but it is you who are the subjects of a teacher.

Conversely, "You teach yourselves" would be in the Reflexive Voice, since you are not teaching anyone else, only yourselves. Please note, if you will, that there is a form, very similar to the Reflexive, which is expressed in the phrase "You teach each other". This is by no means the Reflexive Voice, but is simply the Active Voice with the personal pronoun of the Accusative relating directly to the subject. That much is clear.

Let us commence with

The Passive Voice.

All the tenses of the Passive Voice commence with the letter **p**. Therefore, the passive tense-prefixes are:

Present	**pa–**	palilob,	I am heard.
Imperfect	**pä–**	pälogol,	you were seen.
Perfect	**pe–**	penetegom,	he has been discovered.
Pluperfect	**pi–**	pifanof,	she had been caught.
Future	**po–**	posagos,	it will be said.
Future Perfect	**pu–**	pununon,	one will have been informed.

In English, a *present* passive is often really *perfect* in signification; as in, "the duty is finished", is the same as "the duty has been finished": **blig pefinom**.

On the other hand we use what is, apparently, an Active form in a Passive sense, as in, "the plot thickens", meaning "the plot is being thickened", **klän pabigom**. In all such cases we must consider the sense and not the sound.

The Infinitive in the Passive Voice is formed in the same way, and is subject to the same rules.

- **Pamilagön**, to be admired.
- **Pevunön**, to have been wounded.
- **Polibön**, to be about to be freed, to be going to be freed.

- **Paketöl**, imprisoned, being imprisoned.
- **Peketöl**, imprisoned, having been imprisoned.
- **Poketöl**, about to be imprisoned.

It is often necessary to examine English passive participles very carefully, to determine what tense they really signify:

The castle seen in the distance, **kased palogöl in fag**.
The castle built on a rock, **kased pebumöl su klif**.

If we turn the sentence into the Active form it will be clearer:

The castle which *we see* in the distance.
The castle which *someone has built* (not *is* building) on a rock.

It is clear, is it not, that the Passive Voice is also the voice of Mastery, by which responsibility may be denied, by which persons may be concealed from justice? "It is said", "A tax was raised", "A war was declared", "People were killed", "A regrettable mistake was made" – in these phrases, no named guilty party, no one to take responsibility. And, by the same token, it is the voice of the Dispossessed, the people who are done-to, never doing things for themselves: "my family was evicted", "all our money was lost", "my man was thrown out of work".

There is another form of the participle, slightly differing from the future, and having the prefix ö instead of o. Its meaning is "that which must" or "ought to do something", or "that which must" or "ought to be done".

> **Öbinöl,** that which ought to be.
> **Pöfinöl,** to be finished.
> **Pöks pömenodöl,** errors *(which ought)* to be corrected.
> **Pöks pomenodöl,** errors which will be corrected.

I was about to test whether my pupils had been paying attention, with Exercise 22, when I discovered, to my despair, that both had curled up in the thick atmosphere of the chapel, and had fallen asleep. I was about to come down upon them, wrathful with the rage of Cödel Yagöl, scimitar in hand ready to strike at their slothfulness, when I decided that, perhaps, it was not worth the trouble. It was so peaceful here, so calm and quiet after all our troubles. So I let them slumber on: Bosman was stretched out upon a black table which, I noticed with some grim amusement, had a neatly-lettered notice framed above it, announcing it to be, "the mortuary table upon which the executed Covenanters were laid, prior to their entombment in the kirkyard of Greyfriars".

Feeling my own senses to be dulled, I decided to join my companions in a brief sleep. I therefore wrote the exercise upon some paper, which I transfixed to the side of the balcony with the point of my scimitar; then I wrapped my cloak around me, and drifted into slumber.

Exercise 22.

- **Volapük popükom in läns mödik.**
- **Mans pecödoms, pelägoms e peseitoms in sepi.**
- Errors will have been corrected.
- Errors which will have to be corrected.

When I awoke and had, after a few moments, re-discovered where I was, I saw to my horror that I was alone once more. Neither Bosman nor Downie was anywhere to be seen! I struggled to my feet and shouted, but none heard. Outside, the height of the sun showed that it must be close on mid-day. I noticed then that a smaller note had been pinned underneath Exercise 22; it stated, in Downie's neat copper-plate: "Apologies. Tardiness awakening, incipient panic, departed Hope." By the last two words, I could only suppose he meant Hope Park Terrace, where the District Registrar had his office.

I cursed them for their stupidity, and rushed out into the Cowgate; there was, of course, no sign of them. Sweeping aside anyone who strayed into my path, shouting the war-cry of *"Cödel Yagöl yagom!"*, I strode down the Cowgate, and darted up Infirmary Street. When I reached the South Bridge and paused to look at my watch, I saw that it was barely twelve o'clock; I became desperate, realising that my companions were in danger of ruining our entire plan. I waved my scimitar and prepared to march upon the District Registry. But events now over-took me. For, rattling down the street towards me, from the direction of Newington, I saw a carriage, from which two heads poked out in turn – those of Bosman and Downie – and just as suddenly disappeared. The carriage swept past, and I could see that two policeman were also inside: my fellow-conspirators had been captured! Gathering up my cloak, I ran after them, along South Bridge, past the Wax-Work Museum and Grand Historical Galleries, from which a number of pleasure-seekers emerged, who now tried to entrap me, imagining me to be another exhibit in that famous display of kings, queens, warriors and statesmen. But I dodged adroitly, and crossed the High Street, across the North Bridge, avoiding snakes and errant decapitated fowls, making no ground upon the carriage, but neither losing sight of it. I saw it halt outside the grand edifice of the Registry Office, and beheld, to my horror, Bosman and Mr. Downie bundled out of the carriage, and up the steps into the building; I strode across the end of Princes Street, and through the heavy doors of the Registry Office.

As soon as I entered, it was evident that I had stumbled upon a scene of great moment to Civil Government. An imperious-looking man, his face black with anger and with shouting, stood in the centre of a large room, while his attendants ran around in confusion. He was

clearly labelled "Registrar for Scotland". In front of him stood two
large constables, with Bosman and Downie between them; to one side,
another gentleman, the very picture of indignation and righteousness;
his label noted him as the "District Registrar".

"This is an outrage!" shouted the larger party, over and over. "Who is
this man Bosman, who thinks he can cock a snook at the very face of
Civil Government?" He shook his fist at a gentleman beside him. "This
is an outrage, Mr. Murray! The district of Newington is embroiled in a
scandal! Who is this Bosman, which one is he, I repeat?"

A finger was dramatically raised by Mr. Murray, the District Registrar, and jabbed in the direction of Bosman. As if struck by a trident,
Bosman visibly jerked. The more imperious gentleman, the Registrar
for Scotland himself, glared upon Bosman for several moments.

"You are a disgrace, sir!" he shouted. "A disgrace to your country
and your Queen. What have you to say for yourself? – no! I will not
hear it! There can be no justification for your acts of anarchy and
subversion! Waste not your words, sir, on me! I will teach you to
respect the Law of the Land!"

It was time for Cödel Yagöl to take action. I stepped forward, and
sundry clerks fell back before me. My movement attracted some
attention, as did the cries of fear of those around me. The Registrar
looked up, distracted for the moment.

"You, sir!" he demanded. "What do you mean by this interruption?
Are you with the Police?"

I shook my head, and now took a step or two backwards, preparing
myself for precipitate flight, should it be called for.

"Then why are you wearing that helmet?" he demanded, advancing
upon me still. "Is there a fire? Do you represent the Fire Brigade?"
He gasped, eyes wide open. "The Lord have mercy!" he exclaimed,
twirling as he stood. "Fire! There's a fire! Save the records, take all
that you can and run! Fire! Fire!"

In the ensuing confusion, both Bosman and Downie fled. As clerks
scattered about the building, some clutching piles of Census Books,
others only their overcoats, I took the opportunity to retreat to the
door, and stepped out under the bright skies over Edinburgh, just in
front of a wave of men in suits, who bellowed for pails of water. I
hastened down the steps which led into the station, and sought my
companions.

I found them at length, huddled together behind a porter's trolley, piled high with leather trunks and suit-cases of a grander sort. Enraged, I threatened them with the Scimitar of Justice, and hauled them out into the open. I demanded to know what had possessed them to ruin all of our plans, and advised them that I had only just escaped with my liberty, as I had secured theirs. "Already," I said, "there is a hue and cry upon the streets above us. It is only a matter of time before they look down here, and we will be discovered!"

"*Ponetegobs!*" stated Downie, rather unhelpfully, although I am sure that he meant it well.

"Indeed," I said. "The Passive Voice: we will be discovered! Would that you had listened to our plan as carefully as you listened to my lesson on the Passive! You, Bosman, what have you to say for yourself?"

Bosman shrugged his shoulders, looked at me balefully, and lit one of his infernal cigarettes. Downie, for his part, seemed about to burst into tears, as he had done during the affair of the Leibnitzians. There seemed little point in haranguing them now, so I found a safer place to hide, within sight of the platform from which the Eskbank train would depart at twenty minutes before two; but out of sight of passers-by.

As we lay in hiding, I was horrified to receive a tap on the shoulder. Fearing that we had now lived our last moment of freedom, I turned round swiftly, ready to flee. To my astonishment, standing behind me were Mr. Kobayashi and Mr. Kumakura. "Gridis, respected samurai Shodel!" said the former, bowing, while his companion looked on impassively. "Glidis!" I said in return. Downie and Bosman looked on, open-mouthed. "Famous samurai wait for train?" Mr. Kobayashi enquired further, looking slightly puzzled.

"No, no," I thought it best to explain. "We lie in ambush – fierce enemies – many swords – honour in danger."

This explanation, once it had been simplified back and forth, greatly pleased Mr. Kumakura, who bowed deeply at all three of us. Mr. Downie gravely bowed back. Mr. Kobayashi explained that they were momentarily catching a train to Dalmeny, to "scrutinise great Forth Bridge"; we said farewell with all dignity; and were left alone once more.

From the streets above, we could hear bells of fire-engines; but there seemed to be no immediate search for the falsifiers of the Population Census. After a further agonising wait, we climbed aboard our train and, each breathing a sigh of relief, set off round the flank of Arthur's Seat.

Reaching Eskbank efficiently and precisely at eight minutes past two, we disembarked and pondered what we should do. Bosman was all for sitting in the waiting-room for over two hours, and catching the Polton train. For my part, I felt greatly un-nerved, and proposed that we should not attract any unwelcome attention, and that we walk to Polton by road. Downie, by this time, had lost all of his good humour, and any ambition of his own, and was willing to become a passive object to any suggestion.

After a scientific application of the scimitar, we agreed to set out from Eskbank by road, under a sky which alternately soaked us with showers and dried us with bright sun-shine. It was no great distance, perhaps three miles or so to Broomieknowe, followed by a mile along the road which led past the policies of Polton House, and down into the glen at Polton itself. All along that road, however, both Downie and Bosman complained and moaned and shuffled, and stopped to rest tired feet. I urged them on every so often, amusing myself by claiming that I had heard a police whistle; or that I had seen a troop of horses galloping towards us. At those moments, my two friends were galvanised into action, throwing themselves into the ditch, or hiding behind a convenient bush. But such energy lasted barely a minute or two; and it took us two long hours to walk to Polton, which any man could do in one.

I whiled away the time in the profitable matter of

The Reflexive Voice.

I reminded my students that the Reflexive meant that an action came back on oneself – "a coward shoots himself", "a wise man hides himself", "a lazy person sits himself down every five minutes".

The Reflexive form of the verb is the same as the Active Voice with the addition of the suffix **-ok**.

Thus:

Plidob, I amuse	**plidobok**, I amuse myself
Siedol, you sit	**siedolok**, you sit yourself down
Lägom, he hangs	**lägomok**, he hangs himself

In the plural the **-s** usually follows the **-ok**, but may be made to precede it, if that form is thought more euphonious:

Plidoboks, or **plidobsok**, we amuse ourselves
Lägomoks, they hang themselves

Note that an equivalent expression, sometimes used, is **Plidob obi**. However, this form can be very confusing:

Plidol, you amuse, **plidolok**; or, **plidol oli**, you amuse yourself
Plidomok or **plidom oki**, he amuses himself (**Plidom omi** would mean *he* amuses *him*, one person amusing another person).

If the object is expressed by a separate pronoun in the plural it is translated "each other".

Pükomoks, they speak to themselves
Pükoms okis, they speak to each other
Pükobsok, we speak to ourselves
Pükobs obis, we speak to each other

As we came closer to Polton, and saw the valley of the River Esk opening out below us on our right hand, I was delighted to find that both Mr. Downie and Dr. Bosman were taking some real pleasure in analysing the grammar of our situation. On my right, I detected Mr. Downie repeating over and over, in time with the wringing of his hands, that "we have been discovered!" (or, more precisely, "repeatedly, discovered, apologies!", which I understood in the Passive Voice); Bosman, on my left, expressed a view, with sidelong glances which were filled with hatred and resentment, that "we have discovered each other". I, for my part, considered that we had, finally "discovered ourselves". Thus, with a certain amount of truth, we were able to state in Volapük, firstly:

Penetegobs!   We have been discovered!

Secondly:

Enetegoboks! We have discovered ourselves!

And thirdly:

Enetegobs obis! We have discovered each other!

Despite these insights into the Passive and Reflexive Voices, which my companions had gained in this exciting day, I could scarcely persuade them to respond to my questions for

Exercise 23.

- **Logobok in lok at.**
- **Aikel löfomok gudikumo ka kopanali omik, no binom volutel velatik; ab voluteis velatik löfoms okis.**
- I have struck myself with this walking-stick.
- You will kill yourself! *Etcetera.*

– so I shall leave this exercise to be completed by my Readers. *Fin tidüpa balselulid.*

A few moments before we began our descent of the leafy lane which led to Polton, we were alerted to a strange sight in the skies beyond Mavisbank, further to the north, above Loanhead. It was, Bosman explained excitedly, a "hot-air balloon, or a dirigible". I had come across many hot-air balloons in my life, and seen them tethered for the Common Excitement at fair-grounds the length and breadth of the land, from Aberdour to Zetland (where, once every two years, because of a commitment to one who had been a friend to me in my youth, I was obliged to place my life in the hands of silent sailors, and visit the over-used harmonium of Burravoe). But this one was not at all the shape of such a balloon: it was in the form of a fish, of a dark-brown colour; and it was moving towards us at a slow speed, wallowing from side to side, emitting a great buzzing noise, and leaving a trail of smoke behind. The flying-machine slowly came closer, then, plummeting, disappeared from our sight.

Dr. Bosman was as pleased as I had seen him since he was gloating in my rooms, a fortnight earlier. He explained to us that he was a great admirer of "The Air-Ship", and assured us that it was the "mode of transport of the future", capable, if captained skilfully, of long journeys. He gave us to understand that a German colonel had taken up the ideas of Mr. Ericksson of America, and was making considerable progress with his inventions, which would, some day, open up vast areas of unexplored land. The French, too, had made great advances with machines known as "*dirigibles*", which signified balloons, filled with light gas, which could be directed towards a distant goal. Mr. Downie expressed his view that anyone who flew in such a thing was throwing down a gauntlet to the gods, and deserved to die the death of Icarus. Dr. Bosman begged to differ, and the pair of them fell to arguing fiercely. Eventually, I was obliged to smite between them with my scimitar, and thus restore order.

Our final half-a-mile, down the hill to Polton, was filled with Bosman's delight at having seen such an invention in the air above Mid-Lothian, and Mr. Downie's lamentations at the state of his boots, and the blood which, he surmised, must even now be pouring from his flayed feet.

We came down to the river, and turned right into the lane which led to Mavisbank House. And immediately were over-taken by a throng of boys and girls, women and a few men, who were hastening in the direction of the field used by the Lasswade Cricket Club, just to the east of the walled garden of the House. In the confusion, I could hear news that the "flying machine" had landed on the cricket field. Dr. Bosman recovered his energies with miraculous speed, and ran off like an excited school-boy with the crowd. Mr. Downie was terrified by the throng; he crossed his arms over his chest, thrust down his chin, and hastened up the lane which led to the House, with never a backward look. For my part, curious to learn more, I followed the crowd at a steady pace, came round the corner of the garden, and found a strange object lying on the grass, like a whale washed up, and of similar dimensions. A figure in a heavy overcoat stood dizzily beside it, explaining some of the mechanisms to the local scientists.

As I came closer, the figure hailed me and lurched in my direction, most unsteady in its balance. The crowd parted, enthralled. I saw, as he removed hat, muffler, gloves, and greeted me once more, that it was none other than Mr. Jo!

Katel Balsefolid, the Fourteenth Chapter:
Prefixes and Suffixes

"Lugleklimels obinoms"

I was, I confess, astonished to find our old companion, Mr. Jo, among us at Mavisbank. But, to all appearances, I was not as astonished at that, as he was at being alive.

"Oh, what a journey, Mr. Justice!" he exclaimed, shaking me furiously by the hand, quivering in every limb. "I began to suppose I would never land my aerostat upon *terra firma* again!"

I told him that I had seen his balloon swaying dangerously in the afternoon sky, and that I wondered why it did so.

"My investigations into the cause have not yet yielded a conclusion, Mr. Justice," he answered, "as I was just explaining to these kind people. It began shortly after I departed the policies at Woodhouselee, and has not ceased since. I suspect—" he waved vaguely in the direction of his now-deflated balloon. "I suspect one of my guiding-ropes may have twisted. Or something." He shook his head in mystification, then brightened up again. "But, what a great shock to find you here! Would you like to see my aerostat? I call it the 'Aberbrothic Dirigible'. Only it is not very. Not very dirigible."

Grasping me by the arm, he dragged me to the billowing pile of material, and showed me the wickerwork of the basket, or *"nacelle"* ("A French word, Mr. Justice"), in which he claimed to have travelled the length and breadth of the land. The cascading piles of material, some kind of light cotton, as far as I could determine, were painted an interesting brown or orange. "The people of Arbroath," he confided in me, in hushed tones, "have christened it 'The Smokie'." He nodded sagely at me. "For its colour, you see. And its shape."

I realised now that, from the great distance at which we had first seen the balloon, it had reminded me precisely of that – a smoked haddock, open mouth at the front, twisted tails flapping in the breeze at the rear.

I informed him that I admired his flying-machine greatly. I discovered

Bosman at my elbow, anxious for an introduction to the great aeronaut. I performed this duty, and Bosman pumped Mr. Jo for a detailed explanation of every rope, every fold of cloth, the mysteries of the burner which – we were advised – had a double purpose: firstly, it heated the air which allowed the balloon to rise; secondly, it drove a small engine with a blade or propeller attached, which moved the whole affair forwards through the air. It seems that the bag of gas is in three portions: a central one which contains heated air, being the larger of the three; and two outer pockets, to front and rear, containing a light coal-gas, which is not permitted to escape. Mr. Jo proudly displayed this "combinatorial envelope" to us, announcing that it was his own invention. I noticed that Dr. Bosman paled slightly when he discovered that a flame would be so close to the coal-gas pockets, and stood well back. However, a considerable number of Poltonians clustered around, forcing me somewhat into the background.

At length, however, the crowd thinned, complaining loudly that the balloon was unlikely to rise again that day. Dusk was already falling. Hastily, Mr. Jo collected a team of those who could not sneak away, and arranged for ropes to be tied to the balloon, and for it to be tethered securely to the Cricket Pavilion which jutted out from the garden wall. On the previous day, at the insistence of Mr. Deans, our rickshaw had been dragged down here "for tidiness", and it stood propped against the wall. The securing of the aerostat lasted some thirty minutes, at the end of which it was so dark that we had difficulty seeing to whom we spoke. We were left almost alone on the cricket-field.

"Now, Mr. Justice," said Mr. Jo, rubbing his hands keenly. "Is Sir Thomas still with you? I am eager to speak with him again!"

Accompanied by Bosman, we made our way up the path and steps to the House. On the way, Mr. Jo explained his purpose. It seemed that he was writing an article for his innovative Encyclopaedia, on the subject of James Tytler, innovative Encyclopaedist and Balloonist himself; and had thought to make a journey to another famous family of Tytlers, at Woodhouselee, near Penicuik. Unfortunately, the Tytlers there claimed to be, to a man, unrelated to James; unsympathetic to an unauthorised landing on their grounds by any aeronaut, they had chased off Mr. Jo with a pack of hounds and a brace of shotguns, which came perilously close to puncturing the balloon.

"Not a single piece of information would they give me on James Tytler," lamented Mr. Jo. "The learned Mr. Fraser-Tytler, who holds the Chair of Conveyancing at Edinburgh University, conveyed to me that he wished to have nothing to do with Radicals, Fantasists, and anyone from north of the Forth. He also gave me to understand that his esteemed ancestor, Mr. Frazer Tytler, Advocate and Professor of Civil History, equally had nothing to do with the arrant nonsense of the foolhardy Mr. Tytler. And when I tried to persuade him that Mr. James Tytler was a relative of whom he could be proud, having been the first to ascend in a balloon in the entire Kingdom of Great Britain, he called his factor and his game-keeper and suggested they fill my balloon with lead." Mr. Jo shuddered: he was visibly upset at the memory. "I barely escaped with my life, Mr. Justice, barely with my life! And so much to do! I am too young to die at the hands of wealthy land-owners!"

I made some appropriate soothing comments, to raise his spirits. Are we not all, I said, too young to die in such a way? "Never fear, Mr. Jo," I said, clapping him on the shoulder. "The bearers of truth will always be remembered, and never die in the memory of the People!"

"Maybe so, Mr. Justice," he acknowledged, with even more agitation than previously, as we reached the top of the rise and came to a side-door into the House. After a few moments of reflection, he took a deep breath. "So, I thought to take myself to Edinburgh, to seek you out. But the wind drove me eastwards instead, and I was obliged to put down in some haste. But what a surprise to find you here!"

Keeping to myself my thoughts on the nature of surprises – sometimes pleasant, sometimes otherwise – I ushered Mr. Jo indoors, and sought out Urquhart. We found him, as usual, holding court in the midst of a throng of ladies of a certain age. The greetings exchanged between Urquhart and Jo were fulsome, formulated in Volapük, and fatuous. I left them in close conversation, and tracked down Mr. Deans, to advise him of our adventures in Edinburgh.

*   *   *

Mr. Deans was a worried man. "Well, Mr. Justice," he said thoughtfully, after hearing me out, "I think we may yet have trouble on our hands. If anyone at the Register Office recognised our Mr. Downie, they might think to follow him out here . . . "

It was a possibility which I also had been turning over in my mind, but had been loath to express. I was down-cast to hear my own thoughts thus confirmed. I made up my mind then to leave Mavis-bank, just as soon as I could think what to do with Bosman and Urquhart – and now Mr. Jo as well. I cursed the aeronaut for his accidental plunge into our midst. Could he not have pursued his search after knowledge in his own home county?

To compound my troubles, Mr. Deans now handed me a letter which, he said, had arrived that very afternoon. It had been sent from Leith at noon, and was addressed to "Mr. Justice, at Mavis-bank Private Lunatic Asylum". I opened it. I could tell from the hand-writing that it had been composed by Mr. Gunn. It was signed by a good dozen of the principal members of The Edinburgh Society for the Propagation of a Universal Language; and it cited Article Four of our Rules, which admitted the possibility of calling an Extra-ordinary General Meeting of the Society, should a simple majority of the members so request. The purpose of this Meeting, said the letter, would be to censure both myself and Dr. Bosman, for our "indecorous, undemocratic, and ill-conducted manouevres" at the recent Annual General Meeting. Taking into account our "pre-cipitate" departure from Edinburgh, to which no known purpose could be attributed, the Members had voted to hold the Extra-ordinary Meeting, on the Sunday after next, the nineteenth day of April. A flat refusal having been received from the Gael Mr. Mac-Donald, for the use of his premises, Mr. Dewar had agreed to permit the meeting to be held in his shop. If Bosman and I did not attend that meeting, the remaining Members would "hold a vote" on a motion to expel us. Expel us – from our own Society!! I detected the promptings of Mr. Kilpatrick in all of this, and made a mental note to have him ejected from the Society at the earliest opportunity.

"Bad news, Mr. Justice?" asked Mr. Deans, seeing the look of despair on my face.

I sat down wearily in a chair. "No, Mr. Deans, just more trouble which I shall have to deal with." I did not wish him to learn of any present challenge to my authority within the Society.

"I'm sure you will do that just admirably," said my friend politely, and went off to look after his own affairs, which included the urgent pacification of Mrs. Flowers, long convinced that she was the unhappy

Lady Grange, concealed among the savages of St. Kilda by an interesting husband. On this evening, Mrs. Flowers was persuaded that Mr. Jo's balloon was a vessel sent from the mainland to carry her from her rocky imprisonment, back to the sparkling lights of Edinburgh Society; and was making repeated attempts to run, in her night-attire, to the cricket-square and be "up-lifted". Mr. Deans was therefore greatly occupied.

*   *   *

I spent the early part of the evening in writing up the events of the day, and the lessons which were learned; and in considering my affairs. My great plans for trans-forming the Society into an instrument of the Volapük Academy seemed now to lie in tatters at my feet. For this, I cast blame at Sir Thomas Urquhart, for his grand promises of abetment. But every success which I had achieved while in the guise of the Cödel Yagöl was soon destroyed by the ability of people to suffer blows and rise again. Not one of them – as far as I could determine from the list of signatories at the foot of Gunn's letter – had remained true to Volapük. I took small comfort from the fact that the members also wished to bring Bosman to charge – all that this told me was that they resented his own petty attempts to steer the Society towards Esperanto. The thought which would not leave my mind was this: that perhaps I had brought my troubles upon myself. This was not the passive mood, but the reflexive.

I cannot wholly explain why I now did so; but, as the Residents chaotically and noisily prepared themselves for another interesting night, I left my room to seek out both Dr. Bosman and Sir Thomas, shook each solemnly by the hand, and embraced them, with tears in my eyes. To my great surprise, and – dare I say it? – comfort, both of them reciprocated in similar mood. Urquhart then ruined the whole thing by bursting out into gales of laughter and hitting me around the legs with his infernal stick. But he soon repented of his boisterous behaviour, and proclaimed me, before the assembled lunatics, "the greatest living Volapükian in the Realm!" Mr. Jo was inordinately impressed by this accolade, and shook me and Dr. Bosman warmly by the hand, several times over.

To divert attention from my tears, I sat down in a corner of the drawing-room with Bosman and Sir Thomas, and asked Mr. Jo to read us his article concerning James Tytler. Which he proceeded to do, for the next twenty-three minutes precisely, for it was a very long article. As he read on and on, I reflected that, if all of his articles ran to this length, then he would never reach the goal of fifty-thousand, which Urquhart had set him; and would therefore never see publication. In the course of that half-an-hour of relative peace and quiet, I learned of Mr. Tytler's boyhood in some forgotten hamlet of Forfar-Shire; of his insatiable appetite for learning; of his character as a shining example to all other encyclopaedists who came after (or before); of his repeated, and finally successful, arrangements to be the first living Briton to ascend in a balloon; of his subsequent humiliation by charlatans and *ignorami* of Edinburgh; and finally of his emigration to America, and sad extinction there in a puddle. It was scarcely a story to enliven my spirits, and I found in it, rightly or wrongly, too many echoes of my own life; but the recitation cheered Mr. Jo enormously, and he was keen to read me other recent works – on the nature of "Vexatious Litigants Resident in Montrose", on "Several Howtowdies of Forfar", on "Scientific Investigations into the Daichies at Buddon Ness". But my companions and I, having reached a new reconciliation and understanding, looked at each other and slowly shook our heads at each proposal. Finally, it was Sir Thomas who stood up, clapped Mr. Jo on the back and advised him to persevere with his Labours, "for your Light of Understanding illuminates the Stygian Waters of the Tay like the Colossus of Rhodes". Our encyclopaedist gave every indication of supreme satisfaction, and allowed us to retire for the night.

*   *   *

On the following morning, just as we completed an early breakfast, a Constable Campbell sought entrance. He had, he intimated, been despatched from the Police-Station at Bonnyrigg, on an Investigation of Great Importance. When it was explained to him that the super-intendent was unfortunately absent from the Institution, due to a tem-porary incapacity, he was content to be led into the presence of Miss Davidson. Miss Davidson scolded him thoroughly for having arrived "at the worst possible time", displaying with an all-encompassing wave of her hand the ferment, babble and turmoil over which she presided at this time in the morning, as the Residents arranged themselves into a suitable hierarchy for the day. Grandly, she sent the constable down to the kitchens, where he examined his boots for a good hour and clutched successive cups of tea.

At around nine o'clock, frustrated in his duties, the constable decided to pursue his enquiries without reference to the matron, who had either forgotten about him altogether, or had chosen to ignore him. Mr. Campbell therefore ventured out from the kitchens, located the nearest crowd of Residents by the simple police procedure of following the ceaseless noise, and ended up in the drawing-room of the south-wing.

Finding himself surrounded by a host of interested gentlemen, Constable Campbell drew out his notebook, licked his pencil and called for silence. He was a very tall, thin man, hair slightly greying, and with a moustache which bore the unmistakable stamp of authority. I am told, for I was not there at that time, that silence was instantaneous and profound.

"My orders," called out Campbell, "are to identify and apprehend a Mr. Alexander Downie, late of Her Majesty's General Register House in Edinburgh, and to accompany the said Mr. Downie to Edinburgh for further questioning." His remarks caused considerable excitement among the Residents: cries went up of "Edinburgh, O Heaven!", "Apprehension!", and "God Bless Her Majesty, thrice and thrice again!" Within moments, a man stood up, pointed dramatically at his own chest and declared: "I am that man, sir. You may arrest me! I will not resist!" Gratified, Constable Campbell put away his notebook, took the man by the arm and began to lead him away.

"Stay your hand, Constable!" came a shout. It was Mr. Oliver, the medical student. "That man, whom you hold by the arm, is but an impostor!" There were shouts of outrage around him, and a general cry of "Impostor! Charlatan!" Mr. Oliver continued, holding up his hand for silence: "I am Mr. Downie, and I will not let another man take my place." Great roars of approval from the on-lookers. Mr. Campbell pushed his captive away in disgust and laid hands upon Mr. Oliver, whom he proceeded to lead to the stairs with a dignified show of officiousness.

But no sooner had he reached the head of the stair-case than Mr. Gordon, the sheep-farmer, burst from the ranks, and threw himself upon the policeman.

"Where do you think you are taking that man, Constable?" he demanded to know.

"Have a care, sir!" exclaimed Mr. Campbell, drawing his truncheon. "Stand back, or it will be the worse for you!"

Mr. Gordon fell back. "That man is no more Mr. Downie than I am!" he proclaimed. "There is the man you seek!" He pointed dramatically at the hapless Mr. Glegg, the Aberdonian druggist, now a mere shadow of his former self, after several severe discussions with Miss Smyth.

"Who? Me?" muttered Glegg, trying to move backwards into the throng.

"Yes – that is the man you want, sir," repeated Mr. Gordon. "See how guilt is written all over his pasty face!"

It was true; for anyone who knew not Mr. Downie's appearance, Mr. Glegg was the picture of ill-concealed guilt. Constable Campbell made up his mind, released Mr. Oliver, and took possession of Mr. Glegg. But at that moment, a dozen other Downies made their presence known, including, as it happened, the real Mr. Downie himself; for they all saw, in arrest and banishment to Edinburgh, the promise of an escape from their day-to-day monotony.

I arrived at the climax of this great commotion, and rapidly pieced together what had been going on. Constable Campbell was becoming quite agitated, as he darted from person to person, trying to effect an arrest, only to find his intended charge being denounced as an impostor.

I thought it best to assist the poor man from his predicament, and, adopting the most urbane and conciliatory tone I could manage, drew the policeman to one side, and asked him to tell me in simple language for whom he was looking. "Thank you, sir," gasped Campbell, running his hands through his hair. "It's nice to hear a sane man again! Now then, I have been asked to look out for—" he consulted his notebook again, "Mr. Alexander Downie and Dr. Henry Bosman." He looked at me hopefully. "I don't suppose you could assist me in this matter?"

I had to disappoint him. "My dear sir," I told him. "How most unfortunate! Mr. Downie and Dr. Bosman both left the Asylum last night. I did wonder why they had fled so precipitately, and now I understand – they had no wish to be arrested by the merciless Arm of the Law, as represented by yourself!"

"Well, sir," admitted the constable, "I take that as a compliment. But I am disappointed. However—" he took out his pencil once more, "I don't suppose you could give me a description of the two suspicious individuals, and maybe an idea of the direction they might have taken?"

Naturally, I told him that I could, and led him off to Bosman's Census Office, where we could discuss the situation in peace. Mr. Deans was good enough to supply us with a pot of tea and some shortbread, and we were left alone (except for a crowd of Residents, who concealed themselves ill behind the door-jambs, whispering and grumbling).

I introduced myself to Constable Campbell in my own name, surmising, correctly, that he had no knowledge of me. We talked of this and that, I gave him the fullest descriptions of the two hunted men, such that the constable might be apprehending every man between the ages of twenty and sixty in the County of Mid-Lothian, in expectation of a "good arrest".

"And now, Sergeant," I said finally, "I am aware that Dr. Bosman is a most learned man in the language of Volapük. It might be to your advantage to acquire some familiarity with that language, if you are to proceed to a successful conclusion."

"Volapük, sir?" asked Campbell suspiciously, taking out his note-book again. "And what kind of animal might that be? How do you spell it?"

I gave him advice on that matter, and he furiously scribbled the name into his notebook, then looked up keenly "So: Volapük, sir. Can you explain it to me? If it makes my job any easier, I am a keen student!"

I sighed with the deepest satisfaction, settled back, and gave him the briefest of lessons:

Tidüp balsemälid – Prefixes and Suffixes.

"If I might be permitted to use an analogy, Mr. Campbell," I began, "I would say that the matter of Prefixes and Suffixes is the burning gas which permits the balloon of Volapük to lift to the skies and sail away on the aether."

Mr. Campbell looked up from his note-taking, a confused expression creasing his face.

I explained that, to a limited number of "base", "radical", or "principal" words, one could add any number of standard prefixes and suffixes to give that one Principal a greater life than it had ever known before.

Consider the following illustration, I said: the word for a criminal in Volapük is **klimel**. With the application of prefixes and suffixes, we may very easily arrive at the following variations in quality of that simple word:

- **klimel,** a criminal or felon
- **smaklimel,** petty-criminal   (small-)
- **leklimel** villain   (large-)
- **gleklimel,** master-criminal   (great-)
- **klimelil,** ruffian   (-little)
- **smaklimelil,** ne'er-do-well   (small-little)
- **luklimel,** thug   (bad-)
- **luklimelil,** delinquent   (bad-little)
- **luleklimel,** convict   (bad, big-)
- **lugleklimel,** jail-bird   (bad, great-)
- **legleklimel,** outlaw   (large, great-)
- **lusmaklimelil,** wretch   (bad, small-little)

Thus, Mr. Campbell, from one word, four prefixes and one suffix, we gain an additional dozen words, maybe more should we choose to. Words formed by prefixing syllables are, in reality, a kind of compound in which the first part is intimately blended with the second. In our previous example, **gleklimel,** a criminal, the word is composed of a prefix **gle-** followed by a noun **klimel,** great, or master-, criminal; thus, **klimel** is the "principal" and **gle-** the "determinant".

The constable asked me to go through the list once more, and made more notes in his book. Having done so, he looked up to await further enlightenment.

"So you see," I advised him, "by applying these determinants to the principal, we can make almost any word which we choose. Here," I said, reaching into the pocket of my coat, for it is my habit to carry with me a number of important reference-documents for the language of Volapük, for just such occasions as these. The student will find all of these documents included in the "Promptuary" at the end of this book. I passed him now a list of the most common prefixes and suffixes, that he might take them away and study them, of an evening in his Police-Station.

The policeman took them eagerly, and folded the list in at the back of his book, assuring me that he would take great care of it.

I decided to continue with my lesson, for he seemed an enthusiastic student, and firmly believed that this additional knowledge would help him lay hands on Bosman and Downie.

For the suffixes, the endings **-ik**, **-el**, **-am**, are the most common, and almost every radical may assume them. In our vocabulary of Volapük, we frequently give the radical only of one of these derivatives, leaving the others to be inferred, or inflected, by the intelligent student.

From any radical denoting a quality, an adjective attributing that quality may be formed by adding -ik: for example, **gud**, goodness, **gudik**, good; **jap**, sharpness, **japik**, sharp; and so on. Thus, dropping "-ness" is equivalent to adding -ik, or vice versa.

Every root or radical has, or may have, an adjective form ending in -ik, but there is not always a corresponding English adjective. Many adjectives are entirely lacking in English. We have no such word, for example, as "to-daily", and we use instead the possessive "to-day's", as in "to-day's newspaper", which is, in Volapük, **gased adelik**. We have "golden" derived from "gold", but have no adjective derived from "iron". (Constable Campbell nodded sagely at this point, for I had apparently hit upon a mystery which had troubled him for some time. "I suppose, sir," he asked reasonably, "that the word 'ironic' is therefore used in the same way?" I advised him otherwise, and continued.) But in Volapük, the words **golüdik**, **lelik**, **silefik** are regularly formed from **golüd** (gold), **lel** (iron), **silef** (silver). Whole phrases are also rendered by an adjective ending in -ik or an adverb ending in -iko, as my students will have learned in Lesson Eleven (**tidüp balsebalid**).

In similar fashion, any verb may form a noun by applying a suffix **-am**, which expresses the action of the verb, like our words in "-tion": for example,

- **plepalön**, to prepare   **plepalam**, preparation

And almost any verb may form a noun ending in -el, which expresses the doer of the action, as in **plepalel**, one who prepares; **studel**, a student, comes from **studön**, to study. In our example above, **klimel** is formed from **klim**, a crime.

All of this seemed quite clear to Constable Campbell, and I began to have a better opinion of the man. But I did not wish to tax him too far in his first apprehension of Volapük; and the hour for dinner was almost upon us, so I decided to come to the

Fin tidüpa balsemälid.

Constable Campbell was pleased to stay for dinner, at Miss Davidson's insistence; she had come bursting in at the end of our lesson, apologising profusely, and excusing herself for her ill-manners, "but, you know, Constable, the Residents sometimes drive me out of my mind!" Campbell looked askance at this remark, but he let it pass.

We congregated in the dining-room; myself, Campbell, Mr. Jo, Sir Thomas, Bosman and Downie, all to one table. Bosman and Downie were, understandably, in high nervous excitement, and Downie kept his head down at all times, scarcely uttering one word. Bosman never looked directly at the policeman, and affected an accent which hid his Colonial slurs under a quite rude resemblance of the Hebridean style of speech. But Constable Campbell, whose intelligence impressed me the more I saw of him, understood that the curious behaviour of the pair was simply due to their residence at Mavisbank, and politely ignored it. Sir Thomas, on the contrary, fastened his attentions on Campbell in the most ingratiating manner, and plied him with questions. The constable had, it seemed, done military service in his youth, and Sir Thomas was eager to recount to him certain deeds of his own derring-do and chivalry. Campbell listened with extreme courtesy and increasing scepticism, until as soon as the mince and potatoes had been dispatched, he eagerly expressed the view that he had better be on his way. Amidst many heart-felt protests from the Residents, who crowded round, in the sanguine hope that he would arrest at least a half-dozen of them, he took his leave of us and made his way back to Bonnyrigg by bicycle.

*   *   *

As we attended to a plate of rhubarb tart, a curious incident occurred. A tall, grey-faced man appeared in the door-way, fidgeting with a bundle of papers and talking with Mr. Deans and Miss Davidson. He peered at us all. Some of the Residents called out greetings of a more or less impolite nature, and we learned that his name was Mr. Pollard. It seemed that our small group stood out amongst the people in the room, although I could not imagine why, for Mr. Pollard came across to us directly. He was at least six feet and six inches in height, and had very little flesh about his person. Under his mouth, in place of a chin, grew a beard which was spread far too thin for comfort. His brow sweated as he progressed, leering, in our direction.

Coming up beside us, he coughed discreetly and asked if he might interrupt our dinner. "I am Mr. Pollard, the Secretary and Treasurer of the Mavisbank Private Lunatic Asylum Company (Limited), at your service."

Sir Thomas stood, and looked him up and down. "And I, sir," he replied majestically, "am Sir Thomas Urquhart, Baron of Cromarty, hereditary Sheriff there, patron of the three churches there, admiral of the seas between Caithness and Inverness, and proprietor of all the lands, estates, and fortified places of the Black Isle!"

Mr. Pollard appeared overcome with awe and gratitude. "My pleasure, sir, my pleasure entirely. Oh," he groaned, "that we have a Knight of the Realm staying within these walls – what a happy, happy day!"

Absurdly, Mr. Pollard made a deep bow before Sir Thomas. The latter smirked, and waved his hand magnanimously: "Please rise, my good fellow," he said, "and join us for dinner."

"Oh no, Sir Thomas, I could not do that. No, no, that would not do at all." Pollard shook his head decisively. "I beg you to continue, you and your friends—" He looked in an interrogative manner at the rest of us around the table.

Sir Thomas waved an arm vaguely in our direction. "Oh, these are not my friends, merely my servants. It amuses me sometimes, to have them dine with me. Let me present them – this is Mr. Jo, my secretary and biographist . . . " Mr. Jo inclined his forehead over his place-mat. "This is Dr. Bosman, my personal physician and occasional posterior ablutionary . . . " Bosman burned red in the face, but pursed his lips to remain silent. "And this is Mr. Justice, my valet, acolyte and procurer."

Pollard acknowledged us all, but was disturbed to find another physician in his establishment. "Oh dear, oh dear," he stuttered. "I fear that my superintendent, Dr. Keay, may have some reservations about the presence of Dr. Bosman, Sir Thomas. It is not normally permitted . . . "

"Fiddle-de-dee and poppycock, Mr. Pollard!" responded Sir Thomas, clapping Bosman upon the head to make his point. "Here is the finest physician you will ever meet! Do you know that he once cured no fewer than five hundred souls, on the battle-field of Verona, of the King's Evil?" Sir Thomas looked proudly upon Bosman. "I think he and your own doctor will find themselves to be kindred spirits!"

Mr. Pollard looked doubtful, but was too overcome by his awe of Sir Thomas to make any further objection. "Perhaps, Sir Thomas, we could meet after dinner – I have some matters that will need to be cleared up. That is, if you can spare me the time?"

Sir Thomas shook his head fiercely. "No, sir, I have no time for that. There are a dozen pretty wenches," here, he blew some gallant kisses in the direction of a neighbouring table, whose sexagenarian occupants gazed at us, simpering or slack-jawed, "who have assignations with me this afternoon. No, sir, if you wish to discuss business, you may talk to my valet, Mr. Justice."

"Very good, your Lordship, very good," mumbled Pollard, and he retreated backwards to the door, then vanished.

*   *   *

When dinner was completed to everyone's satisfaction, I felt obliged to seek out Mr. Pollard, whom I found in a small office at the foot of the main staircase.

"Ah, Mr. Justice," he greeted me, rather less obsequiously than he had done with Sir Thomas. "A small matter of administration which you can help me with. I am advised that the account of Sir Thomas and his retinue has not been paid in full, a matter I find highly irregular. I am a regular man, Mr. Justice, very regular indeed. I think you will find that I manage all of my affairs in a regular manner, very regular indeed, if I may say so." Mr. Pollard became quite emboldened, a different man from the one we had witnessed in the dining-room, barely twenty minutes earlier.

"So regular am I, Mr. Justice, that I have built a very regular business at my registered office in St. David Street, in the very heart of Edinburgh. I have not merely this grand Asylum in my care, to which we will only accept persons of distinction and—" He paused, the better to prepare the implication, "of distinction and, I repeat, a certain income. Not merely this Asylum, I say, but I have also in my trust the Home for Destitute Girls in Bonnyrigg, the Orphans' Corrective Home at Portobello, the Ravenscroft Convalescent Home for Veteran Gentlemen, and the Metropolitan Cemetery Company Limited: I have, I think you will find, all the regularities of Life in my port-folio."

Just then, my friend walked past. "Mr. Deans!" commanded Mr. Pollard, now quite enlivened with excitement. "Mr. Deans, come in here."

Mr. Deans duly complied, and stood placidly by the door as Pollard continued. "I am the regular and sole authority in this place, whether or not Dr. Keay, the Superintending Physician, is present! Am I not, Mr. Deans?" Mr. Deans confirmed this fact. "Oh yes, indeed, and my knowledge of my business is very regular indeed: I can cite you every paragraph and every provision of the 'Trial of Lunatics Act' of 1883, of the 'Criminal Lunatics Act' of 1884, of the 'Lunacy Act' of 1885, of the 'Lunacy (Vacation of Seats) Act' of 1886, of Her Majesty's 'Idiots Act' of 1886, of the 'Inebriates Act' of 1888, of the 'Imbeciles Act' of 1889, and of the 'Lunacy Act' of 1890 . . . " he licked his index-finger for each of these great Acts and checked them off on his other hand proudly. "And every man Jack of them states this: that I make the decisions here!"

Mr. Pollard paused to consider, as if unsure how he had arrived at such a state of agitation. He fanned himself and sat down behind his desk. "Now where was I? Ah, and Sir Thomas Urquhart, sir," he addressed me. "I am a regular man, but I am also a worried man. How is it that Sir Thomas has been with us for almost a week, and that I have no record of any payments in my accounts? Neither for himself, nor for his three servants? Can you explain it, Mr. Justice?"

I had no idea how to reply, and wondered whether I should perhaps deny all knowledge of financial matters. Mr. Pollard interpreted my hesitation as a sign of guilt. "Mr. Justice: let me make this easy for you. Is Sir Thomas curable?"

"Curable, Mr. Pollard?" I was rather startled by the question. Sir Thomas, being dead, was scarcely curable.

"Yes, curable, sir. Can he be cured? What is Dr. Bosman's mental prognosis? I will not have any incurables in this establishment – it does my business no good at all! Incurables worry me, and they bring no profit, either to themselves or to the Mavisbank Private Lunatic Asylum. Incurables are quite irregular!"

I considered the matter. Clearly, it would do no harm to adjudge Sir Thomas as curable, so I said that Dr. Bosman advised me so. Mr. Pollard was to some degree calmed by this thought. "But I worry about the money, Mr. Justice – it is highly irregular not to have the accounts paid, don't you see? It is not for me to question Sir Thomas' integrity, but the account must be paid! Mr. Justice, I will tell you something." He stepped over to me and, placing a long arm around my shoulders in a complicit manner, lowered his voice. "In the strictest confidence, Mr. Justice, we have, on Monday, a visitation from the Lunacy Commissioners."

This meant nothing to me, and my face must have betrayed this, for he continued: "The Lunacy Commissioners come regularly, twice each year, you understand, to inspect our premises and the facilities offered, and make a report on whether we are regular or not. Despite the regularity of our business, a visit from the Commissioners is always a great worry. For if we are not regular, then we shall receive a bad report, and that is not a good thing, Mr. Justice. Being regular means that all accounts must be paid in full, and all persons found within the Establishment must be either Staff, or Residents, or the servants of Residents. Our entertainments must be regular, our treatments must be sound, our Residents must be found to be contented. But above all, the accounts must be regular. Do you see my problem, Mr. Justice?"

In truth, I saw not just his problem, but also my own. The last thing we wanted, except perhaps the company of Sir Thomas, was an agency of the Government uncovering our place of refuge. It was imperative that we left the place. To be rid of the man, I confirmed my full understanding of his problem, and promised that matters should be expedited to make the accounts just as regular as possible. I left him worrying with Mr. Deans in the small office.

I gathered Bosman and Mr. Jo (Sir Thomas was nowhere to be seen), and we retired to consider our position. We found the store-room above the stables in the north-wing, which was secluded enough for our purpose. In little or no time at all, we had agreed that our best strategy would be to leave Mavisbank as soon as possible. After about a quarter of an hour, as we still sat there in discussion, there was a commotion in the yard, and Pollard emerged from the House, in quite a fit of worry, waving his arms at Mr. Deans and Miss Davidson. The latter was in tears, the former ashen-faced. It seems that Mr. Pollard had found nothing to be regular.

"I come out here to have a quiet Saturday in the country, and what do I find? Nothing but worry! Dr. Keay in his sick-bed. Irregular guests, treating the Asylum as if it were their own fiefdom, without paying a penny! Parochial balloonists dropping in from the skies, as if this were a common pleasure-ground! An idiot policeman poking his nose where it does not concern him! This is not regular at all, by no means! Does this tell me that I need not worry? Does it?"

We could not hear any answers to Pollard's excited interrogation, but it was clear that such answers as were given were not at all placatory.

"What way is this to run a good investment? I have trouble enough on my hands with that mad-man Clouston conspiring to take away all my business to his fairy-tale castles at Craighouse! Oh, what can we do? I will be back at first light on Monday with Dr. Keay, to prepare for the Commissioners; and, if that account has not been paid and any of these people are still here, then we shall have worries, mark my words! Regular worries!" With that threat, he climbed aboard his substantial carriage, flicked regularly at the horse, and bounced off along the drive-way that led to the North Gate.

Katel Balselulid, the Fifteenth Chapter:
The Interjection

"Kautö!!"

After Pollard's departure, I looked for Mr. Deans. He was most apologetic, and cursed the Company Secretary for his ignorance and his worrying – "There was no 'Imbeciles Act' of 1889," he pointed out, "and all the others are just foam on the waters. The man sees nothing beyond his accounts."

But he seemed relieved when I advised him of our plans to depart. "It is probably for the best, Mr. Justice. The Commissioners have keen eyes, I fear. But so they should, after all." We decided that Monday morning would be the best time for a departure, as the trains would be running propitiously. Mr. Jo advised us that he had to make many repairs and adjustments to his machine before he could launch himself into the upper atmosphere.

We therefore spent the Sunday busy at all those arrangements which we must make for our departure. Sir Thomas had that morning made the rather startling discovery that his mice, who had unaccountably accompanied him from Edinburgh, and previously twenty-four in number, had increased even to the third generation: "Gargantua", it seemed, had done Sir Thomas proud, and had impregnated his eleven sisters to such a degree, that no fewer than one hundred and thirty new babies had been born overnight. Sir Thomas was transported to Paradise: "One hundred and fifty-two children, Justice!" he boasted to me. "The very number of generations which separates me from Adam, so Adam has produced." In high spirits, he scuttled off to find Mrs. Bentzen, so that the two of them might plot out names and genealogy. I was, I confess, interested in the co-incidence of number; but less encouraged by Sir Thomas' boast that, "They will all be able to speak my Universal Language!", a prediction, given my experience with the parrot, I found unrealistic. Mr. Deans, on hearing of the new arrivals, suggested that they might require a larger box; and asked his colleague, young John Currie, to knock together something grander.

Sir Thomas demanded that he supervise this construction, and, as I later heard from an exasperated Mr. Currie, was a very hard task-master: the new palace for mice took an entire day to build. Mrs. Kirkaldy was softened by the mere thought of babies, and donated a full canvas bag of oats for their sustenance and well-being, a gift which Sir Thomas, gallant to a fault, acknowledged with a quatrain that brought a blush to the good woman's cheeks.

For his part, Mr. Jo spent hours down at the cricket-square with the architect Mr. Burnie, attending to his flying-machine and preparing it as best he could for the morning flight. Dr. Bosman and I sat with each other, discussing our past antagonism, and the foolishness which had led us to argue that one Universal Language could hold sway over another. I think I finally persuaded him that Esperanto was no better and no worse than Volapük; and that we should work closely together in the future, sharing all that we knew and all of our researches. Even, I suggested, we should conduct mutually beneficial researches into the vocabulary used commonly by Africans, Asians, and Orientals, with a view to advancing to a higher vocabulary altogether. Bosman was enthusiastic. "*Ni venkos!*" he cried in his suspect Esperantist dialect, standing up and shaking hands with me, "*Ni venkos* – we shall win!" "*Lesi ovikobs* – indeed we shall win!" I replied enthusiastically. I began to nurture ambitions of retrieving my position in Mrs. Forbes' house-hold, on our imminent return to Edinburgh – my recon-ciliation with Bosman would surely assist my passage down the attic-stair. Of course, I did not tell Bosman of the imminent Extraordinary General Meeting, proposed for following Sunday. It seemed cruel to upset him further, just when we had effected a reconciliation.

While we worked at our own plans, most of the Residents prepared themselves for a visit to church, and some had high hopes of an afternoon trip to the public park in Loanhead: there was, therefore, great cheer among all the regular parties at Mavisbank.

I occupied the peace and quiet of the Sunday afternoon in bringing all of my notes into order, writing down for posterity those lessons and exercises from the past two days which I present in this volume, and storing them carefully in my tin box. I took the opportunity thus afforded to read over the notes and Transactions which I had written over the previous week, and interrogated myself on the wisdom and meaning of my recent actions. It did not seem, now, to have been a sensible tactic, to have contracted with Urquhart, and to have forced an open conflict with Bosman. Worse than that: I now wondered whether it was right to oblige future generations to adopt a language whose rules permitted little variation and creativity.

These were hours of bleak introspection. But at supper-time, in the company of friends, I regained hope of a brighter future. After supper, I reviewed my recent "Transaction" relating to the rather obscure matter of Writing for the Blind, which was discussed vigorously at an early meeting of the Edinburgh Society; the interested student may, of course, examine that document elsewhere in this volume. From my brief introduction to several different methods of writing for the blind, I found that those of M. Louis Braille or Mr. Thomas Lucas could readily be adopted as the official, authorised, alphabet for blind students of Volapük. It seems clear that a method of dots, lines or other simple symbols could be used to represent the constituent parts of a Volapük word – the prefix, the radical, the suffix. The matter is so simple that even Dr. Bosman – no, even Mr. Gunn! – might be able to understand it.

The one thing which was clear from our discussions on these methods of writing was that the most popular method for blind people themselves were those methods which had been developed by other blind people. Truly, a case of the Blind leading the Blind, and neither falling into a ditch! A lesson for those who would try to impose their own standards on others.

I intend to write a paper for the Academy in Paris, outlining my ideas, and proposing the creation of a Committee to examine the matter in more detail. This Committee must take responsibility for developing a written alphabet for the blind; and a sign-language for the deaf and dumb; each of these must be as fundamentally simple as Volapük itself. If ever I return to my habitual life, I should, of course, be honoured to serve on this Committee.

*   *   *

On Monday morning, the thirteenth of April, 1891, the House stirred at about seven o'clock, and we breakfasted at nine. Immediately thereafter, Mr. Jo dressed himself in his heavy coat, gloves and warm hat, and went down to the cricket-square to prepare for flight. "Arbroath awaits my triumphant return," he stated, before swinging dramatically down the path, closely followed by a group of interested admirers, some of whom carried small bags of Mid-Lothian coal to fuel the burner, and to replenish the coal-gas.

I gathered together Dr. Bosman and Sir Thomas, and such small items of luggage as we had accumulated during our brief stay at Mavisbank – mostly papers and such, although Sir Thomas had a bag full of lace handkerchiefs from his regiment of admirers. Dr. Bosman had nothing other than the clothes in which he stood. But he seemed cheerful enough to be departing.

We thought to see Mr. Jo on his way before we ourselves proceeded to the railway-station; in the company of the entire complement of Staff and Residents of the House – excepting the Lady Grange and the nurse, Miss McGarrie, posted to keep her from making an escape from St. Kilda – we made our way down to the meadow by the river. The balloon, under the influence of the hot air arising from the burner, was already fidgeting at its ropes, and the striking resemblance to a smoked haddock was obvious.

At last, all was ready. The wind, so our aeronaut advised us, was set fair for Aberbrothic, and the order was given to cast off; the balloon rose gently and noisily into the air, directly upwards, as if reeled in by some heavenly fishing-line, its engine sputtering and its propeller swishing. Mr. Jo continued to shout out his farewells, and wave a flag (on which the Volapük legend: "*No man obi oviatom!*" had been extended overnight to: "*No lusmamanil obi oviatom!*"), as he rose higher and higher. Leaning backwards to watch him, we detected of a sudden a note of panic in his voice. He dropped the flag at his feet and hastily began to fiddle with the mechanisms and ropes. In an instant, the balloon began a precipitous descent, plunging earthwards to the very spot from which it had just lifted. As it approached the ground, we could hear Mr. Jo shouting to us: "Quick, stop, climb aboard, flee!" and similar interjections.

I took a moment to provide Dr. Bosman quickly with

Tidüp balsevelid – Interjections.
The ending for interjections is **-ö**. Therefore, take the imperative mood of any verb, simply drop the letter **-d**, and omit any personal ending. Thus:

- **Spidö!**   Run!   (from the Imperative form **Spidöd**)
- **Stopö!**   Halt!
- **Bafö!**   Bravo!
- **Kautö!**   Look out!
- **Bunö!**   Jump!

Fin tidüpa balsevelid.

before we ran to the basket, which had now landed on the wet grass with a thud and crack, to find out what had so disturbed our friend.

"They're all here!" he gasped. "The Police, the Authorities – they have surrounded us! There's no way out!" He pointed distractedly in all directions, and the fear painted on his face was enough to make us aware of our danger.

"Quick!" he advised, grabbing Sir Thomas roughly and dragging him over the lip of the basket. "Climb aboard, there's no time to be lost!"

But it was clear that Mr. Jo's basket was built for one man alone, and would not contain even Sir Thomas as an extra passenger. But then the inventive Mr. Burnie hit upon an idea: "The rickshaw!" he shouted. Immediately, the rickshaw was dragged from its resting-place, willing hands secured ropes to it at various supportive points, and tied those ropes back to any suitable point on the under-belly of the dirigible. In less than five minutes, we had an additional *nacelle* suspended from the balloon. Into which, throwing caution to one side, Sir Thomas, Bosman and I hastily climbed, pushing before us the tin-box with all my documents, and the mouse-palace with its unsuspecting occupants and their essential bag of oats.

Back in his own basket, Mr. Jo applied his burner at full flame, and we rose slowly but steadily from the ground, leaving behind us a lake of upturned faces. Our rickshaw swung perilously some ten feet below Jo's basket, wheels twirling idly in the wind; but seemed secure enough. We brushed the tops of the trees, rapidly attained and overtook the height of the House itself, and then caught a breeze which moved us slowly in the direction of Lasswade, over the lake and doocot. But before we had gone very far, we saw the sight which had so terrified our spy in the sky:

Our persecutors were swarming from three directions simultan-eously. Issuing from the drive-way which led to the North Gate, with access from Loanhead, were a good half-dozen carriages, filled with Alienists and Lunacy Commissioners (or so we supposed, for they seemed be-spectacled and respectable enough, being led by Mr. Pollard); from the direction of Polton, along the little lane which led from the Lodge, around twenty or thirty policeman on foot, having arrived, as far as we could tell, on board a "special" train from Eskbank, and led by Constable Campbell; from the East Gate, several speeding black carriages, and leaning out of the fore-most of these, the avenging Registrar General for Scotland himself, urging on his teams of horses and clerks.

But they were all soon past us, Alienists, Lunacy Commissioners, Registrars and Constables all, as we swung high above Lasswade, and touched the cold upper airs, on our way to the Extraordinary General Meeting of The Edinburgh Society for the Propagation of a Universal Language, and to liberty.

Katel Balsemälid, the Sixteenth Chapter:
The Frequentative and Aorist Forms, the Prepositions and Derived Prepositions; Idiomatic Expressions; and *Miscellania*

"Päistimobs, no poistimobs"

The wind carried us beyond Lasswade and then, as we came out of the valley, bore us northwards towards the *leglezif* of Edinburgh. We sat huddled in the rickshaw, clinging on to each other for safety, as it swung steadily backwards and forwards. It was bitterly cold. Sir Thomas had put on his embroidered mittens, and amused himself – and infuriated us – by engaging in a game of *bal pötet, tel pötets, kil pötet*, and so forth, on the knuckles of myself and Bosman. For their safe-keeping, he sat upon the splendid new box which was the home for his one hundred and fifty-four mice and their bag of oats, the first flying mice in Mid-Lothian; but was concerned for their health, for "it is thanatostically hyperboreal up here, Mr. Jo!" Sir Thomas wished to know whether our pilot had any spare straw, to keep the mice snug; but the answer was regrettably in the negative. The many ladies' handkerchiefs were therefore sacrificed for rodent comfort.

Nervously, his teeth chattering from fear or cold, Bosman shouted up to Mr. Jo, to ask when we should arrive in Edinburgh. Ten feet above us, Mr. Jo muttered some answer, but the wind caught his words and bore them away. For my part, the only additional clothing which I possessed was the helmet, cloak and gauntlets of Cödel Yagöl. I pulled on the gauntlets and, in a fit of humanity, wrapped the cloak around myself and Dr. Bosman, if only to stop his infernal shaking. The helmet, or mask of Cödel Yagöl, I left to one side, for I no longer wished to wear it; and Sir Thomas used it as further protection for his generations of mice.

Our view of Edinburgh was totally obscured by a fog, which lay thickly in every direction along the coast. The top-most knob of Arthur's Seat poked out, and, over to the west, the Pentland Hills rose dramatically out of the clouds. But for miles to our north, east and west, there was nothing else to be seen. To make our situation worse, the dirigible now veered slightly, and promised to carry us, not to Edinburgh, but in the general direction of East-Lothian.

Mr. Jo peered out over the featureless expanse before us and shrugged his shoulders. "Well," he said, "it seems that we will not make Edinburgh."

"What?" shouted Bosman, enraged. "What do you mean?"

Mr. Jo earnestly explained that he had very little control over the flying device, because some of the ropes, by which eager hands had attached our rickshaw to the balloon, had "fouled" the controls for steering. I asked Mr. Jo to explain this more clearly. Which he did, to our utter mystification. All we could see was a jumble of ropes and pulleys, here and there a metal object like a horse-shoe, and great knots where, according to Mr. Jo, there should have been free-running wires. "The thing is," he concluded, "that I can no longer steer the ship!"

As if in confirmation of this gloomy prognosis, the dirigible now began to shift its nose towards the south-east.

Dr. Bosman became agitated. He stood up, threatening to tip all three of us from the rickshaw into the mist below. "Put the balloon down here," he demanded, "and we'll walk to Edinburgh!"

Mr. Jo shook his head sadly. "I cannot do that. Look—" and he pointed directly downwards, over the edge of the basket, where the ground was already quite obscured from view. "I have no idea what is down there. If we descend, I may end up in a river, down a chimney, in a fire – we would be destroyed utterly! We might even—" Here, Mr. Jo wiped perspiration from his face, and I could see that his eyes widened at the thought, "We might even put down in some land-owner's park, and be peppered with bullets until we are dead!"

"Never mind that!" Dr. Bosman shook his fist impotently at the pilot above us, "Put us down anyway – sudden death is better than this madness!"

Mr. Jo shrugged his shoulders and began to pull levers and adjust ropes, peering upwards as he did so. It looked marvellously com-plicated. After a lengthy pause, and with no apparent adjustment in our height, he looked down at us again, a perplexed expression on his face.

"We cannot go down, I fear," he said apologetically. "I think that Mr. Burnie's Perpetual Motion Device has taken over."

I queried this. "What device is this, Mr. Jo?"

Our pilot seemed a little embarrassed. "Mr. Burnie persuaded me yesterday that his new invention for perpetual motion, or perpetual energy, could readily be fitted to my dirigible. I permitted him to do so. Hence these horse-shoes and pulleys and cables. Unfortunately," here he rubbed his forehead in despair, "he has fitted it so that, when I open the valves to descend, his machine closes them and stokes up the fires, so that we ascend again. There's no fooling it." Mr. Jo looked sad. "The only way for you to descend is if I cut the ropes which support you . . . "

Bosman collapsed in on himself, and leaned against me for support. "Then my fate is sealed," he whispered. Of a sudden, I shared his despair, and the words came un-bidden to my mouth: "*adyö – adelo deilobs!*"

*   *   *

For hours, it seemed, we drifted silently over the cloud. We were suspended, as if in a dream, between blue sky and white sky. Our course altered gradually to south, south-west, west – in short, we were cruising in a wide circle. All that could be heard was the steady drone of the propeller, the whistling of the breeze through the ropes, the flapping of the gills of the giant haddock, the chattering of Bosman's teeth, and the occasional grumble from Sir Thomas, as he worried about his mice.

The perceptive Reader may inquire how it is that I continue to write these words in our Hand-Book and Manual. Let it never be said of a serious champion of the Universal Language, that the biting winds of eastern Scotland even once prevented him from writing his text-book: I therefore distracted myself from the dizzying air below us, by completing my notes on the events of the past day. And let it never be said that the education of my comrades would stop just because we hung fearful, suspended between life and death. *Fanöd deli!* For, though we die tonight, then we die with our knowledge of Volapük enriched! I therefore proposed to Bosman that I give him a brief lesson:

Tidüp balsejölid – The Frequentative Mood and the Aorist Tense.
In Volapük, I explained, there is a distinction made between the

expression "I walked on the ground" and "I used to walk on the ground", the former suggesting one specific occasion, the latter indicating a frequent occurrence. In Volapük, the phrase "I walked on the ground" is rendered simply as *äspatob su gluni*. But for the phrase "I used to walk on the ground", an additional vowel -i- is introduced, thus: *äispatob su gluni*.

So, I advised Dr. Bosman (who, disappointingly, took very little interest in my lesson), when a verb refers to the habitual, "frequent", performance of an action, this may be indicated by adding the letter -i (pronounced as a separate syllable) to the tense augment. Thus,

- **ai-, äi-, ei-, ii-, oi-, ui-.**
- **pai-, päi-, pei-, pii-, poi-, pui-.**

Urquhart interrupted here with one his impertinent remarks: "So, I would render 'I had frequently made love to that woman' as *ülöfob et vomi?*"

As befits a good teacher, I ignored his interruption and his imbecilic giggling. I explained to my companions that, for grammaticians, the mood we had been discussing was termed "The Frequentative", while the simple past tense was known as "The Aorist" – *Pästimob* – "I was once honoured".

And, despite appearances, Bosman had indeed been taking account of all my lessons, for he groaned then, and said to me un-prompted: "*Päistimob!*"

Astonished, I looked at him. "Indeed, Dr. Bosman," I replied, "you were once in the habit of being honoured!"

"And from now on, I will no longer be honoured . . . " he muttered.

"*No poistimom,*" said Urquhart, rather unnecessarily. Mr. Jo, who was leaning dangerously out of his basket to attend to my lesson, nodded glumly, then returned his attention to the milky wastelands below. *Fin tidüpa balsejölid.*

Our journey continued eastwards; at around one o'clock, a break in the cloud showed us a large house on a hill below us. Our pilot recognised this as the Mid-Lothian and Peebles District Asylum at Rosslynlee, barely three or four miles south of Mavisbank. Sure enough, a number of the patients stood on the ground surrounding the house, and waved to us. Only Sir Thomas waved back. Then the clouds closed in again.

When night fell, the clouds began to thin below us, and, by the light of a dim moon, we were able to make out Mavisbank House as we passed over it. We have done so several times during this cold night, following a circle some five miles in diameter. I can barely see to write these words. My fingers are numb. I will pick up my pen again to-morrow.

[. . .]

Exercise 24.

Translate into Volapük:

- In that house down there, they see things not seen by other men.
- Do you drink wine? I used to drink wine, but now I am drinking rain-water.
- Do you eat meat? We used to eat meat, but now we are chewing leather.
- I write, in order to teach.
- I am writing, in order to teach.

[. . .]

It is four-and-twenty hours since we first escaped from the clutches of inimical authority, and still we sail over Mavisbank and the smoking valleys of Mid-Lothian. Sir Thomas has loaned me his gloves, so that I might continue to transcribe for the education of the Common Man, even in our Peril. I reward his selflessness by providing

Tidüp balsezülid – Prepositions of Time and Motion.
The ending **i** is sometimes added to adverbs of place, giving them the meaning of motion towards. Thus,

- **Ebinobs in et dom de lienet**, we have been *in* that house of madness.
- **Nekanobs golön in at domi de lienet**, or **nekanobs golön ini at dom de lienet**, we cannot go *into* this (other) house of madness.

Similarly the ending **a** is used to denote motion *from* in a few words.

Is, isa, isi,	here, hence, hither
Us, usa, usi,	there, thence, thither
Kiöp, kiöpa, kiöpi,	where, whence, whither

To express duration of time the preposition **du** is used. But sometimes the preposition is omitted (as in English) and then the noun may remain in the nominative or be put into the accusative. Thus, there are three forms of expression:

•	**Blibobsöx in sil du dels tel,**	We might remain
•	**Blibobsöx in sil dels tel,**	(for) two days in
•	**Blibobsöx in sil delis tel,**	the sky.

But we prefer to retain the preposition **du**.
Fin tidüpa balsezülid.
[. . .]

*   *   *

Note by the Contributing Editor of Logic:
This is, I regret to say, the final chapter, or, if I may be permitted to borrow an expression to which we are now greatly accustomed, Katel Finik, of this Hand-Book. It will be understood that I have been put to great pains to decipher the hand-writing of the author in this last chapter, for in several places the penmanship, to my chagrin, is seen to falter. It is also most lamentable that several pages have been lost from the manuscript; we have been to great trouble to mark the lacunae with ellipses, to guide the Reader. We can only surmise that these missing passages are, even now, impaled on bramble-bushes, hawthorn-trees, and similar sports of Mother Nature, in the mountainous wastes south-west of Dalkeith.

An additional calamity is that the "key" to Exercise 24 has been lost, so the serious Student will have to determine for himself if his rendering of the translation is correct.

We would request that, if any person comes across these missing pages, he be pleased to dispatch them to myself, Dr. Lyon, or to my colleagues Dr. Chartres or Professor Cordiner, at the Mavisbank Institute for Pantology, for correction and inclusion in any future edition of this work. You have been very patient. I, too, have been very patient. I thank you for your patience. We are, *ergo*, thanked. (FRL)

Postscript

A note from Dr. William Chartres, Episcopalian,
concerning the mysterious writings at Roslin:-

No doubt many Readers have been as greatly disturbed as I by the signification and meaning of the writings within the garden of the Roslin Manse, and by the curious chant kept up by the unfortunate Sir Thomas Urquhart throughout his stay at Mavisbank Academy. It is our greatest good fortune to have found a mind of such amiability, such clarity, and such affinity, in the person of Professor Sigismond Bugarschitz of Vienna, that we may pass on to the Readers of this volume his enlightening translations of these writings. The esteemed Professor is, of course, familiar to us all for his recent interpretations of the Rosetta Stone, which reveal the intercourse between the Ancient Egyptians and Voyagers from the Furthest Stars; and we are certain that his forth-coming sixteen-volume *Kurzweilige epistopaläentologisch-wissenschaftliche Forschungsberichte über den Syllogismen des Grafen Hubertus von und zu Hause* will cause a revolution in the studies of the Neo-Platonic Civilisations.

We received, only yesterday, a letter from Professor Bugarschitz, containing his excellent and fluent translation of some words which we had telegraphed to him on the sixteenth day of April. Since they require no further revision from a poor scholar such as myself, we reproduce them as follows:

"I am by your recent Telegraph excitedly aroused. Here in Wien believes Everyman, that a great scientific Event in Roslin succeeds. Later will I my Observation explain. For now, let me Light on the unknown Words bring.

"Ebo payagobs e pacödobs, ibo dels ebeigoloms kü äyagobs. Eketobs, ab esötobs libön. Elitobs adelaliti nabik su vegi nefinik kel dugos äl odelo; e sikod efalobs.

"My good Sir, these Words are clearly from a Volapük-Language Diktum extracted. Volapük-Language was recently here in Wien very spread; I myself have on some Occasions the Meetings attended, and naturally with the leading Exponents at length Themes into Discussion taken. The Words, which you kindly sent have, can thus translated become:

"Now are we hunted become and are we judged become, for the Days have by us passed, in which we ourselves have hunted. We have in Chains placed, when we have oughted at Liberty to set. We have with a narrow Today-Light the Road without End lighted, which leads into the Morrow; and thus have we fallen.

"This Diktum shares with the Dead Cult of the Egyptian many interesting Characteristics. It is certain, that the Weighing of the Heart before Thoth in these Words encompassed is. And when we next the short Song or Verse (or 'Rime', if I the Poet Coleridge correctly cite) study, which an interesting Metre not common here in Europe pursues, find we quite clear, that it Matter holds, which for very certain to the Astronomical Secrets of the Pharaohs new Understanding brings.

> Baltumlulsefol mugs ebinoms,
> Glekalodik in sil esenoms.
> Efidoms lieni,
> Emekoms vam bedi,
> Obik vab e mugs efaloms.

"This will translated become:

> One hundred four and fifty Mouses they have been,
> Greatly cold in the Heaven they have felt themselves.
> They have eaten Ropes,
> They have a warm Bedding made,
> The Wagon mine and the Mouses have fallen.

"My dear Herr Professor! Here are the Clues not to avoid! This Rime tells us, that a Visitation from the Stars in the nearest Future to be expected is. Consider: One Hundred Four and Fifty – this is the product of twenty-two and seven, the Dividend and Divisor of *Pi*, written π. Can that an Accident be? In no Event! π helps us, the Sizes of Circles to comprehend. The inverse Product helps us therefore, the Size of the Universe outside our Circle to comprehend. And then follow the References to 'the Heaven' and to 'the Wagon' – in my Country refers 'the Wagon' to The Wain, alternatively The

Great Bear, alternatively The Plough. The Visitation will of course Origins in the Constellation known as The Plough have. And let us further extrapolate: the little 'Mouses' must as the Visitors themselves understood become, who search for a new Homeland. This is, how the Visitors on the Walls of the Necropolis of Giza depicted were.

"When we this Rime in Conjunction with the other Text together sit, clear understood will it be, that the Visitors in the Judging Chair sit will, as states the demotic Book of the Dead, which in the Tomb of Tuthmosis III found was.

"My dear Herr Doktor Chartres, these Texts are the most exciting Discoveries of our Century! My serious Colleague, Herr Professor Etzel of Hünsrück, arranges even today an Expedition to Roslin, so that he may for the Visitors from the Stars be preparing. My own dear Son, young Hartmut, travels with him, these Matters to annotate and to study. Their Arrival in four Weeks should expected become!"

Napolel Balid, the First Addendum:
A Promptuary of Volapük

Readers should not be inclined to examine this "Synopsis of Inflections" until after they have mastered all the previous exercises. They are then recommended to make a copy of the Synopsis, leaving blanks for the Volapük letters, which they will afterwards fill up from memory.

Plural Ending	-s					
Negation	ne-					

Case	Nominative	Possessive	Dative	Accusative		
endings	–	-a	-e	-i		

Gender	Feminine	Masculine	Neuter			
prefixes	ji-	om-	os-			

Adjective		Ordinal	Comparative	Superlative		
endings	-ik	-id	-ikum	-ikün		

Adverb						
endings	-iko	-na	-ikumo	-iküno		

Preposition	Among	In/into	From	During		
endings	-ü	-i	-a	-du		

Person endings	1st Person	2nd Person	3rd (Masculine)	3rd (Feminine)	3rd (Neuter)	Indefinite
Singular	-ob	-ol	-om	-of	-os	-on
Plural	-obs	-ols	-oms	-ofs	–	–

Tense Arguments	Present	Imperfect	Perfect	Pluperfect	Future	Future Perfect
– Active	–	ä-	e-	i-	o-	u-
– Passive	pa-	pä-	pe-	pi-	po-	pu-

Frequentative						
– Active	ai-	äi-	ei-	ii-	oi-	ui-
– Passive	pai-	päi-	pei-	pii-	poi-	pui-

Gerundives	Present
– *Active*	ö-
– *Passive*	pö-

Mood	Participle (-ing, -ed)	Infinitive	Imperative	Soft imperative (Optative)	Harsh imperative (Jussive)	Potential
endings	-öl	-ön	-öd	-ös	-öz	-öx
	Conditional	Conjunctive	Interrogative	Reflexive		
	-öv	-la	-li	-ok		

Interjection	
ending	-ö!

Thus: *joke* – **cog**

Plural Ending	cogs		
Negation	necogön		

Case	Nominative	Possessive	Dative	Accusative
endings	cog	coga	coge	cogi

Gender	Feminine	Masculine	Neuter
prefixes	jicog	omcog	oscog

Adjective		Comparative	Superlative
endings	cogik	cogikum	cogikün

Adverb			
endings	cogiko	cogikumo	cogiküno

Preposition	Among	In/into	From	During
endings	cogü	cogi	coga	cogdu

Person endings	1st Person	2nd Person	3rd (Masculine)	3rd (Feminine)	3rd (Neuter)	Indefinite
Singular	cogob	cogol	cogom	cogof	cogos	cogon
Plural	cogobs	cogols	cogoms	cogofs	-	-

Tense Arguments	Present	Imperfect	Perfect	Pluperfect	Future	Future Perfect
– *Active*	-	äcogob	ecogob	icogob	ocogob	ucogob
– *Passive*	pacogob	päcogob	pecogob	picogob	pocogob	pucogob

Frequentative	Present	Imperfect	Perfect	Pluperfect	Future	Future Perfect
–Active	aicogob	äicogob	eicogob	iicogob	oicogob	uicogob
–Passive	paicogob	päicogob	peicogob	piicogob	poicogob	puicogob

Gerundives
  –Active öcogöl
  –Passive pöcogöl

Mood endings	Participle (-ing, -ed)	Infinitive	Imperative	Soft imperative (Optative)	Harsh imperative (Jussive)	Potential
	cogöl	cogön	cogöd	cogös	cogöz	cogöx

	Conditional	Conjunctive	Interrogative	Reflexive
	cogöv	cog-la	cog-li	cogok

Interjection ending cogö!

Prefixes

Prefix	Significance	Example	
Ba–	One	**Bafom**	Uniformity
Bä–	Low	**Bälän**	Low-land(s)
Bevü–	Between	**Bevünetik**	International
Bi–	Before, pre–	**Bisiedön**	To preside
Blä–	Black	**Blädeil**	Black Death
Da–	Completion	**Dalabön**	To possess
De–	De-, ab-, off-, away	**Deklinön**	To decline
Dei–	– until death	**Deifeit**	A struggle until death
Ge–	Back, re–	**Gepük**	Reply
Gle–	Great, extremely	**Glezif**	City
Ko–, Ke–	With, co-, com-, syn–	**Kokömön**	Come together
Le–	Very, Highly, Chief	**Leplidik**	Very satisfactory
Lefü–	East	**Lefüfifän**	East Fife
Len–	Towards, ad–	**Lenpük**	Address
Love–	Over, super–	**Lovelogön**	To over-look
Lu–	Small, bad	**Lufat, lulak**	Step-father, pond
Mö–	Many	**Möpükik**	Polyglot

Prefix	Significance	Example	
Ne-	Un-, in-, dis-	Neflen, Nedat	
			Enemy, left
Nolü-	North	Nolümelop	North America
Si-	Heavenly	Sijutel	Sagittarius
Sma-	Small	Smabed	Nest (of vipers)
Sulü-	South	Sulüfikop	South Africa
Vä-	All	Vägödelo	Every morning
Vesü-	West	Vesülodän	West-Lothian
Vie-	White	Viebod	White bread

Suffixes

Suffix	Significance	Example	
-af	Names of animals	Wulaf	Wolf
-al	Person (dignified, superior)	Kademal	Academician
-am	Action, -tion	Spodam	Correspondence
-an	Person (professional)	Dokan	Doctor
-av	Names of sciences	Tikav, Kiemav	
			Logic, chemistry
-äl	Abstract noun	Tikäl	Mind
-än	Country (from **län**)	Skotän	Scotland
-ef	Collection of persons	Kongef	Congress
-el	Person, doer	Mekel, Skotel	
			Maker, Scotsman
-em	Collection of things	Vödem	Glossary
-il	Diminutive	Glupil	Clique
-in	Names of substances	Dülin	Steel
-ip	Names of diseases	Kolip	Cholera
-it	Names of birds	Palit	Parrot
-op	Place (from **top**)	Yulop	Europe
-öf	Quality or state	Nedeilöf	Immortality
-öm	Apparatus	Tomöm	An instrument of torture
-öp	A place for (from **top**)	Malädöp	Hospital
-ul	Month (from **mül**)	Balul	January
-üp	Hour (from **düp**)	Tidüp	Lesson

Example of Derivation.
(From Dr. Auguste Kerckhoff's "Complete Course".)

From **Pük,** language, speech:
Pükik, linguistic, pertaining to language; **pükatidel,** language
  teacher; **pükapök,** defect of speech; **pükön,** to speak;
  pükönabid, pükönamod, manner of speech; **motapük,**
  mother tongue; **volapük,** universal language.
Pükat, oration; **pükatil,** short speech; **pükatel,** orator; **telapükat,**
  dialogue.
Pükav, philology; **pükavik,** philological.
Püked, saying; **pükedik,** sententious; **pükedavöd,** proverb;
  pükedavödik, proverbial; **valapüked,** motto.
Pükel, orator, speaker; **pükelik,** oratorical; **möpükel,** polyglot,
  speaker of many languages.
Püköf, eloquence; **püköfik,** eloquent; **püköfav,** rhetoric;
  püköfavik, rhetorical.
Pükot, talk; **pükotik,** talkative; **okopükot,** soliloquy.
Bepük, discussion; **bepükön,** to discuss.
Bipük, preface.
Gepük, answer; **gepükön,** to answer.
Lepük, assertion, affirmation; **lepükön,** to assert, to affirm.
Lenpük, address; **lenpükön,** to address.
Libapük, acquittal; **libapükön,** to acquit ("speak free").
Lupük, chatter; **lupükön,** to chatter; **lupükem,** gossip; **lupükot,**
  gossip (that which is said); **lupüklam,** stammering; **lupüklön,**
  to stammer.
Mipük, mis-speaking, slip of the tongue; **mipükön,** to mis-speak.
Nepük, silence; **nepükik,** silent; **nepükön,** to keep still.
Sepük, pronunciation; **sepükik,** pronounceable; **sepükad,**
  pronouncement (rendering of decision); **sepükam,** act of
  pronouncing; **sepükön,** to pronounce.
Tapük, contradiction; **tapükik,** contradictory; **tapükön,** to
  contradict.

The Numbers

0	nos	10	bals	20	tels
1	bal	11	balsebal	30	kils
2	tel	12	balsetel	40	fols
3	kil	13	balsekil	50	luls
4	fol	14	balsefol	60	mäls
5	lul	15	balselul	70	vels
6	mäl	16	balsemäl	80	jöls
7	vel	17	balsevel	90	züls
8	jöl	18	balsejöl	100	tum
9	zül	19	balsezül	1,000	mil
				1,000,000	balion

The Days of the Week

Sunday	balüdel	Thursday	lulüdel
Monday	telüdel	Friday	mälüdel
Tuesday	kilüdel	Saturday	velüdel
Wednesday	folüdel		

The Months of the Year

January	balul	July	velul
February	telul	August	jölul
March	kilul	September	zülul
April	folul	October	balsul
May	lulul	November	balsebalul
June	mälul	December	balsetelul

English to Volapük

to be able, *kanön*

to accuse, *kusadön*

address, speech, *lenpük*

adieu, *adyö*

to admire, *milagön*

again, *denu*

all, *valik*

almost, nearly, *ti*

also, *i*

America, *Melop*

and, *e*

angel, *lanel*

angry, *zunik*

to announce, *nunön*

ape, *lep*

April, *folul*

to arrive, *lükömön*

arm, *lam*

as, similarly to, *äs*

to ask, *säkön*

a-going astray, *pölivegam*

August, *jölul*

author, *lautel*

authorship, *laut*

bad, *badik*

badly, *badiko*

bag, *sak*

to bake, *bakön*

to be, *binön*

beautiful, *jönik*

to become, *vedön*

bed, *bed*

beer, *bil*

to believe, trust, *klödön*

to belong, *lönön*

best, *gudikün*

better, *gudikum*

beware, watch out!, *kautö*

black, *blägik*

blood, *blud*

blue, *yulibik*

boat, *bot*

bone, *bom*

book, *buk*

boy, *pul*

bravo!, *bafö*

bread, *bod*

to break, *blekön*

to bring, *blinön*

brother, *blod*

to build, *bumön*

but, only, *sod*

but (conjunction), *ab*

by, *a*

Capitalist, *katadel*

castle, *kased*

cat, *kat*

to catch, *fanön*

central, *zenodik*

century, *yeltum*

to chain up, imprison, *ketön*

chapter, *katel*

character, *kalad*

cheap, *nedelidik*

chief, director, *cif*

child, *cil*

church, *glüg*

cloth, *klöf*

cold, *kalod*

to come, *kömön*

commerce, trade, *ted*

companion, member, *kopanal*

to be compelled, *mutön*

contented, happy, *kotenik*

to correct, *menodön*

to count, *numön*

cow, *kun*

coward, *temipel*

crime, *klim*

criminal, *klimel*

to cry out, *kreiön*

currier, *skitatölatel*

dangerous, *pöligik*

to dare, *dalön*

daughter, *jison*

day, *del*

day before yesterday, *edelo*

dear, *löfik*

dear, beloved, *divik*

dear, costly, *delidik*

dearly, *delidiko*

to deceive, cheat, *citön*

dictionary, *vödasbuk*

difficult, *fikulik*

to die, *deilön*

to discover, *netegön*

distance, *fag*

district, part of town, *zifadil*

to do, act, *dunön*

does – ?, verb suffix used to denote an interrogative, *-li*

dog, *dog*

to drink, *dlinön*

drop, water-drop, *tof*
duty, *blig*
to eat, *fidön*
eight, *jöl*
to employ, *cälön*
empty, vacant, *vagik*
end, *fin*
enemy, *neflen*
English, *nelijik*
English language,
  nelijapük
Esperanto (a bas-tard
  language),
  esperantapük
Europe, *yulop*
every morning,
  vägödelo
eye, *log*
to fall, *falön*
father, *fat*
favour, *gön*
to fear, *dledön*
February, *telul*
to feel, *senön*
female friend, *jiflen*
female scholar, *jijulel*
female teacher, *jitidel*
female teacher of
  Volapük,
  jivolapükatidel
feminine, *jilik*
few, not much, *nemödik*
final, *finik*
to finish, *finön*
first, *balid*
fish, *fit*
five, *lul*
to flee, *fugön*
food, *fid*
fool, *fop*
foot, *fut*
for (because), *ibo*
for me, *obi*

for the first time,
  balidna
to forget, *fögetön*
to forgive, *fögivön*
four, *fol*
free, *libik*
French, *flentik*
Frenchman, *flentel*
Friday, *mälüdel*
friend, *flen*
from, *de*
garden, *gad*
gender, *gen*
general, common,
  valemik
gift, *giv*
girl, *jipul*
to give, *givön*
to go, *golön*
to go past, by, *beigolön*
gold, *golüd*
golden, *golüdik*
good, *gudik*
goodness, *gud*
goose, *gan*
gradually, *pianik*
grain, *glen*
grass, *yeb*
great, *gletik*
greater, *gletikum*
greatness, *glet*
green, *glünik*
grief, *dol*
ground, earth, *glun*
to guide, direct, *dugön*
guiding, leading,
  dugöfik
hand, *nam*
to hang [anything],
  lägön
happy, *beatik*
to have, *labön*
he, it, *om*

head, *kap*
health, *saun*
healthful, *saunlik*
healthy, well, *saunik*
to hear, *lilön*
height, *geil*
helmet, *häm*
to help, *yufön*
her, *ofik*
here, *is*
to hide, *sävön*
his, *omik*
to hold, *kipön*
home (native country),
  lom
honey, *miel*
to honour, *stimön*
to hope, *spelön*
horse, *jeval*
hour, *düp*
house, *dom*
how?, *liko*
hundred, *tum*
hungry, *pötütik*
to hunt, *yagön*
hunting, *yagöl*
hunting-dog, *yagadog*
husband, *matel*
I, myself, *ob*
if, *if*
if, verb suffix used to
  denote the
  conditional, *-la*
immediately, "right
  away", *fovikiko*
immortal, *nedeilik*
in, *in*
Indian, *nidian*
instruction, *tid*
to interrupt, *ropön*
iron, *lel*
it (not referring to any
  noun), *os*

January, *balul*

Japan, *Capän*

joke, *cog*

Journal of Volapük, *volapükabled*

journey, travel, *täv*

judge, *cödel*

to judge, *cödön*

July, *velul*

to jump, *bunön*

June, *mälul*

just such, *söm*

just the same, the very same, *öt*

to keep silent, *seilön*

to kill, *funön*

kiss, *kid*

to know, *nolön*

to know, be acquainted with, *sevön*

lady, *läd*

land (not water), country (one's own), *län*

language, *pük*

last, *lätik*

to lay, *seitön*

leaf (of tree or paper), *bled*

to learn, *lenadön*

leather, *skit*

to leave, let, permit, *letön*

lesson, lesson-time, *tidüp*

to liberate, free, *libön*

to lie, tell falsehood, *lugön*

light (noun), *lit*

to light up, *litön*

lightness (not heavy), *leitik*

line, rope, *lien*

litre, *liät*

to live, *lifön*

to live, dwell, *lödön*

logical, *tikavik*

long, *lonedik*

to lose, *pölüdön*

love, *löf*

to love, *löfön*

lovely, *löflik*

low, *bapik*

lunacy, madness, *lienet*

lunatic, mad (adjective), *lienitik*

to make, *mekön*

a maker of machine parts for a linoleum-press, *linomapeda-cinadilabumel*

man (human being), *men*

man (not woman), *man*

many, much, *mödik*

March, *kilul*

mare, *jijeval*

to marry, *matön*

masculine, *manik*

May, *lulul*

meat, *mit*

merchandise, *can*

metre (39 inches), *met*

Mid-Lothian, *Zen-Lodän*

million, *balion*

mine, *oba*

mirror, *lok*

Miss, *vomül*

mistake, *pök*

Monday, *telüdel*

money, *mon*

month, *mul*

mortal, *deilik*

most sinful, *sinikün*

mother, *mot*

mother, *jifat*

mouse, *mug*

murder, *mölod*

my, *obik*

mystery, confusion, *kofud*

narrow, *nabik*

nation, *net*

to be necessary, *zesüdön*

new, *nulik*

New Year, *nulayel*

newspaper, *gased*

night, *neit*

nine, *zül*

noise, *böset*

none, no (adjective), *nonik*

nose, *nud*

not at all, indeed not, *leno*

not, no, *no*

not, un-, *ne-*

nothing, zero, *nos*

now, just now, *ebo*

to obey, *lobedön*

October, *balsul*

often, *ofen*

on, *su*

once, formerly, *vöno*

one, *bal*

one's self, *ok*

organ (musical), *gel*

to ought, should, *sötön*

our, *obsik*

own self, *iet*

oyster, *huit*

part, *dil*

person, *pösod*

physician, *sanel*
to play, *pledön*
to please, amuse,
   plidön
pleasurable, *gälik*
pleasure, *gälod*
policeman, *polel*
postal, *potik*
potato, *pötet*
pound sterling, £,
   steab
power, *valüd*
preparation, *plepalam*
to prepare, *plepalön*
to prevent, *viatön*
professor, *plofed*
project, *ployeg*
to purchase, *lemön*
to be quiet, stop,
   takön
rage, *vut*
rage, *zun*
to rain, *lömibön*
to read, *lilädön*
to receive, *getön*
red, *ledik*
to remain, *blibön*
to return (to), *gegolön*
river, *flum*
road, *veg*
robbery, *lapin*
rock, cliff, *klif*
rose, *lol*
to run, make haste,
   spidön
same, *ot*
Saturday, *velüdel*
scholar, *julel*
scimitar, *flekaden*
Scotland, *skotän*
Scotsman, *skotel*
sea, *mel*
seat, *sied*

secret, plot, *klän*
to see, *logön*
-self, *it*
to sell, *selön*
September, *zülul*
seven, *vel*
sharpness, *jap*
she, *of*
sheep, *jip*
shoe, *juk*
shore, *jol*
short, brief, *blefik*
a short time ago,
   bletimo
silver, *silef*
sin, *sin*
Sir, Mr, *söl*
sister, *jiblod*
sister, *sör*
to sit, *siedön*
six, *mäl*
sky, heaven, *sil*
small, *smalik*
smaller, *smalikum*
snow, *nif*
to snow, *nifön*
so, thus, *so*
society, club, *klub*
solitary, alone, *soalik*
some, *anik*
son, *son*
song, *kanit*
South African,
   sulfikopel
to speak, *pükön*
stallion, *omjeval*
star, *stel*
to be in a certain
   state or condition,
   stadön
state (government), *tat*
station, depot, *stejen*
stop!, *stopö!*

story, *kon*
stove, *fön*
to strike, hit, *flapön*
strong, *stenüdik*
to struggle, fight,
   kämpön
student, pupil, *studel*
to study, *studön*
such, *som*
Sunday, *balüdel*
swift, *vifik*
to take, *sumön*
tall, *geiliko*
to teach, *tidön*
teacher, *tidel*
teacher of the world-
   language,
   volapükatidel
telegraph, *telegaf*
to tell, *sagön*
ten, *bals*
tenth, *balsid*
terror, *jek*
test, *bluf*
than, *ka*
to thank, *danön*
that (before relative), *ut*
that (demonstrative), *et*
that very, *üt*
that very one, *eit*
their, *omsik*
there, *us*
therefore, *sikod*
thief, *tif*
to think, *tikön*
this, this one, *at*
this month, *amulo*
this very one, *ät*
thousand, *mil*
three, *kil*
through, by means
   of, *dub*
Thursday, *lulüdel*

ticket, *zöt*
time, *tim*
to, *al*
to-day, *adelo*
to-morrow, *odelo*
tomb, *sep*
to torment, *tomön*
towards, *äl*
town, *zif*
train, railway, *tlen*
to travel, *tävön*
treachery, *tlät*
to treat, *tölatön*
to tremble, *dlemön*
truth, *velatik*
Tuesday, *kilüdel*
two, *tel*
umbrella, *lömibajel*
to understand,
  kapälön
unpleasurable,
  nebeatik
useful, *pöfüdik*
wagon, carriage, *vab*
walk, *spat*

to walk, *spatön*
walking-stick, *spatin*
warmth, *vam*
to wash, *vatükön*
water, *vat*
watery, *vatik*
weakly, feebly, *fibiko*
Wednesday, *folüdel*
week, *vig*
to weep, *dlenön*
well, *gudiko*
what?, *kis*
when, *kü*
when?, *kitim*
when?, *kiüp*
where?, *kiöp*
where?, *kiplad*
while, for, *du*
white, *vietik*
who (feminine), *kif*
who (masculine), *kim*
who, which, *kel*
whoever, *aikel*
whole, *lölik*
why?, *kikod*

wide, *vidik*
widower, *viudel*
to will, *vilön*
to win, *vikön*
wine, *vin*
with, *ko*
woman, *vom*
woman, *jiman*
word, *vöd*
world, *vol*
world-language,
  volapük
worse, *badikum*
to wound, *vunön*
to write, *penön*
year, *yel*
yearly, *yelsik*
yes, *si*
yes, of course, *lesi*
yesterday, *ädelo*
you (thou), *ol*
young, *yunik*
your, *olik*
your (plural), *olsik*
zeal, *zil*

Volapük to English

a, *by*
ab, *but (conjunction)*
adelo, *to-day*
ädelo, *yesterday*
adyö, *adieu*
aikel, *whoever*
al, *to*
äl, *towards*
amulo, *this month*
anik, *some*
äs, *as, similarly to*
at, *this, this one*
ät, *this very one*
badik, *bad*

badiko, *badly*
badikum, *worse*
bafö, *bravo!*
bakön, *to bake*
bal, *one*
balid, *first*
balidna, *for the first
  time*
balion, *million*
bals, *ten*
balsid, *tenth*
balsul, *October*
balüdel, *Sunday*
balul, *January*

bapik, *low*
beatik, *happy*
bed, *bed*
beigolön, *to go past, by*
bil, *beer*
binön, *to be*
blägik, *black*
bled, *leaf (of tree or
  paper)*
blefik, *short, brief*
blekön, *to break*
bletimo, *a short time
  ago*
blibön, *to remain*

blig, *duty*
blinön, *to bring*
blod, *brother*
blud, *blood*
bluf, *test*
bod, *bread*
bom, *bone*
böset, *noise*
bot, *boat*
buk, *book*
bumön, *to build*
bunön, *to jump*
cälön, *to employ*
can, *merchandise*
Capän, *Japan*
cif, *chief, director*
cil, *child*
citön, *to deceive, cheat*
cödel, *judge*
cödön, *to judge*
cog, *joke*
dalön, *to dare*
danön, *to thank*
de, *from*
deilik, *mortal*
deilön, *to die*
del, *day*
delidik, *dear, costly*
delidiko, *dearly*
denu, *again*
dil, *part*
divik, *dear, beloved*
dledön, *to fear*
dlemön, *to tremble*
dlenön, *to weep*
dlinön, *to drink*
dog, *dog*
dol, *grief*
dom, *house*
du, *while, for*
dub, *through, by means of*
dugön, *to guide, direct*

dugöfik, *guiding, leading*
dunön, *to do, act*
düp, *hour*
e, *and*
ebo, *now, just now*
edelo, *day before yesterday*
eit, *that very one*
esperantapük, *Esperanto (a bastard language)*
et, *that (demonstrative)*
fag, *distance*
falön, *to fall*
fanön, *to catch*
fat, *father*
fibiko, *weakly, feebly*
fid, *food*
fidön, *to eat*
fikulik, *difficult*
fin, *end*
finik, *final*
finön, *to finish*
fit, *fish*
flapön, *to strike, hit*
flekaden, *scimitar*
flen, *friend*
flentapük, *the French language*
flentel, *Frenchman*
flentik, *French*
flum, *river*
fögetön, *to forget*
fögivön, *to forgive*
fol, *four*
folüdel, *Wednesday*
folul, *April*
fön, *stove*
fop, *fool*
fovikiko, *immediately, "right away"*
fugön, *to flee*

funön, *to kill*
fut, *foot*
gad, *garden*
gälik, *pleasurable*
gälod, *pleasure*
gan, *goose*
gased, *newspaper*
gegolön, *to return (to)*
geil, *height*
geiliko, *tall*
gel, *organ (musical)*
gen, *gender*
getön, *to receive*
giv, *gift*
givön, *to give*
glen, *grain*
glet, *greatness*
gletik, *great*
gletikum, *greater*
glüg, *church*
glun, *ground, earth*
glünik, *green*
golön, *to go*
golüd, *gold*
golüdik, *golden*
gön, *favour*
gud, *goodness*
gudik, *good*
gudiko, *well*
gudikum, *better*
gudikün, *best*
häm, *helmet*
huit, *oyster*
i, *also*
ibo, *for (because)*
iet, *own self*
if, *if*
in, *in*
is, *here*
it, *-self*
jap, *sharpness*
jek, *terror*
jeval, *horse*

jiblod, *sister*
jifat, *mother*
jiflen, *female friend*
jijeval, *mare*
jijulel, *female scholar*
jilik, *feminine*
jiman, *woman*
jip, *sheep*
jipul, *girl*
jison, *daughter*
jitidel, *female teacher*
jivolapükatidel, *female teacher of Volapük*
jol, *shore*
jöl, *eight*
jölul, *August*
jönik, *beautiful*
juk, *shoe*
julel, *scholar*
ka, *than*
kalad, *character*
kalod, *cold*
kämpön, *to struggle, fight*
kanit, *song*
kanön, *to be able*
kap, *head*
kapälön, *to understand*
kased, *castle*
kat, *cat*
katadel, *Capitalist*
katel, *chapter*
kautö, *beware, watch out!*
kel, *who, which*
ketön, *to chain up, imprison*
kid, *kiss*
kif, *who (feminine)*
kikod, *why?*
kil, *three*
kilüdel, *Tuesday*
kilul, *March*

kim, *who (masculine)*
kiöp, *where?*
kiplad, *where?*
kipön, *to hold*
kis, *what?*
kitim, *when?*
kiüp, *when?*
klän, *secret, plot*
klif, *rock, cliff*
klim, *crime*
klimel, *criminal*
klödön, *to believe, trust*
klöf, *cloth*
klub, *society, club*
ko, *with*
kofud, *mystery, confusion*
kömön, *to come*
kon, *story*
kopanal, *companion, member*
kotenik, *contented, happy*
kreiön, *to cry out*
kü, *when*
kun, *cow*
kusadon, *to accuse*
-la, *verb suffix used to denote the conditional (if—)*
labön, *to have*
läd, *lady*
lägön, *to hang [anything]*
lam, *arm*
län, *land (not water), country (one's own)*
lanel, *angel*
lapin, *robbery*
lätik, *last*
laut, *authorship*
lautel, *author*
ledik, *red*
leitik, *lightness (not heavy)*

lel, *iron*
lemön, *to purchase*
lenadön, *to learn*
leno, *not at all, indeed not*
lenpük, *address, speech*
lep, *ape*
lesi, *yes, of course*
letön, *to leave, let, permit*
-li, *verb suffix used to denote an interrogative (does —?)*
liät, *litre*
libik, *free*
libön, *to liberate, free*
lien, *line, rope*
lienet, *lunacy, madness*
lienitik, *lunatic, mad (adjective)*
lifön, *to live*
liko, *how?*
lilädön, *to read*
lilön, *to hear*
linomapedacina-linabumel, *a maker of machine parts for a linoleum-press*
lit, *light (noun)*
litön, *to light up*
lobedön, *to obey*
lödön, *to live, dwell*
löf, *love*
löfik, *dear*
löflik, *lovely*
löfön, *to love*
log, *eye*
logön, *to see*
lok, *mirror*
lol, *rose*
lölik, *whole*
lom, *home (native country)*
lömibajel, *umbrella*

lömibön, *to rain*
lonedik, *long*
lönön, *to belong*
lugön, *to lie, tell*
  falsehood
lükömön, *to arrive*
lul, *five*
lulüdel, *Thursday*
lulul, *May*
mäl, *six*
mälüdel, *Friday*
mälul, *June*
man, *man (not woman)*
manik, *masculine*
matel, *husband*
matön, *to marry*
mekön, *to make*
mel, *sea*
Melop, *America*
men, *man (human being)*
menodön, *to correct*
met, *metre (39 inches)*
miel, *honey*
mil, *thousand*
milagön, *to admire*
mit, *meat*
mödik, *many, much*
mölod, *murder*
mon, *money*
mot, *mother*
mug, *mouse*
mul, *month*
mutön, *to be compelled*
nabik, *narrow*
nam, *hand*
ne-, *not, un-*
nebeatik, *unpleasurable*
nedeilik, *immortal*
nedelidik, *cheap*
neflen, *enemy*
neit, *night*
nelijapük, *English*
  language

nelijik, *English*
nemödik, *few, not much*
net, *nation*
netegön, *to discover*
nidian, *Indian*
nif, *snow*
nifön, *to snow*
no, *not, no*
nolön, *to know*
nonik, *none, no*
  (adjective)
nos, *nothing, zero*
nud, *nose*
nulayel, *New Year*
nulik, *new*
numön, *to count*
nunön, *to announce*
ob, *I, myself*
oba, *mine*
obi, *for me*
obik, *my*
obsik, *our*
odelo, *to-morrow*
of, *she*
ofen, *often*
ofik, *her*
ok, *one's self*
ol, *you (thou)*
olik, *your*
olsik, *your (plural)*
om, *he, it*
omik, *his*
omjeval, *stallion*
omsik, *their*
os, *it (not referring to*
  any noun)
ot, *same*
öt, *just the same, the very*
  same
penön, *to write*
pianik, *gradually*
pledön, *to play*
plepalam, *preparation*

plepalön, *to prepare*
plidön, *to please, amuse*
plofed, *professor*
ployeg, *project*
pöfüdik, *useful*
pök, *mistake*
polel, *policeman*
pöligik, *dangerous*
pölivegam, *a-going*
  astray
pölüdön, *to lose*
pösod, *person*
pötet, *potato*
potik, *postal*
pötütik, *hungry*
pük, *language*
pükön, *to speak*
pul, *boy*
ropön, *to interrupt*
sagön, *to tell*
sak, *bag*
säkön, *to ask*
sanel, *physician*
saun, *health*
saunik, *healthy, well*
saunlik, *healthful*
sävön, *to hide*
seilön, *to keep silent*
seitön, *to lay*
selön, *to sell*
senön, *to feel*
sep, *tomb*
sevön, *to know, be*
  acquainted with
si, *yes*
sied, *seat*
siedön, *to sit*
sikod, *therefore*
sil, *sky, heaven*
silef, *silver*
sin, *sin*
sinikün, *most sinful*
skit, *leather*

skitatölatel, *currier*
skotän, *Scotland*
skotel, *Scotsman*
smalik, *small*
smalikum, *smaller*
so, *so, thus*
soalik, *solitary, alone*
sod, *but, only*
söl, *Sir, Mr.*
som, *such*
söm, *just such*
son, *son*
sör, *sister*
sötön, *to ought, should*
spat, *walk*
spatin, *walking-stick*
spatön, *to walk*
spelön, *to hope*
spidön, *to run, make*
 haste
stadön, *to be in a certain*
 state or condition
steab, *pound sterling,* £
stejen, *station, depot*
stel, *star*
stenüdik, *strong*
stimön, *to honour*
stopö!, *stop!*
studel, *student, pupil*
studön, *to study*
su, *on, upon*
sulfikopel, *South*
 African
sumön, *to take*
takön, *to be quiet, stop*
tat, *state (government)*
täv, *journey, travel*
tävön, *to travel*
ted, *commerce, trade*
tel, *two*
telegaf, *telegraph*
telüdel, *Monday*
telul, *February*

temipel, *coward*
ti, *almost, nearly*
tid, *instruction*
tidel, *teacher*
tidön, *to teach*
tidüp, *lesson, lesson-time*
tif, *thief*
tikavik, *logical*
tikön, *to think*
tim, *time*
tlät, *treachery*
tlen, *train, railway*
tof, *drop, water-drop*
tölatön, *to treat*
tomön, *to torment*
tum, *hundred*
udelo, *the day-after-*
 tomorrow
us, *there*
ut, *that (before relative)*
üt, *that very*
uyelo, *the year-after-*
 next
vab, *wagon, carriage*
vagik, *empty, vacant*
vägödelo, *every morning*
valemik, *general,*
 common
valik, *all*
valüd, *power*
vam, *warmth*
vat, *water*
vatik, *watery*
vatükön, *to wash*
vedön, *to become*
veg, *road*
vel, *seven*
velatik, *truth*
velüdel, *Saturday*
velul, *July*
viatön, *to prevent*
vidik, *wide*
vietik, *white*

vifik, *swift*
vig, *week*
vikön, *to win*
vilön, *to will*
vin, *wine*
viudel, *widower*
vöd, *word*
vödasbuk, *dictionary*
vol, *world*
volapük, *world-language*
volapükabled, *Journal*
 of Volapük
volapükatidel, *teacher*
 of the world-language
vom, *woman*
vomül, *Miss*
vöno, *once, formerly*
vunön, *to wound*
vut, *rage*
yagadog, *hunting-dog*
yagöl, *hunting*
yagön, *to hunt*
yeb, *grass*
yel, *year*
yelsik, *yearly*
yeltum, *century*
yufön, *to help*
yulibik, *blue*
yulop, *Europe*
yunik, *young*
Zen-Lodän, *Mid-*
 Lothian
zenodik, *central*
zesüdön, *to be necessary*
zif, *town*
zifadil, *district, part of*
 town
zil, *zeal*
zül, *nine*
zülul, *September*
zun, *rage*
zunik, *angry*
zöt, *ticket*

Napolel Telid, the Second Addendum:
Key to the Exercises

Exercise 2.

The boy's mouse	**Mug pula**
For the men	**Manis**
To a father	**Fate**
The house of the dog	**Dom doga**
The geese	**Gans**

Exercise 3.

Man labom dogi.	The man has a dog.
Man labom dogis tel.	The man has two dogs.
Dog logom gani.	The dog sees the goose.
Dog blinom gani mane.	The dog brings the goose to the man.
Man pin labom gani.	The fat man has the goose.
Pul labom dogis tel e jipi bal.	The boy has two dogs and one sheep.
Man givom dogi pule.	The man gives the dog to the boy.
Man givom steabis kil pule.	The man gives three Pounds to the boy.
Dog labom futis fol.	The dog has four feet.

Exercise 4.

Kim labom dogi?	**Man labom dogi.**
Kim givom dogi pule?	**Man givom dogi pule.**
Kimi man givom pule?	**Dogi givom man pule.**
Kime man givom dogi?	**Man givom pule dogi.**

Miss Coqually's answers to Exercise 5:

The fat man has seven geese. **Man pin labom ganis vel.**
The four dogs have twelve feet.

Dogs fol laboms futis balsetel.

Who has three hands? **Kim labom namis kil?**

The boy's father gives 100 Pounds to the man.	**Fat pula givom steabis tum mane.**
Who has the dog?	**Kim labom dogi?**
The boy has two dogs.	**Pul labom dogis tel.**
The man has three dogs.	**Man labom dogis kil.**
The dog has four feet.	**Dog labom futis fol.**
The boy has two feet.	**Pul labom futis tel.**
Who has two hands?	**Kim labom namis tel?**
The man gives money.	**Man givom moni.**
Who sees the dog?	**Kim logom dogi?**

Exercise 6.

Binob.	I am.
Givol.	You (singular) give.
Lobedom.	He obeys.
Kreiof.	She cries out.
Golos.	It goes.
Dledon.	One fears.

I speak.	**Pükob.**
I obey.	**Lobedob.**
We go to the tomb.	**Golobs sepe.**
I have the power.	**Labob valüdi.**
We bring a man to the tomb.	**Blinobs mani sepe.**
He brings the food.	**Blinom fidi.**

Exercise 7.

Labol valüdi.	You have the power.
Pükol.	You speak.
Golol.	You go.
Kömols e fugobs.	You (plural) come and we flee.
Pükobs e lilobs.	We speak and you listen.

He has a tomb.	**Labom sepi.**
You go and I come.	**Golol e kömob.**
You obey me.	**Lobedol obe.**
He cries out.	**Kreiom.**
She flees.	**Fugof.**
He brings a man to the tomb.	**Blinom mani sepe.**

Exercise 8.

Man löf– vom–.	**Man löfom vomi.**
Neflen– man– giv–	**Neflen mana givom moni**
mon– vom–.	**vome.**
Vom– dlin– blud–.	**Voms dlinofs bludi.**
Vom– lem– vin– neflen–.	**Vom lemof vini neflene.**

Exercise 9.

A lady-friend	**Jiflen**
A female merchant.	**Jitedel**
Sister	**Sör**
Widow	**Jiviudel**
A female president.	**Jibisiedel**
Mare	**Jijeval**
Wife	**Vom**
Japanese Lady	**Jicapel**
Bitch	**Jidog**

Exercise 10.

Liko stadol, o söl !? Stadob gudiko, danob ole.

How do you do, sir? I am well, thank you.

Li-binol lonedo in zif? No lonedo, gomob bletimo al Daisart.

Are you in this town for a long time? Not a long time, I go to Dysart in a short time.

Binom-li Daisart zif jönik? Binom lejönik.

Is Dysart a beautiful town? It is very beautiful.

Have you seen my wife to-day? No, sir; is she not in the house?

Li-elogol vomi obik adelo? No, o söl! no-li binof in dom?

How is your daughter to-day? Thanks; she is much better.

Liko jison olik stadof adelo? Dani; stadof mödo gudikumo.

Exercise 11.

Sevob mani, kel tomom obi.

I know the man who torments me.

Man, keli sevob, tomom obi.

The man, whom I know, torments me.

Kif binof läd et, kel labof lömibajeli?
Who is that lady who has the umbrella?

I see the man who speaks to the woman. He is my tormentor.
Logob mani ut kel pükom vome. Binom tomel obik.
That woman is the wife of my tormentor.
Vom et binof vom tomela obik.
Does this lady know the character of her husband?
Vom sevof-li kaladi mana ofik?

Exercise 12.
Klub obsik labom kopanalis telselul.
Our society has twenty-five members.
Kis binom pük ola?
What is your language?
Flen oba löfom pükis obik.
My friend loves his language.
Neflens obik löfoms pükis omsik.
My enemies loves their language.

My language is Volapük.
Pük oba binom Volapük.
Who is your friend?
Kim binom flen ola?
Our enemies are members of that group.
Neflens obas binoms kopanals et glupa.

Exercise 13.
Pük at binom pük obsik.
This language is our language.
Man et labom flenis kil; löfob flenis ab no mani it.
That man has three friends; I like the friends but not the
man himself.
Sevol kopanalis kluba obsik; ob sevob manis ot.
You know the members of our Society; I myself know the
same people.
Man ut, kel lödom in dom at, binom fop, e sevom nosi.
The man who lives in this house is a fool and knows nothing.

This language is ours. **Pük at binom obsik.**
I do not trust that man. **No klödob mani et.**
We live in the same town. **Lödobs in zif ot.**

Exercise 14.
Sil binom blägik. The sky is black.
Blud obik binom ledik; blud omik binom yulibik.
My blood is red; his blood is blue.
Valüd oba binom gletik; valüd ola binom smalik.
My power is great; your power is small.
Tidob vöds valik kel sevol.
I teach all the words which you know.

No, Esperanto is bad!
No! Esperantapük binom badik!
Yes, indeed, Volapük is good!
Lesi! Volapük binom gudik!
All good men have good hearts, and love a good language.
Valiks mans gudik laboms ladis gudik e löfoms
püki gudik.
You are a quick pupil.
Binol julel vidik.

Exercise 15.
Lenadobs kilna in del, telsebalna in vig.
We learn three times a day, twenty-one times a week.
Buk gudik ät tidom volapüki ole balidna.
Just this good book teaches Volapük to you for the first time.
Düps goloms vifik, e no labobs timi mödik.
The hours go past quickly and we have not much time.

You speak Volapük badly.
Pükol Volapüki badiko.
The Capitalist buys cheap and sells dear.
Katadel lemom nedelidiko e selom delidiko.
You write well.
Penol gudiko.

Exercise 16.

Tlät obik no binom so gletik äs olik : binom smalikum.
My treachery is not as big as yours: it is smaller.
Volapük binom pük nefikulikün in vol lölik.
Volapük is the easiest language in the whole world.
Binob yunikum ka ol.
I am younger than you.

You are more cowardly than I.
Binob temipikumo ka ol.
I do not know a language which is easier than Volapük.
No sevob püki kel binom nefikulikum ka volapük.

Exercise 17.

Löfob bligi dunön.
I like to do my duty.
Kim kanom numön stelis sila u tofis mela?
Who can count the stars in the sky or the drops in the ocean?
Binob in vol al tikön, no al pledön.
I am here on earth to think, not to play.
Sötol studön volapüki al kanön pükön ko nets valik.
You ought to study Volapük so that you can speak with
    every nation.

To travel is better than to arrive.
Tävön binos gudikum ka lükömön.
We ought to travel by train if we can buy a ticket.
Sötobs tävön dub tleni if kanobs züt lemön.
It is better to have loved and lost, than not to have loved.
Gudikum binos elöfön e epölüdön, ka no elöfön.

Exercise 18.

Present	Imperfect	Perfect	Pluperfect	Future	Future Perfect
Kusadob I accuse	**äkusadob** I was accusing	**ekusadob** I have accused	**ikusadob** I had accused	**okusadob** I will accuse	**ukusadob** I will have accused
Kautol You beware	**äkautol** You were taking care	**ekautol** You have taken care	**ikautol** You had taken care	**okautol** You will beware	**ukautol** You will have taken care
Ketom He imprisons	**äketom** He was imprisoning	**eketom** He imprisoned	**iketom** He had imprisoned	**oketom** He will imprison	**uketom** He will have imprisoned
Libof She liberates	**älibof** She was liberating	**clibof** She liberated	**ilibof** She had liberated	**olibof** She will liberate	**ulibof** She will have liberated
Lömibos It rains	**älömibos** It was raining	**elömibos** It rained	**ilömibos** It had rained	**olömibos** It will rain	**ulömibos** It will have rained
Logon People lie	**älogon** People were lying	**elogon** People lied	**ilogon** People had lied	**ologon** People will lie	**ulogon** People will have lied
Vikobs We win	**ävikobs** We were winning	**evikobs** We have won	**ivikobs** We had won	**ovikobs** We will win	**uvikobs** We will have won
Dugols You lead lead	**ädugols** You were leading	**edugols** You led	**idugols** You had led	**odugols** You will lead	**udugols** You will have led
Netegoms They discover	**änetegoms** They were discovering	**enetegoms** They discovered	**inetegoms** They had discovered	**onetegoms** They will discover	**unetegoms** They will have discovered

I have been the best, I was better yesterday, I am good to-day,
to-morrow I will be worse

Ebinob gudikün, edelo äbinob gudikum, adelo binob gudik, odelo binob badikum.

Exercise 19.

Golobsös al stejen.	Let us go to the station
Takolös dlenön	Please, stop crying.
Takolöd böseti!	You must stop this noise!

Polel ogekomom – standolöz!
The policeman will return – stand up, now!

Make haste, for the policeman is angry!
Spidolöd, polel binom zunik !
Please take this bag and run!
Sumolöd saki e gonolös!
Be a man, you weakest of persons!
Man binolöz, pösod fibikün!

Exercise 21.

Älöfoböv mani at, if äbinom-la nestupikum
I would like this man if he were less stupid.

If no äbinos-la so pöligik, älöfoböv gegolön domi obik in zif
If it were not so dangerous, I would like to return to my
house in town.

Pölüdobsöx.
We might possibly lose.

This book would be useful to you if you should wish to study
the language of Volapük.
Buk at äbinomöv pöfüdik ole, if vilol-la studön Volapüki.
If you had helped, I would have forgiven you.
If iyufol-la, ifögivomöv oli.
If you had seen this woman in the garden, she would have talked
to you.
If ilogol-la vomi at in gad, ipükoföv oli.

Exercise 22.

Volapük popükom in läns mödik.
Volapük will be spoken in many lands.
Mans pecödoms, pelägoms e peseitoms in sepi.
The men were judged, hanged, and laid in a tomb.
Man gletik pununom.
The great man will have been informed.

Errors will have been corrected.
Pöks pumenodoms.
Errors which will have to be corrected.
Pöks pömenodöl.
What language is spoken in Scotland?
Kiom pük papükom in skotän?

Exercise 23.
Logobok in lok at.
I see myself in this mirror.
Aikel löfomok gudikumo ka kopanali omik, no binom volutel velatik; ab volutels velatik löfoms okis.
Whoever loves himself more than his comrade is not a true revolutionary; but true revolutionaries love each other.

I have struck myself with this walking stick.
Eflapobok me ko spatin at.
You will kill yourself!
Ofunolok!

"The Mechanic's Reference Library"

Foolscap, 4to, cloth boards, circuit edges, 1*s.* 6*d.* each.

Messrs. Blundell & Howard,
"Hot Air and the Future of Guided Flight."

Cory, F.W.,
"How to Foretell the Weather , complete with Pocket Spectroscope. With 10 illustrations."

Donelan, Fr. J-M.,
"Electric Phaetons and Their Maintenance."

Gray, Major Antonio (Retd.),
"The Complete Art of Making Fireworks; or, The Pyrotechnist's Treasury."

Hepworth, T.C.,
"The Magic Lantern and its Management; including full Practical Directions. 10 illustrations."

Kininmonth, A.A.S.,
"An Abridged History of the Construction of the Railway Line between Garve, Ullapool and Lochinver." *Water-stained, uncut.*

Paul, Col. Aviator,
"The Pump-House Engines of Estonia."

Proctor, Richard A. (BA),
"Wages and Wants of Science Workers."

Miss Alison Rae,
"Harmonia Mundi: A Practical Guide to the Economy of Church Organs."

Schnieke, Dr. A. (of Munich),
"The Moebius Enigma and Its Application to the *Perpetuum Mobile* - A Machine for Perpetual Motion. With Directions on how to repair Gears, Strips, Gyroscopes etc., in the event of Arrest."

Shaw, John,
"To the Moon by Balloon: my Journey to Thirty-Seven Thousand feet. And back again."

Many other volumes available from this extensive Library!

" L U N A T I C A "

a Library of Scientific Works on Nervous Disturbances from Dobie & Mackintosh

"Similar works could find a place upon my groaning shelves."
Dr. Thomas Clouston, of Edinburgh.

Many illustrated, crown 8vo, foxed, cloth extra, 3s. 6d. each volume.

BELL, DR. JOSEPH,
"Mania, Melancholia and Dementia Among Pipe-Smokers - An Analytical Study."

CALVERT, MISS,
"The Home Companion for Cases of Derangement."

THE HON. LADY CAWSTON,
"Common Accidents in Moral Management, and How to Rectify Them."

CHRISTIE, CHAS.,
"An Address to Humanity, containing an accusatory letter
to Mr. William Pollard; a Recipe to make a Lunatic, and seize
his Estate; and a Sketch of a True Smiling Hyena."

COCKTON, H.,
"The Life and Adventures of Valentine Vox, the Ventriloquist."

CORDINER, DR. CHAS.,
Proceedings of the Caledonian Phrenological Society." 3 Vols., half-bound.

CRISTALIS, MISS IRENE,
"Pneumatic Magnetism Evident in the Elastic Worrying Engine."

HUTCHISON, DR. I.,
"Choice Pickings from Comparative Nosology."

MCDOWELL, L.,
"On Obscure Diseases of the Brain, and Disorders of the Mind."

MATTISSON, PROF. A.,
"An Understanding of Nervous Ailments, and their Successful Treatment
by the Incomparable *Oleum Svedicum.*"

MILTON, J.L.
"The Bath in Maladies of the Skin."

MOORE, WM.,
"Neurosyphilitic Treatment without the Use of Mechanical Restraints."

ROSIE, GEO.,
"The Acquisition of Grammar and Vocabulary as an
Alleviation to Cephalic Distraction."

No subject is greater than the Human Brain!

"The Academy of Language"

"A copious horn of learning from Dobie & Mackintosh."
The Laurencekirk Presbyter.

Post 8vo, divinity calf boards, 7s. 6d. per volume.

BARBER, DR. CHARLES CLYDE,
"A Collection of Every Alphabet in the Civilised World."

BURNIE, MR. D.B.,
" 'A Man Crouching Backwards Over Our Lady, by Victor Hugo'.
A Translation from the French, Made Entirely by Mr. Burnie's
Metamorphologikon, Unassisted and Unedited."

CAMPBELL, PROF. I.,
"A Strange Manuscript Found in a Cylinder Hat."

GOETHE, J.W.,
"Pun: Dil Balid."

LYON, DR. FELIX,
"The Rosetta Stone - a Rosicrucian Hoax." *In preparation.*

MACPHERSON, JAMES
"Kanits Ossianik." *A Delight in Volapük!*

MARX, C.,
"Katad. Dils balid e telid." *Dil kilid in plepalam.*

MURISET, MONS. E.,
"Ti : Best Taken with Bread and Jam? The Sound of Solresol."

PASSINGHAM, REV. D.,
"Ni Venkos: We Will Win.
A Practitioner's Introduction to Esperanto."

TAYLOR, QUERCUS ROBERT SIMPSON,
"Unusual Variations on Well-known Examples of the Yukon Zeugma.
A Bed-side Companion, Describing Essential Features of the
Glottal Hiatus and Imparting Judicious Knowledge of Linguistics by
Mnemonics; Newly Over-hauled for Publication." *In preparation*

MISS RUTH WILSON,
"The Shorter Standard English Usage. In Seventeen Volumes."

To subscribe to the "Academy of Language", send 30 stamps to:
Miss Gibson at West Newington House. On our receipt of this sum,
the name and address of the Reader will be registered on our
"Professorial Roll", to benefit from a Discount of no less
than 9d. per volume on all future publications.

The "Edifying Entertainment" Library

"Instruction without Pain, Amusement without Guilt:
These books are Wondrous, Hilarious, Uplifting, Erudite.
Dobie & Mackintosh have done it again!"
Reverend M. Goodfellow, of Marchmont.

"EXCELLENT FINISH." PRICED INDIVIDUALLY.

Mrs. Brown
"Post-Prandial Philosophy." Royal 8vo, wormed, 3s 6d.

Clodd, Edward, (FRAS)
"Myths and Dreams. Revised edition."
Imperial 4to, doublures, oblong, 3s 6d.

Cremer, W.H.,
"Hanky-Panky: Easy Tricks, White Magic, Sleight of Hand, &c.
With 200 illustrations." Foolscap 8vo, cont. cloth, 4s 6d.

Ebmeier, Dr. K.,
"Forty-Five Fascinating Feats with a Flute." *By the acclaimed
author of "Twenty-Two Tempting Tricks with a Trombone."*
Imperial 8vo, half-Morocco, marbled edge, 21s.

Farsier, Donald,
"True Serfs. Or; Let the Winds Blow Low." 12mo, forel.

Fraser-Tytler, C.C
"Mistress Judith: A Novel." Post 8vo, illustr. boards, 2s.

Ferguson, Mr. Neil (M.A., M.A.),
"Bacteria, Yeast Fungi and Allied Species, A Synopsis.
With 87 Illustrations." Crown 8vo, tabby, 3s 6d.

Mrs. Hazelwood,
"The Autocrat of the Breakfast Table. Illustrated by J.Gordon
Thomson." Post 8vo, cloth limp, 2s 6d. "The Autocrat of the Breakfast Table" and "The Professor at the Breakfast Table" in one volume,
post 8vo, half-bound, 4s.

Kind, Dr. A.,
"Amusements with a Microscope: Merry Instruction for Young
Scamps." Pott 8vo, shagreen, rough finish, 3s 6d.

McKelvie, Bro. Peter (late of Airdrie),
"Puniana: Riddles and Jokes With numerous illustrations by the
Author." Royal 4to, China paper, linen boards, 2s 6d.

Write to us for our full Catalogue of Wit and Wisdom !